Gods of War

Sovereign Stars Book 2

Blair C. Howard

Cleveland, TN

ISBN: 979-8-9862563-1-3

Library of Congress Control Number: 2022912172

Dedication

For Jo, as always

Prologue

Jackknife looked frantically back over his shoulder as he ran through the narrow corridors of the abandoned osmium mine on Asteroid K1437, trying to keep up with his captain, Tiger Wok, while dodging the blasts from the plasma weapons of the pursuing Blues, now slowly closing in on them from behind.

Jackknife had convinced Tiger it would be an easy job. After all, the mine had been abandoned for years and the amount of osmium ore left behind was well worth the risk. Unfortunately, that risk had turned out to be much greater than he'd thought. Apparently, the Blues had the same idea.

Jackknife turned, planted his feet firmly on the metal floor, raised his railgun with both hands and waited.

"Come on, Jack," Wok yelled. "What the hell are you doing?"

"Give me a minute," Jackknife shouted. He was tired of these Blue bastards getting the drop on them. He remained still as the sounds of the approaching aliens reached the curve. He saw the first one appear and fired a barrage of three-millimeter depleted uranium projectiles that slammed into the rock walls filling the entire area with dust and debris.

Jackknife didn't wait to see if he'd hit any of the invaders. Instead, he turned and sprinted after his captain.

"The main intersection is up ahead," Tiger Wok shouted.

"Go, go, go," Jackknife yelled, breathing hard. "I'm right behind you." He rounded the last curve to find Wok already at the corner of the large intersection, half-hidden behind the rock wall, his blaster aimed down the corridor covering Jackknife's frantic run.

Jackknife slowed, dodged around the corner, stopped, leaned his back against the rock wall and gasped. "That last volley I threw at them should slow them down a bit. What now, Captain?"

Wok lowered his weapon and touched the comm button on his forearm. "Wok to Red Dragon."

"This is Red Dragon. Go ahead, Captain," the voice cracked through the speaker.

"We're headed your way," Wok said as he jerked his head, and he and the still-recovering Jackknife began jogging again. "We ran into a pack of Blues. They're right behind us. We're going to need backup."

"Copy that, Captain. I have your position on the FLIR. We'll be ready for you on approach."

"Copy that! Wok out," Wok said as he turned the jog

into a sprint. Then to Jackknife he shouted, "Let's get back to the docking bay."

The two pirates took the middle tunnel, the shortest way back to their ship, hoping the intersection of the three tunnels would stall the Blues for a few extra minutes. *But who the hell knows how or what those bastards think?* Wok thought as he ran. *I'll have Jack's balls for this.*

They emerged from the tunnel into a large docking bay where Wok's ship, the *Red Dragon*, was waiting, its grav engines running and three of its crew, armed with railguns, moving into position to cover them.

But the crates of osmium had still not been fully loaded. The mech loaders were still carrying them into the *Red Dragon*'s cargo hold.

"Damn it, Ratelli," Wok spat as he skidded to a stop at the still open cargo door. "What the hell's going on?"

"We're almost done, Captain." Ratelli, the First Mate, typed on this data screen.

"You should have been done ten minutes ago," Wok yelled in between breaths. "We've got Blues on our tail and we need to get out of here, now."

Realizing they weren't going to be taking off any time soon, Jackknife stopped running, and with his lungs heaving he checked his ammo count. The digital display on the side of the magazine read two-hundred-six. He still had plenty. He walked back towards the mouth of the tunnel, knowing they would have to fight a little longer.

There were many such abandoned mines scattered throughout the Sovereign Systems. Mining companies came, picked the asteroids clean of the low-hanging fruit and then moved on to greener pastures, of which there were too many to count. At least in the Galactic West there were, especially after the invading Swarm armies had destroyed so many settlements and colonies.

Jackknife had done the research, studied the scouting reports, so it was just his luck to pick one the Blues had also chosen.

He readied his railgun and braced himself against the wall, his eyes on the tunnel, knowing the Blues would be spilling out in a matter of moments.

"Leave the rest and get those mechs on board," Wok yelled at the loading crew. "Finish setting the charges. We need to launch. Go, go, go!"

The loading and demolition crews went to work with a will. When Tiger Wok spoke, everyone took notice.

"Step aside, Jack," Wok shouted.

Jackknife nodded, smiled to himself and did as he was told, knowing what was about to happen. He retreated twenty meters or so and then watched as Wok turned, narrowed his eyes and began to concentrate, his face set as if turned to stone. Almost immediately, metal railings began tearing themselves out of the rocky floors; crates full of osmium, desks, chairs, machinery, and tools, flew through the air into the tunnel opening, completely blocking it.

"That should buy us some time," Wok said. "Come on, Jack. Let's get the hell out of here." And he turned and ran towards the ship.

Jackknife made sure the way was clear, giving the area one last scan, then he, too, sprinted back to the *Red*

Dragon, jumped onto the ramp, hit the retract lever and the ramp began to close, even as the whine of the *Red Dragon*'s grav engines increased and she lifted off.

The ramp closed. Jackknife secured his railgun in its rack and made his way to the flight deck to find Tiger Wok already seated in his captain's chair.

"Where to, Captain?" the pilot asked.

"Find the nearest Slip point," Wok replied, "and stay away from any that will take us into USF-controlled territory. Then, find the quickest route back to the Freyja. It's time to go home."

"Anybody seen Clintok?" Jackknife asked.

Chapter One

Desperate Measures

The alarm buzzed and Prince Elio Lorne woke up with a start. He lay still for a moment, slightly disoriented. It was earlier than usual, but he needed to get his workout routine in before the day started. He was tired and cold, and part of him wanted to stay under the covers and sleep a little longer. No one would notice anyway. Then he remembered his commitment to the USF and his friends. Images and emotions from the battle with the Swarm came rushing back. The fighting back on Tor and in the Beta Cephei System was almost fourteen standard months in the past, but still too real, and always foremost in his mind.

That day the Swarm had invaded Pricus City had changed his life, as it had that of every human all across the Sovereign Systems. No one, anywhere, was safe, and no one knew when or where they would strike next.

He glanced at the screen on his forearm—these days

he slept with it on his arm; only rarely did he take it off—and closed his eyes and shook his head when he saw the list of his appointments for the morning. He had a Sovereign treaty meeting with the scribe committee at 9 a.m. An envoy from the Bithica System was supposed to arrive at 10:00 a.m. and he and his father were scheduled to greet them on the landing pad. Then, a holo conference with the prince of the Yanakuku System at 10:30 a.m. His weekly meeting with the Dukes was scheduled for noon.

Damn, he thought, sliding out of bed, *my day's filled up before it's even began.*

And he knew from past experience that each and every one of them would run longer than its allotted time.

Then, to make matters worse, he received a new notification. He was now scheduled to be present at an oversight committee meeting with the governors of Orso South in ten minutes.

Ever since his return from the battle of the Beta Cephei system, his father, the king, had been overloading him with royal duties and responsibilities: meetings, etiquette classes, studies, and he didn't like it; not one bit. And on top of all that, Marshal Ugo Tan, commander in chief of the Orso military, had taken him under his wing and laid out a punishing training schedule for him.

And so he had to make a choice. He knew if he didn't get his workout in now, the day would be lost and he would fall behind Tan's schedule, and he couldn't allow that to happen. It was too important.

"Screw it," he muttered, tapping the screen to get rid of the itinerary. "I've better things to do with my time."

So, after a quick shower and a light breakfast, he donned his navy blue USF jumpsuit and his halo, picked up his gear and walked the short distance across the palace courtyard to the training facility and into the holo suite.

Once inside, he closed the door, walked to the far side of the room, placed his gear in the locker and took an FTK Interactive Railgun from its rack, turned it on and walked back to the center of the room.

The training weapon was an exact replica of the real thing, a more modern and much lighter version of the old Z9s they'd used in Pricus City. The weapon also operated like the real thing, but instead of shooting .2-caliber depleted uranium projectiles, it fired invisible laser beams that interacted with the hologram. He tapped the touch-sensitive area on the left side of his halo to turn it on and felt the familiar tingle of the nerve jack. He waited several seconds, then took a deep breath and said, "Begin training program Ugo Tan, Tactical Module Seventeen."

Module seventeen was all about ground combat—inner-city street fighting—developed by Tan from the USF Marine training manuals especially for Elio.

The lights seemed to flicker and dim as Elio found himself transported to the virtual world of a half-ruined city that reminded him, uncomfortably so, of Pricus City. He was part of an advanced virtual reality—VR—game, moving quickly along a street flanked by two-story buildings on either side. He brought his railgun to his shoulder and scanned the rooftops, doors and windows.

He hadn't gone more than a dozen meters when his

first target, a Swarm soldier, appeared in a second-story window to his left. Elio stopped, went to a half-crouch and leveled his railgun at the alien. The Blue brought its own weapon to bear, but it wasn't quick enough. Elio fired two short bursts and the alien fell back into the building. A few steps farther on, two more Blues appeared on the roof of the building to his left. He fired, dropped them both and continued on, keeping an eye on both sides of the street and his stats scrolling along the bottom of his vision.

Everything was being measured and computed in real time: reaction times from his eyes to the target, gun sights to target, transitions between targets and firing times, his brainwaves, heart rate, and breathing were all measured to the nano-second. To pass to the next level, he had to achieve an average overall reaction time of less than .7 seconds.

A movement to the right caught his eye and he turned to see three figures inside a shop window. He trained his railgun on the figure to the left and fired. The window shattered. He fired again and a Blue went down. He swung his weapon to the right, his finger on the trigger. The second figure was a human hostage. He swung the weapon to the third individual, another Blue and fired again. All in less than two seconds.

And so it went on, Elio moving along the virtual streets, in and out of buildings and rooms, finding shoot and no-shoot targets at every turn until, when almost twenty minutes later, he'd finished the module and emerged on the other side of the town.

The VR shut off automatically and Elio removed his

halo and replaced the weapon in its rack. His overall average reaction time was .68. Better than last time, but his goal was to get the time below .5. His target discrimination score was still 100%. He'd passed and would be able to commence module eighteen tomorrow.

He picked up his gear and halo and took the elevator down to the gym. The Palace Militia was already done with the gym for the day so Elio had it to himself until noon. He tapped the data pad on his forearm, pulled up the physical fitness module and transferred the feed to the giant wall screen.

Marshal Ugo Tan's image appeared on the screen. It was a recorded message. "Hello, Elio. You are on day twenty-three of the program. You have four minutes to warm up before the workout begins. As always, your target times, blood pressure and average heart rate will be displayed on screen. Good luck."

But before he could begin, his data pad buzzed. He had a message from his father, the king, wanting to know where he was, why he'd missed the governor's meeting and why he wasn't answering his calls. Elio tapped the screen and dismissed the message.

After a light jog around the exterior track, he stretched his hamstrings and waited for the start timer to begin.

"Your first set," Marshal Ugo Tan's image said, "is twenty burpees, ten sandbag carries and five pull-ups. As many reps as possible for twelve minutes, then you can rest for two minutes before you begin the next set."

"Ten, nine, eight..." the automated voice of the timer began.

Elio eyed the pull-up bar and the two forty-pound sandbags that lay at either end of the gym. The bare, concrete floor in front of him did not look inviting. He hated burpees. *How can a simple exercise using nothing but the floor and gravity be so difficult?* he wondered.

"Three, two, one." The voice stopped and the high-pitched tone sounded. Elio crouched down for his first burpee, put his hands on the floor in front of him, flung his legs out to the rear putting himself into the pushup position, drew them back in again and jumped into the air.

"One," he shouted as he started the next one.

Twelve minutes later the timer stopped and Elio, having completed the set, barely, bent over and rested his hands on his knees. He gasped with each breath and sweat dripped from his forehead to the concrete floor.

It was almost thirty minutes later when he finished the final two sets, completely drained physically and mentally and doing his best not to vomit. His chest heaved uncontrollably. He walked around in circles with his hands over his head, trying to help his body recover. All he wanted to do was lie down on the floor and rest, but he couldn't. His body needed to learn active recovery.

He took a drink from his hydro pack and checked his stats. His pulse rate was one-hundred-twenty-four and dropping; his blood pressure one-ten over sixty. He could feel his heart beating steadily. His body was recovering quickly.

After more stretching and walking around to cool

down, he tapped his screen and brought up Ugo Tan's next workout regimen.

"Your final workout for today, Elio, is TK," Tan's image said. "Although, as yet, we don't know exactly how these powers work, we do know that stress and practice make them stronger so, now that you're suitably stressed after your workout, it makes sense to commence your TK training sessions immediately. You need to be able to employ TK on demand, even when you're physically exhausted. Your first task, then, is to move each of the four one-kilo dumbbells from the rack to the bench on the other side of the room. You have six minutes to complete the task. The timer will start in ten seconds."

The giant screen went black and then flashed a giant number ten and began counting down.

Elio took a deep breath in through his nose and rolled his shoulders, trying to slow his heart rate. The timer sounded and Elio began to concentrate on one of the weights.

He stared at the weight and concentrated, willing it to move. Nothing. He took another deep breath and tried again. Still nothing. He couldn't understand why he couldn't make it happen. Never, since that first time in Pricus City, had he been able to understand how it worked. He just knew that when he needed it, it happened. During the battle of Beta Cephei, he'd been able to take the controls of a Class A carrier, not to mention a half-dozen other ships of varying sizes. Now, so it seemed, he was unable to move even a small, one-kilo dumbbell.

It's too soon, Elio thought. *We still don't know much*

about how TK and Psy work, why some people have it and others don't, and why TK doesn't appear to be available on demand, when Psy almost always is.

Elio shook his head and tried again, and again he couldn't do it. Ugo Tan was of the opinion the powers were like a muscle and that the more you exercised them, the stronger they became.

Elio wasn't sure that he was right. *But what do I know?* he thought.

But Elio wasn't one to give up easily. He tried to ignore his physical weariness and concentrated on his breathing. *Slow breaths in through the nose, slow breaths out through the mouth. Repeat, and repeat, and repeat.* He continued to stare at the weight, and, in his mind's eye, he watched it rise off the rack... and it did. Elio almost fell over in surprise, and the weight dropped back onto the rack.

Stars, he thought. *Is that all it takes?*

He relaxed, tried again, his mind scribing an arc from the rack to a bench on the far side of the room. Obediently, the weight lifted off the rack and followed the imaginary arc across the room and settled down on the bench.

Elio grinned and tried again, this time adding a little speed. The second weight streaked across the room and smashed into the bench, shattering it.

"Oh, yes," Elio yelled. "Now that's more like it."

Elio, crown prince of Orso, was a typical royal: six-feet seven inches tall, of average build—though fit and finely muscled—with shoulder-length blond hair and intense blue eyes. He was half in and half out of the hydro and was still drying his hair when his data pad, on the table in his bedroom, buzzed. He crossed the room, naked, slipped the unit onto his left forearm and waited the obligatory three seconds while the nano probes entered his skin and completed the connection. Then he tapped the screen and brought up the notification that Tenilo had scheduled a call in ten minutes. The icon that displayed the message was still programmed to route his notifications through Dinka's account, and he still couldn't bring himself to change it.

Dinka, his personal robot companion, had been destroyed back on Tor, but the programming and the thumbnail icons still showed Dinka's image. Dinka was a robot, just a piece of tech, but Elio had grown up with him and found it hard to remove and replace the bot's programming.

Elio quickly finished dressing and grabbed his halo just in time to jack into a virtual meeting with Tenilo.

"Good morning, my prince," Tenilo said. "How was the workout?"

"Better today," Elio replied. "I think I'm beginning to get the hang of this TK thing. I managed to fling a dumbbell across the gym and destroy one of the benches." Elio grinned.

"That's... very... That's good to hear," Tenilo said and leaned back in his chair. "I wish all the TK identifiers were training as hard as you. We're going to need them, I think. How's your father doing with the contracts with the USF?"

Elio shrugged. "All right... I think, but there's so much to do. Thousands of ships have to be retrofitted and, to be honest, it seems to me that things are moving much too slowly. Then again, maybe I'm just impatient."

Tenilo nodded. "It is indeed a vast project he's taken on. Progress here in R&D is also slower than I would like, but there's little we can do about it, I think."

"Then maybe things *are* slowing down," Elio said. "It seems to me the sense of urgency we all had right after the first attack has turned to... well, complacency."

Tenilo tilted his head to one side, widened his eyes and looked at the prince. "People do have short memories sometimes," the little man said. "The fleet is being retrofitted based on the *Avenger*'s weaponry and armor, as we suggested, but I do think they're having a more difficult time of it than they expected."

"What's the holdup, d'you think?" Elio asked.

"I don't know." Tenilo shook his head. "Ships are stacked up, waiting in line at the yards to be fitted with armor and new weaponry. There are plenty of skilled personnel; more than we need, in fact, but their skills are not compatible with the new systems. There are plenty of technicians familiar with the fleet's energy-based weapon systems and the multi-ray shielding and we have scores of teams who can program a phased-proton shielding array or configure the ranges for deflector or dispersant capabilities, but there are very few teams with experience in advanced fiber-reinforced polymer iron or AR five thousand Dutrinium, let alone any that specialize in them."

"Yes, that old tech, the old iron shielding, was discarded decades ago. We should have kept more of those old ships, like the *Avenger*, around," Elio said, remembering the last series of meetings with the fleet leadership and the engineering officers he'd attended. "Sometimes the USF is too big and too complex for its own good," he continued. "What I wouldn't give for a fleet of the old Defender or Guardian Class warships right about now."

"Yes," Tenilo agreed. "And while you're at it, add in a half-dozen shipyards equipped to make repairs to them and retrofit the new Angel class ships."

Elio nodded and said, "We need an entirely new class of ships and new shipyards capable of building them."

"Agreed," Tenilo said, "and as you know, I've been overseeing a new starship class design, the Avenger Class, but it is still sixteen months from production. You wouldn't believe the bureaucratic roadblocks we're running into. You know how it is; the constant bickering and arguing over who gets what contract and for how much. It's always the same. It comes with the territory."

"Yes, I heard about that," Elio said, "and from what I've heard, the new ships are going to be quite special and everyone's going to love them. You've seen the plans, of course. Where will they be built?"

"That's one of the biggest hang-ups we keep running into," Tenilo said. "We don't know for sure. The USF is still taking bids, but there are very few shipyards that can even take it on. It's a long process."

"And they will be the same size as Defender Class starships?" Elio asked.

Tenilo nodded, looked at his data pad and touched the screen, bringing up a graphic on the virtual screen in front of them so they could both see it. "Yes, pretty much," he replied. "As you can see, there are four shipyards in the Orso System that were used to build the old Defender Class starships. They have all been reassigned and retooled. Two of them are being used to build star freighters. It seems the increase in demand for goods and materials since the Swarm invasion, and the degradation of the supply chain, has created a need for them almost as dire as the need for warships. Trading and transportation demands are through the roof."

"Wait a minute," Elio said. "What about existing facilities?"

"What do you mean?" Tenilo asked, narrowing his eyes.

"I mean... what about the old ports, the old shipyards?" Elio asked. "Why should we have to wait for new shipyards to be built?" He began typing and searching on his data screen while he was talking. "What about the old shipyards where the Guardian Class ships were built?"

"I told you," Tenilo said squinting at him, trying to figure out what Elio was getting at. "All of those old yards are being refurbished."

"Not them," Elio said. "You said there are four of them, right? There must be more than four. Surely, the USF didn't update them all."

"I don't know what you mean," Tenilo replied.

"Send me that list of shipyards," Elio said.

Tenilo sent the file.

"Yes, I knew it," Elio said, his excitement growing.

"This is quite a list. I suggest we take a look at the histories, see what their status is. Look, if some of these old shipyards were decommissioned... we could... We need to check the personnel records."

"Why?" Tenilo asked.

"Because..." Elio said, "I want to know if the yards were all decommissioned and if so, what happened to the personnel. Were they transferred or just let go? Were the yards abandoned? If so, can they be recommissioned? And the people... we need qualified people."

Tenilo shook his head and said, "I think you're wasting your time, my prince. The Guardian-Class yards that weren't refurbished and restructured, if there are any, would have long been abandoned and stripped; they would be beyond redemption."

"I don't think so," Elio said. "If there's one thing I've learned while attending these high-level meetings over the last twelve months, it's that the fleet's number one priority is to save money, in every way possible. Think about it. It would cost more money to strip those yards than it's worth. No, I think they would simply have walked away, abandoned them."

"So... you're suggesting there might be Guardian-Class yards still out there somewhere," Tenilo said skeptically, "ready to be fired up and capable of producing Dutrinium armor?"

Elio looked up at him. "Yes, that's exactly what I'm saying."

Tenilo tilted his head, narrowed his eyes, frowned, then he nodded and began talking softly to his data pad.

After a few minutes, Elio looked up and said, "All

right, Tenny, I've found three possibilities. There are three systems that once operated at least one shipyard. The last one closed down back in sixty-two. That's only sixteen years ago."

"Yes, three," Tenilo said. "And the one you're talking about is in the Beta Ariatis System in the constellation of Aries. That shipyard was producing heavy cruisers until thirty-two-twenty-two, fifty-six years ago, when it was restructured to build Starstream transports."

"Aries... Hmm," Elio said thoughtfully. "The Greek god of war. How appropriate... What if I could get my father to approve a mission to Beta Ariatis, to take a look at it? You know, scout it out, see if it's worth recommissioning?"

"Do you think he would do that?"

"If he saw the value in it, he might," Elio said. "You and I both know we need more systems working together. If I'm right, the Beta Ariatis System has huge potential. If that facility could be used to manufacture only armored panels for the new Avenger Class ships, it would be a huge plus. I need to persuade my father to see this."

"Yes, of course," Tenilo said. "But I think you should take a look at these Slipstream logs." He put them up on the screen and continued, "There's a lot of unregistered activity in the Beta Ariatis System. That could mean pirates. That system is far away from the nearest fleet station. If you were attacked, it would be hours before help could arrive. Something tells me your father isn't going to approve you going to Beta Ariatis."

Elio looked at Tenilo and smiled. "Ah, but you see, I have an idea."

This could be perfect, Elio thought. *He's always challenging me to do more... It could work.*

"What is it?" Tenilo asked.

"Look, I need to go," Elio said. "I'll get back to you as soon as I can."

"But—"

Elio ended the call and removed his halo. *I need to see my father.*

Chapter Two

Royal Gambit

It was later that day when Elio walked confidently into his father's business office. The king himself was there, seated behind his massive desk, flanked by a wall of antique books that had gone out of print even before The Purge. Facing him, seated on ornate red and gold chairs, were Duke Rutta and Marshal Ugo Tan. The three of them were finishing up the last item on their agenda. Elio didn't know what that was, nor did he care; he was there to sell them on his idea.

"Ah, Elio," King Orson Lorne said. "I hope this won't take long. I have meetings all afternoon. You mentioned in your post this morning that you have something of importance to discuss. So, sit down and tell us what it's about."

"Yes, I do," Elio said as he sat down next to the marshal, then tapped on his forearm screen, connected with the holo generator at the center of his father's desktop, and then hesitated for a moment and said, "But before I begin, I would ask a question of you all. Right now, at this very moment, if we are to win against the Swarm, what would you say is our greatest need?"

The marshal narrowed his eyes, frowned and said, "What do you mean, my prince?"

"I mean," Elio said, a little more impatiently than he intended. "What do we need most, right now?"

Ugo Tan and Duke Rutta exchanged glances. "My prince, we all know that we urgently need ships with armored hulls," Rutta said. "Which is why we're building new shipyards and refurbishing the old ones."

"And there's the problem," Elio said.

"What?" all three men asked in unison.

Duke Rutta leaned forward so he could see him and was about to speak.

"Hear me out," Elio said, holding up his hand and moving to the edge of his seat. "Do we have even one shipyard capable of refitting an Angel Class in less than three months? I don't think we do. In fact I know we don't. It's going to take at least another year to bring the four shipyards on line, and in the meantime, we remain vulnerable to Swarm attacks."

The king nodded thoughtfully.

"So what are you proposing?" Tan asked. "And why do you think you're qualified to talk about such things?"

Elio ignored the last question and said, "What if we had more shipyards? Shipyards that are big enough to not only build the new Avenger Class ships, but also big enough to retrofit our Angel Class ships as well? What if there were shipyards just sitting there waiting for us to start them up again?"

The king smiled and said, "That would be a wonderful thing, my son, but what the hell are you talking about?"

"I'm talking about the shipyards beyond the USF systems. The ones we walked away from because it was too expensive to strip them." That was a bit of a stretch, even for Elio; he had no idea if the shipyards were stripped or not, or even if they were still there.

The three men looked at one another again, each daring the other to speak.

"My prince," Rutta said finally. "I can understand your enthusiasm, but we are not aware of any such shipyards. If there are any, they were abandoned long ago and would be... I'm afraid they no longer exist."

"But you don't know that for sure?" Elio leaned forward and pointed a finger at the duke.

"Well... I uh," the duke stammered. "I'd have to look into it and—"

"And there you have it," Elio said triumphantly. "I *have* looked into it. I've had my team looking into it and I'd like to show you what we've found." He tapped his screen and a three-dimensional hologram of the galaxy appeared above his father's desk.

"And what exactly are we supposed to be looking at?" Rutta asked.

Elio tapped several times more and the hologram morphed to show the Aries constellation. "This is the Aries System... I mean the constellation of Aries." Elio tapped his screen again and the relevant data appeared above the hologram.

"This is a readout of the specs for the abandoned shipyard in the Beta Ariatis System or, as it's sometimes known, the Sheratan System, and these are the specs for the shipyard on the planet Freyja." Elio tapped again and an image of a vast industrial complex appeared. "I believe that shipyard is still intact. If so, it could be used to manufacture the new Avenger Class ships *and* repair and refit the Angel Class ships. This is a major resource and it's just sitting there, unused."

"I remember that yard," Tan said. "It's been abandoned for at least a century. You're talking rub—"

"With respect, marshal, you're wrong," Elio said, interrupting him.

"The Freyja Shipyard closed down early in thirty-two-sixty-two, just sixteen years ago. In fact, the last Starstream transport was launched in February of that year, but here's the thing: until thirty-two-twenty-two, until they were phased out, that shipyard was producing heavy cruisers, Guardian and Defender Class cruisers, like the *Avenger*. That was only fifty-six years ago."

The king leaned in to get a closer look, resting his chin in his hand.

Duke Rutta shook his head decisively. "We've talked about this before, Your Grace," he said and turned to look at the king. "The retrofitting of the Angel Class ships is expensive enough. Why build more ships at this time? Our resources are finite."

"I disagree," Elio said. "Aren't you forgetting about the Swarm? They are still out there and they're still attacking the outlying systems, but that could change. They could attack this system at any time."

Duke Rutta waved his hand and scoffed. "The main thrust of the Swarm was destroyed months ago. Yes, there are small groups here and there, but they're little more than a nuisance and easily dealt with."

Images of the close contact fighting and the devastation back on Tor flashed through Elio's mind. *How could these people forget so quickly?* he wondered.

"Have you forgotten already, my lord?" Elio said slowly, a hard edge to his voice. "Have you forgotten the destruction and the millions of lives that were lost on Tor and in the Pallas System and in the fleet not much more than a year ago? I haven't. I was there. I saw what the Blues did to our people and our cities, and I believe we, as a royal family, have an obligation to make sure it never happens again. And the only way to do that is to build new ships *and* retrofit our fleet with the proper weaponry and armor and develop new technologies."

Elio tapped his screen again and the hologram changed to display a three-dimensional map of the known battles with the Swarm.

"You must also remember that, as far as we know, the Swarm does not use the Slipstreams, which means they either have true FTL travel or they can generate traversable wormholes on demand. They can travel in between systems in a way of which we have no knowledge. That means, my lord, that we can't just sit around on our asses and guard the Slip Gates."

Rutta and the king looked suitably shocked at Elio's

language and apparent disrespect for the duke. Marshal Tan simply smiled.

"We *must*," Elio continued, "have enough ships available for a quick response to a surprise attack, and that's entirely possible considering there's evidence the Swarm threat is increasing."

"Why would you say that?" Rutta asked skeptically, a sneer on his lips.

"Look at the map, my lord," Elio replied. "It doesn't take a genius to see that the number of attacks is increasing. Time is of the essence. We... need... more... ships, and we need them quickly. Therefore, I propose we send a ship on a scouting mission to confirm this data." He tapped his screen and the hologram changed again, back to the image of the abandoned shipyard. "We need to confirm that the dockyard is viable and... available."

Everyone sat quietly, staring at the great dockyard. The duke looked down in frustration. The king rubbed his chin, frowning deeply.

"I agree with Prince Elio," Ugo Tan said finally. Everyone turned to look at him. "We must do whatever we can to be prepared in the event of another major attack. I also agree with Prince Elio that such an attack could come at any time. Therefore, we must learn to be creative. We must find new resources, and... we *do* need to build more ships." He tapped his own data pad and the hologram changed back to the Beta Ariatis System. "But the planet Frejya, here... This system... I'm sure I've heard reports of pirate activity."

"As did I," Elio said, "and I checked." He brought up another set of reports and pie charts on the holo-graph. "This is data sent back by the last USF patrol ship that visited the system just before the first Swarm attack. As you can see, they reported no unusual activity. The Beta Ariatis System has no other inhabitable planets than Freyja. They found nothing, and they left."

Ugo Tan looked confused as he scanned the reports. Elio became nervous but tried to hide it. There were indeed reports of pirate activity but Elio, knowing his father would never sign off on a mission that might put his only son in danger, had hacked into the system and doctored the reports. He also knew that the USF fleet was busy enough defending the occupied systems from the Swarm to worry too much about pirates and ne'er-do-wells.

"I understand," Rutta said shaking his head and waving a hand at the hologram. "This is all very impressive; it really is. But the Beta Ariatis System is too far out of USF jurisdiction... and let me remind you of some logistical hurdles that still exist."

"I'm listening," Elio said.

"First, even if we knew for sure this shipyard still exists, which we do not, we would need to transport large numbers of the existing shipyard workforce to that location. That would require a large number of transports. Each ship and each team would need supplies, clean water treatment, excavation capabilities, settlement support, and infrastructure. We're talking about recolonizing an entire planet in... what? A matter of weeks? You can't simply land, flip a switch and begin operations."

"I agree, but what if Freyja already has people living there?" Elio asked.

"Bah." Rutta scoffed. "Unlikely. From the dates of the last transmissions on your charts, extremely unlikely."

"Unlikely, but not impossible," Elio said.

"Please let me finish," Duke Rutta said sharply.

Elio bowed his head in respect.

"To transport large numbers of qualified tradesmen and engineers from our existing facilities would deplete the workforce—"

"That's true," Tan interrupted. "But we do have a surplus of shipyard personnel, many of them qualified, some, unfortunately, not. However, since the Swarm attacks began and we put out the call for builders and engineers, we've had a massive influx of candidates and students, many of whom already have significant experience in related careers. It will take but a few months to integrate them into the workforce. Plus, we have even more that will be graduating within the year. So, my lord, we have plenty of able-bodied workers. We just need to put them to work. If what Prince Elio is suggesting turns out to be true, we could begin moving them out almost immediately."

Rutta nodded, then continued, "Very well, so let's say that these shipyards do indeed exist, and let's take another huge leap and say there's a population and infrastructure already in place. And," he said and held up a finger for emphasis, "let's also say that we have enough existing personnel and we actually transport them out there without incident..."

Again, he paused for emphasis. "And this you haven't

thought of: every one of those engineers and specialists is trained and qualified to work the modern energy-based technology used on the present Angel Class ships. Not one of them knows the first thing about Dutrinium armor or kinetic weapons technology. No one is qualified to run the tech for those old systems. Everything is outdated. And we can't spare anyone from the existing yards."

"Then don't you think we need to get them up to speed as quickly as possible?" Tan asked impatiently. "New shipyards or old; they're going to have to learn anyway; some of them already have. We can have them go to work... today in our existing shipyards and learn on the job. So why not now? I suggest you get as many of them as you can into training as soon as possible. In the meantime, I still think Prince Elio's suggestion has a great deal of merit."

So, Elio thought, *the marshal is with me. Good, I'm not so sure about my father. I need to give him a push.*

"Thank you, Marshal Tan," Elio said. "I agree with everything you say, which is why I'm proposing we send a scouting mission to Freyja... One ship to confirm the existence and viability of the shipyard or... not."

"One ship?" Ugo Tan asked skeptically.

"Yes, you yourself said we have limited resources."

"My prince," Rutta said. "It is not prudent for us to squander our resources on... wild goose chases such as you suggest. Furthermore, we have to consider the safety of the crew and the ship. Such a venture would put the ship far beyond the reach of USF support. If the ship was unfortunate enough to make contact with the Swarm, it could take many hours, even days, and many

Slip jumps before reinforcements could arrive. It's just too risky."

"And who would want to take on this crazy mission?" the king asked. "None of our captains would want such an assignment out beyond USF-controlled space."

"Which is why I'm volunteering to lead it," Elio said quietly and then held his breath. The three men looked at him in amazement. No one said a word.

"Think about it," Elio continued. "I'm doing little enough hanging around here, other than attending meetings I have no interest in. I have no interest in politics. You said it yourself, Father. I need to be doing something productive. I'm almost thirty-two years old. There are starship captains younger than me. I need to get back out into the field where I can do something useful, earn some respect."

"Son," the king said with a sigh. "We all respect you, and one day you will become a great leader and a worthy king. But you were involved in a great deal of combat on Tor and in the Beta Cephei System. Those were rare events, and I do not wish to see them repeated. Yes, you fought heroically, but that doesn't mean you should go off into the unknowns of space on your own. There's no telling what you'll find. Besides, I need you here. Your people need you here. They need you to lead."

"They need me to lead from the front," Elio said. "Not from behind a podium or a hologram."

"Elio." The king grimaced. "I understand your youthful vigor... and your patriotism. But you cannot let your thirst for adventure override your duty to your people."

"Who said anything about adventure?" Elio retorted. "I'm talking about helping the fleet, helping all of the sovereign systems, helping the war effort by securing the resources we need. And what we need are shipyards."

"We've had this conversation before, Elio," the king said shaking his head. "I will not allow it. You have much to learn about politics and royal responsibilities and—"

"Oh, for God's sake, Father," Elio snapped. "When are you going to wake up?" The force of his eruption surprised even Elio himself.

The king's eyes opened wide at the sudden interruption. It was unprecedented. No one interrupted the king, not even his son.

Ugo Tan's and Duke Rutta's mouths dropped open. They were stunned.

"Don't you see?" Elio said loudly, waving his hands. "Of what use is it to any of us if I learn to give better speeches and attend boring meetings if we are all dead, killed by the Swarm? What good is it if we manage to join Orso and Tor and Illith and all the other strategic mining systems under one political banner, if the rest of the systems are ruled by the Swarm? Don't you see the big picture? What good is it if we build new shipyards that can't begin production for more than a year? What we need is existing shipyards, and we need them now. We can't wait around. In fact, I'm not going to wait around. I'm not going to sit here and discuss budgets and strategies while we have valid data that needs to be investigated and confirmed. I have my own ship, *The Queen's Pleasure*, and I will do it on my own if I have to. I don't need authorization from anyone at this table..."

He stopped his rant, more than a little embarrassed that he'd let his emotions take over.

Stars, he thought. *I've gone too far this time. Now he'll never let me go.*

Silently, he cursed himself, shook his head and leaned back in his chair, waiting for the explosion, but all were silent.

"May I say something, Your Grace?" Ugo Tan said finally, breaking the silence.

The king nodded, staring over the desk at his son.

"I won't deny having thought at length myself about our needs," Ugo Tan said. "There's no doubt it will take more than a year to bring even one new shipyard online; we need to do better. I think Prince Elio makes some valid points. And sometimes in politics and in military strategy, we have to go with our gut feelings. As for myself, I have never been wrong when I've gone with my gut and put a leader in charge who is passionate about the mission. Prince Elio has clearly done his research. I don't know of anyone else who would be more qualified to lead such a mission, and I *do* think it to be a worthy mission. I say we do as he suggests and send one ship. A simple mission, there and back, to reconnoiter and confirm. I think we owe him that much. We all know the *Avenger,* and possibly the entire USF fleet, would have been destroyed at Beta Cephei had it not been for his contribution during the battle, not to mention the potential upside if that shipyard does still exist and is viable."

Tan sat back in his seat. The king and Duke Rutta stared at Elio.

"Give me a crew and a ship," Elio said earnestly as he

leaned forward on his seat, his elbows on the arms of his chair, his hands clasped together in front of him. "If I'm wrong... I'll forget it, and I'll sit in all the political meetings you want."

The king clenched his jaw and continued to stare at him. Neither Ugo Tan or the duke had seen him so indecisive. Inwardly, Elio was smiling to himself. He knew his father well. He had a chance now.

"For the record," Rutta said, "I disagree with the marshal and the prince."

"Big surprise," Elio said, much to the duke's chagrin.

The king stood, stretching himself to his full height of six-feet-seven-inches. He took a deep breath, expanded his chest then exhaled slowly as he read the data and the charts hovering above the hologram.

"The Beta Ariatis System?" the king said thoughtfully, his left arm across his massive chest, his right hand stroking his beard.

"Yes, Father."

"How long will you be gone?" the king asked, still staring at the hologram.

Elio had no idea. It would depend on the Slipstreams and the route. He hadn't yet bothered to figure that out, and he could have kicked himself for his negligence. But he couldn't show any hesitation. He needed to convince them that he had indeed figured it out.

"A week," Elio said without hesitation. His political training was finally beginning to pay off.

The king looked away from the hologram, swallowed, eyed each man in turn and finally settled his intimidating stare on the marshal.

Far from intimidated, Ugo Tan leaned back, folded his arms and maintained eye contact with the king.

"What do you think, Ugo?" the king asked.

"I think we should do it," he replied.

Elio looked at his father. The king sighed, shook his head, looked at his son and said, "I will approve the mission on one condition."

"Yes, Father?" Elio asked.

"I want, in advance, a detailed plan, a threat assessment and a full set of mission op orders. You, that is we..." He glanced at Tan and Rutta before continuing, "will treat this operation as if it's a combat mission into enemy territory. And I will only approve it if there has been no recent Swarm or pirate activity in the Beta Ariatis System."

Elio hid his concern, thinking it was a good thing he'd once again hacked the military database and adjusted the intel, deleting any mention of recent pirate activity.

"I can do that," Elio said. "I'll have the reports on your desk by the end of the day."

"We can spare one squadron of F32A fighters to escort you through the first Slip. As long as you're going via a core system, that is," Ugo Tan said.

"All right," the king said, "that leaves only one question, the answer to which I think I already know. Who would you take with you on this mission?"

Elio smiled and said, "The *Avenger*, of course, with Captain Morian in command."

The king smiled, his eyes saying, *Well done, my son.* "The *Avenger* has been undergoing extensive repairs, Ugo," he said. "Do you have a progress report?"

Ugo Tan tapped his data pad, looked at the data and said, "She's due to leave the dry dock in less than forty-eight hours."

The king nodded, then said, "Draw up the orders and I'll sign them."

Far away, in the Canis System, Tenilo was pacing back and forth inside his room, wondering why Elio had cut him off so abruptly. *What's going on?* he wondered.

It was at that precise moment that the data pad on his forearm buzzed to let him know he had a notification. He tapped the screen and opened the message. It was from Prince Elio.

Finally, he thought.

"The mission to Beta Ariatis to confirm the shipyard is a go," the message read. "My father has approved it. I'm to lead the mission. I have the *Avenger*. Captain Morian is on board with it. Operation Royal Gambit is approved."

Tenilo smiled and closed the message. He was pleased for Prince Elio and wished he could join him.

Chapter Three

Pins and Needles

Commander Manda Haal, *Avenger's* First Officer, entered Commodore Richard Morian's stateroom to find him seated at his desk waiting for her.

Morian nodded at her and said as he picked up his halo, "Please sit down, Commander." He gestured to the halo on the table in front of a chair. She sat, picked it up and, together, they slipped them onto their heads.

Haal was an attractive woman of what once would have been called Nordic extraction. She was unusually tall—almost six-feet-six—fair-haired, in her mid-forties and smart. She'd entered the Fleet Academy on her seventeenth birthday, graduated five years later and climbed rapidly through the ranks to her present rank of full commander.

Their avatars were instantly transported into a virtual

meeting in a large room attended by some one-hundred-fifty USF fleet officers.

The meeting had already begun. Marshal Ugo Tan was standing on a slightly elevated stage facing a giant, globe-shaped hologram depicting the entire United Sovereign Systems.

"...Swarm attacks on the outlying systems have increased by twenty-one percent over the last ten days," Tan said, pointing out several spots on the hologram. "These attacks were small compared to those of more than a year ago and have resulted only in minor damage. We believe these attacks to be little more than enemy probes designed to test our defenses and weaponry. We know from past experience that the Blues learn quickly and adapt. General Kimmel?" Tan turned and looked down at the gray-haired man seated next to him.

Manda had met General Kimmel once before. He was an older man in charge of the fleet's Engineering Corps.

Kimmel stood, cleared his throat, tapped the data pad on his forearm and the hologram changed from a globe to a graph.

"In total," he began, "twenty-two systems, including the initial four major conflicts culminating in the Battle of Beta Cephei, have suffered Swarm attacks." He paused, checked his data pad, then continued, "And even though the new enemy advances were, in all cases, successfully repulsed, many of the systems involved are still without communications. However, I'm pleased to be able to tell you that recently discovered tactics involving retro weaponry have aided in these battles greatly."

Morian gave Haal a sly smile. This was intel they were already aware of; Morian having developed most of them himself.

Manda smiled back at him, then jumped as she felt a tingling in the back of her head. Fear? Anxiety? She couldn't tell. Whatever it was, it was something she'd never experienced before. It was as if she was experiencing someone else's emotions. She couldn't explain it. All she knew was that the emotions weren't hers, and if they weren't hers, then whose were they and why, all of a sudden, was she able to feel them?

"We are making every effort possible to refit our vessels with railguns, smart kinetic weapons and Dutrinium armor which, in and of itself, is a major challenge." Kimmel paused again, looked around the virtual room, then continued. "All of this takes time, practically and logistically. The USF has not produced these weapons, and especially this obsolete armor, on this scale for generations, so we are experiencing... challenges. We know many of you here have put in requests to have your ships retrofitted, but I'm sorry to have to tell you that we have a huge backlog, and I'm unable to provide you with a time frame."

Many in the room groaned and shook their heads.

"I know, I know." Kimmel held up his hands trying to calm the room. "We're doing all we can, but we're dealing with a supply chain battle the likes of which we've never experienced before. We don't have any inventory of the old weapons. Everything has to be manufactured from scratch, including and particularly the armored panels. The entire fleet has to be retrofitted, and even if we had what we need on hand, it would take years. Once the parts have been manufactured, they, along with your ships, have to be delivered to the shipyards and that's another problem: the shipyards. There are very few that can accommodate this kind of work without being completely rebuilt... or refitted. We're using every possible resource."

He continued and turned and looked at Tan, "We are, so I'm told, trying to locate more shipyards. We have to retrain thousands of people. We're having to transport supplies and goods between systems at a rate we've never done before. And, at the same time, we have to protect the systems from Swarm attacks with what we have available. So, I'm asking you to be patient as we work through the backlog. You'll be notified of your ship's status as soon as possible."

The room was silent. Everyone knew Kimmel was trying to figure it all out as best he could. And even though they didn't like it, the captains and officers, from Tan to the lowest rank present, knew there was nothing they could do but be patient.

Despite this, there were still murmurs of discontent among the officers, but not from Morian whose ship, *Avenger*, was undergoing repairs and refit in the Orso military dockyards.

Manda was still experiencing the enigmatic feelings and emotions. Something was going on inside her head and she didn't like it.

The meeting eventually ended and they removed their halos.

Manda was relieved. She knew Morian had some Psy

abilities, and she wanted to ask him about what she'd been feeling.

She set her halo down on the table in front of her, then turned to Morian and said, "Captain, I—"

But before she could finish her question, he glanced at his data screen, then held up a hand, interrupting her and said, "I'm sorry, Commander. I have to jack into a meeting with Prince Elio. Can we talk later?" And, without giving her time to respond, he picked up his halo and slipped it onto his head.

Inwardly, Manda sighed and shook her head. Morian's response was nothing new. As Captain of the *Avenger* and one of only a handful of veterans of three Swarm battles, Commodore Richard Morian had many new responsibilities and was always in demand.

Later would have to do.

Chapter Four

Is she, or isn't she?

Manda Haal made her way down to Deck 5 and the medical bay. She touched the icon on the pad next to the door and it slid open to reveal Doctor Jyra Dowd, *Avenger's* chief medical officer, reading a holographic chart hovering above her desk.

"Commander Haal," Doctor Dowd said, tapping the screen on her forearm. The hologram disappeared. "How can I help you?"

"I'd like to check myself in for a... a screening."

Dowd nodded. "Of course, but why? Are you not feeling well?"

"Yes... well not exactly."

"All right, come on in, close the door and sit down."

Manda sat down in front of the desk while Dowd typed on her data screen and accessed Manda's medical records.

She gave the records a cursory glance, nodded, and

said, "Well, commander, everything seems to be in order. Your last screening was only four weeks ago and, unless something's changed, you're in the peak of condition."

"That's just it, doctor," Manda replied. "Something has changed, but I don't know what it is. I... sometimes think..." She stopped talking, knowing she was on the verge of making a terrible mistake. Any hint of mental instability and the doctor had the authority to remove her from duty.

Dowd peered at her over her old-fashioned glasses, antiquated instruments that had been rendered unnecessary by nano eye surgery more than a hundred years earlier. But Dowd—now in her mid-eighties, and even with her white hair, looked no older than thirty—liked how she looked wearing them; not only that, but they were always sure to raise questions and thus a conversation wherever she wore them.

Manda didn't speak. The truth was she didn't know what to say. Dowd took the hint, rose from her seat and said, "I see. Well, you'd better come with me and we'll see if we can sort it out."

Manda nodded, stood and followed Dowd out of her office and into the hall to a plain white door. Dowd waved her forearm over the scanner. The lock clicked and the door opened. "Room One is open," she said. "Come on in."

Manda followed her inside and sat down on the anti-grav couch. Dowd ran the standard diagnostic download from her forearm data pad, providing herself with a scan of Manda's vital medical and biological activity over the last twenty-four hours. Then she had Manda slip her right arm into a diagnostic cuff and took the current readings.

"Everything appears to be in order, Commander... So why don't you tell me what's going on?" Dowd took a seat beside her.

Manda took a deep breath then said, "I think I have Psy, doctor," and then she did her best to describe the emotional flashes she'd experienced during the meeting.

Dowd listened intently. Then, once Manda had finished, she smiled, leaned forward, clasped her hands together and said, "Here's what we know. Ever since the first Swarm invasion, medical facilities in many systems have been receiving patients who appear to be experiencing either TK or Psy."

"Do you think that's what it is?" Manda asked, furrowing her brow. "As far as I know, I don't have any royal lineage."

"It's possible, I suppose," Dowd replied. "There has been a small number of confirmed cases where people of non-royal descent have experienced one gift or the other, but such cases are rare."

"Really? So the answer is no?"

"Not necessarily," Dowd said as she stood up. "The USF is eager to identify anyone with the gifts. If you'll accompany me to the lab, I can run some tests."

Five minutes later, Manda was seated at a table in Dowd's lab.

"This is a modified halo jacked into the ship's AI," Dowd said, handing it to her. "The neuro link will feed your brainwave activity, sensory and limbic system rhythms into our Psy Diagnostic Sequencer."

"Krista?" Manda said, using the AI's nickname as she slipped the device onto her head. "I take it the process is painless?"

Dowd smiled and nodded. "You won't feel a thing," she said as she rolled her chair to a bench upon which was a small holo generator. "Just relax and work your way through the exercise."

Dowd waved her hand over the holo generator and a hologram of Manda's brain appeared above it.

The sequencer took Manda through a series of tests, situations, challenges and obstacles, some of which she found easy to solve, some impossible, many of them solvable but frustrating.

One of the tests put her inside a virtual room. From there she was taken to a hallway and instructed to choose a door she believed was the room she was shown. She was asked to do this several times. Sometimes she was right; sometimes she wasn't.

Once she completed all the tests, Manda removed the halo and rubbed her eyes, feeling as if she'd been testing for hours, but on checking her chron she was shocked to see it had been only sixteen minutes.

Dowd handed her a hydro pack. "You did well, commander. That test can drain you. Krista will... Ah, and here are the results."

Manda took a drink and looked at the doctor expectantly.

"I'm afraid everything is quite normal," Dowd said, scanning the lines and rows of data scrolling above the hologram. "You're officially designated non-TK and non-Psy capable."

Manda sighed. "Well," she said, "I'm not sure if that's a relief or a disappointment. I'm sorry, Doctor Dowd. I hope I didn't waste too much of your time."

"Not at all. But remember, if at any time you feel anything out of the ordinary, USF code states you must report to the nearest medical facility as soon as possible."

"I will," she replied. "Thank you, Doctor."

So, it must have been my imagination, she thought as she strode down the hall to the elevator that would take her to Deck 9 and the bridge. *Maybe it's stress. Maybe it's... Maybe I should just quit daydreaming and get on with it. Hell, what I really need is a good hot cup of coffee and something to eat.*

She nodded to herself and exited the elevator at Deck 8 and headed for the officer's mess. She was almost there when she turned left at a T-junction and almost ran into Jiksar.

"Oh, sorry," Jiksar said.

"Excuse me, I'm sorry." Manda laughed. "I was lost in thought."

"Commander Haal, it is good to see you, ma'am."

Jiksar, a junior lieutenant in Tactical, worked for Lieutenant Commander Omario Kingston, Chief Tactical Officer, as part of the bridge crew. He was also from the Bossian System, which is why he had no first name. He, too, was tall, slim with shoulder-length brown hair, thin features and almond-shaped eyes.

"Yes, it's good to see you, too, Lieutenant," she replied, puzzled. She tilted her head slightly and furrowed her brow. "Are you... Is everything all right?"

"Yes... ma'am. All is well." Jiksar hesitated as if he

wanted to say more, his eyes almost level with hers but not quite. He was one of the few men on the *Avenger* who was as tall as she was.

Manda was self-conscious of her extreme height. It made her stand out... everywhere, and sometimes feel out of place, and she knew she was an intimidating presence, which was probably the reason she'd had little luck with men.

There was an awkward pause, a long moment when neither of them knew what to say.

"I'm just headed to the cafeteria for some coffee before I head back up to the bridge," she said finally, for want of something better to say.

"Er... yes," Jiksar said, "I was on my way there myself; to the bridge, that is."

"Very well," she said. "Please inform Commander Jadern I'll join him shortly." Then she turned and walked away thinking, *That was strange. Jiksar's usually a very confident and articulate communicator. He must have had something on his mind... Wait, you don't think he...* She stopped walking and turned to look after him, just in time to see him enter the elevator. *No! Of course not!* She shook her head, smiled, continued on to the mess hall and quickly forgot about him.

Chapter Five

Level E-9

Gian Vastum, a veteran of the Battle of Tor, banked his fighter hard to port, the Swarm fighters close behind. It was three of them against his one, and he was not having a good day.

He checked his scanners. Two of them were still on his tail. *Where the hell's the third one?* he thought as he jinked hard to starboard. It had disappeared off his scanners, or so he thought. *Stars, where is it? It has to be somewhere. Whoa, there it is.*

It was moving faster than he thought possible, taking the angle, anticipating where he was going to be. *Damn it. I hate these things.*

He reversed his thrusters. The two enemy craft behind him were taken by surprise and flashed past him. He reversed his thrusters again, changed direction and went after them, but they were too fast. *Damn, damn, damn!*

Now all three enemy fighters were ahead of him and peeling off in different directions. *Stars*, he thought. *What the hell do I do now?*

And then he made a mistake; he hesitated, unable to make up his mind. He switched his direction, turned hard to starboard, dissecting the angle between himself and the enemy craft that was making a long, looped turn to the right, and went after it.

If I can get him... and... and he overshot. The enemy was now once again on his tail.

He flipped the body of the F32 end-over-end and, still traveling in the same direction at something more than Mach 20, his railguns armed and ready, his thumbs on the trigger buttons on the yoke. He could now see the enemy craft ahead of him, but now the other two Swarm ships were closing in on him from the rear. His targeting system locked on to the one in front of him.

Two? he yelled. *Where the hell did the other one come from?*

He thumbed the trigger buttons. Two streams of white light—fifty-caliber, depleted uranium rounds— streaked out in front of him as he twisted the fighter hard to port, and the enemy ship exploded in a flash of brilliant blue fire.

The second enemy ship fired its plasma weapons as it flew past. The F32, twisting like a corkscrew, was able to dodge the lethal streams of blue plasma, just.

Where it went, Gian had no idea, but he could now see the third enemy fighter on his screen to the rear. He flipped the fighter, mentally computed the enemy's arc, hit the throttle and went after it. Its arc was greater than he'd thought and the enemy fighter was still out of range. He was losing ground. The enemy craft was much faster than the F32. He held the yoke hard to starboard, dissecting the arc, his thrusters at maximum. He couldn't let up. If he did, he wouldn't have time to re-acquire either of the two remaining enemy ships, but by cutting across the arc his disadvantage in speed was somewhat nullified, if his math was correct.

It was coming together. He straightened out. The Swarm ship was now in front of him, slowly increasing the distance between them. *Just a couple of seconds more...*

His targeting systems lit up and locked on. He jammed his thumbs down on the buttons and hundreds of rounds streaked toward the enemy fighter, ripping it apart in a blaze of blue fire.

Gian relaxed back in his seat, heaved a sigh of relief and... his proximity alarms sounded, startled him, and his screens flashed red. Something had him targeted.

"Warning," the system's cold, digital voice sounded. "Target Lock. Target Lock."

"I know. I know," Gian yelled back at the voice, knowing it was futile.

Instinctively, he rolled the ship to port and pulled up hard, trying to break the lock, but to no avail. He hit the Electronic Countermeasure switch.

"Warning. Target Lock. Target Lock."

The enemy ship must have been close. Try as he might, he couldn't lose it. He looked at his screens, trying to get a visual on the enemy's position. It was on his tail, and close.

He shoved the yoke forward and maxed all four thrusters, putting the F32 into an inverted loop.

"Warning. Target Lock. Target Lock." The digital voice spoke faster. The throbbing of the alarm increased, as did the intensity of the flashing red screens. He glanced at the proximity screen. The alien craft was still there and closing fast.

"Impact in five seconds."

"Damn, damn, damn!" he yelled and banked hard to starboard, jinking left, then right, up and down, left again and... Nothing worked. The enemy ship still had a solid lock.

"Impact in three seconds."

Sweat dripped into his eyes. He blinked it away, trying to see through the haze. He didn't have the time to take his hand off the stick to clear his vision.

The engines were at maximum thrust. He couldn't...

"Impact!"

Stars!

His screens turned solid red and then blinked off. A high-pitched siren sounded and Gian winced from the pain in his ears.

"Plasma impact. Mission Failure. Mission Failure," the digital voice repeated.

The cabin depressurized and he felt the simulator slowly settle back onto its docking station. The canopy opened and Gian pulled off his helmet.

"Mission Failure," the digital voice said, loud enough for anyone in the vicinity to hear. "Level E-nine incomplete. Overall score, thirty-seven percent." *Oh... that's embarrassing,* he thought as he looked around the lab.

"Stupid computer," he snarled as he unbuckled and stood up. He stepped out, turned and threw his helmet into the seat in frustration.

That was his third and final attempt to pass level E-9. Now he would have to start over, go all the way back to E-one.

He downloaded his score from the simulator onto the data pad on his forearm and logged it in, knowing that Danis would be disappointed. She'd pulled a lot of strings to get him this opportunity, and he didn't want to let her down.

He was on detachment from the fleet academy after finishing his first year, now a second-year rookie on summer break with little to no military experience. But what he did have was a natural, perhaps even supernatural, flair for all things flight, and Danis had recognized it.

Disgusted with his performance, Gian headed down to Deck 3 and his quarters, having had just about enough of the simulator to last him a lifetime. *Who the hell can beat an AI anyway?* he thought as he threw himself down on his bed.

Chapter Six

Rogue Pilot

Gian, a tall, stocky man of twenty-six with short-cropped blond hair, lay back on his bed and slipped his halo onto his head. He'd woken early that morning, at just after four standard time. Unable to go back to sleep, he'd hit the hydro, dressed and then gone to the simulator lab where he was able to get in two runs on the F32A simulator—both of which he'd failed—with enough time left to call his friend Andra.

Andra Graynir, daughter of Raymar Graynir, Governor of the Pricus System, was on Caerus, the Orso home planet, with her family. Her relationship with Gian began with a treasonous plot to kidnap Prince Elio Lorne, a venture that ended badly for all concerned when the Swarm attacked the system's home planet, Tor, the seat of local government and Andra's home world.

Following a running battle through the streets of Pricus City, during which all of the conspirators except Andra and Gian had been killed, Elio had not revealed the ill-fated plot against him. More than that, he'd elevated them both to hero status and had facilitated their entry into the Orso Fleet Academy. Gian had been inducted immediately. Andra, because of her age—she was twenty at the time—had to wait another year until she graduated from her local university.

Gian tapped the side of his halo, closed his eyes, spoke the command, and his avatar entered the virtual garden setting. Andra's avatar joined him a moment later.

"Hey, you," he said, giving her a friendly hug.

The nerve-jack was realistic but not quite the same as the real thing.

"I wish I could be up there with you," Andra said. "It's been more than a year since I've seen you."

"I know," he replied, "but my probationary period will be over in a couple of months, then I'll be able to get leave to visit you. Did you get your application in?"

"Yes. Elio and Marshal Tan both signed off on it, and I submitted it to the academy yesterday," Andra said. "I should hear back in two to three weeks."

"You'll have no trouble being accepted, not with those two on your side," Gian said. "Besides, the USF is hungry for applicants now."

"I just didn't think you would be gone this long," she said.

Gian pulled away from their embrace and held both of her hands. "I know. Neither did I, but when Danis offered me this three-month detachment to the *Avenger* for flight training, I couldn't pass it up. She's the fleet's top pilot, you know."

"Yes, of course I know," Andra replied. "So when will you be home?"

"I'll be back at the Academy in less than four weeks. *Avenger* is still undergoing repairs. She's due for her shakedown cruise sometime around the middle of next month; I don't know exactly when, but I'll be heading home before then."

Andra nodded. "That's good. I miss you. You're the only decent friend I have."

"I miss you too."

"You're lucky to be out there, doing all the exciting stuff." Andra folded her arms in a mocking pose. "Meanwhile, I'm stuck on Caerus, waiting to hear back from the Academy."

"Well, it's not all exciting," Gian said. "It's mostly classroom stuff. You know, written and oral tests, and simulations. I hardly ever get to fly a real fighter. They keep telling me I'm not ready yet. Who knew training to be a fighter pilot could be so boring?"

"I'd still rather be up there with you," Andra said. "Then at least we could be bored together."

Gian smiled. That's why he liked her. She always lifted his spirits.

Andra's data pad beeped. She lifted her arm and checked it. "I have to go," she said.

"All right," he said. "Just... send me a message whenever you can. I'll see you soon, goodbye."

She told him goodbye, promised to stay in touch and then cut the connection. Gian elbowed himself up, slid off the bed, set his halo on his bedside locker and sighed. His relationship with Andra wasn't a romantic one; they were just good friends, at least that's what he thought. What Andra thought... well, that could be something entirely different.

He changed into his navy blue USF jumpsuit, tidied his tiny room, then stepped out into the corridor and made his way to the main elevator and took it down to the Hangar Deck where the training facility was located.

Lieutenant Commander Danis Morian had also been involved in the Battle of Pricus City, having been shot down by Swarm fighters when she was sent to rescue Prince Elio after the initial attack on the planet. It was there that she'd recognized Gian's natural abilities.

She was forty-two, but looked to be no more than thirty, a little more than five-feet-ten-inches tall, dark-skinned with green eyes and raven-black hair and... she was Commodore Richard Morian's twin sister, younger than her brother by four minutes.

She was already in the training facility when Gian arrived. She checked her chron. He was two minutes early. She smiled to herself, then said, "Simulator?"

"Yes," he replied, taking his seat at the front of the empty classroom. "They've all been submitted... Danis, can we... do it for real this morning?"

Danis narrowed her eyes and said, "You know better than to call me by my given name, Vastum. You either call me Commander or ma'am, understood?

He nodded. "Sorry, I just—"

"I know you just, but you're a probationary naval officer now and you must learn to abide by the military protocols." She stared down at him, smiling inwardly. His enthusiasm was infectious.

"So, you want to fly?" she asked.

He nodded. She looked at her chron again. It was already eight-fifteen and she had an appointment with her brother at ten.

"I don't know," she said, her tone serious. "I've seen the results of your sims this morning. You failed E-nine again, and your score was only thirty-seven percent. I don't think you're ready yet."

"Oh, come on, Dan... Commander," he pleaded. "Please. You said it yourself; flying is all about muscle memory and natural instinct. I can't learn if I don't get any cockpit time. And who knows when we'll get a stretch of downtime like this again. I just want to make the most of it, and besides—"

"All right, all right," Danis said, holding up a hand to stop him from talking. "I also said it took a lot of practical sim and theoretical training. Flying an F32A is inordinately difficult. All four engines operate independently, which makes it so maneuverable. It also makes it one of the most dangerous fighter aircraft ever designed, and not just for the enemy but also for the pilot. You have to be able to fly it by touch and—most important—by instinct, which is where the muscle memory comes in."

"I know all of that," Gian said, "and I can do it. Just because I didn't pass E-nine doesn't mean I can't fly. I can."

She stared at him for a long moment, then, having

already made up her mind when he broached the subject, said, "Very well, but it will have to be quick. I have a meeting at ten."

"Thank you," Gian said, the delight in his voice undeniable.

"Gear up," she said. "I'll meet you in the hangar in fifteen minutes."

* * *

Gian increased power to the F32A fighter's grav drive and followed Danis out of the hangar into the blackness.

Once clear of the ship, they brought their main engines online. The controls felt natural in his hands; it was as if he was part of the ship, unlike anything he'd felt in the simulator. He smiled to himself as he made tiny adjustments to each of the four engines. The craft altered its attitude slightly in response. His smile increased; the four engines on the tips of the four stabilizers, each independent of the other three, made the F32 infinitely maneuverable. The controls were located just to his left. All he had to do was drop his left hand and let his fingers do the walking. It required a level of dexterity learned only after long hours of practice, and he'd certainly put those in over the past several weeks, but he still had to be careful. The throttles were sensitive to the touch, and the touch had to be instinctive and precise.

Danis made a turn to port out of the hangar doors with Gian on her tail, matching her moves.

"Domino to Avenger Control," Danis's voice came over the comm.

"Go ahead, Domino."

"Ranger One and Ranger Trainee out on training maneuvers."

"Copy that, Ranger One."

Gian grimaced and spoke into the comm. "Can't I get a better call sign than 'Ranger Trainee'?"

"What's the matter?" Danis laughed. "You are a probationary trainee, correct?"

"Yeah, but. I was thinking, they used to call me Danger Zone back home in Pricus City, in the grav car races. I was the best. How about that? I could be Danger Zone."

"That's not how it works, rookie," Danis said. "You don't get to pick your own call sign. Someone has to give it to you... Wait! I have it. Yes, that's perfect."

"What?"

"Joker. That's you."

"No way. I'm not funny, just the opposite, in fact."

"I know. That's why it's perfect. So that's it, Joker. You have your new call sign. I just made it official. It can't be changed now."

Gian rolled his eyes. He hated it, but he had no choice. He was going to have to work his way up from the bottom, just like everyone else.

"All right, Joker. We'll go through the standard formations. Stand by."

"Joker, standing by." He cringed at the call sign.

"All right. Formation grouping one. Double Wing. On me. Go."

Gian increased power slightly, caught up with Domino and moved into the first position. Matching her trajectory and speed, he pulled back into the first position. Before he had time to settle in, Danis streaked away and ordered him into position two. He complied. Then again, and again so fast he barely had time to think. He had to get into position quickly and smoothly, knowing that Danis was timing him and recording the exercise.

Gian had the formations memorized, but Danis was doing her best to throw him off while he did his best to thwart her.

They were on grouping six when Danis called a break.

"So far, so good, Joker. A little ragged and a little slow now and then, but I've seen worse."

You've got to be kidding me, Gian thought. *I was damn near perfect.*

"Now I want you to reduce thruster three to ten percent, then we'll go to grouping seven."

"Copy that," Gian said as he tapped controls and reduced power to the thruster. It was standard practice. An F32 could fly on one engine if it had to. Grouping seven was designed to simulate protection for a fighter with an engine shot away, something that had happened to Danis a little more than a year ago back on Tor.

Maneuvering with an engine out was extremely difficult, but it was a real-life skill that had to be learned.

He was learning fast. All those hours in the simulator were beginning to pay off. He was hitting the marks quicker and quicker. His fingers flickered over the controls. The F32 responded like a well-trained racehorse. *Surely, Danis is impressed,* he thought.

His thoughts were rudely interrupted when his consoles flashed orange then red, and the "all-ships" warning lights began to blink.

"This is an all-ship emergency," the automated voice filled the cockpit. "I repeat. This is an all-ship emergency. Enemy activity detected. Enemy activity detected. Proceed to coordinates..."

Gian checked his screens. The coordinates were already scrolling up on his screen. "Domino," he shouted. "What's going on?"

"Blues have been detected at the Slip Gate," Danis replied. "Go back to *Avenger* and dock. I'll take it from here. The rest of the squadron is launching now. They'll catch up."

"No, Danis," he shouted. "I can help."

"Negative, Joker," Danis's voice was calm, but it had an edge to it. "Training is over. Return to *Avenger* immediately."

"No! I can't let you take off after them by yourself." Gian checked his screens. "We're already more than halfway to the Slip Gate. The rest of the squadron is eight minutes away at best."

"Negative, Joker," she said, her voice hardening still further. "You're a rookie trainee. You will return to *Avenger* immediately."

She switched tones and channels, then said calmly, "Avenger, this is Domino. Coordinates confirmed. My ETA is five-minutes-forty-seven seconds. Joker is returning to *Avenger*. I say again, Joker is returning to *Avenger*."

"Copy that, Domino. Ranger Squadron is deploying. ETA coordinates eleven minutes."

"Copy that," Danis said. "How many Blues?"

"Three Blues in tight formation."

"Copy," Danis replied.

Gian gritted his teeth. Three Swarm ships only minutes away and he'd been wanting to kill some Blues ever since he left Tor; ever since they'd killed all his friends. He checked his scanners. *There are only three of them*, he thought, his mind racing. *Me and Danis can take them out easily.*

"With all due respect, Domino," he said. "Those ships could be back into the Slipstream and gone before the rest of the squadron gets here. You know our best chances are to engage now."

"Damn it, Joker," she replied. "I told you to stand down. You're not certified. If anything happens to you on an unsanctioned run, it's my rank and my ass that's on the line."

Just because I'm the new guy doesn't mean I'm worthless, he thought angrily, *and this is my chance to prove it. I can do this. If Danis can see me in a real battle, maybe she'll change her opinion of me.*

What Gian was contemplating, to disobey a direct order from his squadron commander, was a risk. *But what the hell—I've taken risks before. What about when we kidnapped Elio? I got away with that one because of how well I performed under fire.* That wasn't exactly true, but Gian was going to believe whatever would justify what he was about to do.

"And I wasn't certified in the Battle of Tor, either," he

muttered to himself as he fired up thruster number three to full power and pushed the fighter to full speed, passing Danis as he went.

"Damn it, Gian," Danis shouted as she increased speed and went after him.

Chapter Seven

It Takes Two

By the time Danis caught up with Gian, it was too late to turn back. Gian knew Danis was angry, but his adrenaline was pumping and he didn't care. All he cared about was that he now had a chance to prove himself.

And then, there they were. He had visuals of the three Swarm ships, still in tight formation.

"Three marks, twelve o'clock," Gian said.

"I see them," Danis said as she moved up almost in line with him.

They didn't expect such a quick USF response, he thought. *They're probably just a small detachment probing our defenses.*

He was about to communicate his thoughts to Danis when six more Swarm ships appeared.

"Domino..."

"I see them. Nine marks total," Danis said. "You go left. I'll go right."

"Copy that."

One of the first three enemy ships locked onto Gian, but he was already locked on and fired first. His enhanced lasers cut through the enemy's shields and stunned it. It lost momentum. Its shields flickered. Its blue halo dimmed, but he saw none of that; he was already going after a second enemy ship.

Danis flew by, out of his line of sight, but he was unable to see her position on his scanners. Nor did he see the now quickly recovering enemy ship explode in a blinding flash of blue fire. All he could see... all he wanted to see was the enemy formation in front of him and, instead of staying on the periphery as he'd been taught, he aimed the F32 for the center of the enemy formation and pushed the throttles to the max.

The F32 rocketed straight toward the still tight enemy formation, his lasers blazing. He hit one and streaked past it, through the enemy formation and beyond.

His proximity screens blinked red, warning him an enemy had locked onto him, then blinked green again. And again, he didn't see the Swarm ship explode as Danis's railguns took it out. He was focused only on one thing, and that was to destroy as many of the enemy ships as he could and thus earn the respect he thought he so richly deserved.

He reversed his thrusters, waited for the F32 to slow, then flipped the fuselage of the fighter end-over end. He dodged an incoming bolt of blue plasma, then flung the ship hard to starboard while firing twin bolts of laser fire at a third ship, clipping one of its upper weapons platforms, but doing little damage.

Somehow, he managed to insert himself into a firing position between two of another three Swarm ships. His targeting systems locked on. He fired four short bursts, jinked to port, then up, rolled and came in again for another shot. He fired again, slammed the throttles wide open and put the craft into a rolling turn to starboard. His shots had landed smack on target. The halos of two enemy fighters had faded almost to white.

That's three, he thought. *Pretty damn good for a rookie, huh, Danis?*

He looked around. Hunting more targets. Then, he happened to glance at one of his screens. Both of his hits were recovering. *What the hell?*

And then all three of his proximity screens changed from green to red. One of them had locked onto him.

He didn't think about dying; he didn't think about getting hit or losing a thruster. Instinctively, he cut the thrust to his two port engines and opened the throttles of his two starboard engines to the max. The F32 flipped hard to port and began spinning like a top. He cut power to the starboard thrusters, reversed all four engines, and flipped the F32 end-over-end, dodging a plasma bolt from the second now fully recovered enemy ship. He fired a long burst, and again, the ship's halo flickered and died.

Five more enemy ships appeared near the Slip Gate, but before he could react to them, two energy bolts grazed his port side, almost taking out an engine.

He turned to get a look at the ship that had fired at

him. It was moving fast, far faster than anything he'd experienced in the simulator. He put the F32 into a vertical climb, all four engines at maximum thrust. He glanced at the screens. The enemy was still closing fast. Gian cut the thrust on his upper port engine and, with three engines at maximum thrust, he put the F32 into a long, spiraling dive.

The alien craft fired again and missed, but it was still on his tail and still closing.

And suddenly, Gian lost his concentration. He'd tried everything he knew to shake the Blue, but nothing was working. It was turning sharper and moving faster than anything he remembered seeing in the training footage from previous engagements. *They must have upgraded,* he thought, throwing his ship hard to starboard.

His mind went blank. He didn't know what to do. Another alien ship appeared some five hundred meters away to his right. Now he had a real problem. There were two of them and he couldn't outrun or outmaneuver either of them.

Then both upper weapons platforms on the second Swarm fighter began to swing in his direction.

Damn, damn. "Damn!" he shouted.

And then the alien ship seemed to burst into a million pieces. The flash of exploding plasma lit up the sky and Danis flew by, her railguns firing streams of depleted uranium slugs at the enemy still on his tail. It, too, went out in a blaze of blue fire. She'd gotten them both.

A deep feeling of relief flooded Gian's mind. He

wiped his face with his gloved hand. He looked at the palm of his hand. The glove was wet. He was sweating.

Before he could think about what Danis had just done, his focus switched to the five new enemy ships.

"Gian, follow me. We're going home," Danis said calmly. "Formation Three, Starboard."

"Copy that," Gian said and slipped into position behind and to her right.

"Domino, this is Ranger Two at your five o'clock."

Gian checked his scanners. Ten fighters, the rest of Ranger Squadron, were approaching.

"Copy that, Ranger Two. You can take it from here. I'm just about out of ammo. I need to rearm. I'll check in with you when I get back to *Avenger*."

"Copy that. Two out!"

Chapter Eight

Unforgivable

Nothing much was said during the flight back to the *Avenger*. Danis spent most of it wondering what she was going to do with her wayward rookie. *Yes, he has the makings of a good... no, great pilot,* she thought, *but he's egotistical, insubordinate, unruly and hard-headed, none of which are good qualities. I'm either going to have to break him or dismiss him from the program.*

They entered the hangar, Gian first, then Danis.

The first thing she did, even before the hangar pressurized and her canopy opened, was to check in with Ranger Two.

"All clear, Domino," Ranger Two, call sign Strawberry—her real name was Lieutenant Tara Berry—said in response to her request for a status report. "All enemy craft have either been destroyed or have left the system. They did *not* use the Slipstream. They just headed out beyond the sun at speeds my scanners estimated at close to point-four lightspeed, and then they just... disappeared. We're on our way home. Zero casualties."

"Keep your eyes peeled, Strawberry. Domino out!"

The green lights lit up, signaling pressurization was complete and she opened the canopy.

Her helmet was still on as she descended the ladder to meet Gian.

One of the hangar crew chiefs stepped up to the bottom of the ladder to receive the formal verbal handoff of the craft, but Danis stepped off the ladder, turned and walked past him. She had Gian in her sights. He was just stepping down off the ladder when she let him have it.

"What the hell do you think you were doing out there?" she snapped, raising her hand and shoving his shoulder.

Gian flinched and turned to face her, the color draining from his face.

"I gave you a direct order. You ignored it, not once but three times. You were insubordinate and stupid, and you almost got yourself killed."

It was that last sentence that Gian took umbrage to. He furrowed his eyebrows in, bared his teeth and snarled, "What the hell, Danis? We took them all out. I did my fair share of flying and shooting and—"

Danis cut him off and stepped forward. "You will address me either as Commander or ma'am. Do not let me have to tell you again. You think you did your fair share? You didn't. You got lucky, is all. What don't you understand, rookie? We're not a bunch of solo cowboys, each trying to outdo the other. We're all part of a team;

something you have yet to learn. You were insubordinate. You don't get to fly around, doing your own thing and disobeying orders. How long have you been in training?"

He opened his mouth to speak, but again she cut him off. "Shut up and listen for once. The answer is almost fourteen months, and you still haven't picked up on that yet?"

Gian crossed his arms. "Well, I think I did a pretty damn good job out there. I didn't get hit once."

Danis shook her head. He had no idea.

"Flying as part of a USF squadron is not like racing gravcars on some third world planet like Tor. So, you managed to hit a couple of targets. Congratulations, *Joker*. What do you want, a medal?"

"I want some damn respect," Gian snapped. "And maybe you off my ass."

"You really do think you're something special, don't you?" Danis threw her arms up in frustration. "Well, you're not. You're a hair-brained rookie with no business inside an F32. I should put you on the next shuttle back to Caerus."

Gian stared back at her, not liking what he was hearing. Never for a moment had he thought his disobeying her would provoke such an extreme reaction.

"But guess what, *Joker*." Danis stepped in closer, putting her face within inches of his, even if she did have to look up at him. "While you were out there doing your solo routine, I was behind you all the way, covering your ass. Flying in formation like we're trained to do, working together."

"What?" He was stunned.

"Oh yeah. I was right behind you the entire time. And if you could put that big, insecure ego to one side for a minute, maybe you could take an objective look at what *actually* happened out there."

His attitude changed from defensive to confusion. "What are you talking about?" he asked.

"I'm talking about us working together. Since this is clearly a new concept to you, why don't you take the time to review the sensor data and FLIR footage from both of our fighters. You will see there were multiple times you almost died and I saved your butt."

"No!" he replied. "That's not true. I—"

"Yes, it's true," she interrupted him again. "You were so damned focused on only what was in front of you that you had no idea what was behind, below and above. Not only did I have to keep myself from getting hit, but I also had to save your sorry, rookie ass. You're grounded, Trainee Vastum. Now get the hell out of my sight, and stay out, while I decide what the hell I'm going to do with you."

She was inches away from his nose. His eyes blinked and he backed up. Danis didn't realize she had been shouting. Her words echoed off the hangar walls. Several officers and members of the hangar crew stood frozen, watching them, taking it all in. Never had they seen their squadron commander so angry.

The look on Gian's face told her he had gotten the message.

"I'm sorr—" he began, but she interrupted him yet again.

"I said... *you're grounded!*" she snapped, her voice

low, threatening. "Now go. Get out of my sight." She would have said more, but she was herself interrupted by a spike of emotion from her brother. It was nothing tangible, nothing she could decipher, but it was there and she knew she was needed elsewhere.

Chapter Nine

Hidden Agendas

1 0:25am Standard Time

Elio, in his office on Caerus, and Morian, in his stateroom on the *Avenger,* were jacked into a virtual meeting room going over the plans for Elio's mission.

"I can't believe the king approved this," Morian said, shaking his head.

"Hah, me neither," Elio replied. "I had to do a lot of talking, but I pulled it off, mainly because my father and Marshal Tan know how important it is for us to find available shipyards. This is our chance, Captain. If we're successful, the benefits will be incalculable."

"The Aries Constellation..." Morian said, looking at the hologram floating above the center of the table. "It's so far from... anything. It's in the middle of nowhere. To my knowledge, the USF hasn't had a real presence in that system for... more than twenty years. If there are any settlements out there, they'll be either pirates or free people."

Morian leaned in to study the bullet points of the mission parameters. "So this is actually just a recon mission."

Elio nodded. "Basically, yes," he replied guardedly.

Morian nodded absentmindedly and continued scanning the data. "If the intel is correct," he said, "the Beta Ariatis System once had the largest shipyard in the entire Sovereign System."

"That's why we're going," Elio said. "The Beta Ariatis System is little known today, but back in its day it was a major hub for all kinds of engineering, including the shipyard. Captain, they built Guardian and Defender Class ships there. The last one, the *Argo*, was commissioned in thirty-two-twenty-two. As you say, Captain, if the intel is correct, it's big enough to build the new Avenger Class ships and refit the Angels."

"But we don't know for sure?" Morian said thoughtfully.

"No, that's why we need eyes on it," Elio said. "We need boots on the ground to confirm."

Morian nodded thoughtfully, then said, "If we find only a portion of what's listed in this last readout, it will still be a massive addition to the fleet's resources."

"It will indeed," Elio said enthusiastically. "Now you know why the mission was approved so quickly."

It was at that moment that Ugo Tan's avatar appeared

in the room. "Good afternoon, Commodore, Prince Elio," he said, taking a seat at the table.

"Thank you, Marshal," Morian said, nodding his head.

"I assume Prince Elio has given you the specifics for the proposed mission?" Ugo Tan asked.

"He has," Morian said. "In fact, we were just going over the mission specs, but why me? Surely you have other captains that would jump at the chance to take on such a mission."

"Firstly, because Prince Elio asked for you. Second, the *Avenger* is one of only a half-dozen ships with the firepower and armor to defend herself in case of attack," the marshal explained. "And third, there's no one I trust more to carry the mission to a successful conclusion... Captain Morian, these resources in Beta Ariatis, if they exist, are incredibly important to the war effort. But if they are precious to us, it's fair to assume they will also be precious to the enemy. Would you not agree, sir?"

Richard nodded. "So, it's a race to see who can secure these decommissioned shipyards first?" he asked.

"We hope not, but we have to assume so," the marshal said. "If the shipyard on Freyja is viable—and it very well could be; it was decommissioned only sixteen years ago—it's safe to assume there will be others. We need you and your crew to confirm what's out there and who's out there and find out if the Freyja shipyard is operable, and if it's not, what it will take to make it operable. Once you confirm its status, we'll send engineers, labor and machinery and get the shipyard up and running again."

"I understand, marshal," Morian said, "and you can rest assured: if it's there, we'll find it."

"Outstanding, Captain," Tan said, then continued. "I knew we could rely on you... There's... something else you should know. We've received multiple transmissions over the last forty-eight hours, indicating the Swarm is hacking into our data when they make their scouting advances into our systems through the Slipstream."

"Really?" Elio and Morian asked together.

"I thought they're not using the Slipstreams," Morian said.

"Not generally, no," Tan replied. "But they can, and they are when it suits them. And it suits them to hack into our flight data. For what reason we are not sure, but we have to assume they're assessing our strength and tracking our destinations."

"So, it's possible they will be tracking us, then?" Morian said.

"It's a possibility," Tan said, "and a concern."

"That adds a whole new level of complexity," Elio said.

Tan nodded and said, "In which case, it seems prudent to adjust your flight plan and complete your Slip jumps via random destinations."

Morian sighed and thoughtfully shook his head. "So, our jump to the Aries constellation is not going to be quick?" he said.

"No, you're going to take the scenic route. So, prepare your crew for a long flight. Your final destination will, until you make the final jump into the Beta Ariatis System, be known only to you and Prince Elio."

"Understood, sir," Morian said.

"I'll need your final mission brief within the next two hours," Tan said. "Prince Elio, you will leave immediately to join the *Avenger*. You'll leave as soon as I issue the order."

"Yes, sir," Morian said.

"I'll be on my way within the hour," Elio said. "D'you have room for *The Queen's Pleasure,* Captain?"

"I think we can find room," Morian said, smiling.

"That is all. I wish you good hunting," Ugo Tan said as his avatar blinked out.

Elio looked at Morian and said, "Well, that's it then. The mission is a go. You do know my father is backing it, and that he expects nothing less than success?"

"And we are grateful for his backing," Morian said. "As to success... well, we'll do our best, of course."

As he looked at Elio, a feeling of... was it a warning from his Psy? If so, what was it about? Was Elio hiding something? Surely not. Everyone's emotions were running ragged. Everyone had been working around the clock to finish the repairs to *Avenger*'s hull and armament. And, because of the increase in the frequency of the Swarm attacks, emotions were running high.

Morian opened his mouth to speak, to question the prince, then thought better of it and dismissed the feeling.

"So, are we done, you and I?" Morian asked. "If so, I need to inform the crew and ready the ship."

"I think so, Captain," Elio replied. "I'll join you as soon as I can." And with that, he signed off, leaving Morian more than a little... uneasy. Why, he didn't know and, as he was never one to worry about things he couldn't change, he again shrugged off the feeling of disquiet.

He removed his halo, sat back in his chair, clasped his hands behind his neck, closed his eyes and breathed deeply and slowly, enjoying a few moments of quiet before... the storm? Perhaps, perhaps not.

Chapter Ten

For Your Ears Only

Manda Haal and Michael Jadern, Morian's XO, were at their posts on the bridge when the word filtered through that something was up and that the captain was due on the bridge momentarily.

The door hissed as it slid open. Morian walked onto the bridge, stepped up to the command rail, grasped it with both hands and looked around.

"Attention on deck," Jadern shouted, and everyone stood with their hands clasped behind their backs.

"At ease!" Morian said and everyone relaxed... but only slightly.

Morian, a tall, dark-skinned man of forty-two, six-six with piercing black eyes, stood for a moment staring at the forward screen, gathering his thoughts.

The command deck with the captain's chair and the

rail at which Morian was standing was elevated some two meters above the bridge deck: the helm, comms, navigation, weapons, tactical and damage control. From this elevated position, he could see the entire bridge deck and had an uncluttered view of the giant forward screen and the six smaller screens to his left and right that provided views of starboard, port, above, below, and to the rear.

Two meters below the rail, in the center of the bridge deck and directly in front of him, a circular holo generator, some three meters in diameter, could project a hologram of the entire galaxy or a single planet—and everything in between—all in real-time. It could project a hologram of whatever the ship's active and passive scanners might detect. In battle, such as the three that *Avenger* had participated in more than a standard year earlier, it was an indispensable tool.

"Thank you, everyone," Morian said finally. "I have just come from a mission briefing, and I can now inform you that the rumors are true. *Avenger* will deploy within the next twenty-four hours under sealed orders. The mission is top secret. That being so, as of now, all informal communications off-ship are locked. See to it, Lieutenant Lowry."

Lowry nodded, turned to her console, sat down, and entered the necessary commands while Morian waited.

"Comms are locked, sir," she said. "Incoming with command-level access only. I have sent the access codes to your data pad and copied Commanders Haal, Morian and Jadern only."

Morian nodded and continued, "We are about to

embark on a mission to one of the outer systems. That's as much as I can tell you. Lieutenant Lowry, you may notify the crew to prepare for imminent departure and inform them of the communications lock. I'm sure they'll not be happy to hear they will be unable to communicate with their loved ones, but you can assure them they'll be able to as soon as it's safe to do so."

"Aye, Captain," Lowry said and turned again to her console.

"Mr. DeLong," Morian said to the navigations officer. "We will be taking a number of seemingly random jumps to our destination. You will be informed of the coordinates of each jump as we go. No one other than myself, my two senior officers and... No one will know our final destination until we make the final jump. No one on this bridge will communicate any information pertaining to the mission to any member of the crew other than those present. Are there any questions?"

Manda Haal had plenty, but this wasn't the time to ask them. The question was a mere formality, and no answer was required or expected.

"Very well, then," Morian said. "Prepare the ship for departure. Lieutenant Fargo, I want a full weapons report and ammunition inventory on my desk within the hour. Officer of the deck?"

"Aye, sir," Lieutenant Jiksar took a step forward.

"Report to sick bay and inform Dr. Dowd that all sick personnel must be transferred to the med unit on Caerus before we depart. She can use Shuttle 2. See to it, Mr. Jiksar, and give her all the help she needs."

"Aye, sir," Jiksar said and quickly left the bridge.

Morian looked around and said, "Where's Commander Morian?"

"She's conducting a training exercise off-ship, Captain," Jadern said.

"Lieutenant Lowry," Morian said. "Inform Commander Morian she's needed in my ready room ASAP."

"Aye, sir. Doing it now."

Morian nodded and said, "That's it, for now. Thank you."

He turned away from the rail and headed for the door. "Commander Haal, Commander Jadern, my ready room, now, if you please."

* * *

"Please sit down," Morian said as he sat down behind his desk. "To follow up on what I said on the bridge, nothing said in here leaves this room. Is that clear?"

Haal said yes and Jadern nodded as they sat down in front of his desk.

"For the record, please, Mr. Jadern," Morian said.

"Yes, of course, Captain," Jadern said.

"You must be wondering what this is all about," Morian said, his elbows on the arms of his chair, his fingers steepled together in front of him. "As you know, we have literally thousands of ships that, if we're to defeat the Swarm, must be refitted and upgraded. You will also know that the USF is woefully short of shipyards capable of handling not only the refits, but also the construction of the new Avenger Class warships. New yards are being constructed, but the earliest any of them can be brought online is at least twelve standard months. That being so, in less than twenty-four hours, we will depart for the Beta Ariatis System in the Constellation of Aries to conduct a reconnaissance of what once was one of the largest ship-yards and manufacturing facilities in the Sovereign System."

He paused and looked at them each in turn, then continued, "Due to the increased Swarm activity, our route to Beta Ariatis will be... irregular. We'll be making at least nine jumps, all seemingly random. The jump coordinates will be revealed to Navigation only minutes before the actual jump. The reason for this is because we have reliable intelligence that the Swarm is now able to track us through the Slipstreams."

That tidbit of information caused Jadern to gasp.

"Only myself, you two, Commander Morian and our... guest know our ultimate destination, and it's to remain that way. Beyond the first jump we will have no escort and, if we're attacked, will be many hours from the nearest USF fleet. There will be no rescue."

"How long before we leave, Captain?" Haal asked.

"As soon as we have clearance from Marshal Tan," he replied.

"And our guest?" Jadern asked.

Morian looked at him, frowned, then said, "Prince Elio Lorne... and he's not actually our guest. The king has designated him to lead the mission."

"*Excuse* me," Haal said and immediately apologized.

"I'm sorry, Captain. That's a bit of a shock. He's to lead the mission?"

Morian smiled and then said, "Those are my orders. Though I'm hoping it's figurative rather than practical. Prince Elio is... gifted in many ways, but he's not qualified to command a starship. Now, unless you have any more questions, I suggest we all go about our business and ready ourselves and the ship for departure."

They both stood to leave but, while Jadern stepped over to the door, Haal hesitated.

Morian looked up at her and said, "What is it, Commander?"

She looked around at Jadern who was standing at the open door waiting for her.

She raised her eyebrows. He got the message, nodded and left, closing the door behind him.

"I was wondering if I might have a private word?" she said.

"Of course, but please make it quick. I have a lot to get through before we depart. Please, sit down."

She sat down and looked at the edge of his desk, wondering how to begin, then took a deep breath and said, "Well, I'm not sure how to say this... and I'm sure... but..."

Morian looked at her, concerned. "What is it, Manda?"

"Well, when we were at the briefing earlier, I... I had... I was almost overcome by some very weird emotions. Emotions I'm sure were not my own. I know... I... Oh hell, I thought I was experiencing some kind of Psy."

Morian narrowed his eyes and said, "And?"

"I don't know. That's why I'm asking you. I know you have the gift, but... I had Doc Dowd run the standard tests and they were all negative. But, Captain, it was so real. I've never experienced anything like it."

Morian nodded, ran his hand over the top of his head, sighed and said, "I think, Commander, that what you were experiencing was probably my fault."

Haal's eyes widened. "What do you mean?" she asked.

Morian looked a little unsure of how to answer her. "These... gifts, as everyone seems to be calling them; we still know very little about them, or why or how they manifest themselves. I first experienced telepathy, or Psy, more than fourteen months ago in a time of extreme stress. Since then, my own Psy abilities appear to be developing, growing stronger.

"Doctor Dowd and I are working on it but, as yet, I have little control over it." He paused, thought for a moment, then continued, "I think what you experienced may have been some sort of... overflow from me."

She stared at him, not knowing what to say.

"Sometimes, when emotions run high," he continued, "we think it's possible for others to pick up on them. During the meeting, I was trying hard to feel out the emotions of the other officers. I think that's perhaps what you experienced. I wouldn't worry too much about it... unless it happens again. Then I would want to know about it."

"Of course, Captain," she said, then continued, "If I may be so bold, sir; did you?"

"Did I what?"

"Did you learn anything from the other officers?" she asked.

"No, well, not really..." he replied and then lapsed into thought.

"Sir?" she asked.

He looked at her and said, "Nothing. I was just trying to figure it out myself. So... if that's all..."

"It is," she replied as she stood up. "Thank you, Captain. I'll leave you alone."

"Any time, Commander. Oh, and don't forget. Any more out-of-body experiences... I want to know about them."

"Of course. You'll be the first to know, sir."

She closed the door behind her with a deep feeling of disappointment. Deep down, she'd still been hoping she had at least some Psy potential. *Oh well*, she thought, *but...*

* * *

Morian looked at the door, deep in thought. Unlike Doctor Dowd, he had an open mind about his own abilities and those of others, and what Manda Haal had just told him had made him wonder.

There was a knock on the door, it opened and Danis stuck her head inside and said, "You wanted to see me?"

"Yes, how did you know?"

"Oh please," she said as she came in and sat down. "What's going on?"

And he told her, and he told her about his conversation with Haal.

"Really?" she asked. "And you think... what?"

"That's the problem," he replied, "I don't know what to think, but I do think we should both keep an eye on her."

Chapter Eleven

Secrets

Elio was seated at his desk in his private office making the final preparations for the mission. He was scheduled to leave the planet in forty-five minutes for the *Avenger*.

His fingers flew over the hologram as he highlighted and transferred files to the data pad on his forearm.

The *Avenger* was under communications lockdown so he couldn't send them through the net as he normally would have. He had to take them with him.

He shook his head as he looked over the mass of holographic files, knowing he couldn't take them all; not that he wanted to take them all, but he did want to be sure he had those he needed. And that was the problem; he didn't have time to sort through them.

He tapped the secure files labeled "Recent Activity" with his forefinger, opened it, found the file he was looking for—it was labeled "Tiger Wok"—and opened it. He'd heard of this prominent pirate several times.

Oh... yes! he thought. *Now that's exactly what I'm looking for.*

Under Wok's picture was a list of intel reports detailing the pirate's many activities, but that wasn't what interested Elio. What did interest him was Wok's small fleet, a hodge-podge of Defender and Guardian Class ships. Old designs, like the *Avenger*, heavily armored and armed with railguns, cannons and missiles.

Oh, my beautiful stars, he thought. *It could be one hell of a gamble, but what if we could get those beautiful old ships to fight for us? What if I could persuade him... It's got to be worth a try.*

He continued to muse and scheme about how he might go about such a crazy and obviously dangerous enterprise as he closed the file, encrypted it, locked it, and then transferred it to his data pad, smiling hugely at what he figured would be the outcome if he could pull it off.

He closed out the Wok file, opened another labeled "Crowe, Sasha" and looked at the image of a beautiful young woman aged thirty-eight with brilliant blue eyes and a mane of blonde hair. And he couldn't help but think there was something vaguely familiar about her.

It was then his thoughts were interrupted by an incoming call. It was from Andra Graynir.

What does she want, I wonder? he thought as he closed out the file and took the call.

Chapter Twelve

Pulling Strings

Gian was in the mess hall eating lunch. The food wasn't bad, but it wasn't that great either. And he was depressed. It had been less than an hour since his dressing down by Danis, and now he was grounded. *Grounded,* he thought savagely. *Insubordination? Stars. What was I thinking?*

Lieutenant Jiksar set his tray down across from him and sat. Although Gian was new, he'd been doing his best to make friends with as many of the crew as possible. Jiksar was one, a guy he got along with and liked.

"How's it going, Joker?" Jiksar smiled.

Gian rolled his eyes. "How'd you hear about that?" he asked truculently. "It only happened this morning and I hate it."

"Word travels fast on this ship, rookie," Jiksar replied. "What's to hate? I've heard worse."

Gian shook his head and ate another spoonful.

"I wouldn't worry about it," Jiksar said. "Hey... I guess you heard the news?"

"No. What news?" Gian asked, taking another spoonful.

"We're about to get out of here, to deploy. We leave sometime in the next twenty-four hours."

Gian perked up. "Really?" Finally, he was going to get a chance to go on an official deployment. "Where to?"

"Don't exactly know," Jiksar replied. "One of the outer systems, from what the captain said. That's all I know."

Haltar Sen, the senior helmsman, joined them and sat down next to Jiksar. "Did you tell him?"

"Yeah. Sounds like some crazy mission," Jiksar said.

"I don't care how crazy it is," Gian said, taking another bite. "I'm just happy we're finally getting out of here."

Haltar Sen looked at Gian, frowned and said, "You... don't..." Then back at Jiksar. "You didn't tell him, did you? He doesn't know... does he?"

Gian stopped chewing, looked first at one, then the other and said, "What?"

"I'm sorry, Gian," Sen said. "They should have told you already. You're not going."

Gian's world came crashing down. *What? Why? Why are they doing this to me?* He put down his spoon, stared down at his plate then pushed it violently away. Jiksar and Haltar Sen didn't say a word.

Gian rubbed his eyes and looked around. He was so

angry he was afraid to say anything, afraid of what it might be.

He looked up and saw none other than Danis entering the mess hall, obviously looking for someone.

Gian saw red, stood up and, without thinking, started across the room toward her.

"What's going on, ma'am?" he asked, even before he'd quite caught up with her. People at the tables nearby looked up in surprise.

She looked surprised to see him. "Not now, Vastum," she said and turned away and continued walking.

"Yes, right now," Gian said, following her. "If you're going to remove me from *Avenger*, I think I'm entitled to know why. And I'd appreciate it if I'm told by my direct supervisor and not have to learn it from second-hand gossip in the mess hall."

Danis stopped walking and turned to face him. "Who told you?" she asked, obviously annoyed.

Gian looked back where he'd been sitting, but Jiksar and Sen were already gone. "It doesn't matter," he said. "Why didn't you tell me? I thought we were friends."

Danis sighed, crossed her arms, and said, "Gian, what happened on Tor was another time and another place. Yes, we were friends. We were all friends, thrown together under circumstances over which we had no control. That was then. This is now. I'm not your friend. I'm your commanding officer, and you are a second-year Fleet Academy trainee."

He stared at her for a long moment, not knowing what to say.

She sighed, shook her head and said, "I was going to tell you. I was going to call you into my office right after I took care of something else. I want to know who told you."

"I told you it doesn't matter," he replied. "Why am I not going on the mission? I'm entitled to—"

"No," she cut him off. "You're entitled to nothing. If you're going to remain part of this fleet, you'll have to learn to eliminate words such as 'entitled' and 'appreciate' from your vocabulary, especially when you're speaking to a superior officer."

"Why am I not going?" he persisted.

"Are you really that dumb?" she asked.

"I must be," he said sarcastically. "So why don't you explain it to me?"

"Are you serious?" she asked. "Just listen to yourself. You're not going partly because of the way you're speaking to me right now."

That hurt. He was stunned. He hadn't expected that.

"That's right," she said. "If you cannot address me, as your commanding officer, with the common courtesy and respect I've *earned,* you don't deserve my consideration, but primarily you're not going because you can't, or won't, follow orders. You almost got yourself killed this morning. I can no longer trust you, and I cannot put my pilots and myself at risk because you refuse to obey orders."

Gian looked down at the floor. He finally understood why all the seemingly insignificant little details she had been harassing him about were so important.

"It's nothing personal," she said. "You're not the first to learn this lesson, nor will you be the last. You still have a lot to learn."

Gian was... chastened. "I'm... I'm sorry, Danis. I mean, ma'am. I didn't understand why you were being so hard on me," he said, suddenly realizing he'd pushed her to the limit apparently for the last time, and that if he had any hope of getting her to change her mind, he had better own up to it.

He straightened up, feet apart, hands clasped behind his back and said, "I'm sorry, ma'am. No excuses. You're right. I was wrong. I've been wrong all along. But I've learned from my mistakes. I didn't realize—"

"Did you even review the data from the last flight?" she asked

"Yes, I did. And you were right. There was a lot more going on during the battle than I thought. But that's why I want to learn, ma'am. I want to learn to see the battlefield the way you do. I know I'm not perfect. I know I'm going to screw up sometimes. But I'm willing to learn, and the only way I can do that is by trying. I promise you I'll do better."

She stared at him, not saying a word. Was that a good thing? He didn't know. What he did know was that he had to own his mistakes. It was the only way he was going to retain any shred of self-respect he still had left.

"I'm sorry for disobeying you earlier, ma'am. I am. I really am. I... just didn't realize the consequences of my actions. Damn it, Dan... Commander. I just... I just wanted to impress you. I'm honored to be able to learn from the best pilot in the fleet." He shook his head, turned away and wiped his forehead with the back of his hand. "I'm sorry," he muttered, just loud enough for her to hear. "I guess I just blow it sometimes." He kicked himself mentally and was ready to walk away.

"So, what did you learn from the data?" she asked.

He looked back at her. She still had her hands on her hips, a hard expression on her face.

"I... saw that there were at least three times when an enemy ship had me locked on," he replied, "and that you destroyed them. You saved my life multiple times."

"And?" she pressed him.

"And I learned that I need to keep a better watch on my scanners and not get tunnel-vision on my targeting sensors."

"Yes and?" she snapped.

"I learned that I need to see the whole battlefield. That I have to learn to be part of the team. That if we try to fight them alone, one on one, they'll win. I learned that by supporting each other and maintaining the correct battle formations, we multiply our firepower and enhance our chances of winning."

"Well," she said, "that's a start, at least."

"I must also apologize for accosting you like this," he said. "In the future, if I have any further questions about your orders, I will request an interview and direct them to you only in your office and with your permission. I'm sorry, ma'am. I really am. I understand why you don't want me to stay. I guess I'm not as ready as I thought."

He turned away. Ashamed to face her anymore, wondering how he could have been such a jackass? Here he was, stationed on the *Avenger* under Captain Richard Morian and Danis Domino Morian. It was the assignment of a lifetime and he'd screwed it up. *Damn it!*

He walked back to his table, picked up his tray, walked over to the trash incinerator, scraped what was left of his meal into the unit and set the tray on the counter. Then he turned again to find Danis standing in front of him.

"Oh..." he said.

She had the beginnings of a smile on one side of her mouth. "Probationary Pilot Vastum, I accept your apologies. Even so, I should have you sent planet-side on the first available shuttle, but I won't. Stop!" She held up her hand as he was about to speak.

"You're one lucky rookie, Vastum," she said. "You're lucky I'm in a forgiving mood. And you're lucky we're strapped for people and that we need every available body."

Gian perked up. "Really?"

"Perhaps." She held up a finger. "I'll consider re-assigning you to the mission under three conditions. If you fail even one of them, I'll send you back to a permanent ground assignment."

"I know where I screwed up," he said enthusiastically. "I can do better. I promise."

"All right, here it is," she said. "I want a detailed written After Action Report of what happened this morning, and I want a list of at least ten tactical and operational mistakes you made during the engagement. And I want it all on my screen within the next twelve hours."

"Yes, ma'am."

"No typos."

"No, ma'am."

"The second condition is this," she continued. "I want you in the simulator twelve hours a day from now on, unless I tell you otherwise."

"Yes, ma'am."

"Third, if you ever disobey an order from a superior officer—and that includes non-commissioned officers—I'll have you thrown in the brig for the duration. Do you understand?"

"Yes, ma'am."

"And Gian?"

"Yes, ma'am?"

"If you call me ma'am one more time, I'll throw you out an airlock."

"Yes, ma—" He caught himself, grinned and said, "Copy that, Domino."

* * *

Gian almost ran down to the flight deck. He was so excited. His intention was to begin working on his After Action Report, but first he wanted to check on the simulator availability for the day. He wanted to start logging hours and, if Danis wanted him in there for twelve hours a day, he would do thirteen.

He stepped out of the elevator and walked quickly toward the hangar bay doors. He held his arm up to the sensor expecting the door to open immediately, but it didn't. He glanced at the portal and saw that the great doors were open and that the landing lights were on. Someone was arriving.

He waited patiently and was surprised to see a small but familiar ship slip smoothly inside and dock in one of the empty guest slots. The yacht's grav engines whined as *The Queen's Pleasure* hovered for a few seconds, then settled gently down. The hangar doors closed and re-pressurized. The warning lights turned from red to green, and the access door slid open allowing him to enter.

The hangar crew scurried around the yacht. The ramp lowered and Prince Elio appeared and stood for a moment, then stepped out and walked down to the hangar floor.

It had been more than a year since Gian had last seen Elio, but he noted that he'd changed hardly at all. He was dressed in a one-piece, royal blue flight suit sans rank insignia, but with the collar trimmed in gold. He was an imposing figure, but his smile was as genuine and warm as ever.

"Gian," Elio said, smiling. "What the hell are you doing here?"

"I'm on detachment from the Academy," he replied as he stepped forward and shook the prince's hand. "But why are you here?"

"Can't say, not now anyway, but it's great to see you, Gian," Elio replied, wrapping his arm around his shoulder. "How are you doing? Well, I hope."

"Oh yeah," Gian said, "I'm... doing well." He felt a little guilty as he said it, in light of the mess he'd gotten himself into during the last several hours, but Gian had come to think of Elio more as a brother rather than a royal prince. Their fighting together back on Tor during the first Swarm invasion had brought them closer together than any of Gian's friends, and he knew he didn't always follow protocol when talking to the prince, but to Gian, friendship was more powerful than rank.

"Well," Elio said, slapping him on the back, "I have someone else with me I'm sure you'll be glad to see." He turned to look back at his yacht. Andra Graynir had just stepped onto the ramp.

"Andra!" Gian said.

"Hey, Gian." Andra smiled as she strutted down the ramp.

"Whoa. What? How...?" Gian stuttered.

Andra shrugged and stepped forward for a hug. Gian wrapped his arms around her.

"I have friends in high places," she said lightly, smiling at Elio. "Prince Elio was kind enough to approve my request. I've still not received my acceptance to the Academy, but he's working on that, too. In the meantime, he's arranged for me to work here on the flight deck, just for the duration of this mission."

"What?" Gian threw his head back and laughed. "You've got to be kidding me."

"Nope. It's true," Elio said. "But it wasn't all me. Andra's excellent rating on her fleet application earned her some good points. I simply urged the powers that be to give her a non-fleet job on the *Avenger* until her application is approved and she joins the Academy. Now, I have to report to the commodore. We'll get together later, yes?"

He didn't wait for an answer. He slapped Gian on the shoulder again and walked away toward the elevators, leaving Gian alone with Andra. But then he stopped, turned and said, "Oh, and by the way, Gian, please do me a favor and introduce Andra to the Crew Chief."

Chapter Thirteen

Into the Black

"Good afternoon, my prince," Morian said when Elio stepped into his ready room. He stood and walked around his desk to greet him and shake hands.

"It's good to see you again. Please sit down."

"And you, Commodore," Elio said as he sat down opposite Morian.

They passed the next several moments exchanging pleasantries and reminiscing about times past, then Morian said, "Do you really think the shipyard on Freyja is viable?"

"One has to hope so, Commodore," Elio replied. "If not, well... it doesn't bear thinking about, does it?"

He was right, and Morian knew it, but he was also a realist and knew the chances of finding a viable shipyard after being so long abandoned were zero to none, but he also knew he had to remain positive, so he nodded and said, "Of course... My prince... please don't call me Commodore. It may be my rank, but aboard ship I'm the captain, and that would be the correct term of address."

Elio stared at him, then grinned. "I knew that. Please accept my apology, *Captain*."

"None needed, my prince—"

"Elio," the prince said, interrupting him. "My name is Elio."

"That will not happen," Morian said, "at least not in front of the crew."

"As you wish," Elio said and then changed the subject. "When do you expect to cast off?"

Morian checked his chron. "As soon as I get the word from Marshal Tan which, now that you're aboard, should be quite soon."

Quite soon turned out to be almost two hours. That being so, it was some three hours after Elio's arrival on the *Avenger* that she was approaching the Caerus Slip Gate.

Commander Haal was seated at her post next to Morian's chair on the command deck of the main bridge watching the bridge crew prepare to make the first jump. The captain was not yet present.

"Avenger, this is Lieutenant Commander John Jackson, Sigma Three leader. D'you copy?" a voice said over the comms.

"We copy. Go ahead, Sigma Three," Lieutenant Sandra Lowry, the senior communications officer, replied.

"Sigma Three on approach," Jackson said. "We are to accompany you through your first Slip jump. We have word that a small fleet of Swarm ships is present in the

Tema System near the gate. We will engage ahead of your arrival and clear the way for you."

Lowry turned her head and looked up to Haal. Haal nodded. Lowry turned again to her console and said, "Copy that, Sigma Three. Thank you for your help. We'll follow you in. Good hunting. Avenger out."

Looks like the fun is already about to begin, Haal thought as she sent the news to Captain Morian.

She waited for a reply, but none came. She glanced around the bridge, noting that everyone was busy at their stations and nothing was out of order. She checked her chron again, more out of concern than a need to know.

"This is Slipstream control. Please identify yourself."

Haal, who was watching the forward screens, watched as the rim of a giant wormhole slowly came into view, the familiar purple haze shimmering against the black of space.

"Slipstream control, this is USF1736 Avenger, requesting access."

"Copy that, Avenger. You have authorization. Send coordinates when ready."

Lieutenant Simon DeLong, *Avenger's* Navigations Officer, tapped in the coordinates and said, "Authorization received and logged. Sending coordinates now."

"Coordinates received, Avenger. You are approved for Slipstream approach. Proceed on heading five-one point seven-five."

"Avenger proceeding on five-one point seven-five," Haltar Sen said, giving a thumbs-up to DeLong.

Commander Jackson, leading the Sigma Three fighter squadron, also confirmed the heading. Haal sat back in her chair, rested her elbows on the arms, and steepled her fingers in front of her, watching as *Avenger* approached and entered the wormhole and wondering if she should call the ship to battle stations. The jump to Tema was a short one, just sixteen minutes. Not much time, but she decided to give it a couple more minutes.

She glanced at Lieutenant Commander Jadern, the ship's XO, who was standing at the command rail, his hands linked together behind his back. He raised his eyebrows in question and mouthed the words, "battle stations?"

She shook her head and raised five fingers at him. He nodded.

The screens all turned black as they entered the Slipstream. The ship tremored slightly and Haal experienced the familiar, never-to-be-forgotten feeling as her stomach lifted for a second.

A few minutes after they'd entered the Slipstream, Captain Morian stepped onto the bridge.

"Commander, how are we doing?" he asked.

"All's in order, Captain," Haal said. "Sigma Three is ahead of us. They have all the data they need. I recommend we go to battle stations at once and when we exit the Slip, we deploy Ranger Squadron to back them up."

"How big is this Swarm fleet?" Morian asked.

"We don't know for sure, Captain. The most accurate readings from the Tema Control Station is eleven, but our best guess is twelve to fifteen craft."

"Thank you, Commander," he replied, then to his XO he said, "Order the ship to battle stations, Mr. Jadern."

"Aye, sir," Jadern replied, then, "Now hear this, now hear this. All hands to battle stations. All hands to battle stations." The words echoed throughout the ship.

Some nine minutes later, Haal turned to look at Morian and said, "Six minutes to Slipstream exit, Captain."

Morian nodded. "Attention, all hands," Morian said over the ship-wide comms. "Slipstream exit in five minutes."

The bridge was quiet as everyone watched the countdown clock. At the two-minute mark, Morian said, "Shields up, Mr. Jadern."

"Aye, Captain. Shields at one hundred percent."

"Status report?" Morian said.

"All six reactors at one hundred percent. All four engines fully functional. All thrusters functional."

"Lieutenant Fargo," Morian said. "Armaments please."

"All armaments at one hundred percent. All stations fully functional," Fargo snapped.

"Prepare all hands," Jadern's voice echoed around the ship. "Slipstream exit in... sixty seconds."

It was the longest sixty seconds of Haal's life until, finally, the ship lurched slightly, her stomach flipped, the screens lit up, the blackness melted away and stars came into view, but that wasn't all.

The screens were filled with Sigma Three fighters already engaged with the Swarm.

Morian stood, brought up the giant hologram in the well deck in the center of the bridge and stepped to the command rail. He tapped the data pad on his arm and a second hologram above the first began scrolling numbers and stats.

He tapped again. The globe-shaped holo changed to a three-dimensional, real-time view of the battlefield: the USF forces represented by green dots, the Swarm ships by blue dots. He glanced and checked the numbers. He counted seventeen swarm ships and twelve USF fighters, plus the *Avenger*. And, he noted, most of the Swarm ships were located to their starboard side.

"Sigma Three Leader to Avenger," Jackson's voice filled the bridge.

"Go ahead, Sigma Leader," Lowry replied.

"We could sure use a little help from your railguns at my three o'clock position."

"Copy, Sigma Three," Lowry said, glanced at Morian —who nodded—and then said, "Tactical, go."

"Targeting is up," Corin Fargo replied from Tactical. "Turrets one through five; fire at will as they come to bear. Requesting thrusters go to full burn, on my mark... Mark!"

Haal felt the ship surge as the thrusters kicked in.

"Full burn is a go," Haltar Sen confirmed from the helm.

Haal stepped up to the rail beside Morian, and together they watched as the heavy 80mm railguns from turrets one through five began to make short work of the enemy craft.

"The new weapons are looking good, Commander," he said without turning to look at her.

She glanced sideways at him. He was standing tall, feet slightly apart, hands clasped behind his back.

"Aye, Captain," she replied, smiling to herself.

She appreciated that Morian wasn't one to micro-manage the bridge, though he had every right to, and there were many captains who did just that. He trusted his commanders to do their jobs, and she knew she was free, and expected, to make whatever tactical decisions she thought necessary without having to run to him for approval of every little decision. He trusted her, and she trusted him. It was an almost symbiotic relationship, and she wasn't the only one. Most of the bridge officers felt the same.

The battle was a short one. So short, in fact, that Morian decided not to launch Danis's squadron. The new 80mm rail cannons were a vast improvement over the old 50mm weapons now carried by some of the F32A fighters.

The *Avenger* moved into position, protecting the starboard side and the Sigma Three fighters.

Several Swarm ships took shots at the *Avenger,* and some of them hit home. And while her shields held, two or three managed to get through, but the new, enhanced Dutrinium armor held with little damage. Tension on the bridge was low as the engagement quickly turned into a turkey shoot. In less than fifteen minutes, most of the Swarm ships had been destroyed, and those that weren't had hightailed it out of range. For, while the USF now seemed to hold an advantage in weaponry, the Swarm ships were still much faster and infinitely more maneuverable than they had been fourteen months ago. And that worried Morian. If they had been able to improve their drives and maneuvering capabilities, how long would it be before their weaponry showed similar improvements?

"Sigma Leader to Avenger, all enemy activity has ceased. You're clear for the next jump."

"Copy that, Sigma Leader," Lowry said, "and thank you for your help."

Morian tapped his data pad and said, "Morian to Sigma Leader. Thank you. I wish you were coming with us."

"Thank you, Captain," Jackson said. "I wish we were too, but our orders are to remain in Tema and await reinforcements. We're expecting a Swarm reaction force to arrive any minute. Now I suggest you get the hell out of here while the gate's clear. Good luck and good hunting, Captain."

"Thanks again, Commander. Morian out," he said and closed the connection.

"Very well, Commander Haal, let's make that next jump."

"Aye, Captain."

Chapter Fourteen

I Can See Clearly Now

As the *Avenger* entered the wormhole for a second time for their jump to the Apiia System, Haal was experiencing an uneasy feeling deep in her gut; not the usual flip as the Slipstream drive kicked, but more a feeling that all was not quite as it should be.

She was sure that something was wrong, but what? She didn't know, and that in itself only enhanced the feeling. She looked around the bridge. The giant hologram in the center of the well-deck showed only the undulating blackness of the inside of the wormhole.

She bit her bottom lip. The feeling persisted. Was it her women's intuition?

"Commander, are you all right?" Morian asked, interrupting her thoughts.

Haal regained her composure. "Yes, Captain. I'm fine."

"Commander, now is not the time to play tough." Morian knew his crew well. "If you're not well, I need to know."

Haal shook her head, trying to drive the feeling of impending doom out of her head. She turned to look at him and said, "I'm fine... It's just... Captain, I have a bad feeling about our exit. I can't tell you why. It's just... I don't know what it is."

Captain Morian studied her for a long moment. She shrugged helplessly. His lips tightened and he nodded. "It's all right, Manda. You don't have to know why." He tapped his data pad and opened the ship's comms.

"Now hear this," he said, his voice steady. "We will exit the Slip in seventeen minutes. All hands to battle stations. Ranger Squadron, make ready to deploy."

Haal watched as the bridge crew swung into action, then she stepped away from the rail, descended the six steps down to the well-deck and made one last round of the crew now checking their systems. Then, she walked back up onto the bridge, took a hydro-pack from the dispenser, ripped open the top and drank half its contents. She breathed deeply, resealed the pack and stowed it away. Then she rejoined Morian back at the rail, waiting for the scanning systems to come back online as they exited the Slip.

Nothing could have prepared Manda for what she saw when the *Avenger* exited the Slipstream. The screens lit up, the hologram flashed once, steadied, and displayed an area surrounding the ship of several thousands of cubic kilometers. The area in the immediate vicinity of the wormhole was alive with Swarm ships.

"Shields up," Morian snapped. "All batteries prepare to engage. Fire at will as they come to bear."

The *Avenger* began to take fire. Manda couldn't help but remember how during the fighting in the Beta Cephei system, plasma blasts from the Swarm ships had rocked her and eventually disabled her, leaving her dead in space with more than a hundred casualties. But now, with better physical shields and updated power shields, they were much more protected.

"Rotating hull sixty degrees," the helm officer said.

"Turrets two through forty, concentrate on the closest targets," Fargo said into her comms.

"Scanners showing fifty percent more targets topside," another voice rang out.

"All turrets, fire as you come to bear," Fargo said, her voice calm. "Missile batteries go to Harpoons and fire as you come to bear."

Manda watched as the railguns and cannons opened fire. The view in front of her, on the screens and hologram, was alive with enemy ships and the blue flashes of their plasma weapons.

As *Avenger* rotated, the views changed, but the enemy's numbers didn't. There were far more of them than she originally thought, hundreds of them.

"This is Domino requesting permission to deploy Ranger Squadron," Danis's voice came over the comms.

"Negative, Domino," Morian snapped. "There are too many of them. Stand down."

Manda thoughtfully nodded her agreement. She glanced up at the stats scrolling above the hologram. They were showing the number of enemy ships was six-hundred-thirty-two, much too high for the squadron to engage. *Avenger* wouldn't be able to fight and protect her fighters at the same time.

It was also true, she knew, that even with her newly enhanced shields and armor, and her second-generation railguns and the new, fifteen-kilogram smart Harpoon missiles, *Avenger* was no match for so many. It was only a matter of time before they'd wear her down. No, the only answer was to fight and run.

Manda knew Danis wouldn't like the order, but she would trust her brother to know what he was doing.

She gripped the rail and stared down at the hologram. It looked like a wasp's nest. Swarm was a good name for the enemy. They were everywhere.

Without thinking about it, she began to analyze the battlefield. It was only then that an overwhelming sense of urgency came upon her.

Somewhere, seemingly off in the distance, she could hear Morian conducting the battle, relaying orders to the bridge in response to incoming tactical information.

"Engine three is under attack," one of the junior tactical officers shouted. "Seven bogies, port side, seven o'clock low."

"Shields to port and rear. Turrets sixteen through twenty-four, concentrate on those seven bogies and fire at will," Morian said calmly. "Damn, there's a lot of them. Not quite the start to the mission I was hoping for."

The new 80mm rail cannons were taking their toll. It took only one hit from one of the heavy slugs of depleted uranium to destroy a Swarm ship, either completely or leave it dead in space. And the area all around the

Avenger was already littered with debris. It should have been an easy task to wipe them all out, but it wasn't turning out that way.

In the fourteen months since the last major battle, the enemy had learned much about the USF ships, weaponry and tactics. Their ships were now faster and much more maneuverable, making them harder to hit. Not only that, but their plasma weapons were also more powerful.

Manda shook her head. *It's taking too long,* she thought. *We're taking hits.* She looked up at the stats. The number of enemy craft had dropped to six-hundred-three. *Only twenty-nine. We've taken out only twenty-nine. We'll be overwhelmed. We have to get out of here. But how?*

It was at that moment she felt a slight tingling inside her head, near the base of her skull. She leaned over the rail, gazing intently at the hologram, trying to make sense of the enemy formations. *Which way?* she wondered. *Which... way...?*

Everything she'd ever learned throughout her career was telling her the best direction to take the ship was to reverse course and head toward the mass of Swarm ships that were farthest away. She knew that would give them more time. But something else was telling her she was wrong.

The tingling feeling increased. Something was telling her that she must choose a different route and head toward the sun. *But that's right into...* She cut off the thought and tapped her data pad. The hologram changed slightly, providing her with a different point of view. At first glance, it seemed that a main engine burn toward the sun would take them directly into the area from which they were taking the most fire. That didn't feel right. Anyone with a modicum of experience knows when you're losing a battle, you don't charge right into the teeth of the enemy... *Or do you?* she thought. Something was telling her that's exactly what she had to do. She leaned further over the rail, trying to figure it out. She couldn't.

"Commander Haal, we need to get out of here, and quickly," Morian said, breaking into her thoughts. "I don't want to stay here and fight it out."

"Enemy craft flanking aft and under," one of the tactical officers said.

Manda decided to go with her gut. She didn't know why, but she knew the route she wanted to take. She also knew she'd have one hell of a job trying to explain it to Morian and Navigation, but she was wrong.

"Commander Haal, what do you have?" Morian asked.

"Mr. Sen," Manda said. "Come to heading seven-four point three-two and go to sector five nine. On my mark."

"Copy that," Morian said. "Go! Mister Sen, I want out of this mess."

"But that will take us straight into the middle of the enemy formation," Simon DeLong, the chief navigation officer, yelped.

"Sector five nine, do it now, Lieutenant Sen," Manda raised her voice.

Delong looked at Morian. Sen looked at Morian. Morian looked at Manda, then nodded.

DeLong shook his head but turned again to his console.

"Proceed to sector five nine, Mr. Sen," Manda said. "Main engines at point seven-five then, on my mark, go to heading thirty-six mark one zero."

"Aye, Commander," Sen said without turning his head.

The great ship began to turn, all forty gun turrets blazing. Sen completed the turn, increased thrusters to seventy-five percent, and *Avenger* headed straight into what both DeLong and Haltar Sen were convinced was certain death.

The change, of course, took the enemy completely by surprise.

"Broadside's starboard and port, Ms. Fargo," Morian said to the weapons officer. "Harpoon and Mark 59 cruise missiles."

"Aye, Captain." Fargo's fingers raced over the screens in front of her sending the message to the twenty-four missile batteries, twelve on either side of the hull.

Less than sixty seconds later, twenty-four smart missiles exited the tubes, each heading for its own computer-designated target. Unfortunately, the Swarm, having learned a hard lesson in past encounters, managed to evade or destroy most of them, but seven did find their targets, destroying them in a blaze of blue fire. The rail cannons, now at close range, did better, destroying some twenty-one enemy ships.

It wasn't much, but it was enough to get them through closely packed formations and before long, as if by some amazing stroke of luck, the *Avenger* was through and was in the clear, heading directly towards the sun.

"Flank speed, Mr. Sen," Manda said quietly. "Go to

sector five nine and reduce speed to Mach twelve, then go to heading thirty-six mark one zero."

Avenger's main engines kicked in and her speed increased rapidly to Mach 40, and the distance between them and the enemy formations began to increase exponentially.

Manda somehow knew that if they could reach the turn before the Swarm could lock onto their new course, the *Avenger* would make it all the way around to the backside of the sun to the new Slip Gate undetected.

"Nice work, Manda," Morian said quietly. "Keep the shields up and notify me when we are in programming distance to the Slip. I'll be in my ready room if you need me."

"Thank you, sir," Manda said and watched him leave, then breathed a sigh of relief, gripped onto the rail, lowered her chin almost to her chest, and closed her eyes.

"Commander?"

She looked up to see Simon DeLong standing beside her.

"Lieutenant?" she replied.

"If I may, ma'am, how the hell did you figure out that course so quickly?"

She looked at him and smiled, knowing she didn't have a reasonable answer. Hell, she didn't even know the answer herself.

She hesitated, then said, "I assessed the battlefield, figured out what I considered to be the best option, and did the calculations. Isn't that what you would have done?" she asked, throwing it back to him.

He looked skeptical, then said, "That makes sense,

but you couldn't have known the route was clear... could you?"

"I didn't," she replied. "I made an... educated guess. Call it a hunch, if you like." She knew that wasn't it at all, but it was the only way she could explain it, even to herself.

DeLong nodded. He looked impressed. That made her feel somewhat better.

"Don't think too much about it, Simon," she said. "We have a long way yet to go, so let's not relax too soon. Let's wait until we're back inside the Slipstream. Now, don't you have something better to do?"

He nodded, looked at her for a moment, then turned and walked away, back to his station.

Manda went to her seat, retrieved her hydro pack and sat down, thinking about what had just happened.

How did she know that heading would work? It was with a feeling of trepidation and no little awe that she realized she couldn't explain it, and she didn't have to.

Chapter Fifteen

Rescue Mission

It was almost five hours later when they finally exited the Apiia System and made the short jump to the Kaplia System. They were heading sunward toward their new Slip point some four-and-a-half hours distant on the far side of the minor star.

Morian, having called a meeting of his senior staff, stepped into the conference room and took his seat at the head of the table. Present were Commander Manda Haal, Lt. Commander Danis Morian, Lt. Commander Michael Jadern, Science Officer Herrick Tobbs, Navigation Officer Simon Delong, Senior Helmsman Haltar Sen, Weapons Officer Corin Fargo, Senior Tactical officer Omario Kingston and Chief Engineer Maxim Volkov.

"Well done, everyone," Morian said as he sat down. Then he looked at the assembled officers, smiled and said, "So, maybe we're not so rusty after the long break after all. What do you have for me, Lieutenant Fargo?" he asked his weapons officer.

"Ion missile stores down to seventy-nine percent. Railgun ammo is at eighty-six percent," Fargo read from her data screen. "All turrets and missile tubes are fully functional. Shields are at one hundred percent."

"Good. Mr. Volkov?"

"Power cell nine is being repaired. It should be fully functional within the hour, Captain. That is all I have to report. All systems are good."

"What about Navigation?" Morian asked.

"Except for the fact we still have no idea where we're going, all systems are fully functional," DeLong said. "When are you going to provide us with our final destination, Captain?"

"When I decide you need to know," Morian said with a smile.

DeLong didn't look happy, but he knew Morian well enough to know there was no point in pursuing the information further. He looked at Morian and nodded.

"Mr. Sen," Morian said. "You did well today, but I would just say this. We, but you in particular, must be alert at all times in case we run into a similar situation as we did today." He paused and looked around the room, then he leaned back in his chair, his left elbow on its arm, his chin cupped in his left hand, then said, "We may not be so lucky next time."

"May I, Captain?" Haal raised her hand.

"Of course. Please."

"Captain, I know we need to be ready for anything. However, the Swarm has no idea where we are going.

That's the tradeoff we took for not broadcasting our jump data to the Slip control stations, so I'm pretty sure their presence in the Apiia System was a coincidence. I think it's very unlikely the Swarm will have a strong presence at any of our other Slip points."

"That's a good point," Morian said, "but it's still a possibility and we must, as you say, be ready for anything."

"Captain?" Jadern said.

"Yes, Commander."

"Lieutenant Lowry has just contacted me," Jadern said. "We have an incoming transmission."

"From within the Kaplia System?" Morian asked.

"Yes, sir," Jadern replied.

"That can't be," Morian said. "No one knows we're here."

"It's confirmed, sir," Jadern said as he looked at his data screen. "It's an automated distress signal."

* * *

Morian ended the meeting early and walked with Jadern back to the command bridge.

"You have the bridge, Commander," he said to Jadern without looking at him, then stepped down onto the well-deck and went to Lieutenant Lowry's comms station.

"What d'you have, Lieutenant?" he said to Lowry.

Lowry looked up at him, then at her screens and said, "A distress signal, Captain. It's coming from sector fifty-one, sir. It's on a loop, and it's been transmitting for... six days."

"What's the format?" Morian asked as he placed a hand on the back of her seat and leaned forward to get a better look. "Is it military, from a ship, the private sector?"

"It appears to be coming from a privately owned mining company, from the asteroid belt," Lowry replied.

"I want to hear it," Morian said, "but keep the volume down. I don't want it broadcast. Not yet."

Lowry nodded, tapped the screen and a male voice, barely loud enough for Morian to hear, said calmly, "Mayday, mayday, mayday. This is the Valecore Asteroid Mining Company requesting immediate rescue. We have survived a Swarm attack, but we are stranded. Life support is dwindling. We don't have much time left. Kaplia Solar Region, sector fifty-one, Asteroid Belt G7, Asteroid K1437. Mayday, mayday, mayday." And the message repeated.

"What do we know about any of this?" Morian asked.

Lowry's hands glided over the touch screen as he searched for the info.

"Not much," Lowry replied. "A USF destroyer on a routine patrol passed through the system a year ago without incident. There are no active USF stations in the Kaplia System. Valecore Mining is active in multiple systems, including this one."

"What do we have?" Commander Haal said as she joined them.

"A distress call," Morian said. "It's a week old. Survivors of a Swarm attack, but I doubt there's anyone still alive now."

"Well, we know the Blues were here about a week ago," Haal said. "So the timing's correct."

Morian straightened, turned to look at her and noted with some annoyance that Prince Elio was standing behind her. There was, however, little he could do about it. The mission was, after all, the prince's project and he was, technically, the mission commander.

Morian turned to his Navigation officer and said, "How long would it take us to reach Asteroid K1437?" Richard asked.

"About forty minutes by shuttle, Captain," DeLong said.

Morian shook his head and said, "We'll file a report and send it in when we reach the Slip Station."

"Excuse me, Captain," Elio said as he stepped around Haal. "You can't be serious? This person is calling for help, and we're right here. We can't just ignore them."

"I'm sorry, my prince," Morian said as he turned to face him. "The message is six days old. The chances of anyone still being alive are zero, and we are on a priority mission. The mission takes priority."

"You can't be serious?" Elio repeated, stunned by what he was hearing.

"I am," Morian said and crossed his arms. "I know these decisions can sometimes be difficult," he continued, "but that's my job; to make difficult decisions."

"I'm very familiar with making difficult decisions, Captain," Elio said coldly.

"Good! Then you'll understand that this is what I must do."

"I most certainly do not," Elio snapped. "We have to go to their aid. I insist."

"You insist?" Morian said, cocking his head to one

side, his voice dangerously low. "You seem to forget, your highness, that I'm the captain here." He paused, thought better of what he'd been about to say, then continued in a much lighter, more conciliatory tone. "Look, as I said, the message is almost a week old, and we don't even know if anyone's still alive down there." He closed his eyes and shook his head, then opened them again and continued. "I would also respectfully remind you once more, sir, that I am Captain of the *Avenger*, and I expect you to respect and comply with my orders as do all members of my crew."

Elio drew himself up to his full height and assumed his political pose: chest out, chin up, feet apart, hands clasped behind his back. "And with all due respect, Captain, I understand your position and I do respect it. However, I must remind you that I was appointed by the king to lead this mission, and I respectfully disagree with your decision."

Morian had to stifle a smile. The boy had come a long way in fourteen months and was now playing dirty. He knew that by invoking the king he would ultimately get what he wanted.

"We are not on some routine mission, Captain," Elio continued. "We're out here to aid the war effort in our struggle against the Swarm. This mission is about humanity fighting to save humanity. What good are those lofty goals if we cannot help one of our own in distress? What are you smiling at, sir? I'm being serious."

"I know you are," Morian said, "and I wasn't smiling at you. I was smiling in admiration. That was quite a political speech. I don't think even your father could have said it better. You're right, of course."

Elio stared at him in wonder, not knowing what to say or even think, so he said nothing.

"Lieutenant DeLong." Morian turned to his navigation officer and said, "How long until we reach the Slip Gate?"

"A little over four hours, sir," DeLong replied.

Morian grimaced, thought for a moment, looked at Elio while slowly nodding his head, and said, "Very well, my prince. I wish we had more time, but we'll do as you ask. We'll check out the mine."

"Thank you, Captain," Elio said with a slight nod of his head, another royal habit. "I appreciate it. And I was wondering if I might lead the excursion?"

Again, Morian smiled, thinking that although Elio was in many ways much changed, he was still the man who wanted to lead from the front. "You may," he said, checking the screen on his forearm. "You'll take Shuttle One and Commander Morian will escort you. You'll take a squad of Marines with you, and you'll be under time constraints." He checked the screen again. "You'll have no more than two hours on the asteroid. Is that understood?"

"Understood. Thank you again, Captain." Again, Elio gave him the royal nod, then turned and walked away, off the bridge.

Chapter Sixteen

It's not what you think

Gian pushed the throttle to the max, twisting, turning, diving, trying to lose the third Swarm ship, but he couldn't. After five frustrating minutes of nerve-rending combat, his screens went red and began blinking.

"Warning. Target Lock. Target Lock," the computer said.

"*Damn it!*" he shouted. "What the hell am I doing wrong?"

"Warning. Target Lock. Impact in five seconds."

"*Damn, damn, damn!*" he yelled as he jerked the yoke back in a futile effort to get away, but no matter what he did, he couldn't outrun the simulated Blue swaying from side to side behind him.

His screens went solid red and his systems shut down.

"Mission Failure," the simulator's computer intoned.

"Level E-9 Incomplete. Overall score forty-eight percent."

Gian took off his helmet and stepped out of the machine to find Danis standing beside the console with her arms crossed, reading the screens.

"Still having trouble getting past E-9?" she said. "What is it about the tactics of the three of them that's holding you back?"

Gian ran his hand through his hair, shook his head, blew out through pursed lips, then said, "I... don't... know. I can always get the first two; no problem, but the third... I don't know. They're just so fast at this level."

"That's not an answer," Danis said.

"What?"

"What you said," she replied. "It's a typical rookie pilot response. Have you even sat down and thought it through? No, don't answer that. I know you haven't. You should. The Swarm ships in the sim are no faster than the real Blues. So, think about what you did. Think like a pilot. What is it that's holding you up?"

Gian nodded and looked down at the floor.

The simulator program set him against three enemy craft. It was up to him to decide how to defeat them. He always took out the first two but, in so doing, the third always managed to get the drop on him.

He rolled his shoulders and looked at her. "No matter which of the three I go after first, I always get the first two, then the third takes me out."

"Stop." Danis held up a hand. "Stop and breathe. Think. Replay it. Break it down and tell me what you did. Each move."

Gian scratched his head. "All right... well, after taking out the first one, I went for the next closest one."

"And then what?"

"I used my speed like you taught me. I got my target locked on and was able to maneuver away from the third as I shot the second."

"And how long does that last?"

"Not very long because by that time, the third one is on my six and I can't shake it. No matter what evasive maneuvers I try, and believe me, I've tried them all."

"Come with me," Danis said as she turned quickly and began to walk to the pilot's briefing room.

"Think about it, Joker," she said. "You can't change the number of enemy targets, right?"

"Right," Gian answered.

"And you can't change their speed, right?"

"Right."

"And you can't shoot more than one at a time, right?"

"Right."

The briefing room door opened as they approached and they walked inside. Gian promptly slumped down in one of the chairs while Danis walked to the front and stood beside the podium.

"So," she said, "nothing you're currently doing is working?"

"No!"

"So, what can you change?"

Gian stared at his feet. "I... I don't know."

"What is the first thing you do when you engage?"

"I go for the closest ship," he replied.

Danis held up a finger. "So?"

Gian raised his eyebrows, then frowned. "So... I could... not go for that one?"

Danis nodded. "Yes, why don't you try that next time?"

Gian held out his hands. "But you said always take out the known first; always go after the closest ship to give yourself the most time."

"No, that's not what I say," she replied. "I say 'take out the closest ship you can.' That's different. You inserted the word 'always.' 'Always' means inflexible. You have to be flexible; you have to adjust. Fighting—on the ground, in the air, in space—is dynamic. You have to change or modify your attack or defense to fit your situation."

"How?"

"Instead of rushing in to kill the closest one, like you always do, wait, stay back. Analyze the battlefield. Find a weakness."

He nodded slowly, thinking about what she was saying. He knew there had to be a way to defeat the three ships and move on to level E-10. *Maybe she's giving me a hint.*

"Remember, strategy and position. Getting to the right spot faster than your opponent and depriving him of the 'high ground' is key." She made finger quotes. "But before you move, in order to get to the right spot, you have to wait. You have to be patient. You have to analyze the battlefield, determine exactly where that 'right spot' is." Again she made with the quotes. "Then you make your move."

"All right," he said, nodding and frowning. "I'll try

that."

"Do you remember Telemanion's Three Rules of Space Combat?"

Gian rolled his eyes. *Not this again?* "Yes. Of course I do."

"What are they?"

"Rule number one. Get there first with the most."

"Right," she said, "but I think he stole that one from someone else. Rule number two?"

"Never underestimate your enemy."

"Good. And rule number three?"

"If you find yourself in a fair fight, you're losing," he said.

"That's it. You need to—" The data pad on her forearm vibrated, interrupting her. She glanced at it. She had a message from the captain. She was needed in the conference room, urgently.

Chapter Seventeen

Friendly Fire

When Danis entered the conference room she found the captain, Manda Haal, Prince Elio and Marine Lieutenant Rene Dubois already seated and waiting for her.

"Ah, there you are," Morian said as she walked in and sat down. "Problems?"

"None that I can't handle," she replied, then looked around at the gathering and said, "We have an emergency?"

Elio grinned at her and said, "Nothing we can't handle."

"Touché, my prince," Danis said, then looked at Morian and said, "This is about the distress call, right?"

Morian nodded and looked at his first officer.

"Commander Morian," Haal began. "As you know, we've received..." and she continued to explain the distress call and the decision to investigate it, ending with, "You will escort the prince and the marine detachment to the asteroid where you will take up a strategic position ten kilometers out, and there you will stay until they are ready to return. Any questions?"

"Just one, ma'am," Danis said. "Is there any enemy activity on or around the asteroid?"

"None that we know of—" Haal replied, suddenly aware of a slight but familiar twinge at the back of her head. It lasted no more than a second and then was gone. "But we can't know for sure, so be careful."

Danis nodded, then said, "When do we leave?"

* * *

"Get into your gear," Danis said to Gian when she returned to the pilot's briefing room. "I'm assigned to escort duty. You're coming with me."

Gian perked up, sat up straight and looked at Danis. "Really?"

"Yes, really," she said, inwardly shaking her head and wondering if she was doing the right thing, taking a rookie on a combat-ready mission. Not that she was expecting trouble. She wasn't. She'd had Jiksar run a series of extensive long-range scans and they'd found nothing. Unless they were hiding, there were no enemy craft anywhere within a million kilometers. As to hiding, the nearest object to K1437, another asteroid, was more than a quarter-million kilometers away; the only place they could hide was either on or behind K1437. And at forty kilometers in length and a third of that in breadth, and weighing more than two trillion tons, there were plenty of places to hide on K1437; it was a small world unto itself. So, she figured her mission was going to be nothing more than a milk run and Gian could tag along and gain a little real-world experience.

She went to the ready room and donned her gear, still wondering in the back of her mind if she was doing the right thing. She pushed such thoughts aside and went to the hangar where she found Gian ready and waiting and grinning like a fool.

"Wipe that smile off your face and listen to me," Danis said. "While we're out there, you do exactly as I say. I won't tolerate another episode like the last one. You disobey me... and you're done. Do you understand, Trainee Vastum?"

He nodded enthusiastically. "Yes, ma'am. You got it. I got it. I'll do exactly as you say. You have my word."

She nodded, then said, "I take the lead with the shuttle to port. You take the starboard position on my wing. No deviations."

"Yes, ma'am... Domino."

"Go to your ship. We leave in..." She checked the data screen built into the left arm of her flight suit. "Seven minutes."

Danis went to her ship, did a quick walk-around inspection, and then climbed the ladder and slid into the cockpit. She glanced across the hangar to see Gian already inside his cockpit and the canopy closing. For a moment, she had a tiny twinge of regret. Gian was excited, and that wasn't something she needed.

"Calm down, Joker," Danis said over the comms as

she brought her systems online. "This is just an escort mission."

He looked up and saw her waving at him from across the hangar. The canopy was closing over her cockpit.

"Copy that, Domino, and understood." He waved back.

"There are no reports of Swarm activity in the area," she continued, "but remember, the shuttle has Prince Elio on board. This little excursion is apparently at his own personal request."

"Copy."

Gian acknowledged and watched as several medical personnel walked up the shuttle's ramp, followed by a squad of Marines.

The forty-minute flight to the asteroid was completed without incident and, according to plan, Danis and Gian took up a position ten kilometers above the facility.

The asteroid hung in space like a giant potato. Gian tuned his holo to provide him with a close-up view of the complex; it was huge, spread out over an area that he judged to be at least a kilometer square.

He watched as the shuttle settled down onto what he assumed must be the main docking port. On closer inspection he could see there were six massive mine entrances, each of them big enough to accommodate a one-hundred-thousand-kilogram Spiker Corp ore transport.

It was obvious, even to Gian, inexperienced as he was, that the mine had suffered some sort of an attack, because three of the massive entrances had taken heavy damage.

Why would the Blues want to attack an asteroid mine? he wondered. *Maybe they needed resources... More to the point, where the hell are they now?*

Gian scanned the space above and in front of them, imagining a fleet of Blue ships hiding behind the asteroid, waiting to jump them. He tuned his scanners and ran a scan of the asteroid and its immediate surroundings.

"Joker," Danis's voice interrupted his thoughts. "You see anything?"

"No. Noth—Wait!"

What's that? Gian squinted, blinked, did a double take, checked his scanners and, sure enough, there it was, a Swarm craft rising slowly above the far end of the asteroid's horizon. It looked tiny, but only because of the distance. He knew it was almost three times the size of his F32.

"Domino, I have one Blue at three o'clock." Gian adjusted his thrusters to reposition his ship and waited for Danis to answer.

"I see it," Domino said. "Wait! There are three of them."

Gian glanced at his scanners and confirmed. "Copy that, Domino. What's the plan?"

"We wait," Danis replied.

"Copy," Gian said, staring at the three strange shapes on his screen. The design of the Swarm ships made no sense to Gian: a flattened oval fuselage with short, stubby swept-back wings that appeared to have no other purpose than to mount its four exposed plasma weapons, two topside—one on each wing—and two below.

There were no visible doors, ports or cockpit. The

shell appeared to be one piece, smooth and sleek. Research had determined that the ships were constructed of some sort of enhanced silicon, a seamless, dark translucent glass-like material. In fact, it was now known that the Blues came from another reality, an alternate universe or dimension, and were a silicon-based lifeform in contrast to humanity's carbon base.

During the first encounters, when the Swarm appeared over Typhon in the Persei System, they seemed to be almost invincible. The alien ships were impervious to USF Directed Energy Weapons, though repeated hits from the powerful lasers did slow them down, but they recovered quickly. The blue halo that surrounded them was later determined to be some kind of shielding that absorbed the energy from the USF's most powerful weapons, including nuclear weapons.

It wasn't until the Battle of The Pricus System that it was discovered they had no defense against kinetic weapons, and in particular, the old-fashioned, long-discarded railguns.

In contrast, the USF ships, tricked out with reflective shields effective against laser weapons, were extremely vulnerable to the Swarm plasma weapons; so much so that two entire USF fleets were lost during the early battles.

The alien drive technology was still largely unknown but thought to be a vastly advanced version of the human grav drives. But while humanity's grav drives were used only for ground maneuvering, the alien engines could accelerate the Blues ships to near-light speeds. But, advanced as they were, the aliens still had to adhere to the laws of physics, and with speed came a lack of maneuverability. On its own, a single Swarm ship used to seem clumsy and relatively easy to destroy. But they learned quickly and fourteen months later they were much slower, still faster than the USF ships, but much more maneuverable.

How the Swarm ships worked, Gian didn't know, nor did he care. And why would he? All he needed to know was how to destroy them. And that, he thought he did.

He armed his railguns as he heard Danis on the frequency.

"Domino to Shuttle One. We've got three enemy craft. Continue docking. We'll take care of them."

"Copy, Domino."

"Joker," Danis said. "Stay on my starboard wing. I'll take the one in the middle. You take the one on the right. We work together, remember?"

"I surely do, Domino," Gian replied, increasing his speed to match Danis's and together, they hurtled toward the oncoming Swarm fighters.

"Expect them to split up, Joker," she warned him and, even as she said it, the three enemy ships broke formation and separated.

"Take it easy, Joker," Danis said. "Stay on my six. We'll take out the middle one, then the other two. You copy?"

"Copy," Gian said. "I'm right behind you."

A bolt of blue plasma shot through space towards them from the Blue now streaking away to the right. He glanced at his targeting screens. The system flashed green, confirming the lock.

He waited for Danis to fire. A stream of white lightning flew from her railguns as hundreds of 50-caliber depleted uranium slugs streaked toward the enemy craft. There was a blinding flash of blue as the craft exploded.

"Watch your six, Joker," Danis said. "Now go get him." And with that she peeled away to the left, going after the second enemy ship.

"Copy that, Domino," he yelled as he made a hard turn to the right that brought him into line some three kilometers behind the Swarm ship. He increased his speed and began to close the distance between them.

The Blue craft suddenly dropped out of his visual. He glanced at his screens. The enemy ship had slowed; he was overshooting. If he didn't do something, and quickly, the Blue would be on his tail.

He flipped all four of his thrusters ninety degrees and slammed on the power. The F32 responded and rocketed upward and over in a classic loop, bringing it back down behind the alien craft.

He had the advantage again but, had it not been for all those hours in the simulator, he would have died right then and there.

But, even as his screens flashed red and the alarm screeched, and the enemy locked on, he threw the F32 into a spiraling, upward turn just as the enemy fired. The blast of blue fire barely missed him. He pushed down hard on the yoke and put the ship into a steep dive, straight at the alien ship now trying to turn away, but it was too late. Gian thumbed both triggers and twin streams of projectiles streaked toward the alien craft and... missed low. He'd over-corrected. The Blue was slowly turning, trying to lose him. Gian followed, but not quite quickly enough.

The enemy craft increased its speed, made a tight turn to port and streaked away.

Gian turned to follow, and suddenly he had a visual on Danis who was making a long, looping turn, chasing her target.

It was then that Gian realized his target was trying to join with hers.

He was perhaps three kilometers away when Danis opened fire.

Gian grinned as he followed his own target as it raced toward its teammate—if that's what they were. He was now in a perfect position to take him out. He increased his speed slightly. His targeting computers flashed green as his weapons locked on.

He saw Danis's projectiles hit home and the enemy ship exploded.

Gian grinned and thumbed the triggers, holding them down, watching them slam into the enemy craft.

Then at the last second, his heart jumped as he watched Danis's fighter continuing its arc, heading straight into Gian's field of fire.

He let up on the triggers, hauled back on the yoke and pulled up, willing his slugs to miss Danis as he watched them streak toward her. Luckily, Danis, at the very last second, saw the twin streaks of white light and threw her ship hard to starboard.

Sparks flew out of her upper starboard strut as several slugs punched through, but she managed to avoid the majority.

Holy shit! he thought, panicking, unable to believe how quickly and easily it had happened. Adrenaline shot through his body; he felt it tingle all the way to his fingers.

"Danis," he shouted. "Are you all right? Talk to me, for God's sake."

There was a long moment of agonizing silence, then, "Yeah, I'm all right. No thanks to you, buddy."

"Whew!" He yelled to himself and breathed a sigh of relief.

"Follow me in, Joker," Danis said as she turned her F32 toward the asteroid. "I need to see what damage you've done to my ship."

"Copy that, Domino... But aren't we supposed to maintain a position ten kilometers out?"

"We are," she replied, "but I need to check the damage and I can't leave you out here alone, so follow me in."

"Look, I'm sorry," he said, embarrassed.

He made the turn, drew alongside her, matched her speed and was rewarded with a clear view of her scowling at him through her canopy.

"Nice one, Joker," she said. "It's a damn good thing your aim isn't any better than your flying, or else you would have killed me back there." Her tone wasn't exactly teasing, but he didn't want to read her wrong. "Luckily," she continued, "I think you only clipped my upper starboard strut. You owe me one."

"Apologies, Domino. I don't know what happened."

"I'll tell you what happened," she said. "You did it again. You and that tunnel vision of yours. All you could see was your target. You didn't confirm your field of fire; that's what happened." Her tone had turned angry. "If I get killed on deployment by one of these Swarm bastards, that's one thing. But I'll be damned if I get killed by one of my own pilots. Watch your field of fire next time. You're not in a flipping simulator anymore. You have to think in a three-hundred-and-sixty-degree global environment, and know that when you fire, your projectiles will continue on into eternity, or until they hit something. In this case, that was me."

"Yes, ma'am."

"So, get your head out of your ass," she snapped, "and watch what the hell you're doing."

"Yes, ma'am," Gian said and winced, remembering she'd told him she didn't want to be called ma'am. But she either didn't notice or she ignored it, saying nothing.

They both remained silent as they made the trip back to the asteroid and the mining complex, and Gian couldn't help but wonder what awaited them there.

Chapter Eighteen

Clintok

Elio, dressed in standard army issue battle armor, stepped off the shuttle's ramp onto the rock surface of the asteroid feeling decidedly uncomfortable. Not with his mission, but with the armor. He found it restrictive in so many ways. He'd been trained on the suit back home on Caerus and had become pretty proficient in its usage, but this was his first time using it in a real, off-world environment—in a vacuum, in extreme low gravity, and... well, he was uncomfortable.

He double checked his regulator connection and his oxygen level readout. Life support was at ninety-eight percent, the power cell at one hundred percent. He activated the suit's grav generator, raised his arms above his head and stretched; the armor creaked. He checked his N70 rifle, charged it, looked around at Lieutenant Rene Dubois and nodded.

"Let's do this, Lieutenant," he said.

The squad of Marines moved off the ramp and formed into two teams, their railguns at the ready. Elio remained beside the ramp for a long moment staring out into the blackness.

The entrance to the mine, lit only by the shuttle's floodlights and the Marines' helmet lamps, was massive, a gigantic cave, large enough to accommodate a Starfreighter, cut from a rock wall some five hundred meters high, and it was empty. Something about the blackness and the emptiness of the space made it appear even larger than it actually was.

"No power, but it seems clear so far, sir," Dubois said and tapped him on the shoulder. "We're good to go."

"We need to find the source of the transmission," Elio said. "Can you trace it? I want to see if there's anyone actually here."

"Copy that," Dubois said and relayed the command to his team. And, together, he and Elio started forward.

The open space between the shuttle and the mine entrance was a maze of ore containers, some stacked on top of each other, some not, some overturned, their contents scattered all over the rocky surface. It was obvious someone had left in a hurry. *The miners?* Elio wondered as they entered the mine.

Inside the mine entrance was a vast open space, a cavern Elio estimated to be at least a hundred meters high and three times that in diameter, a dark and mysterious world of flickering shadows cast by the moving headlamps, and there was more evidence that someone had left in a hurry: dozens of steel containers lay in odd places around the cavern, some overturned, and again, their contents scattered.

To the right of the entrance, set against the wall, was a complex of steel, prefabricated buildings, all dark and seemingly uninhabited.

"Over there," Elio said to Dubois, gesturing at the complex with his rifle. "That looks like the control center."

Dubois checked his display, nodded and said, "The transmission seems to be coming from inside the building. Alpha Team, take up a defensive position at the entrance. Beta team, you're with me." Then he turned to Elio and said, "Whenever you're ready, sir."

"Let's do it, Lieutenant," Elio said and, more out of habit than necessity, checked his weapon for at least the fifth time.

They approached the building in pairs, spread out across a wide area, rifles at the ready. Dubois nodded and one of the team tapped the green icon on the small screen beside the airlock and, with a whoosh of air, it slid open. The first pair stepped inside.

"Clear!"

Elio followed Dubois inside and the rest of the team followed along behind. Someone tapped the red icon on the far wall of the airlock, the door behind them slid shut, the airlock pressurized and the door to the building slid open.

Elio checked his heads-up display and saw that the air was breathable, but he kept his helmet on; he wasn't taking any chances. He followed Dubois out of the airlock and into what was obviously a sophisticated communications and control center.

The power was on, but the lights were off. Elio tapped the screen beside the airlock and the room lit up. The Marines, still in pairs, spread out and moved on, clearing the complex room by room.

Elio stepped over to a bank of desks in front of a wall of monitor screens. The desktops were little more than large touch screens and holo generators. Most of the screens were dark. Several were flickering, but two seemed to be fully operational. At the far end of the bank of desks was a small screen with words scrolling upward. It took only a second to determine that this was the source of the transmission. Elio touched the control screen and turned up the volume, "...ector fifty-one, Asteroid Belt G7, Asteroid K1437. Mayday, mayday, mayday."

"It seems we've found what we're looking for," Elio muttered, more to himself than Dubois who was standing next to him. "It's on a loop. I wonder if there are any survivors?"

He turned, looked at the terminals, and said, "We need to check the data storage and transmit it to *Avenger*."

Dubois nodded, turned his head and said, "Rogers, see to it."

Rogers stepped forward, removed his helmet and gloves and set to work.

"We have a live one," someone said in Elio's ear.

"Lieutenant, we have an unarmed civilian in custody."

"On my way," Dubois said.

Elio followed him out of the control room along a darkened corridor to a small room—a kitchen—where two of his Marines were talking to a man with his back against a countertop, a large knife in his hand and a half-worried half-happy look on his face.

He was wearing a dirty, work-worn gray flight suit; he was overweight, unshaven, almost bald with flabby cheeks, a gold hoop in his left earlobe and a series of symbols of some sort tattooed on the right side of his neck.

"I'm harmless," he said breathlessly. "I'm marooned. They left me for dead. I thought I was going to die. Thank you, thank you," he repeated as he put the knife down on the countertop.

Elio removed his helmet and said, "Who are you? Where are the others?"

"My name is Clintok," the man replied. "There are no others. I told you, they left me. They're all gone."

"You're not a miner," Elio said. "You're a Bossian. What are you doing here?"

"I'm a freighter pilot. I haul... I was on my regular route from Kaplia One with replacement parts... I was... I was unloading when they attacked. They... the Swarm... they disabled my bird. They shot it all to hell. I barely made it out of there. I had to walk for... hell, I don't know. When I got here the place was deserted. I can't believe someone finally heard me. Who are you?"

"Are you hurt?" Elio asked. "Do you need medical attention?"

"No... No! I'm fine."

"And it was you who sent the distress signal?" Elio asked.

"Yes... yes, that was me," Clintok said. "I didn't think anyone would hear it. This system... not many visitors... I thought I was going to die."

"Is there anyone else with you?" Elio asked.

"No, I told you. They left me. I'm alone," he replied. "As far as I know anyway. I haven't seen anyone else since the attack. When I got here... as I said, the place was deserted."

"What about the Swarm? Are they still here?" Dubois asked.

"I don't know," the Bossian said. "I was in Shaft Two, unloading. They came out of the tunnel. They blew everything up; my ship... everything. I think they were here, too, but they were gone when I got here... and so was everybody else. This is the only secure part of the facility there is. Please... you'll take me out of here?"

"Of course," Elio said. "But first we need to know what you saw."

"Yes... yes," he all but shouted. "Anything you want."

The Bossian was obviously suffering, perhaps even on the verge of a breakdown... or was he? Elio tried to get into the man's mind but found himself blocked. That in itself wasn't unusual, especially when dealing with subjects from the outer systems, but it was another red flag. *I'll need to keep an eye on that one,* he thought.

"The rest of the building is clear, Lieutenant," one of the Marines said from the doorway.

"Copy that," Dubois said, then looked at Elio. "We

have the data from the computers. I think it's time we got out of here, don't you?"

"I do," Elio replied. "Let's get back to the shuttle and… why don't you have someone keep an eye on him?" He nodded at Clintok. "I'm not sure I entirely trust him."

"Take him to the shuttle," Dubois said to two Marines, "and keep a close eye on him."

"Thank you, sir. Thank you," Clintok repeated, bowing several times, almost groveling.

The two Marines took him by the arms and then helped him climb into his filthy vacuum suit, then they guided him out into the corridor, back through the complex and out into the blackness of the cavern.

"Shuttle, this is Marine One," Dubois said over the comms.

"Go ahead, Marine One."

"We're clear. We have one survivor. We're coming home."

* * *

Elio and Dubois put on their helmets, took a last look around the control center, then stepped out into the cavern and backed slowly toward the mine entrance.

They were still just inside when the proximity alarms sounded inside their helmets.

Elio scanned the interior of the cavern, his heads-up display flashing red.

"Movement!" he shouted, slapping Dubois on the arm and then pointing in the direction of one of the shafts. "Over there." He brought his N70 Rail Rifle up to his shoulder and started moving backward out of the mine.

"Sergeant Frank," Dubois shouted. "Get your ass back here, *now!* We need cover."

"Copy," Frank shouted. And, seconds later, he and the rest of Alpha squad ran back to join them.

There was an explosion. Elio was lifted off his feet and landed on his back. He shook his head, rolled to one side, then pushed himself up onto one knee, inwardly thanking the uncomfortable suit of armor for saving his life.

He took his bearings. He was still just inside the entrance to the cavern; the Marines, all on one knee, spaced out around him, were shooting back into the darkness.

There was another explosion several meters in front of him. He dropped to the prone position. Someone shouted. He looked around. A Marine was shouting and waving at him from behind one of the steel containers loaded with many metric tons of ore. Elio scrambled to his feet and ran toward it, blast after blast of blue fire slamming into the cavern wall behind him as he went. He threw himself forward, the Marine firing a stream of covering fire up into the darkness. Breathing hard, he leaned back against the container and tried to see what the Marine was shooting at.

"Up there!" he shouted, firing a stream of small caliber slugs at the catwalk. "They have the high ground. We need to get out of here. You make a run for it. I'll cover you."

Elio looked around the corner of the container.

Multiple Blues were approaching from one of the tunnels, firing as they came.

"Not yet," he shouted. "They're trying to flank us."

He raised his rifle. The red dot in the holographic sight lit up. He snapped off two rounds, taking out one of the aliens. A bolt of plasma slammed into the front of the container. The container lifted nearly a half meter then slammed down again, intact except for a gaping, molten hole where the blast had hit.

The Marine beside him stood, trying to find a better angle. He fired. One of the Blues on the catwalk staggered back, hit the rock wall and collapsed. He fired again. Another Blue tipped over the catwalk rail and fell to the floor below. He ranged his weapon back and forth, looking for another target. There was a brilliant flash of blue fire. The Marine twisted sideways, his railgun flying from his fingers, a neat round hole in the center of his chest. His armor bulged. He fell face-first to the rock floor, smoke rising from the exit wound in the back of his armor.

Elio, his back against the container, peeked around the corner and spotted two more Blues marching across the open space toward him, their weapons pointed his way.

He dodged back behind the container just as a flash of blue burned through the corner. He ran to his right, then on to the next nearest container, exposing himself to the single Blue on the catwalk, but he had no choice. He had to find cover from the two Blues still marching toward him.

"Lieutenant," Elio yelled into the comms. "I have two

Blues coming my way and another on the catwalk. I need covering fire."

No response.

Damn!

Elio raised his rifle and began backing away from the container. He scanned the cavern in every direction, looking for them. Nothing. He turned and ran, heading out of the mine toward the stacks of containers to his left, listening as he went to the Marines yelling, the railgun fire and the shrieking of the plasma blasts.

He slowed, looking right and left, went into a low crouch and moved slowly backward. A movement to his left caught his eye. An alien was marching resolutely around the containers, but as yet it hadn't spotted him.

Elio slowly backed up until his back was against one of the containers and waited. Two seconds later, some twenty meters away to his left, the Blue marched around the corner of another container.

Elio stood stock-still, his head and back against steel, and he waited until the pale blue of the alien's armor came into view. He fired. Three slugs slammed into the alien's chest, punched through its armor and it went down, its arms spread wide, its body limp. Its weapon flew up, spinning, and then dropped to the floor at its side.

Elio was already moving, scanning the containers, looking for the second alien? *Where the hell is it?* he wondered as he crept forward toward the next container.

He blocked out the sound of fighting behind him and concentrated, listening, looking. He paused at the corner of the next stack, took a deep breath, then jumped out into the open, his railgun at the ready, almost into the arms of the marching Blue.

Whether or not the Blue was as surprised as Elio was, he didn't know. He just thumbed the trigger button and three slugs ripped into the alien's legs. It went down, raising its weapon as it went, but before it could shoot, Elio fired again, the heavy projectiles punching through its armor and into its chest. A final shot shattered its helmet and it fell on its back, its feet twitching.

Elio stood for a moment, looking down at it. The blue glow of the armor began to fade, as it had when they killed them on Tor, but this time, instead of turning a sickly white, it turned dark brown, a weird, opaque, honey color. Elio knelt down beside it, trying to inspect the holes in its chest. They were ragged, not clean-edged like those he'd seen on Tor. This armor was different. It was more streamlined, had more layers and, even though it looked heavier, it was actually lighter—finer—than he remembered. *They've upgraded it,* he thought. *It's better than it was, but still vulnerable to kinetics.*

The body lay flat on its back. He stood, took a step back, then looked down at it. The body inside the armor was lifeless, but the armor fit it perfectly. It seemed to flow seamlessly around its body and extremities. *Morian was right,* he thought. *They're learning, evolving.*

His thoughts were interrupted by a plasma blast that exploded against a container just to his rear. He quickly ducked out of sight and tried to get eyes on the rest of the Marines.

"Lieutenant," he yelled into his comms. "I'm pinned down. Where the hell are you? Copy?"

"Copy," Dubois shouted. "We have you. We're coming to you. Stay out of sight until we get there."

"Copy," Elio said and backed up against a container.

Less than a minute later, Dubois and four of his Marines charged through the stacks of containers and slid under cover.

"We have to run for it," Dubois shouted. "We've taken care of all but two of them, but we'll soon be taking fire from above." He pointed up.

Elio looked where he was pointing and easily spotted the familiar blue halo of a Swarm ship. It was still quite a distance away but closing fast.

"Come on," Dubois shouted. And with that he grabbed Elio's arm, jerked him forward, let go of him again and began to run, bent at the waist.

Elio, along with the four Marines, followed him, running, ducking from container to container, dodging bolts of plasma and firing at the two remaining Blues whenever he got a clear shot.

"Marine One, this is Shuttle One," the calm voice of the shuttle pilot said. "We have incoming enemy fighters. You might want to hustle it up."

"Copy that," Dubois said. "On our way. Just let us get inside, yes?"

"You got it, Marine One. Just don't take all day."

Elio knew that Danis and Gian would be covering their exit from the mine, but for how long he didn't know. There were just the two of them, and one was a rookie. They had to get the shuttle out of there and back to *Avenger*.

He checked his ammo count. The railgun had just

over one hundred projectiles left. *Not many. Perhaps not enough. Damn it!*

Stars! he thought as he followed Dubois to the next container. *How the hell many are there?* More Blues were pouring out of the mine entrance.

He put one in his sights and fired two shots. The alien dropped. He ducked and dodged as he and Dubois ran toward the shuttle. The first group of Marines were already at the ramp, but instead of going inside, they positioned themselves in the prone position on either side of the ramp, providing a blanket of covering fire.

"Come on. Let's go," Elio yelled as he sprinted across the open space toward the shuttle, Dubois and the rest of Alpha team on his heels.

They sprinted up the ramp and into the shuttle. Beta Team followed them inside, firing wildly at anything that moved.

"Go, go, go!" Dubois yelled.

The shuttle's engines whined. It began to lift. Plasma blasts slammed into its hull, but the enhanced Dutrinium armor cladding easily held against the light, hand-held weapons.

The shuttle banked to starboard as it climbed, its engines screaming at full power as it streaked away into the blackness of space.

Chapter Nineteen

Close Protection

Where they were coming from, Gian had no idea. What he did know was that suddenly, there were more than a dozen enemy ships rising out of the blackness beyond the asteroid's horizon. He also knew that unless he and Danis did something quickly, the shuttle wasn't going to make it back to *Avenger*.

The damage to Danis's ship, she'd determined, was minimal. They'd returned to their designated position ten kilometers above the asteroid to wait and watch until the ground team was ready to depart.

Fourteen! Gian thought and then blew out through pursed lips.

"Domino!" he shouted, staring at his screens. "I make it fourteen. What d'you want me to do?"

There was a moment of silence before she answered. "How's your ammo?"

He looked at his status screen. "Six Rapiers. Railguns at seventy-eight percent."

"Follow me in," she replied. "Discharge your Rapiers first. All of them, but not until I give you the word. Then stay on my starboard wing. We fight them together. As soon as the shuttle clears, we're out of here."

"Copy that, Domino. I'm in position."

"Here we go," Danis said, her voice calm.

She banked hard to port, heading for the nearest group of nine Blues at something close to Mach 30. They were on them in seconds.

"*Now!*" she shouted and all six of her Rapier smart missiles streaked away toward the nine Blues, and she banked hard to port to give Gian an opening.

"*Geronimo!*" he shouted as he hit the icons on his targeting screen one after the other, then followed Danis, banking away to port.

"Stay with me, Joker," she said as she reversed thrust, flipped her fuselage end-over-end, poured on the power and headed back toward the second group of five Blues.

Damn! he thought as he got the first glimpse of the carnage he thought their twelve missiles must have wrought. It wasn't so much. Of the nine in the group, five still remained. *That makes ten left...* he thought. *How?*

"I'll take the two to the left," he heard Danis say as they streaked toward the group of five. "You take those to the right, but for God's sake, try to stay with me."

"Copy," he said, watching his targeting screens. He adjusted his trajectory slightly, bringing his ship into position on the closest Blue. His targeting screen flashed green. He was locked on. He thumbed the twin trigger buttons on the yoke and two streams of 50-caliber depleted uranium rounds streaked away and impacted the enemy craft. It exploded in a brilliant flash of white.

Again, without slowing, he adjusted his trajectory and hit the twin buttons and flashed by the second Blue so fast he didn't have time to see he'd shot its port wing, severing it from the fuselage.

Where the hell is she? he thought as he hurtled away from the asteroid at just over Mach 40: forty-eight-thousand-plus kilometers per hour.

By the time he spotted her, just seconds later, they were both some eighty kilometers beyond the asteroid.

"I'm right behind you, Danis," he yelled.

"I see you, Joker," she replied. "Stay on my starboard wing. We're going again. Reverse thrusters on my mark. *Mark!*"

He reversed thrust. His fighter slowed. He flipped the fuselage just in time to face the other Blue craft coming in from above. He banked hard to starboard, barely avoiding a bolt of blue plasma. Unfortunately, the maneuver put him in the sights of a second Blue streaking toward him. Without thinking, he thumbed the triggers, held them down, watched the enemy ship explode and, unable to avoid the explosion, flew right on through the blinding flash of white so fast he barely noticed it.

And then he was back over the asteroid again.

"Domino—"

"Stay calm, Joker," she interrupted him. "You're doing fine. I'm on your six. The shuttle's lifted off and is headed back to *Avenger*. It's time to go home. We'll follow her in. We can hold them off until we're within range of *Avenger's* guns."

"Copy that, Domino," Gian said.

"Five incoming," Danis said. "Fall in on my starboard and reverse your fuselage."

"Copy," he replied as he adjusted his position and flipped the body of his craft, putting him upside down and flying backward. He rolled the ship, aligning it with Danis and the shuttle, and watched as the five enemy craft slowly overhauled them. It was a daunting sight. The shuttle's top speed was less than half that of the two F32As and, by his estimate, they were still some thirty minutes out from *Avenger*. They were going to have to take out the five enemy craft themselves.

"How are we going to handle this, Danis?"

"We're going to take them by surprise," she said.

"Oh yeah," he said, "and how are we going to do that? They can see us."

"On my mark," she replied. "We reverse thrust and fire together. You take the one to starboard; I'll take the one to port. Then we reverse again. That will put us on their six and we take them out as we find them. Remember, open fire the instant we reverse."

"Copy that, Domino. On your mark."

"Steady... stea...dy, steady... *Mark!*"

Gian reversed thrust and thumbed the triggers so hard it hurt. His ship, traveling at Mach 7, almost stopped dead. His inertia dampeners kicked in. Even so, he was still slammed back into his seat, feeling as if he'd been punched in the back.

The five pursuing Blues were on them in a flash.

Taken completely by surprise, the two outer craft ran straight into two twin streams of railgun fire. They didn't have a chance. Both ships exploded and, suddenly, the remaining three were behind them, just as Danis had predicted.

"Reverse your ship, Joker, and go after them," he heard Danis shout.

He reversed thrust, flipped the fuselage, rolled the ship and poured on the power. Again, his inertia dampeners kicked in and the F32 rocketed after the three remaining Blues.

It took a minute or so to catch them, and then Gian opened fire on the closest alien craft and saw his projectiles, two streams of white, slam into its tail. The craft didn't explode. Instead, it seemed to shatter, from back to front, as the heavy slugs stitched their way along its upper side.

There was a flash of white to his port side. He had no idea what it was, and he had no time to figure it out. By then, he'd adjusted his thrusters and had locked onto the second Blue. He banked slightly to port, his thumbs pushing the triggers, but the craft also banked to port and he missed.

He continued to follow, increasing his arc, knowing the Blue couldn't match his maneuverability, but it did. Slowly, the Blue ship tightened its turn. Gian followed, trying to tighten his own turn fast enough to catch it.

And then, just as he thought he had it, it dropped out of sight, and he panicked.

What the hell? Where... Damn, damn damn!

"Breathe, Joker." The words were Danis's, but they

weren't coming over the comms; they were in his head. "It's below you and to port. You can do this." She was using her Psy to calm him down.

A sudden sense of calm flooded over him. Time seemed to slow down. He looked at his screens. There it was. He rolled the ship and put the F32 into an inverted half-loop that brought him so close to the enemy ship he almost hit it. His targeting screens turned green and he opened fire. His slugs hit home. The alien craft exploded as he banked away to starboard.

"All right, Joker," Danis said over the comms. "It looks like we're in the clear. Shuttle One is less than fifteen minutes out. Take your position on my Starboard wing and let's escort her in."

"Copy that," Gian said.

They were on their final approach when Danis said, "Enemy craft approaching, seven o'clock low."

"I see them," Gian said. "There are at least a dozen of them. I'm almost out of ammunition."

"I think we can leave them to *Avenger*," she said as the shuttle glided through the hangar door. "Let's go home, kid." And together they followed the shuttle into the hangar.

The great doors closed. The hangar pressurized. The warning lights turned from red to green.

"Avenger, this is Domino. We're secure."

"Copy that, Domino," Sandra Lowry replied.

Gian opened his canopy, took a deep breath and sat for a moment, his head spinning, and willed himself to calm down.

He climbed down, his helmet under his arm, started

toward Danis's fighter and stopped when he saw Morian confront her.

He staggered as the great ship began to increase speed. He continued to watch the exchange between Danis and Morian, and he waited. He needed to talk to her.

* * *

By the time Morian exited the elevator, the *Avenger* had left the alien ships far behind and was heading at flank speed to the Slipstream.

He walked quickly out of the elevator onto the hangar floor and made eye contact with Elio, who had just exited the shuttle, still wearing his battle armor. Elio was followed down the ramp by Lieutenant Dubois with the man they'd rescued, Clintok, at his side drinking the last of a hydro-pack.

"Mister Clintok, I'm Richard Morian, Captain of the Avenger," he said, not offering him his hand. "We need to talk. Please escort him to the conference room, Lieutenant. I'll join you there in a minute."

"Yes, sir," Dubois said and ordered Clintok to follow him.

Morian watched them go, then turned to Elio and said, "It's good to see you back in one piece, my prince. If you would rid yourself of the armor, I'd be pleased for you to join us in the conference room. In the meantime, I must ask you to excuse me. I need to talk to my squadron commander."

"Of course, Captain," Elio replied. "I'll join you as soon as I can."

Morian nodded, then turned and, with his hands clasped behind his back, he stepped over to Danis's fighter to find her descending the ladder.

"Commander Morian," he said, his voice cold and formal.

Danis turned to him, frowning, and said, "Is something wrong?"

"Yes, something's wrong," he replied. "Would you like to explain to me why you took a second-year trainee into an active battle zone? He could have died out there and you would be to blame."

"Excuse me, *sir*," she said angrily, emphasizing the word sir. "I was told by both you and tactical that the asteroid was clear of enemy combatants. I was assured by you, yourself, that active and passive scans had detected no enemy presence within a half-million kilometers and that the expedition was, and I quote, 'a milk run.' That being so, I decided, as squadron commander, that it would be a good opportunity to provide my trainee with a little real-world training. Unfortunately, you, Tactical and the scans were wrong. I would also inform you that he performed well, as good as any pilot on the squadron. He downed at least eight enemy craft that I know of, possibly more."

"The boy is not qualified on the F32A. You had no business taking him out there like that," Morian responded.

Danis glared at her brother and said, "Check your records, brother. I qualified him two days ago. Had I known of the enemy presence... no, I wouldn't have taken him. As it is, I stand by my decision."

Morian raised his arm and tapped his data pad, brought up Gian's records, glanced at them, nodded, then said, "It appears I've misread the situation. Please accept my apologies, Commander."

She glared at him and was about to speak, to retort angrily, when she felt him inside her head.

I really am sorry, sis. You were out there on your own with a raw rookie facing God only knows what. I thought I was going to lose you.

She took a deep breath, willed her heart rate to slow down, looked him in the eye, and projected, *Apology accepted... and I understand, but don't ever do that to me again in front of the squadron and the crew. If you want to rip me a new one, do it in private.*

He nodded. *Yes, that was unforgivable. It won't happen again. We good?*

We're good, she replied.

"I need to go talk to this Clintok character," Morian said. "I'd like you to join us."

"I need a few minutes to freshen up."

"Very well. Join us in the conference room as soon as you're ready." Then he turned and walked quickly away, leaving his sister standing there watching him go.

"Commander?"

She turned around. It was Gian.

"Yes?"

"What was that out there?" he asked. "You... you used Psy on me."

"Just a little. It helped, didn't it?"

"It did, but why?" he asked, bewildered. "You could have taken out that enemy fighter."

"I could have, but I knew you could too." She shrugged. "You needed the experience. You still do."

"But what if... What if I failed? What if I—"

"But you didn't."

"But I could have. What then?"

"Then you wouldn't be standing here wasting my time... would you?"

His mouth dropped open. "You would have let me die?" he asked, stunned.

"We'll never know, will we?" she replied. "Now, I must go. I'm expected in the conference room and I have to clean up first... Look, you did really well today. I'm proud of you, Gian. Just relax. Don't keep trying so hard."

Chapter Twenty

All is not as it seems

When Danis arrived in the conference room some thirty minutes later, Elio was seated across the table from Clintok; Dubois was seated next to Clintok, and Morian was standing at the head of the table holding the back of his chair.

"Ah, Commander Morian," he said. "Please take a seat. Sit wherever you like."

She chose to sit next to Elio so she could look the freighter pilot in the eye and, if necessary, probe his mind a little.

"Mister Clintok," Morian began. "Welcome aboard the *Avenger*. You've had a rough time, so I hear."

"I did, and I can't thank you enough, Captain, for saving me. I'm sure the detour to K1437 must have cost you dearly. I cannot tell you how grateful I am to you and your crew and Prince Elio here. You saved my life."

Morian stared at him, narrowed his eyes and, using

his Psy, he looked into the man's mind. It was not quite the revelation he expected. Yes, Clintok was relieved to be saved, and there were true feelings of joy, of recent despair and of fear, but that was all. Morian had expected the man's mind to be... well, an open book; it wasn't. Furthermore, Clintok seemed aware of the intrusion, though he showed no surprise or resentment. *Strange!* Morian thought.

He turned again to Clintok and said, "What d'you remember about the attack?"

Clintok leaned on the table, clasped his hands together in front of him and stared down at the table, apparently deep in thought. "Well..." he began, then paused, then continued, "I'd never seen them before... the Blues, I mean. I'd heard about them, of course, just like everyone else. And I saw the holo footage and all that, but... well, I never expected them to be on the asteroid... or to come out of nowhere like they did. All of a sudden, boom. There they were."

"Where were you when the attack started?" Morian put his foot up on the rail of his chair and leaned in.

"Like I told him," he said and glanced across the table at Elio, "I was in Shaft Two, unloading. They came out of the tunnel. They blew everything up; my ship... everything."

"There were no alarms?" Dubois asked. "What were they doing in the tunnels?"

Clintok shook his head. "No, there was nothing. I don't know why they were there. They were fast; I know that. Like I said, they just showed up and started shooting without warning."

Morian glanced at Elio. Elio shrugged, not knowing what to say.

"I was lucky," Clintok said earnestly. "When they began shooting, I skedaddled out of there, fast, I can tell you. I started to run to the control center, but when I got outside... Those eerie, buggy-looking blue fighters were everywhere. They destroyed everything. I lay down flat between two containers and played dead. For how long, I don't know. Then they were gone. Where? I don't know that either. They were just gone. That's all I know... I had that ship for more than seven years. Now... it's just gone."

"And when did you make the recording?" Elio asked.

"Recording?" Clintok sat up. "What recording?"

"The distress call," Morian said.

"Oh, that." He rubbed his chin. "Yeah, I did that right away, as soon as they left, as soon as I knew I was the only one left alive on the asteroid. I never expected anyone to hear it, not way out there. That's one lonely place, I can tell you." He paused, looked up at Morian as if he'd had a sudden thought, and said, "You know, while I was alone, I had plenty of time to think. Why did they leave me alive? They had to have known, right? I think they left me alive knowing I'd send that call. I think they were hoping someone would come and rescue me. You know... Like a trap, sort of thing."

Elio and Danis both looked at the Captain. Morian grimaced and checked his data pad. It all sounded too far-fetched to him. But then again, if it was true, it meant the aliens really were learning more and more about humanity, and that they were adapting.

Elio didn't like it. He didn't like it at all.

Danis nibbled the knuckle of her left forefinger, then sat back and stared at Clintok. He stared back at her, a tiny smile on his lips. Was the little man flirting with her, or was it something else?

Gently, she tried to read his thoughts. Nothing. His smile broadened slightly.

He's blocking me, she thought.

The silence lasted only for a couple of seconds or so, then Morian pushed himself upright and said, "Well, Mr. Clintok, I think that will about do it, for now. Lieutenant Dubois will show you to the guest quarters where you can freshen up."

Clintok rose and said, "Thank you, Captain, for everything... By the way, where are you taking me? I was hoping you'd drop me off on Kaplia One."

Morian nodded and said, "I'm sure we'll talk about that later."

Clintok nodded, and Dubois escorted him from the room, closing the door behind him.

"What are you thinking, Elio?" Morian asked, forgetting his promise to maintain formality between them.

Elio hung his head. "I don't know. The man's either incredibly lucky, or unlucky, or he's an accomplished liar, or all three."

"I tried to probe his mind," Morian said, "but all I got from him were emotions of gratitude and fear."

"That's more than I did," Danis said. "I got nothing at all, except the feeling that he knew what I was doing. The man was smiling at me. At first, I thought he was flirting with me but... Richard, I think he has Psy, and I think he was blocking me."

She turned to Elio and said, "You said you think he might be lying. If he was, why? He was in a really bad situation. Why would he lie?"

"I don't know," he replied, "but I suggest we watch him carefully. There's something else, Captain. Those Swarm troopers we fought in the mine; they were different."

Morian frowned and said, "How so?"

"They were... better, more agile, quicker, more aggressive. Their battle armor was different too."

"Their armor?"

"Yes. It was layered, supple, but still no match for a 50-caliber slug. Their weapons were more powerful. Back on Tor, it was like... like we were fighting drones, but today... not so much. And, if what Clintok said is true, they used him as bait to lure us into an ambush. That's an entirely new level of intelligence."

"Elio's right," Danis said. "Their tactics in space were more precise. Their fighters were slower, more maneuverable. Didn't Marshal Tan say they're probing the Slipstreams? I think it's more than that. I think they're attacking us in small numbers to learn about us, our tactics, our weapons... And, from what Elio just said about the troopers, they are adapting."

Chapter Twenty-One

Sight

The argument in the well-deck of the bridge—quiet and low-key as it was—between Manda Haal and *Avenger's* chief navigation officer Simon DeLong, had finally been settled when she managed to convince DeLong that her coordinates for the upcoming Slipstream approach would work better than his.

They'd discussed it for several minutes, DeLong wanting to know how she'd figured it out. Unfortunately, she'd been unable to tell him because she didn't know herself. She was, however, absolutely certain she was right, and so she insisted he adopt them. In the end, DeLong had shrugged and reluctantly acquiesced, and her thoughts turned to Captain Morian.

As if on cue, the bridge door opened and he stepped up to the command rail beside her.

"Commander," he said, "you have a status report?"

She nodded. "Aye, sir. We're on Slipstream approach. We should arrive in just under fifteen minutes."

"Excellent." He reached out with both hands, gripped the rail and stared down at the hologram, seemingly deep in thought.

She looked sideways at him, blinked rapidly several times, rubbed her eyes and said, "Something on your mind, Captain?"

"As a matter of fact, there is," he replied without taking his eyes off the hologram. "I want to ask you something; exactly how did you come up with the coordinates for that last burn?"

"What do you mean?" she asked, puzzled.

"I mean, when the shuttle and the fighters docked after they returned from the asteroid, we were all but surrounded by Swarm fighters, yet you managed to figure out the best escape route—instantly—in your head. And you were spot on. You found the three weakest points in their formations, and we went right through them. I've reviewed the data, Commander. What you did is not statistically possible. How did you know how to do it?"

The truth was, she didn't know, but she didn't want to tell Morian that, so she hedged. "I... I saw the first one; that was easy. Then I... calculated the other two from there. I'm sorry. I don't remember the MOAs."

Morian nodded, then turned his head to look at her. He stared at her intently. She began to feel uncomfortable.

"I'm sorry, Captain. I can go back and figure—"

"No, no. There is no need for that. You made a good call... and not for the first time."

"Thank you, Captain."

"But now," he said as he pushed off the rail. "It is time you got some rest."

"Rest?"

"Yes. I want you to stand down. You've pulled a double shift. We'll be in the Slip in a few minutes. Get something to eat and then get some rest."

"Are you sure, Captain?"

"Yes, you're excused," he said and smiled at her.

Manda rolled her shoulders, then leaned back to stretch her lower back. "If you say so, Captain. Thank you."

From the bridge, Manda went straight to the Officer's Mess. It wasn't until the smell of food hit her nostrils that she realized how hungry she was. She ordered a late but light dinner, ate alone, then went to her quarters.

By the time she was out of the hydro, her muscles had relaxed and she was beginning to feel the full effect of working forty-eight hours straight. She sat down on the edge of her bunk, let her chin fall to her chest, closed her eyes and wondered, not for the first time, what was happening to her.

Three times she'd been able to predict future events with some degree of accuracy, but she had no idea how. And now she was facing awkward questions, not only from her captain but also from members of the crew.

She knew it wasn't Psy or TK. The tests had proved it. But what was it? She pondered the problem for several more minutes then gave up, suddenly realizing just how tired she was.

She sat up straight, twisted around and lay down,

killed the lights, closed her eyes and almost instantly fell asleep.

* * *

Manda was alone, standing at the command rail, watching the battle via the giant hologram and the forward screens, watching as one USF ship was destroyed after another. She gripped the rail so hard that her fingers hurt. She shook her head in frustration, knowing there was nothing she could do to help them; she was unable to communicate with them.

She let go of the rail, took a step back and looked around the bridge. *Where is everyone?* she wondered. They were all gone: Captain Morian, Jadern, Jiksar, Haltar Sen, Sandra Lowry... and all the other bridge officers... They were all gone. She was alone.

Proximity alerts began to sound in three sectors, then a targeting alarm, indicating a Swarm ship had locked on. She ran down onto the well-deck looking for Tactical. The hologram was up, but no one was there. She checked the stats. Power cells three and four were down.

She went from station to station, from flickering hologram to flickering hologram, frantically searching for... someone, anyone, but she was alone on the darkened bridge, surrounded by the sights and sounds of the battle.

The familiar, high-pitched whirring sound of the shield alarms began to resonate across the bridge. She turned again to Tactical. *Avenger* had all her topside shields up at full power.

She ran across the well-deck and back up the steps to

the command deck, turned again to the rail, looked down at the hologram and stared at it in horror. It was a swirling mass of Swarm ships, a veritable hornet's nest, with *Avenger* at its very center. She looked up at the screens and saw nothing but hundreds of Swarm ships, all lined up and ready to fire at the bridge.

The screens turned white. The hologram exploded. The entire bridge was filled with blue fire...

Manda sat up on the bed and gasped. Her skin was awash in a cold sweat. The covers beneath her were soaked. Her chest heaved. She tried to control her breathing.

Holy stars, she thought, *what the hell was that?*

She swung her legs off the bed and staggered to the bathroom. Grabbing the handrail beside the hydro in an effort to steady herself, she took several deep breaths and tried to slow her racing heart.

She poured herself some water and downed it, almost in a single gulp. She looked at herself in the mirror, pushed her hair back behind her ears and took another gulp of water.

Manda lifted her forearm and glanced at the screen. She'd been asleep for a little more than three hours. She tapped the screen with her forefinger. They were still in the Slipstream.

She turned her thoughts to her dream. Something didn't feel quite right. *Not that a nightmare ever feels right,* she thought. Was it an omen of things to come? She paced around the room, trying to wrap her head around it. Was something wrong? Was *Avenger* in trouble? Or was it all... just a dream, a nightmare?

No, it was more than a dream. It was more than a nightmare. Something was definitely off. But what? It was like that feeling you get when you can't remember if you locked the door. She had to check. But check what? She decided to go for a walk.

She slipped into her jumpsuit, put her hair back in a ponytail and glanced at her chron. It was almost midnight, ship time. Few people would be out and about the halls at that time of night, which was good because she felt like she looked a mess. She didn't, of course, but her lack of sleep and state of dress did little to alleviate the overall feeling that she looked like hell.

She left the room, watched the door close and lock behind her, and then set off at a fast clip down the hall. Strangely, the more distance she covered, the better she began to feel.

She took the elevator down to the hangar deck; it was deserted. She made a lap around the perimeter, checking each fighter in turn, then the two shuttles and finally, Prince Elio's yacht, *The Queen's Pleasure*.

Everything appeared to be in order. All of the fighters were secured.

From the hangar, she went to Engineering and walked the catwalks. Several members of Maxim Volkov's team were working on various projects, most of which she didn't understand, nor did she want to. Deciding all was in order, her next stop was the gymnasium, where two crewmen were on treadmills and one of the fighter pilots was going through a calisthenics routine. Again, everything was as it should be.

The cafeteria was livelier. With so many crews on so

many different shifts, it was always busy. Busy, but nothing was out of the ordinary.

She decided to check the bridge, then thought better of it. It was, after all, the most secure section of the entire ship, and besides, if she went nosing around after midnight, it would be sure to arouse curiosity and questions for which she had no answers.

And so she kept on walking, one hallway after another, one deck after another, with no idea why, knowing only that it was important that she did.

It was some twenty minutes later that Manda found herself in front of one of the doors to the server rooms. She pulled up the comm room code on her data pad and waved it in front of the security scanner.

"Access approved, Commander Haal. ID number two five nine nine zero seven," Krista's voice said.

The door slid open and Manda walked inside. The immediate drop in temperature caught her off guard, as it always did.

The server room was massive. The cold air changed every ten minutes. Aside from the rush of air, all was quiet. There were not many terminals, but those she could see were unattended. The lights were already on. *That's odd*, she thought. *The lights are on a motion sensor so... why would they be on?*

She stood for a moment, then walked slowly forward, past rows of equipment, turned a corner and... then she knew. *Avenger* was indeed at risk, but not from the Swarm. She was being assaulted from within, in a more sinister way.

The short, fat man that Prince Elio's team had

rescued from the asteroid mine was bent over one of the terminals.

"Don't move, Bossian!" she said loudly.

He froze, then slowly turned his head to look at her.

"This is a secure area," she snapped. "You're not authorized to be here. Step away from the terminal. You're under arrest."

He straightened up, took two steps back and turned to face her, a drive booster in his hand. Clintok had been hacking *Avenger's* systems.

Clintok looked at her, resigned to the fact that the game was up. He shrugged, tilted his head slightly to one side, and smiled at her.

Manda tapped the emergency icon on her forearm. Less than two minutes later, she heard the door slide open and then loud voices.

"Over here!" she shouted.

The ship's security officers had arrived.

Chapter Twenty-Two

Surprises

Morian was stunned when he received the message from his First Officer. *How could something like this happen?* he wondered as he half-walked, half-jogged along the narrow hall on Deck 2 to the brig. How did he not see it, or at least suspect something? *He's obviously more than a damn freighter pilot. What the hell was he doing on the asteroid in the first place? Could he be a spy? If so, for whom? Son of a bitch! Someone's going to pay for this.*

A Marine sergeant, standing outside the brig, saw him coming and opened the door. Morian nodded his thanks to the sergeant and stepped inside to find Prince Elio already there, waiting for him.

"Have you talked to him yet?" Morian asked.

"No. I thought it best to wait for you."

"Good," Morian said. "Where the hell is he?"

"Right this way, Captain," a security officer who'd heard the question said, then turned to escort them to Clintok's cell. They arrived at the entrance to the cell block and the officer tapped his data pad with a finger, brought up his ID and security code and offered it up to the security sensor beside the barred doors. Morian and Elio did the same.

The doors slid open and the officer handed them off to one of the brig's guards.

It was a different Clintok who sat at the table facing the door. He seemed somehow taller, a little less heavy. Perhaps it was how he now carried himself. The Clintok that sat before them was self-assured, confident and certainly no fool.

"I'll be right outside if you need me," the guard said as he closed the door behind them.

"Good evening, Captain." Clintok leaned back in his chair, his hands bound in front of him with a pair of biometric restraints. He looked relaxed, confident, even amused.

"Mister Clintok," Morian said as he stepped up to the table and sat down. Elio took a seat beside him, and together they stared at the man; Morian bubbling with rage while Elio smiled.

"Who are you working for?" Morian asked.

"I... don't think... I don't know what you mean, Captain."

"You were caught in the server room with a tip drive, downloading USF mission data. You're a spy, Mr. Clintok. Caught red-handed. I don't need to put you on trial.

In a time of war, the penalty for spying is death. Tell me why the hell I shouldn't have you thrown out of an airlock."

Clintok looked at him with narrowed eyes but didn't reply.

"I think you'd better start talking, my friend," Elio said, smiling benignly. "I don't think Captain Morian is bluffing. The vacuum is not a nice way to die. You need to talk, and you need to be honest. So come now; what do you have to say?"

Clintok's eyes darted back and forth. He looked first at Elio, then Morian, then Elio again. Then he seemed to make up his mind, and he smiled. "Well, now, my prince, you're in luck, because I am just a simple man—a simple man but an honest one."

"An honest man would not have broken into a secure area and tried to hack the ship's systems," Elio replied.

Clintok threw up his hands and shrugged dramatically. "What can I say?" he said. "All I have is my word. I don't deny the charges. I'll tell you what you want to know... if I can. It's no big secret. I have no secrets."

"First, you can tell me how you managed to get into the server room without tripping the alarms?"

Clintok squinted across the table at him and smiled. "Let's just say I'm not actually a freighter pilot. I have... other skills."

"I see," Morian said. "Your tip drive is being analyzed by my staff. It's... unusual. Advanced technology. Not something I've seen before. You're no common thief. Who are you working for?"

"I am an enterprising man, Captain Morian. I work only for myself."

"I don't believe you," Morian said.

Clintok shrugged.

Morian looked him in the eye. He needed to establish a link so that he could use his Psy and get to the truth. He slowed his breathing and focused.

"What were you going to do with the data you downloaded?" Morian asked. This time he didn't listen to Clintok's answer. Instead, he focused on the Bossian's eyes and reached out to him with his mind.

"What are you doing?" Clintok asked. His eyes wide open. "Wait, no... don't do that. You don't have to."

Morian could tell that the Bossian was scared, but he could also tell Clintok was Psy adept and was putting up a strong resistance. It quickly became a battle of wills, one Morian wasn't sure he could win.

Both men began to sweat. It was a first for Morian. He'd only encountered people with Psy abilities a half-dozen times before and was not as skilled as Clintok seemed to be. The Bossian knew it, and he began to smile.

And then Clintok broke, and Morian was through, into his mind, but not because of anything he did.

Morian glanced to his left, at Elio. He was sitting very still, his hands clasped together in his lap, his eyes closed. He was using his Psy to help break the man's resistance. Together, they were too strong for Clintok, and his defenses began to crumble.

Morian concentrated on the Bossian. He was still resisting, but in such a situation it was the natural way of things for the thoughts he wanted to hide to be foremost in his mind.

He was no common freighter pilot; that was immediately obvious. *Come on, Clintok,* Morian probed. *Who and what are you? What happened back there on the asteroid? Hah! The Independent Militia of the Free People. You're a pirate.*

Morian broke the connection, sat back in his chair, folded his arms across his chest, and stared at Clintok.

Clintok heaved a long, shuddering sigh and put his head in his hands, breathing hard. "That was hardly fair, two against one, now was it?" he asked finally.

"So, you're a pirate?" Morian asked.

Clintok looked up, his face dripping with sweat. "No... well, yes... but not in the true sense of the word. I am a representative of the Independent Militia of the Free People, the IMFP. We don't recognize your USF." He turned his head to look at Elio. "Nor are we subject to your sovereign rule, my *prince.*" He said the last word with no little disdain.

"You were alone on that asteroid," Morian said. "Why?"

"It was unfortunate," Clintok said. "Let's just say I was a little tardy getting back to the ship. They thought I was dead. I missed the boat, literally. My own stupid fault. If you hadn't shown up when you did, I would still have been there, dead."

"How long ago?" Elio asked.

"Six days. I was getting kind of lonely." He grinned at them.

"Why were you there in the first place?" Elio asked.

Clintok shrugged and said, "For the Osmium, of course. That stuff is hard to find. We knew the Swarm had invaded the asteroid and had killed most of the miners. We also knew that those they hadn't killed had abandoned ship, so to speak. Our intel indicated the Blues had left. Unfortunately, the intel was wrong. They were in the tunnels."

"So that's what's in the containers, Osmium?" Morian said.

Clintok nodded.

"Why did you go after our servers?" Elio asked.

"Well, now," he said, lightening up a little. "You people were... you were a gift from the gods. And this ship?" He gazed around the brig. "I couldn't believe I was on a USF ship of the line, a vast treasure trove of military information. And here I was, with a tip drive in my pocket—we all have them, you know. Kind of providential, don't you think?"

"Who is we?" Elio asked.

"My crew. When I realized my good luck, I had to try. You do understand that, right? I mean, your ship is a gold mine. Slipstream frequencies, military intelligence, navigational charts... stuff we've been trying to get our hands on for years."

"And what did you plan to do with this gold mine of stolen data?"

"Ah, well, that's the bit I hadn't quite figured out. I thought you might have dropped me off on Kaplia One. From there I could easily have gotten back to the Beta Ariatis System and my ship. With what I had to offer, I would be a hero and... quite wealthy."

"Beta Ariatis?" Morian asked. "Your ship is in the Beta Ariatis System?"

Clintok tilted his head slightly and opened his eyes wide. "You didn't know?" he asked. "Well now. That's really something... The Beta Ariatis System is our home. Freyja is the IMFP home world."

Chapter Twenty-Three

Deception

Morian slammed his fist down on his desk and shouted, "How could you do this, Elio?"

"Er... it wasn't as if I had a choice," Elio said and raised his hands in a defensive gesture. "Yes, of course I suspected pirates were in Beta Ariatis, but I didn't know for sure. I certainly didn't know how many, and I sure as hell didn't know they would be as active as Clintok says. All of the intel pointed to a small hideout, nothing more."

"And you doctored the reports?" Morian asked as he paced the room.

Elio looked up guiltily, as if he'd been caught in a lie. "I removed the patrol logs."

"So, when the intel team made their initial scans, that's why they thought there was so little activity. You removed the Slipstream data?"

"Not exactly," Elio replied. "I didn't remove all of it. What I did delete... I..."

"So, we're sitting ducks then?" Morian snapped. "We're going in blind."

"Not necessarily," he replied self-consciously. "I still have the data. I just transferred it to a tip drive. It's in my quarters."

"Damn it, Elio." Morian's voice seemed to bounce off the walls. "Why didn't you tell me? You've known pirates were operating in Beta Ariatis all this time?"

"Yes, I knew, damn it," Elio snapped. "I also knew neither my father nor the marshal, or anyone else would approve the mission if they found out. I did what I did, Captain, and I did it because it was the right thing to do for the fleet."

Morian was angry. So was Elio. He wasn't used to being talked to in such a manner and had it been anyone else, he would have had them arrested.

Morian, frustrated, sighed and dropped into his seat, looked at his friend and said, "Not like this, Elio. This isn't how it works. There's a reason they wouldn't have approved the mission. You were wrong, but it's too late now." He shook his head, frustrated. "We'll be there soon. There's no way to turn back now."

"That's good," Elio said. "We have our mission. That's a win."

"No, it's not." Morian sounded tired. "Especially now. Suppose we're ambushed. How d'you think it will be received by your father or Tan if we take damage or, stars forbid, we lose crew members in a skirmish with pirates?"

"I think you're being a little overdramatic," Elio said. "Come on, Captain, this is the *Avenger*: the most formidable warship in the fleet. They would have no chance."

Morian shook his head, never taking his eyes off the prince. He couldn't believe someone as smart as Elio, and his friend, would do something like this.

Elio stared back at him and ran his hand through his hair, clearly frustrated and... a little apprehensive.

"I don't like this, Elio. I can't believe you allowed me to walk into this blind."

Elio nodded and raised his shoulders in a gesture of defeat. "All right, all right. You're right. I agree. This probably wasn't the best way to get the mission approved, and I'm sorry. I truly am. I just... just couldn't find another way. But while I'll admit the method was wrong, I know the mission is right. You have to trust me." He scooted to the edge of his chair, leaned his elbows on Morian's desk, laid his forearms flat on the desktop, and said earnestly, "It is the right mission, Richard. We're supposed to do this. I know it."

"Easy for you to say." Morian leaned back in his chair. "You're not the one they'll blame if the mission goes sideways. I need those files, Elio, and I need them now."

Chapter Twenty-Four

Big Cat

"There... that's it." Elio disconnected the tip drive and returned it to his pocket, then he tapped his data pad and transferred the data to Morian.

The data pad on Morian's forearm activated and his arm itched, indicating the transfer of the Aries constellation reports was complete.

He glanced at the screen, then said, "Got it." He tapped his data pad and brought up the data in the form of a hologram above his desk and began scrolling through images, lines of text, Slipstream activity reports, traffic movements, mostly freighters identified by their transponders and clearly not pirates, but there were a few unregistered ships; red flags? Yes, but the numbers were small.

"I'm forwarding this to Intel and IT," Morian said as he sent it with a request for an updated risk assessment.

Then he went back to scrolling through the data. Finally, he came to the file that contained ship movement information and began to scroll through it.

"Wait! Go back." Elio pointed to the hologram. "What was that?"

Richard pulled up the last few images that showed the broadcast ID numbers. "What?"

"There. See. Those ID numbers, they have no USF tags."

"So?"

"So, that is exactly how Clintok said the pirates coded their ship logs. And look at that."

Richard scrolled down the long list of ship numbers.

"That's a lot of pirate ships. And they are almost all porting to the same location." Elio pointed to the docking port ID numbers.

Morian did a quick search to find that the docking ports were unlisted. He tapped his data pad and called IT.

"That list of ship numbers I sent you," he said to the officer who answered the call. "Many of the docking port ID numbers are unlisted. I need to know exactly where and what they are. Can you do that? Good. How long will it take?"

It took less than five minutes to establish that the ID numbers were for berths at the old, abandoned—so it was thought—shipyards on the planet Freyja in the Beta Ariatis System in the constellation of Aries.

"So," Morian said, "now we know. That shipyard is indeed viable. Good call, Elio."

Elio nodded thoughtfully and said, "Thank you,

Richard. I think we also know, by the number of unregistered ships entering the shipyard, they are probably older models."

"Look at this." Morian pointed to the hologram and highlighted a number. "We see this one over and over. It's by far the busiest ship in the system. Are you sure this data is complete?"

"It's complete. It's everything I had."

Morian looked at him and smiled. "I'm sure you think so. But just as you were holding out on me, someone could be holding out on you."

Elio tilted his head, narrowed his eyes, stared at Morian and said, "I don't..." He hesitated, then continued, "True enough," he agreed.

"Wait, let's try this." He entered the ship's ID number into the Slipstream database. It took but a couple of seconds before the data came back. The number had been allocated to the *Red Dragon*, an old Defender Class light cruiser registered to a Tiger Wok.

"I don't recognize that name, or the ship; do you?" Morian asked.

"No," Elio replied, "but I'm sure we're going to meet him."

"What makes you say that?"

"Look at the times and Slipstream usage," Elio said. "This Tiger Wok seems to be one very busy cat. And the *Red Dragon* is a Defender Class ship, smaller than the *Avenger*, but still a killer of a ship. There's only one type of captain that would be flying such a ship, and that's a pirate. This ship and this... Tiger Wok, are vital to our mission. He must know what is going on in Beta Ariatis.

We have to find him. We need to know how many of these old ships are still in service and, maybe, persuade them to join us in our fight against the Swarm."

Morian shrugged, looked skeptical and said, "I doubt there's much chance of that. These people are criminals, outlaws. Even if you could persuade them to join us, it would be like herding cats. Then again, your chances are zero if you don't ask."

Chapter Twenty-Five

Big Brother

A short time later, Morian was on the bridge seated in his chair before the command rail, waiting for tactical to report the updated threat assessment, when he heard the door slide open behind him.

"Brother?" Danis said quietly as she approached.

Richard stood. "Danis?"

"I just came to... Is everything all right, Richard?"

"Of course. Why?"

Danis looked around to make sure no one was listening. "I could feel that you were going through some sort of... I had the feeling you were... struggling with something."

"Nothing I can't handle." He paused for a second then said, "You know... this gift we've had foisted on us; it's still so new to us. We can't seem to control it. It turns itself on and off in moments of stress, but I think it's always there, always has been, lurking somewhere in the depths of our subconscious. I don't know about you, but I'm not used to people being able to read my mind. No, I'm fine. Really. You probably picked up on an intense meeting I had with Elio about some updated intel we received..." He couldn't lie to her. "I received. Tactical is going over it now."

"Well, I want to help if I can." She crossed her arms. "If I can take any of the burden off of you, I will."

"I appreciate it, Danis," he said and smiled at her, "but there is nothing you can do. I can handle it. I have to. It's why I'm captain. So, everything is fine and I'll know more when the analysts get done with the data and provide me with a report."

"Is it true then?" she asked. "We're going into a pirate haven?"

Morian rolled his eyes. "Where did you hear that? There are only a handful of people who know that, all of them with the highest security clearances."

Danis smiled and said, "True. But this is a Navy ship. Big as she is, *Avenger* is a very small world and word gets around."

Morian shook his head. "Yes. In answer to your question, I have become aware of recent pirate activity in the Beta Ariatis System, and that's just between us, right?"

"Of course... but pirates?"

"Yes, they're pirates, but they refer to themselves as the Independent Militia of the Free People, the IMFP."

"Sounds very dramatic and official," Danis replied. "How many of them are there? D'you think maybe they're wanting to get a voting block for their system?"

"One, I don't know, and two, I doubt it," Morian said, smiling at her. "The USF has always had trouble with the Free People... with systems that refuse to register. In most cases, Free People means pirates, and from what we now know, there seem to be plenty of them in Beta Ariatis."

"Free People, huh? Well, maybe they're not so bad," Danis suggested.

"What do you mean by that?" Morian asked, frowning.

She shrugged. "I was just thinking out loud, I suppose. Maybe there's something about this... this whole humanity fighting for survival against the Swarm thing that can bring us all together. We surely have more in common with pirates than we do with the Swarm."

"I think we can agree on that," Morian replied. "I have to wonder, though, if the pirates would say the same about us. They might prefer the Swarm over the USF?"

"You can't be serious," she said. "I think it would be best not to judge until we know a great deal more about these... Free People. I suggest you keep an open mind, my brother. No one is all good, and no one is all bad. None of us are perfect, but we are all human, so we have to stick together."

Morian nodded, smiled again and said, "Of course. As you were, Commander."

"Thank you, Captain," she said, drew herself to attention, nodded, spun on her heel and left him standing there, wondering at how far she'd come over the past fourteen months.

Chapter Twenty-Six

Flight Plan

Gian walked out onto the flight deck to find Andra putting away a munitions loader. She parked the machine on its charging port, tapped the icon of the small control screen to turn it off and stepped down, surprised to find him watching her.

"Hey you," he said self-consciously. "How're you doing?"

"I'm doing okay," she replied. "But all the better now that I get to see you," she joked.

"Oh yeah, sure," he said. "Me too, though I don't get to see you as much as I thought I would... You know, since you're here on the ship and all."

"I know." She wiped her hands, then stepped up and gave him a hug.

He hugged her back. "I'm busier than I've ever been," he said, looking down at her.

She laughed and said, "It's all the hours you're

spending in that simulator. Have you passed level E-9 yet?"

Gian blushed, embarrassed. "No, not yet. I'm getting closer though. The funny thing is, I ran into just the same situation when I was with Danis at the asteroid. I pulled it off, but... I can't seem to get a handle on it in the Sim."

"So," she said, leaning back in his arms, looking up at him, "you don't think the simulator's cheating anymore?" she teased.

"Nope. It's me. It's operator error. I guess I'm just not good enough... yet, but I will be. You can bet on it."

"You can do it," she said. "I know you can." She gave him one of those lovely smiles he couldn't get enough of. "I believe in you. You're a good pilot. You always have been."

"You think?" Gian said, thinking back on the simple life they'd enjoyed back on Tor, back before the Swarm, before the fighting, before life had thrown them together and sent them in a completely different direction than they'd planned. Back then, his only goals in life had been no more than to spend as much time as possible with Andra and win on the local gravcar circuit. Now here they were: him a fledgling fighter pilot and her about to enter the fleet Academy.

How things have changed, he thought, not for the first time.

"I'm proud of you, Gian," she said. "You do know that?" she asked seriously. "I mean... Look at you. I've never seen you so dedicated or driven. And you're doing so well. You're learning, improving, every day."

"But I still have so much to learn." He let go of her,

stepped away, and gestured to the other fighters parked around them. "And it's frustrating. I'm much older than these other pilots; I have a lot to catch up on."

"Oh come on, Gian," she said. "You're only twenty-six and you're so smart. You'll catch them and pass them. You'll be the best pilot in the whole USF fleet."

He grinned at her. "You think? Thank you, Andra. I'm so glad you're here."

There was a moment of awkward silence as he stared at her. She was beautiful: tall, slender, her long light brown hair was tied back in a perfect ponytail, and those beautiful green eyes... *Stars,* he thought. *How lucky can a simple jerk from a rock at the end of nowhere get?*

"Hey, you two," Danis said as she stepped out from behind her F32A. "Am I interrupting?"

"No, not at all, ma'am," Gian said. "I just stepped out of the simulator. I've logged thirteen and a half hours already today—"

Danis held up a hand, interrupting him and said, "You're doing fine, Gian. But now's not the time to discuss it."

She turned and called the rest of the squadron to order, then asked them to gather around.

"I'd better leave," Andra said, taking a step back.

"No, you're fine," Danis said. "You can stay. I've nothing to say you can't hear. And besides, you'll be going to the Academy soon and this will be good experience for you."

Andra nodded enthusiastically as the rest of the pilots—twelve of them, including the two shuttle pilots—formed a circle around Danis.

"So, here's the deal," she began. "We'll be exiting the Slipstream in..." She glanced at her chron, then continued, "in about thirty minutes. We don't know if the Swarm will be waiting for us or not, but we have to assume that they will be. In which case our mission will be to protect *Avenger*. Nothing more.

"Once we exit to real space, *Avenger* will orbit the sun and proceed to the next Slip point. Our job is to provide close support and be ready to return to the hangar at a moment's notice. Is that understood?" She looked at Gian.

He folded his arms across his chest and nodded. The rest of the pilots either nodded or voiced their agreement.

"Will the whole squadron deploy together?" someone asked.

Danis shook her head and said, "I don't know, and I won't until we exit the Slip. Just be prepared for anything."

"We know our strengths against the Swarm are maneuverability and firepower," another of her officers said. "And we know they try to counter by pre-positioning and superior numbers. So why don't we just go out there and tear them apart?"

"Because that's not the way we do things," she said. "I told you; our mission is to protect *Avenger*. Nothing more. We go from exit to entry as quickly as possible with as little damage as possible. Do you all get that?"

The pilots mumbled and nodded.

"I can't hear you," she shouted. "One more time, like you mean it."

"Ma'am. Yes, ma'am!" they shouted.

"That's better. Now suit up."

* * *

It wasn't ten minutes later that Prince Elio, dressed in a flight suit and carrying a helmet, walked out of the elevator and onto the hangar floor and stepped over to Danis's F32A. He knew the fighter squadron would be getting ready to deploy and he needed to find her. The hangar deck was in turmoil: deck crews making last-minute inspections, armorers checking weapons, and pilots gearing up. He only had minutes before they would deploy.

Elio had felt truly alive only twice in his life. Once during the Battle of Tor and again as leader of the boots on the ground mission to the asteroid mine. He was sure that this was what he'd been born for: to lead, fight and make a difference.

He was grateful for his exalted station in life. It opened doors for him like no other. But ever since the war against the Swarm had begun, he'd come to realize he was not meant to be a politician, to sit around and talk while soldiers and pilots were risking their lives.

But Elio Lorne was born with more than just his station in life; he also was gifted with not just one of the Heroic abilities but two. As far as he knew, he was unique in that he had the ability of TK and Psy. Both of which were unlocked in a moment of supreme distress on Tor.

He couldn't explain it, nor did he question it. How or why it came to be didn't matter. What did matter was that he knew he could use his abilities to sway the tide of battle, as he had already done during the Battle of Beta Cephei.

He stood for a moment, looking around the vast expanse of the hangar. *Where is she?* he wondered.

He was just about to reach out to her telepathically when she stepped out of the locker rooms dressed in her flight suit and carrying her helmet.

He waved at her and caught her eye.

"Prince Elio, what are you doing here?" she asked. "We're about to deploy."

"Danis," he said, "I need to talk to you."

"Better make it quick," she said as she folded the helmet strap back into itself, ready to lift it onto her head.

"I want you to take me with you, as your copilot."

"What?" She'd been in the process of lifting her helmet to her head. "You want what?" she asked, lowering it again. "No! I'm sorry. I don't have the authority to authorize that, and I wouldn't if I could." She slid the helmet onto her head and turned to mount the ladder.

Elio grabbed her by the elbow. "Wait! Please, Danis. Hear me out. I can help. I know I can."

She took her foot off the ladder, turned again to face him, blinked and said, "You can help? How?"

"With my TK," he answered. "I've been training, with Ugo Tan. I can bring it up at will. Watch."

He turned around, looking this way and that, found what he was looking for, concentrated for no more than a second and an empty armorer's missile transporter lifted three meters off the deck and held there. He looked at Danis, smiled and then lowered it gently down again.

"See?" he said. "Danis, I'm an expert pilot, and with me in the copilot's seat, you can't lose. So come on. Let's do it."

"I... I... No. There's no time. I would have to get my brother's approval."

"He's already approved it," Elio said. "Check your messages."

She looked at her forearm screen and tapped it to bring up the current messages. Then she looked up at him, then at her screen, raised her eyebrows and nodded, pursed her lips, then said, "Well, will you look at that? He did approve it."

"He did," Elio said, "but he did say I needed your approval too. He also said I was not to ride with anyone else if you said no. Not that I'd want to, but... Come on, Danis. Let's at least give it a try."

She fiddled with her helmet strap. "I don't know what we'll be jumping into, and this is probably something we should practice before we go jumping right into battle."

"I'm sure you're right," he said, "but we have to start somewhere. Why not now? Just let me try. I won't be a burden, I promise. I'll follow your lead, do exactly as you tell me. I can work with you."

He paused to let her think it over. The corners of her mouth turned up slightly as if she was considering it.

An announcement interrupted their discussion. "Now hear this. Now hear this. All hands to Battle Stations. All hands to Battle Stations."

Danis stared at him, slowly shaking her head.

He grinned at her, raised his shoulders and his eyebrows.

She was being pinched by time. Elio hoped it would work in his favor.

Danis watched as a pilot ran by them and jumped onto the ladder of his fighter. She didn't have time to argue.

"All right," she said, the look on her face saying she wondered if she was doing something she was going to regret. "Get in. Keep quiet. Do exactly what I tell you. If you screw this up, you won't get another chance."

"Yes, ma'am." He quickly slipped the helmet over his head and almost ran up the ladder.

"Ranger Squadron, stand by to deploy on my command," the voice of Lt. Commander Omario Kingston said in her ear as she settled into her seat and tapped the screens bringing her grav engines online.

* * *

Gian leaned forward and looked across the hangar at Danis now in her ship, the canopy slowly closing. He'd been watching the exchange between her and Elio, though he couldn't hear any of it. And, when Elio scampered up the ladder and hopped into the copilot's seat, he couldn't help but wonder what was going on.

First Danis gave him a wave, then Elio, grinning like a fool did the same. Gian smiled back at them, returned the gesture, tightened the strap on his helmet, then ran his fingertips over his screens bringing his systems online, the grav engines whining comfortingly. His canopy closed with a whoosh of air and a clunk. The strip around the seal turned green, telling him the cockpit was secure. He double-checked his connections to make sure his suit was also secure, then he tapped the icon to activate his inertia dampeners. He checked his targeting and proximity systems, his weapons and, with all systems green, he relaxed, settled back into his seat and closed his eyes, but only for a moment.

Danis's voice said, "All right, team. Listen up. You all should have received the new orders. As soon as we exit the slip, *Avenger* will move at flank speed to the next Slip point so we'll need to move quickly. No one flies alone. We fly in pairs. No pair will venture more than fifty kilometers from *Avenger* at any time. Does everyone copy that?"

"This is Joker. Copy!"

And, one by one, the rest of the squadron acknowledged the transmission.

"Good," Danis said. "We still don't know what awaits us when we exit so keep your wits about you. Begin prelaunch sequence."

Gian checked all readouts and displays for the third time. Everything was good to go. He checked oxygen supply, cockpit pressure, fuel cells and batteries. All good.

"Weapons status," Danis said.

Gian checked. His ammo and missile batteries were at one hundred percent.

"Comms, scanners, targeting."

All comm units were up and running. All stations

were online. All connections were reading one hundred percent.

"Slipstream exit in three... two... one," Jadern's voice said in his helmet.

And, once again, Gian experienced that familiar hollow feeling in his gut as *Avenger* dropped out of the black into normal space.

"Ranger Squadron. This is Tactical. Stand by." Commander Kingston's voice was calm.

"Standing by," Danis replied.

The green lights over the hangar doors turned red and the doors began to open.

Gian's stomach floated for a moment as *Avenger* stabilized and then realigned.

"Ranger Squadron. This is Tactical. You are go for launch. Copy?"

"This is Ranger Leader," Danis said. "Copy that... and out."

"You okay back there?" she asked.

"Yes, ma'am," Elio replied.

"Then hang on. Let's go see what's out there. Domino to Ranger Squadron. Deploy in flight order. Flight One leading."

Danis's F32A lifted quickly and smoothly off the deck on its grav engines and headed straight out through the hangar doors. Her wingman, a young pilot, Frances Johnston, call sign Flippy, followed her out.

Gian, in the second flight, was the fourth to lift off. Once outside, he deactivated his grav engines, brought his fusion drives online and joined the formation, traveling in the same direction as *Avenger,* the plan being to slingshot around the smaller of the two suns and enter the next Slipstream.

Even before Gian had found his place in the formation, his long- and short-range scanners turned red: his screens showed dozens of enemy ships. How many exactly, he couldn't tell.

"Domino to Ranger Squadron," Danis said, her voice calm. "Multiple enemy craft in all sectors. Stay in formation. I repeat, stay in formation."

Gian touched the short-range scanner's screen and decreased magnification. The numbers of enemy ships were even harder to read, but it gave him a broader, cosmic view of their space. Swarm ships were everywhere. They were surrounded by hundreds of them, as if they were in a giant fishbowl surrounded by sharks. Fortunately, there were none closer than a thousand kilometers off *Avenger's* port bow.

"Domino to Ranger Squadron. Go to five kilometers and form Pattern Four around *Avenger* and prepare for sync."

Gian maintained his distance from Flight Two leader as they assumed their position five kilometers off *Avenger's* starboard bow, ready to disperse and attack if needed, yet still close enough to return to the ship if she had to abort.

"*Avenger*, this is Domino. Ranger Squadron is in position. Our scanners are synced. You are good to go for burn."

"Copy that, Domino. Prepare for sync."

Gian took in a deep breath, gripped the yoke with both hands, and slowly breathed out.

"Domino to Ranger Squadron. Prepare to sync on my mark."

As her speed increased, *Avenger* began to pull away from their formation.

"Three... two...one. Mark," Danis said calmly.

Gian tapped the icon for the pre-set and felt more than heard his engines increase power as the automatic settings synchronized his speed to that of the *Avenger*.

For almost ten minutes, *Avenger's* speed continued to increase, as did that of its escort of twelve F32As, and all was quiet. There was no sign of any reaction from the Swarm. *They must have seen us*, Gian thought as he watched his scanners. And then Gian spotted a small image at the top right of his scanner begin to move closer.

Their plan was to let the Swarm react to them. *It must be working.*

"Domino to Ranger Squadron," Danis said. "We have incoming at... five-zero-two. Stay in formation."

Bring it on, you Swarmie sons of... he thought.

"Avenger, this is Domino. We have incoming at five-zero-two."

"Copy that, Domino. We'll proceed on course unless you hear different from us."

"Copy," Danis said.

"Domino to Ranger Squadron," Danis said. "All right, people. We have multiple Blues headed our way. They plan to attack *Avenger*. Our job is to protect her. I know you all want to move to engage and take the fight to them, but we stick to the plan. Don't get suckered into an unnecessary dog fight. Don't stray too far away from home. Stay in formation if you can, and within range of *Avenger*. Good hunting. Domino out."

Their formation, a giant circle around *Avenger,* was large enough to give each of them room enough to maneuver and fight while remaining in relatively the same place in the formation.

Gian watched his screens as the enemy ships moved ever closer until, eventually, they were close enough to count. From what he could see, there were thirty-six of them in twelve flights of three. *Oh, nice,* Gian thought. *E-9 all over again, and then some. Yeah, well, today I pass.*

Gian enhanced his FLIR scanner. Sure enough. There they were. He felt a shiver run down his spine, not of fear but of hate, as he remembered what these... things had done to his home planet. It was time for a little payback.

Gian waited, watching his speed, staying in formation with the rest of the squadron encircling *Avenger* like a belt, staying within the boundaries set by Danis until it was time to go to work.

He and his flight leader were on station on *Avenger's* starboard side at her two o'clock position. He watched as the nearest flight of three enemy ships grew closer, content in the knowledge that he had the advantage of maneuverability.

Gian watched as the leading enemy approached, its weapons turning toward him.

At the last second Gian turned sharply to the low right and realigned his fighter. He'd timed it perfectly. The bolt of blue plasma blew by him. His targeting locked. His screens turned green. He thumbed both triggers. His railguns whirred. Two streams of 50-caliber depleted uranium rounds streaked toward the enemy ship and... missed.

His target made a sharp turn to the right, something he'd never seen or heard of before. The Swarm ships were not supposed to be able to maneuver like that. *What the hell?*

Gian flinched and his mouth dropped open, but even before what had just happened had time to sink in, the Swarm ship fired again.

Luckily the enemy was now more than ten kilometers out, and Gian's long hours in the simulator were about to pay off. Without thinking, he slammed the yoke hard to port and shoved it forward, putting the F32 into a steep, twisting dive. Again the bolt of blue fire scorched harmlessly by.

"Holy stars," he yelled, throwing comms protocol to the wind. "Did you see that?" No one answered.

He shook his head and then, contrary to Danis's instructions, he concentrated on his target, forgetting about anything but the Swarmie that had almost nailed him twice.

He poured on the power and closed the distance between them, his fingers flying over his thruster controls. He angled the F32 to the side, moving in time with the enemy craft, trying to achieve a lock, but every time he thought he had him, the Swarmie seemed to anticipate it and moved accordingly, out of his target lock, the screens flashing red, then green, then red... "Damn it," he shouted.

He did a quick double check of his scanners to make

sure no other Blues were after him, as it was quickly becoming apparent that his first target wasn't going down easily.

He weaved the F32 to port, then to starboard, increased speed, his targeting screens flashing red and green. The alien fired back at him, but Gian dodged it easily. He couldn't understand what was happening. The enemy ship was maneuvering like a USF fighter.

Gian got close and fired. The Swarmie ducked out of sight. Gian increased speed and put the fighter into a steep dive. His targeting screens turned green; he had the lock. The Swarmie turned to port. This time Gian anticipated the move and was already turning to port, matching the enemy's trajectory. He glanced at his screens. They were still green. He grinned. *Gotcha, you bastard.*

It was at that moment he heard the deep buzzing sound of his proximity system warning him he was only seconds away from breaching the fifty-kilometer perimeter of protection around *Avenger*. He only had a matter of seconds.

He increased his speed, tightened his turn, closed with the enemy and... fired.

Yet again, the Swarmie changed course and Gian's rounds missed. This time, however, Gian kept his thumbs on the triggers, matching the enemy's turn, and increased his speed, walking the rounds in. *Hold... hold...*

The slugs impacted the enemy ship, stitching twin lines across its fuselage until, finally, it exploded in a blinding flash of blue fire.

Gian cut his thrust to zero, reversed his thrusters,

then poured on the power. He was barely a kilometer out from the perimeter when he made the turn. He checked his positioning. All was good. He was still within mission parameters. *Time to find another target.*

"Domino to Ranger Squadron," Danis said. "Stay in formation. These Swarm ships seem to be new and improved models. They're slower but more maneuverable. Stay sharp. Watch each other's six."

Gian nodded. So his target wasn't an anomaly.

"Yeah," Ranger Five said. "Looks like they got upgrades. Where the hell are you, Joker?"

"Right behind you, Blackbird," Gian said.

"You pushed the fifty-click limits on that one, Joker," Blackbird said.

"It was close, but I got him," Gian replied.

"Cut the chat, you two," Danis said. "We need to keep the channels open."

"Copy that, Domino," Blackbird said.

Then, as if on cue, "Ranger Squadron, this is Avenger."

"This is Domino. Go ahead, Avenger."

"It's time to come home, Domino. We'll commence solar orbit in... seventeen minutes."

"Copy that, Avenger. We're on our way," Danis said.

Gian followed Blackbird through the hangar doors on his grav engines and brought the F32A to a hover above his designated landing bay. He turned the ship until it was facing the hangar doors, settled her down onto the deck and leaned back in his seat and closed his eyes.

Another couple of minutes later all twelve fighters had successfully docked, the hangar had pressurized and the red lights had turned green, confirming pressurization and life support. He opened his canopy, took off his helmet and crawled out.

"Now hear this, now hear this," Commander Jadern's voice echoed around the hangar. "Five minutes to Slipstream entry. I say again, five minutes to Slipstream entry."

Chapter Twenty-Seven

Skipping Stone

Commander Manda Haal stepped down off the bridge onto the well deck. Travel through the Slip was going as planned; it was time to prepare for the next exit.

"Mr. DeLong," she said as she approached the navigation station.

"Yes, Commander." DeLong stood to greet her.

"We'll be entering the Felisian System in about twenty minutes, correct?"

DeLong bent over to check the navigation screen. "Yes, that's right."

"Very well," she said. "Commander Morian and her squadron performed well."

"Commander Haal?" Omario Kingston, the Tactical Officer, said as he joined her.

"Yes, Commander?"

"We just received the debrief from Commander

Morian. Apparently, the Swarm ships they encountered are much improved, especially their maneuverability. They were able to evade railgun fire, seemingly with ease. This is a first. The squadron is intact: a few minor hits but no casualties. Casualties among the enemy are estimated to be less than half the usual."

"So," Haal said, her hands behind her back, head down. "Our enemies are learning, and quickly. What is Commander Morian doing now?"

"She's preparing for the exit, re-strategizing with her team leaders."

"Very well," Haal replied. "Maintain an open channel with her. I want to know if our proximity strategy needs to change. It worked well enough last time, but who knows?"

"Yes, ma'am," Kingston said and turned away.

"Mr. Jadern," she called out to the XO. "A minute of your time, if you please?"

"Yes, Commander," Jadern said and stepped across the well deck to join her at Navigation.

"D'you have the Swarm numbers for the Felisian System?"

Jadern checked the screen on his forearm, tapped on it several times, then said, "The last report shows there should be considerably less Swarm activity there. Approximately..." Again he checked his screen. "Approximately seventy percent of what we saw in the last system."

"How recent are those numbers?"

"They're a little more than twelve hours old, Commander. It's the most recent intel we have."

Haal nodded. "Inform me immediately if anything changes."

"Yes, ma'am."

Haal turned back to the navigation officer. "Now then, Mr. DeLong," she said. "Do we have anything that might tell us where the Slip points are in the Felisian System?"

"No, ma'am," DeLong replied. "But our latest surveys indicate we'll have to make a similar orbit around the sun, as we just did. We don't know the exact Slip times or locations."

Haal nodded. It was not what she wanted to hear.

"But we do know that the Slips orbit at a much faster rate than many other systems," DeLong said.

"And the size of the star?"

DeLong checked his screen again. "Felisian is a... massive F2, Commander. Surface temperature seven-thousand-two-hundred degrees Kelvin."

Manda looked around, spotted the senior helmsman, Haltar Sen, waved to get his attention and beckoned for him to join them.

"We were discussing the locations of the Felisian Slip points," she said to Sen by way of explanation, then turned again to DeLong. "As they are unknown, and Felisian is a massive F2 star, we'll have to make the calculations in real space and time. I want you to give me an estimate of the three most likely sets of navigation points. It's unlikely they will be accurate, but we might as well try to have something ready to give us an edge when we exit into the system."

"Yes, Commander," DeLong said.

"Mr. Sen," Haal continued. "As we'll have no idea of where to go once we do exit the Slip, I want you to pre-program all three sets of Mr. DeLong's possible coordinates into your system and be ready to execute on my command."

Haltar Sen blinked and looked at DeLong. DeLong shrugged. This level of preparation was something new.

"I know this isn't standard protocol," Haal said, "but you have to trust me. We can't afford to lose any fighters or take any more damage. We have a lot of work to do once we reach our final destination."

"Yes, Commander," Sen said.

She dismissed them back to their stations and returned to the command deck and her seat next to the captain's. It wasn't more than two minutes later that Morian joined her.

"Are we ready to exit the Slip, Commander?" he said as he sat down.

"We are, Captain," she replied. "Well... as ready as we can be considering we know almost nothing about the Felisian System. What little intel we have indicates only a small Swarm presence, but we're not taking anything for granted. We're prepared for the worst and hoping for the best."

"Very good," Morian said. "Commander Morian is concerned about the Swarm's new capabilities and has adjusted her strategy accordingly. Let's hope it works."

"Our biggest problem, Captain, is the fact that we don't know exactly where the Slip points are. Felisian is an F2, a Type two Cepheid yellow giant. The magnetic fields in the system are wild and violent, making forward predictions almost impossible."

"Even for you," Morian said quietly and without looking at her.

She looked sharply at him, opened her mouth to speak, then thought better of it. She *was* worried, though.

From her experiences in less trying times, she knew that trying to establish positional bearings in such a system as Felisian took time, which in normal circumstances was not a problem. But now, with the Swarm breathing down their necks, it was a huge problem. Since the Slipstreams orbited the sun, in a stable system such as Orso, the entry points—and there could be from one to as many as fifteen, but usually only two or three—were easily predictable.

But with a system like Felisian, that wasn't the case. The Slipstreams orbited the yellow giant at random distances and speeds; one could never guess where they might be at any given time. The calculations could take anywhere from as little as several minutes to as much as an hour, which is why she'd asked DeLong to try to predict the three most likely sets of coordinates and have Haltar Sen pre-program them into his systems.

It was a haphazard way of doing things, but better than sitting around waiting for the computers to figure it out. If just one of Sen's predictions worked, it could save them precious minutes, and possibly even lives.

Manda watched as Morian stood, stepped up to the command rail, clasped it with both hands and rocked himself back and forth, then turned again, returned to his chair and slumped down with his chin resting in his hand.

Manda, knowing he needed time to think, double-checked the status of each bridge officer. At ten minutes to exit, she ordered the ship to battle stations, received the estimated coordinates from DeLong and confirmed that Haltar Sen had them pre-programmed into his systems.

The ship exited the Slip into the bright light of the giant yellow star.

"Active scans, Mr. Kingston," Morian shouted as he jumped to his feet and stepped quickly to the rail.

"Aye, Captain," Kingston replied. "Enemy craft off the port bow. Range... four-thousand-two-hundred kilometers."

"How many?" Manda said as she joined Morian at the rail.

"I count... eighteen," Kingston replied.

"Mr. DeLong?" Morian snapped.

"Captain, it looks like the exit has put us into sector three," DeLong said.

"How long until you have the coordinates for the next Slip point?"

"Maybe six... seven minutes."

"Captain," Manda said. "Shall I order the squadron to launch?"

"No. Not yet. It will take those Swarm ships several minutes to get here. We'll be out of here in six. Have them stand by, just in case."

"Aye, Captain."

Morian nodded and returned to his chair.

Manda sent the information to Danis then turned again to look down at the well deck and said, "Mr. Sen, belay those pre-programmed coordinates and wait for orders from Mr. DeLong."

"Aye, Commander," Sen replied.

But the Swarm ships made no attempt to close with the *Avenger*.

Evidently, their learning curve isn't restricted just to improving their ships, she thought as she stared down at the eighteen blue icons on the hologram.

"I have the coordinates," DeLong said. "Sending them to Helm now."

Manda turned to Morian, her eyebrows raised in question.

He nodded, and she turned and gave the order, "Take us in, Mr. Sen. Two-thirds standard. Tactical, keep an eye on those enemy craft. No surprises, please."

"Aye, aye, Commander," Kingston said. "No surprises."

The Slip point was on the far side of the sun; no small distance, considering Felisian's size. But the journey was uneventful. The Swarm ships maintained their position and were soon left behind as *Avenger* accelerated to one-tenth light-speed, and Manda couldn't help but wonder why. *Maybe they really are learning*, she thought. And Manda heaved a sigh of relief as they entered the Slipstream without incident.

* * *

With *Avenger* safely inside the Slipstream, Manda, and no doubt everyone else on the ship, breathed a little easier. But with only forty minutes between entry and exit, there was little time to do much other than prepare for what might lie ahead.

Manda descended once again to the well deck, more for something to do than out of need.

"How long until we exit, Mr. Sen?" she asked.

"Twenty-two minutes, Commander."

She nodded, clasped her hands behind her back, looked around the well deck, then headed back up to the command deck to update the captain.

It wasn't that she was worried as she ascended the six steps... well, she was, just a little. They were headed to yet another anomalous star system, this time a binary: two stars, one a red dwarf, the other a yellow dwarf. Two suns orbiting a common mass. Manda knew why the powers that be back on Orso had chosen these obscure, anomalous systems for their route to Aries. The consensus was that the Swarm wouldn't expect USF presence in such systems and, in ordinary times, they would have been right. But these were not ordinary times.

Thus, once again, the location of the Slipstreams therein was a mystery and this time, there was no time to guestimate. And who knew what they would face once they arrived?

She placed her foot on the top step and was about to reenter the command deck when, suddenly, she felt dizzy. She staggered, almost fell, grabbed the handrail and steadied herself.

"Commander, are you all right?" Morian asked, jumping up from his chair.

"Yes... yes, I'm fine." She wasn't fine at all, but she wasn't going to show weakness in front of the captain and everyone else on the bridge. She had a momentary weird feeling in her stomach, but by the time Morian had reached her it was gone, and so was the dizziness.

He reached out to take her arm and help her up the final step but again, not wanting to show weakness, she lifted her arm to avoid his hand.

She stepped up onto the command bridge and turned to go to the rail and... it was then that it hit her. She stopped dead. She had an overwhelming feeling that she knew where the next Slip point would be. Not just the location; she knew the exact coordinates for their exit and the Slip point. She had no explanation, and she knew that for her to know the coordinates was impossible. But she was absolutely certain she was right.

"Commander, are you—" Morian asked.

"I know where the next Slipstream will be," she said, interrupting him with conviction. She didn't wait for him to respond. She turned again and headed back down onto the well deck and Navigation with Morian close behind.

"Mr. DeLong."

"Yes, Commander."

"Prepare to input coordinates."

"Uh... what coordinates, Commander?"

"We'll be exiting the Slip in sector nine, at five seven zero."

"What? How do you know?" DeLong asked.

"The next Slip point will be at three-two-two seven-one-six point four. Input that into the system and be ready to execute on my mark."

"How? What?" DeLong stuttered, confused. "Commander, we know the Slip points orbit the two stars in unpredictable ways."

"Trust me, Mr. DeLong, and just do it."

"With all due respect, Commander, I don't think it is wise to input a set of Slipstream coordinates into the Nav system. It's impossible to know, even generally, where the Slip points are. When we exit... if you're wrong... it will take time to clear the systems and re-route. It's—"

"You're going to have to trust me, DeLong," she snapped. "I know what I'm doing."

"But it is against protocol to pre-program something this large and—"

"Don't worry about the protocol, DeLong," Morian said. "This is the new protocol. Just do as Commander Haal asks."

"Yes, sir. I mean... yes, Commander." DeLong turned again to his console and began inputting the numbers.

"Lieutenant Lowry?" Manda asked.

"Yes?" Sandra Lowry stood and joined the small group around the Navigation console.

"Please inform Commander Morian that we'll reenter the Slipstream within minutes of the exit, and that she will not be required to deploy Ranger Squadron."

Lowry looked at Morian. Morian simply tilted his head slightly, raised his eyebrows, smiled at Manda and said, "You heard the first officer, Lieutenant. Do as she says."

"Copy that, Captain," Lowry said.

Manda tried to do the calculations in her head. She couldn't, but still she knew that if everything went as planned, they would have only about three minutes in real space before the Swarm could attack in overwhelming numbers.

"It's done, Commander," DeLong said as he stood up and turned to face her. "I don't know how you know what you know, but I *do* trust you. You haven't failed us in the past, and I don't expect you to start now."

"Thank you, Simon," she replied. "Please send the coordinates to the Helm." Then she turned to the helmsman.

"Mr. Sen?"

"Yes, Commander." Haltar Sen turned in his seat.

"Nav will relay the coordinates for the next Slip point," she said. "I want you to pre-program them and be ready to steer six points to port as soon as we exit."

Sen nodded. "Aye, Commander. Six points to port it is."

She felt someone touch her arm. She turned. Morian was standing beside her.

"Gut feeling, Commander?" he asked almost in a whisper.

She shrugged, pulled a wry face and said, "Yes. That's probably the best way to explain it. Although it's... It's more than a gut feeling. I can't explain it."

"And you don't have to," Morian said, "but I hope you're right. I'd hate for us to have to sit there like sitting ducks, waiting for the Swarm to blow us into Andromeda."

"There's no need to worry, Captain," she said with more confidence than she felt. "I know it will work."

There was a lot of tension in the air around the bridge. Everyone knew what Manda was doing was unheard of. She was breaking every protocol in the manual. And if she was wrong...

The *Avenger* dropped out of the Slip and Manda, at the command rail with Morian, felt that familiar hollow feeling in the pit of her stomach, but it soon passed, to be replaced by one of fear as she stared at the forward screens and the hundreds of Swarm ships before them. Several members of the bridge crew gasped.

"Execute, Mr. Sen. Do it now," Morian said calmly.

"Aye, Captain," Sen replied. "Six points to port."

The ship yawed as she came about, and again Manda's stomach lifted.

Together, Manda and Morian watched as the Swarm craft began to maneuver. She looked at navnet scrolling above the holo. The nearest group was less than seven hundred kilometers out. Close enough for them to launch an attack but far enough away that if she was right, *Avenger* just might make it into the Slipstream.

Manda watched as Haltar Sen completed the turn. His fingers danced over the touchscreens. The engines fired and *Avenger* surged forward toward Manda's pre-programmed coordinates.

The bridge was deathly quiet. No one dared say a word.

Manda, her face pale, her hands gripping the rail so hard her knuckles turned white, began to second-guess herself. *What if it doesn't work?* she thought.

Even though she believed with all her heart she was doing the right thing, she couldn't help wondering about the consequences if she was wrong and sending them into a death trap. She felt her heart rate increase as she began to anticipate the worst. She breathed deeply, sucked her bottom lip...

"*Captain!*" Haltar Sen shouted.

Oh no, Manda thought.

"Mr. Sen?" Morian said.

"It's the Slip point, sir. We're here."

The bridge crew all stood, waved their arms in the air and cheered.

Manda visibly heaved a sigh of relief and relaxed her grip on the rail. She'd been right after all.

Four minutes after exiting the Slipstream, *Avenger* was back inside and heading for her next destination.

Morian sat in the command chair with Manda seated next to him. As soon as he was sure that all was well, he rose and asked Manda to join him in his ready room.

"That was a good job, out there, Commander," Morian said as he closed the door behind them. "Please, sit down."

She did as she was asked and sat down in front of his desk, folded her hands together in her lap and, knowing what was to come, waited for him to speak.

He stared at her for a long moment, then said, "How did you know those coordinates?"

She rolled her shoulders, took a deep breath and said,

"I... I wish I knew, Captain, but I don't. You saw me almost fall on the bridge deck steps. That was the moment when I knew."

Morian nodded. "Yes, I saw that. I can only assume you have some form of Psy."

"But Doctor Dowd said I was negative on all the tests."

"I know, but there's still so much we don't know about these strange new abilities. Yours may be presenting differently, that's all."

Manda nodded, deep in thought.

"The coordinates? Did you see them in your head? Or did you hear them?"

"Neither. I don't know. I just... I just knew; that's all I can say. I also knew the Swarm would be present in large numbers; too many for us to fight and survive."

After studying her for a moment, Morian smiled and said, "All right, Manda. You don't have to explain it. But I want you to know that you not only saved us from a massive fight, you probably saved the lives of everyone aboard. So... Thank you and well done, Commander."

"Thank you, sir."

"Take a few moments then return to the bridge," he said. "I'll join you there shortly."

"Aye, aye, Captain."

After freshening up and getting a quick bite to eat, Manda returned to the bridge, spent several minutes at the rail visually checking each of the stations, then she stepped back and settled into her seat; Morian joined her a few moments later.

"Everything shipshape, Commander?"

"It is, sir. We're ready to exit into the Beta Ariatis System."

"Thank the stars for that," Morian said. "Any word of Swarm activity?"

"None, Captain."

"And… you're not…?"

"No, sir. I'm feeling nothing, which is a good sign, I hope."

"So do I, Commander; so do I," he said.

"Bridge to Domino," Morian said into his personal comms.

"Go ahead, Captain," Danis said.

"I'm told there's no Swarm activity in Beta Ariatis, but we're about to exit so you'd better be ready for anything."

"I'm ready, brother. Ranger Squadron is good to go."

"Stay safe, Danis. Morian out."

Several moments later, *Avenger* dropped out of the Slipstream into the Beta Ariatis System.

Unfortunately, Manda had only been half right when she said there was no Swarm presence.

The screens all lit up, flashing red. The proximity alarms sounded throughout the ship, warning them that an enemy had locked onto them. The screens cleared…

They were completely surrounded by a fleet of pirate ships. All of them with weapons hot and locked on.

They'd been waiting for *Avenger* to arrive. But how did they know?

Chapter Twenty-Eight

Welcome to Freyja

Elio climbed out of Danis's fighter and joined her on the flight deck. They'd just received word from the bridge that there would be no fighting and that the squadron was to stand down. Apparently, the pirates wanted to talk terms and, in a gesture of goodwill, one of the pirate captains was going to come aboard.

Elio was... enthusiastic. Diplomacy was something he'd done all his adult life, though reluctantly, and he was good at it. Now all that royal training was about to pay off; at least he hoped so.

Danis stood beside him as the pirate's shuttle depressurized and its ramp opened.

Instead of a diplomat or someone wearing a captain's uniform, a ragtag group of five pirates stepped out and walked down the ramp. Four men and a woman with long blonde hair. Ragtag was the word. Each of them wore either a combination of civilian clothes or quasi-military uniforms from a dozen different star systems. The hairstyles were all different. Two of the men were clean-shaven; the other two had long straggly beards. *What? No eye patch?* Danis thought.

The woman was tall, very tall, almost as tall as Elio. He looked at her. She stared back at him. They made eye contact and, for a brief moment, Elio considered reaching out to her with his Psy but then changed his mind. *That must be Sasha Crowe,* he thought. *I've seen her somewhere before, but where... and when?*

The pirates appeared to be... unconcerned... not at all impressed by the number of crewmen and Marines present on the flight deck, much less by Danis and the other uniforms present. One of them, a giant of a man, was even wearing a pair of mech boots and what once was a USF flight suit.

"I am Prince Elio Lorne." Elio stood with his hands behind his back. "I'd like to speak to your captain."

The visitors looked at him, then looked at one another. A tall man aged about forty, muscular, handsome, with shoulder-length black hair and a beard, stepped forward, a sardonic smile on his lips, and said, "That would be me, my friend. My name is Tiger Wok." His voice was deep, smooth, without a hint of an accent. "But I'm not here to talk to a sovereign prince. I'll talk only to your Captain Morian. So, I suggest you take me to him."

Elio smirked. "I'm afraid that is not how it works. You're on our ship and will therefore do as we say."

"I'm afraid not," Wok replied, totally at ease. "Your ship is surrounded by our fleet." The pirate took a step closer to Elio, obviously a power play, and said quietly, "So, that puts us in charge, my friend. We showed our good faith by coming aboard. The least you can do is show us some professionalism and respect."

"You're outlaws," Elio replied. "I do not respect criminals."

"Is that so?" Wok said, smiling, revealing a perfect set of gleaming white teeth that reminded Danis of a krellfish.

Elio didn't move, nor did he speak.

The pirate looked him up and down. "What kind of prince are you, wearing a pilot's jumpsuit? Are you sure you're a prince, my friend?" His four companions chuckled.

Elio then felt a sudden hard push on his chest, forcing him to take a half-step backward. Tiger Wok was using TK on him. Elio half-closed his eyes, concentrated and pushed back, taking Wok by surprise.

Wok narrowed his eyes, frowned, and pushed. So did Elio. Neither man moved, both clearly surprised by the power of the other. It was clear that Wok had not expected any resistance, or to become engaged in a mental arm-wrestling contest in front of his crew.

He let go, smiled, then laughed and said, "You win, my friend. Perhaps you truly are a prince."

Elio let go, knowing good and well that he hadn't won at all, that it was all a show for the pirate's crew.

"Tiger Wok?" Morian said as he stepped up beside Danis, startling them, offering his hand to the pirate captain. "I'm Richard Morian, captain of the *Avenger.*

Welcome aboard. You said you want to talk. So let's do it."

"Ah, Captain," Wok said, taking his hand and shaking it vigorously. "It is so good to finally meet you. Thank you for providing such a..." He waved a hand in Elio's general direction but never lost eye contact with Morian, "a *prestigious* welcoming party."

"You're welcome, sir. Now, if you'll come with me, I'll escort you to the bridge. Elio, you too. Danis, you can stand down."

What? Elio and Danis thought in unison.

* * *

Elio, raging inside, followed Morian, Tiger Wok and his four crewmen to the elevator. Danis stood staring after them wondering what in the name of Orso her brother was doing escorting five pirates to the bridge.

As they rode the gravrail to the bridge elevator, Elio felt Morian reach out to him, telling him not to worry and to trust him.

Elio, unable to help himself, thought, *I hope you know what the hell you're doing. If not, you're about to hand the ship and crew over to the pirates.*

I don't have a choice, Morian replied. *They have the advantage. I know what I'm doing. Trust me.*

Elio did trust his friend, but he certainly didn't trust Tiger Wok and his band of buccaneers. *Why is he doing this?* Elio wondered. *These people are criminals. In any other situation they'd be arrested...*

The bridge door slid open and Morian led the

group in.

"Captain on deck," Manda Haal shouted.

Every officer stood, turned to face the command deck and came to attention.

Commander Haal stood at parade rest, her back to the rail with her hands clasped behind her back.

"At ease," Morian said and waited until everyone had settled down, then continued, "This is Captain Tiger Wok of the *Red Dragon*. He and his crew are... taking command, temporarily. You will do as he asks without question or argument. Is that understood?"

"Aye, Captain," most of the bridge crew answered, though some of them merely nodded.

Morian turned to Wok and said, "My ship is at your command, Captain."

What? Elio thought. *What's he doing?* Elio opened his mouth to speak, but before he could, Morian was in his head.

Don't say anything, Elio. Be patient. Trust me.

Elio stared at him, his mouth half-open. Morian looked at him, smiling, and nodded.

Elio nodded back.

Tiger Wok, obviously unaware of the discourse between Morian and the prince, smiled and said, "Thank you, Captain. Your hospitality is most gracious, my friend." He turned to his four crewmen. "Go to your stations. Jackknife, you take Tactical; Karl, Navigation; Rudy, Helm. Sasha, you stay with me."

The tall blonde woman nodded but didn't speak. Instead, she turned to look at Elio and smiled. *Stars... she's beautiful.*

Sasha Crowe was easily as tall as Elio, in her late thirties, he knew, slim with brilliant blue eyes and a smile that men through the ages had been willing to die for.

Again, he thought of reaching out to her with his Psy, and again he thought better of it. *The less these people know about my abilities, the better... but Sasha Crowe? Who is she really? Look at her. She's a... No! She can't be. She's a pirate, but...*

Totally aware of her close proximity, he stood beside her, his hands clasped behind his back, two steps behind Wok, Morian, Haal and Jadern, and watched the forward view screens as the pirate crew flew *Avenger* down to the nearest planet, escorted by the rest of the pirate fleet.

It was sometime later, perhaps an hour later, when the *Avenger* entered Freyja's exosphere and began to descend to the planet's surface.

"How are you holding up, Elio?" Morian asked quietly.

"How can I put it?" Elio replied. "Other than the fact we've handed our ship over to a gang of criminals and are now descending into their lair where God only knows what fate awaits us, I'm holding up quite well, I think."

"You should trust me, Elio," Morian said, staring at the screens.

"I'll fully trust you once we're out of this mess, if that ever happens."

"Look," Morian said. "We were outnumbered and outgunned. This seemed to me to be the best way to gain their confidence. Besides, this is what you wanted, what we came for, is it not?"

"You could at least have prepared us first," Elio replied.

"I had no time," Morian said. "It's not like I expected any of this, and they had us surrounded."

"How did they do that?" Elio asked. "Surely, they couldn't have known we were coming. Not from the crazy roundabout route we took."

"I don't know," Morian replied. "I wondered that myself. It was the first thing I asked their captain, Tiger Wok. He ignored me."

"As you can see, Captain Morian." They turned to see Tiger Wok behind them. "We are men of our word. And I will provide you with the answers you seek. But I think it best not to try to explain it to you. What is it they say, a picture is worth a thousand words? It's best that I show you."

The ship descended through the cloud cover and flew slowly over a massive spaceport. Ships of all kinds and sizes were coming and going. It was one of the busiest civilian ports Elio had ever seen.

The pirate Wok had called Jackknife keyed the comms. "Haven control, this is Black Flag requesting docking instructions."

"Roger, Black Flag. We have visual. Please identify your ship."

"This is USF1736 *Avenger* temporarily under the command of Captain Tiger Wok. We're expected."

"That you are, Avenger. Maintain altitude at twelve hundred meters and follow the beacon. You are cleared for docking, bay seventy-three."

"Roger that. Bay seventy-three it is." Jackknife turned and winked at Elio.

What the hell's going on? Elio wondered as he watched the screens as *Avenger* flew slowly on her grav engines over the vast spaceport. He could identify a variety of ships, merchant and military: Starfreighters, Super Galaxy transports. Starliners, Defender class cruisers, antique Guardian class destroyers, even a couple of Battleships and an antique carrier.

"This is Haven control to Avenger. Slow to fifteen knots and go to and maintain altitude at five hundred meters."

The closer they got to the surface, the more detail Elio could identify and the more astounded he became. He could make out a variety of shuttles and fighters. He'd had no idea of the enormity of the complex and couldn't help but wonder why the intel was so out of date. Either the USF patrols were negligent or the pirates were somehow able to hide the true nature of the complex.

Whatever! he thought. *This is exactly what we're looking for. Mission accomplished.*

Tiger Wok's crew were nothing if not skilled pilots. Some thirty minutes after descending through the exosphere, *Avenger* slipped smoothly into docking bay seventy-three and came to a halt.

"There," Wok said to Morian, a huge smile on his lips, "nicely done, wouldn't you say, Captain?"

Reluctantly, Morian agreed that it was.

"So," Wok continued, "let's go. I suggest you take with you no more than two or three of your most senior officers. My crew will maintain good order aboard the *Avenger* while you're away."

"Is that just a nice way of saying you'll keep her under guard, Captain?" Morian asked sarcastically.

Wok grinned and replied, "Very astute, Captain, and very droll, I might add. Shall we go?"

Morian nodded, turned and said, "Elio, Commander Haal. With me. Mr. Jadern, you have the bridge." He paused and glanced at Wok, then corrected himself, "Do as they ask, Commander."

"Aye, Captain," Jadern said, glancing sideways at the smiling Jackknife.

That done, Morian, Elio and Manda followed Wok and Jackknife from the bridge main airlock and from there onto a boarding lift and waited as the huge platform lowered them to the ground and a large crowd of people all waving and cheering, as if they were welcoming home a long-lost ship and its crew.

"Who are all these people?" Commander Haal asked, a look of total confusion on her face.

"They are supporters of the Independent Militia of the Free People," Tiger Wok replied. "They're here to welcome you."

Sovereign stars, Elio thought. *This is... what the hell is going on here?* he asked himself for the umpteenth time.

The crowd parted and they walked through, and Elio was amazed at the diversity of the people. There were very few of them that could be identified as pirates. Most of them were just regular people: men, women, children, spacers, all kinds of people. *What are they all doing here in a pirate haven?* he wondered.

"Welcome to the Freyja, my friends," Tiger Wok said as he turned to face the crowd. "Look around you." He raised his arms to the crowd. "See? They are excited to welcome you."

"You talk as if they knew we were coming," Morian said.

Wok looked at Morian, smiled and said, "In a sense, yes, they did. But patience, my friend, and all will be explained to you."

* * *

They boarded a hover shuttle and the big man they called Jackknife closed the gate behind them. Manda watched through the window as the crowd began to thin.

The shuttle lifted off and flew along the docking bay toward the tall buildings some ten kilometers away. *This is more than a small pirate haven,* she thought as they flew past markets, restaurants and shops. *It's a city.*

How could they have known? she wondered. Her mind began to wander, to speculate. *There has to be a spy on board Avenger. No, that can't be it. Only myself, the prince and Captain Morian had access to the final destination... Someone with Psy? Clintok? Danis? Not Danis... Clintok, though. Not likely. According to the captain, his Psy is weak. Is it possible to communicate across star systems? I don't think so... and he's been confined to a cell ever since he was caught. Could he have read my mind, or Elio's, or the captain's?* Her thoughts were interrupted by Tiger Wok.

"As you can see," he said, acting the tour guide.

"Haven is an impressive city. People of all ethnicities, all walks of life from around the galaxy have come here seeking protection from the Swarm. This, my friend," he said addressing Morian and waving his hand expansively, "is our stronghold. Here, we, the Independent Militia of the Free People, can protect them."

"How can this many people be off-grid?" Haal asked. "Are they not registered with the USF?"

"You will find, Commander, that the star systems are far broader than you, and the USF, can imagine." He smiled and laughed and turned to Morian and said, "My friend, you have no idea of the untold numbers of undocumented colonies there are across the galaxy. You people see no further than the end of your noses. Ah..." He put up his hand, interrupting Morian as he was about to speak. "But, please, you should not take it personally, Captain. What I'm telling you is just the reality. You cannot suppress freedom."

"There must be more going on here," Elio said. "This is more than just a band of pirates."

"Yes, you are correct, Prince," Tiger Wok said. "If you must call us pirates, then you must," he said with a shrug. "I, however, prefer the term free people. Be that as it may, there are *many* bands of *pirates* here. We have banded together because of the Swarm threat, forming a sort of... alliance, you could say. Yes, we may have our differences, but when it comes to the Swarm, we have more in common than not."

Manda was beginning to pick up on what was going on. This was so much larger than they expected, in so many ways. But pirates working together? It was unheard of. Pirates were too independent, untrustworthy, unruly. How had they made it work?

The shuttle, after a ten-minute flight, docked inside a hangar on the second floor of the tallest building in the city.

"Here we are, my friends. Come." Tiger Wok stood, waved for them to follow him and exited the shuttle and, together, they walked into a vast atrium filled with people.

"So," Morian said as they walked together across the atrium, "you have this... alliance. Might I ask who's running it?"

"Ah," Tiger Wok said as he stepped closer to Morian and draped his arm over the captain's shoulder. Morian managed to contain himself and allowed the arm to stay, but Manda could tell he was more than a little uncomfortable at the unwanted gesture of pseudo friendship.

"Our leader," Wok said conspiratorially, "or should I say leaders, are actually a board of directors."

"A board of directors?" Manda asked. "That sounds more like a corporation than a band of pirates."

"There you go again with that word, but yes, I agree," Tiger Wok said. "But it's an historical fact that the pirates of old ran their ships like a business; every member of the crew had a say in the running of the ship, I believe, and a fair share of the booty, depending upon rank, of course. I, myself, was against the label, but you know how things go, and one has to be... flexible in these situations. So, the board of directors it is. And that's who I am going to introduce you to. But first, I have something to show you."

Chapter Twenty-Nine

Now you see me

Morian was beginning to feel somewhat better about Tiger Wok and his organization. The more the pirate captain said, the more it became clear that he and his people were not his enemy, but he still didn't understand why and so he decided to play along with him but still keep his guard up.

Wok steered them across the atrium to a large service elevator that took them down three floors, and from there along a seemingly endless hallway to a large double door that opened into another hallway that led to another building.

As they passed through the double doors, Manda looked at Elio and raised her eyebrows in question. He nodded, then reached out to Morian, expressing his concern.

Morian merely nodded, as if to say, "trust me."

Manda caught a little of the calming influence, but something she couldn't quite grasp was causing her serious concern. It wasn't the fear that they might possibly be taken captive by pirates; it was something quite different, but she couldn't figure out what it was.

The small group continued on along a long stainless steel-walled hallway inset with multiple, blue-painted doors until finally, Wok stopped in front of a large double door.

"This is what we've brought you to see," Wok said after turning to face them. "Before we go in, I should tell you that what you're about to see is... unprecedented, remarkable. I also want you to know that we're thankful you're here. We've been waiting for this moment for a long time."

Morian didn't know what to say, so he merely nodded.

The pirate captain returned the gesture, turned to the door, punched a code into his data pad, then offered the screen to the sensor beside the door. The sensor turned green and the lock clicked. Wok pushed the door open, and they followed him into a large, dimly lit, windowless room full of people all seemingly talking to one another, their voices blending together.

Most of them were on their feet, some standing still, some walking around muttering to themselves, and some were seated at large desks.

The walls were covered with touch screens and marker boards, all covered with handwritten notes, formulas, symbols and images. Every once in a while, one of them would rush to one of the screens or a board and write or draw something on it. The place was a hive of disorganized activity that seemed to have no rhyme or reason to it.

The group took a few steps further inside, then Wok held up his hand, turned to face them and said proudly, "Here they are."

Morian, Elio and Manda looked around the room, bemused. *What the hell is all this?* Morian thought. *It's like... a zoo. Who and what are these people?*

The occupants of the room were men and women ranging in age from about twenty to more than one-hundred-twenty-five. As Morian watched, he noticed that most of them were not talking to one another at all; they seemed to be talking to themselves and, from what he could hear, nothing they were saying made sense. It all sounded like gibberish. And the images and symbols on the walls? They didn't look like anything intelligible either.

Morian, his patience fast running out, turned and looked at Elio and Manda, shook his head in frustration, turned back to Wok and said, "What is all this, Captain? What are we looking at? Who are these people and why have you brought us here?"

Wok smiled benevolently, stroked his beard and said, "So many questions, Captain Morian, and understand-ably so." He waved a hand in an expansive gesture that encompassed the entire room and continued, "Here, my friends, you see what we call the Seers. The people in this room all possess the third of the three abilities granted to the heroes of old. These people possess the ability to peer, although imperfectly, into the future. It is called... The Sight. The ability to see what is to come."

"So that's it," Elio said, not really surprised.

Morian nodded, turned his head to look at Manda, then turned again to Wok and said, "So, the stories are true. This is the third gift."

Manda felt relieved, suddenly realizing she wasn't unique. What she didn't understand was what all these people were doing. There seemed to be no order to it; it wasn't even organized chaos.

"That's right, my friend. Yes," Wok said to Morian. "Of course, the stories are true. You see it right here, in front of you."

"But why here?" Richard asked. "And why are they with you?"

"These people started exhibiting their abilities shortly after the Swarm attacks began, just as others began to develop TK and Psy. Although, the numbers of people with the Sight are much smaller than those with TK and Psy. But to answer your question, a small number of them got together and formed a working group, the nucleus of this working group, in fact. There's no mystery about why they're here; they all just happened to be in the Beta Ariatis System. One of them was even a member of my crew. So the word traveled, and one by one new Seers joined the group. The strange thing is, though, that none of them are able to fully grasp..." He paused, seemingly lost for words, then continued. "And, of course, we knew the USF would take and swallow up these people, so we had to protect them. They are free people and so they want to remain; free and outside any USF registry."

"What do you mean?" Elio asked. "They couldn't fully grasp... What couldn't they grasp?"

Wok thought for a moment, considering how to best answer the question, then said, "As you see, the Seers are working together. The ability seems to manifest itself on different levels, similar to TK and Psy. One Seer might see more than another. One Seer might have a more... developed skill to make sense of what they see. Most, however, need to work with others. It appears that most of them can only see small portions of the future. Or they can see things without context. It's not until another Seer comes along and connects the... dots, as they say, almost as if they are working on a puzzle, that they can make any sense of what they're seeing. They predicted your arrival with great accuracy, which is why we were waiting for you."

"I see," Morian said, still trying to get his head around the complexity of what he was seeing and what Wok was trying his best to explain. It was clear to Morian that Wok understood little more than he did.

"They have been incredibly accurate in forecasting not only Swarm activity," Wok continued, "but many other dangers. Which is why these shipyards have remained safe for as long as they have."

"And that, I suppose, is another reason the population has grown so much?" Elio asked.

"Yes, the free peoples across the galactic network

connect with and find one another. The Seers," he said and turned his head to look at them, "continue to work together to keep Freyja safe, and the population continues to grow. Fortunately we have plenty of room for them, and as the population grows, so does the number of Seers."

Morian was amazed by Wok's story but not all that surprised by what he heard. For several weeks he'd watched as Manda's fledgling abilities began to mature. At first he was unsure, but that had changed during the long journey to Aries.

Aries, god of war, he thought. *These Seers... Are they then the gods of war? This new ability offers endless potential... and possibilities for the USF in the fight against the Swarm.*

He watched a middle-aged man walk across the room in front of him, his head down and his hands clasped behind his back, lost in thought.

Richard reached out to him, trying to make contact, but there was nothing, just blackness. It was as if the Seer had built a wall around himself that blocked Morian's attempts. He tried again, concentrating harder, trying to force his way into the man's mind. Again, he was unsuccessful.

"It's no use, my friend," Wok said, smiling. "When a Seer is using the Sight, there is no way to read their minds. Both Psy and TK are useless against them. Why that is, we don't know."

"I see," Morian said, making eye contact with the pirate, tempted to try reaching out to him. But he didn't. Partly because he wanted the man to trust him and partly because he was beginning to like him. *Maybe these pirates are not all we think they are. Maybe this is why we're here*, he thought, remembering Danis's words returned to him. 'Good people aren't all good, and bad people aren't all bad.' *In other words, there's good and bad in all people.*

Chapter Thirty

The Board of Directors

"Come, my friends," Tiger Wok said, smiling at the group. "It is time. Let us go and meet our Board of Directors. I know they are waiting for you and will be just as pleased to meet you as I am."

They left the Seers to their work, Elio sure that not one of them had known they were in the room.

Tiger Wok took them back to the elevator and up to the fourth floor.

Throughout their time with Wok, Elio had said little, taking in the sights of the city on the ride from the space-port and the strange encounter with the Seers. Now he was about to meet the rulers of Freyja and he was... a little excited. While he'd had no idea of what they would find when they finally reached Beta Ariatis, he had been preparing for some sort of meeting the entire mission.

Wok led them into a large lobby with floor-to-ceiling windows that offered a magnificent view of the city, its busy streets filled with people, a public square with fountains, and even a large church.

Jackknife joined them a few minutes later, his heavy mech boot clicking on the concrete floor. Elio hadn't even noticed the big man had left them.

"The board's ready, Captain," he said to Wok.

"Good, good. Thank you, my friend." Wok waved his hands again and said, "Come, follow me. They are waiting to meet you." He turned and walked toward a double door with two huge, rather rough-looking pirates standing one on either side. Neither one looked impressed by the two uniformed USF officers, or the royal, but they let them pass without a word.

The council chamber was typical of those Elio had attended across the Sovereign Systems. Some two-dozen people were seated behind the elevated, semi-circular bench.

Behind a long narrow table placed at the center of the room facing the bench were three empty chairs. Wok gestured to them and whispered, "You are to take a seat at the table. I will be waiting for you."

Morian took the center chair, Elio took the one to his left, and Manda the one to his right. Wok, Jackknife and several other members of his crew retired to the back of the room.

This was certainly a more formal setting than Elio had imagined when he first had the idea of aligning with pirates. Most of them had gray hair and looked older than any Elio had seen so far during his short time on the planet.

"The chair recognizes the delegation from the USF

Avenger," an older woman seated at the center of the bench said. "Who will speak for you?"

Elio looked at Morian. Morian nodded and Elio cleared his throat and said, "Thank you, ma'am. I am Prince Elio Lorne of the Orso System. Thank you for your welcome. We are grateful and honored to be here. To my right is Captain Richard Morian, and to his right is Commander Manda Haal of the *Avenger.*"

Morian and Haal nodded.

"We have heard of you, Captain Morian," a heavy-set man with a gray, braided beard said. "We have been waiting for you. You are all welcome. Our Seers have been telling us for many months that you would come, although we do not know why. Please, tell us why you are here."

"We are here because the USF needs your help." Elio's statement was answered by laughter from several members of the board. It was clearly unexpected.

Elio waited for the laughing to die down, then said, "Yes, I understand your reaction, but we are all facing a common enemy, the Swarm. This enemy from another reality has destroyed many of our worlds, and from what Captain Wok has told us, you have not gone unscathed yourselves. We have had some successes in our war against them, but the USF does not have unlimited resources and the Swarm is learning, evolving. We need your help, your ships and access to your shipyards and ports."

"Surely, you jest, Prince Elio," the man with the beard said. "We are but a handful of free people. Our system is a small one. What could we possibly do to help the combined Sovereign Stars and its massive fleet? Very little, I think, especially when we all know that less than eighteen standard months ago you were hunting us down like rabid dogs." The old man's voice was mild but with an edge to it.

"That's what we are here to find out," Elio said earnestly, leaning his elbows on the table. "And what you say is true, but times and circumstances change. We are all humans. Our fight is with the Swarm, as is yours. We do not want a war with you. Yes, we have different ideologies, different wants and needs, but I say again, we are all human and our battle against the Swarm is a battle for all humanity. You must see this."

"We have survived against the Swarm quite well without you," a woman at the far end of the bench said. "Our Seers are our best protection. We do not need the USF."

"I think you do," Elio said, "as we need you. The USF does not have the resources to protect humanity... all of humanity. And we know from our experiences that you do not have the resources to protect this system... even in the short term. The Swarm appears to have developed true faster than light travel. They appear out of nowhere. Yes, we have the Slipstream and it is very effective, but it's also predictable. Entry and exit points are fixed. We must defend those entry and exit points. If they take or destroy them, no one will be able to help anyone. It's not just the USF that needs your help; it's all of humanity. Your resources, your abilities, your Seers can make the difference between victory or defeat. Think of how many people, families, women and children can be saved with the help of the Seers."

"And what would keep the USF from using the Seers against us?" another, much younger man asked. He was thin and wore a black, neatly trimmed goatee. He had piercing brown eyes and wore a miss-matched wardrobe that gave him the look of someone who, had he been anywhere else in the Sovereign Systems, was homeless. "We all know that if we were to share the Seers with you now, as soon as the threat is removed, the USF would turn on us. You have never wanted anything but to subjugate us. Why should we believe any different of you now?"

"True! Yes! Hear, hear," several voices along the bench called out in support of the thin man.

"I know, I know," Elio said, standing and holding up both hands. "We understand your concerns. That's why I'm here; to show you a true expression of our integrity. We need your help. Humanity needs your help. Please... let us forge an alliance and defeat the Swarm together."

Elio sat down and looked at Morian. Morian didn't seem too impressed.

The members of the board began to talk amongst themselves. Finally, they seemed to take a vote. Thumbs along the bench were presented either up or down; most of them down.

"We understand why you came," the woman at the center of the bench said. "But we have decided that what you propose is not in our best interest. We have survived well enough without the USF thus far."

"We would need a guarantee," another woman shouted. "We would need a guarantee that we would retain our freedom and independence. Even then—"

"My crew would not work with the USF even with a guarantee," another man shouted.

"Why are you really here?" shouted yet another.

Voices rang out all along the bench, each trying to be heard over the others.

Morian closed his eyes and shook his head, feeling sorry for his friend. Elio had tried his best, but they obviously didn't trust him. The Board of Directors was suspicious, and rightly so. Elio's political arguments were not going to work with this group. These people were practical. They were survivors to whom other world politics meant nothing.

Not only did Morian have a lot riding on this mission, but so did Elio. They both needed the mission to succeed.

Morian reached out to them, trying to feel them out, to find a sympathetic mind, but all he found was an overwhelming aura of contempt. He sat still for a moment longer, listening to the angry voices. Finally, he'd had enough and rose to his feet.

"I suggest you all calm down and listen for a minute. Maybe you'll learn something," Morian said, gaining their attention. The noise died away. Every member of the board stared down at him.

"We know you're running out of the essentials, food in particular. We also know the Beta Ariatis System doesn't have the resources to support its rapidly growing population. And we know that this, plus the extra logistical burden of the war, has brought you to a place where you need us as much as we need you."

"Not so!" someone shouted.

"Hah," Morian snapped. "It's true, and you all know it better than I do. You need food and materials."

"And the USF will supply them?" the thin man asked. "How kind."

"We will," Morian replied. "We have the capacity, and the capability, to transport large quantities of supplies through the Slipstream," Richard said. "We have the ability to travel faster via shorter routes than regular freighter traffic. We have vast stores of military resources that can be diverted to the Beta Ariatis System as needed.

"We know most of you are not pirates and do not consider yourselves outlaws. You are free people, and so you will remain. What we're offering is not some trick designed to lure you into an unwanted alliance with the USF, far from it. We're here to offer help and to ask for your help in return." Again, he reached out with his mind. This time he felt they were a little more receptive; at least they were listening to him.

"I want you all to know," he continued, "that at first I didn't want this mission. I could not see that any good could come of it. Furthermore, I didn't know there were pirates in the Beta Ariatis System. Had I known I certainly wouldn't have agreed to it.

"But we desperately need extended shipyard capabilities. Our original mission was to come and investigate what we thought were long abandoned shipyards here on Freyja, to see if they could be refurbished and brought back online. It seems you've already done that, which makes our mission even more important. We need that resource." He gazed along the bench, taking in each and every silent face.

"I have to be honest; I would not have agreed to take this mission if I knew we would be meeting all of you. King Lorne and the rest of the Sovereign Systems are not aware of your presence here, and I can tell you I would not be here were it not for Prince Elio. He opened my eyes to something much bigger than all of us, and I am proud to be here at his side. I respectfully ask you to reconsider your decision."

The room was silent. Morian reached out to them again trying to get a feel for what they were thinking, but he couldn't get a good read on any of them.

* * *

Elio stood. "It's true this mission was my idea. I knew we had to find you. My father and the entire Orso System will provide you with all the vital and logistical support we can. He is willing to reach out to you as equals, to forget the bureaucratic rules of the Sovereign Systems." It was a bit of a stretch, and Elio knew that unless his father did indeed comply with what he was offering these free people, there would be no alliance, but he decided he would have to cross that bridge later.

"It's also imperative that you know something else,"

Elio continued. "I mentioned that the Swarm is learning, evolving, and it's true. We also know, from what Captain Wok has told us, that you have not yet been involved in a head-to-head conflict with the Swarm. That being so, we have information that will help you when you do meet them head-on, and meet them you surely will, and probably sooner than you think."

Elio paused for effect, then continued, "The modern USF Fleet cannot stand against the Swarm. Our modern armor, shields and weapons are ineffective against them. We have lost hundreds of our ships fighting them.

"The majority of your ships, however, are old, like the *Avenger*. Most of them are unregistered and do not emit locator beacons as required by current Sovereign law. What you don't know is that those outdated ships have two major advantages over the modern ships of the USF Navy. One, they still have their heavy Dutrinium armor which, while not totally impervious to the Swarm's plasma weapons, is much more effective. And two, they still have their outdated kinetic weapons. Weapons that, by themselves, can destroy the Swarm ships."

Several of the board members laughed when they heard that.

"It's true," Elio said. "We know the Swarm comes from a silicon-based reality, which means they have different weaknesses and advantages. Their ships have a tremendous ability to absorb directed energy weapons. But with that strength comes the weakness. Their silicon base makes them molecularly unstable when hit with blunt force. Thus we've had great success with kinetic weapons such as railguns and missiles with kinetic warheads. This has been the key to our success."

The room was quiet. The entire board was listening to his every word.

"Your single fleet of armored ships with its antique weapons," he continued, "will be more effective against the Swarm than anything we have in the USF. As to your shipyards... We need them to update our modern fleet. We need your factories designed to fabricate and repair our old tech and refit our modern ships."

Elio was about to make one final plea when the double doors flew open. Everyone turned to see what the interruption was.

A young man wearing a red rag around his head and a pistol on his hip rushed into the council chamber, his face white.

"What is it, son?" the man with the braided beard asked.

"The Seers, sir. They've made a prediction," the young man said, trying to catch his breath.

"And? Out with it, man. What do they say?"

"The Swarm, sir. They are coming, in great numbers, to attack Freyja. Today."

The old man stood. So did the rest of the board. So did everyone else in the room.

"And the outcome?" the old man asked.

"They are not able to predict the outcome of the attack, only that there will be a major battle."

"This meeting is adjourned," the old man snapped. "Alert the fleet and get them into space."

Morian walked quickly to where Tiger Wok had been sitting and grabbed his arm as he was about to leave.

"We'll fight with you," Morian said.

Wok grinned. "Of course, my friend. I think we are going to need all the help we can get. Follow me. I'll see you back to your ship."

Chapter Thirty-One

Irregular Strategies

It wasn't more than thirty minutes later via fast shuttle that Morian and Haal were back on the bridge of the *Avenger,* Elio having made a mad dash to join Danis on the flight deck.

"Attention Ranger Squadron, this is Tactical," Omario Kingston's voice echoed throughout decks seven, eight and nine. "Prepare to deploy. I say again, prepare to deploy." The message repeated several more times, jerking Gian and Andra out of their... lovemaking. Gian jumped up off the cot and onto his feet, as did Andra, both of them grabbing for their clothes.

"What the hell's going on?" he said, more to himself than to Andra. "We haven't been here for much more than a couple of hours. Why are we suddenly on high alert?" he mumbled as he struggled into his flight suit.

"Gian, let me go with you," Andra pleaded as he grabbed his helmet and gloves.

"What?" He stopped, turned, and looked at her.

"I want to go with you. In your fighter, as your copilot. Like Elio with Danis."

"No, no... No!" he snapped at her. "You know I can't do that."

"But I can help. I can be your second set of eyes out there. You said it yourself; the Blues are getting better and faster. The F32A fighters are designed to carry two people. You need a copilot. I can do that. Let me help."

"I've got to go," he said, then turned away, wrenched open the door and ran through it into the corridor. Andra, now fully dressed in a one-piece jumpsuit, ran after him and followed him all the way to the hangar. They stopped at the foot of the ladder to the fighter's cockpit where Gian put on his gloves.

"Look," he said, turning to face her and grabbing her hands. "We can't do this. I don't have the authority, and I know Danis won't approve it. Andra, I have to go. Please..."

"I know you want to protect me, Gian," she said, hanging onto his hands, "but there's just as much danger here on *Avenger*, perhaps even more."

"But you're not a pilot," he said. "I can't carry a passenger into battle. The captain would have my guts for his dinner."

"No, but I do have TK. I can push the Blues, just like Elio."

"Elio's a pilot." He paused, staring at her. She made a good point. But he knew if he did this, Danis would probably ground him forever. Then again, he hated leaving her behind in the hangar, in danger. He hesitated for a moment longer, then saw Danis and Elio run across the hangar and climb into her fighter. He made up his mind, knowing he'd surely have to pay for what he was about to do.

"All right, grab a flight suit, quick as you can." He pointed to the locker bay. "We could launch at any moment. If we do, I'll have to go without you."

Andra turned and ran. Gian watched her go, hoping she'd be too late, and then climbed up into the F32.

Less than five minutes later, Andra appeared in the locker bay doorway, suited up with gloves and helmet in hand. She ran to the ladder, threw the helmet and gloves to one of the flight crew, scrambled up the ladder—followed by the crewman—and into the rear seat. The crewman handed her the helmet and gloves, wished her good hunting and slid back down the ladder and removed it.

Gian turned to look at her, his face pale, his forehead ridged with frown lines. "You okay?" he asked. "You sure you want to do this?"

She nodded and pulled on her helmet.

"So be it, then," Gian said, then turned and pulled on his own helmet, wondering how the hell he'd let her talk him into it.

He rationalized what he was doing by telling himself he'd had to make a quick decision and—as the canopy closed over them—that he'd figure out how he was going to answer for it later. He took a deep breath, shook his head and began his pre-launch sequence.

"Ranger Leader to Ranger Squadron, listen up, everybody," Danis said. "We have incoming right above us.

Our job is to meet them before they reach the atmosphere and keep the fight off-planet. We go first; the fleet will follow. We fight in pairs. Stay in formation. Let's go."

Gian watched as Danis's F32 lifted and smoothly exited the hangar, followed by her number two, Lt. Tara Berry, call sign Strawberry. Then he took a deep breath, eased the throttles of his grav engines forward, lifting the F32 off the hangar deck, and followed Ranger Five, Blackbird, out into the dockyard. He brought his fusion engines online and put the F32 into a steep climb, reaching for the sky, cutting his gravs as they cleared the tall buildings of the city.

Onward and upward they climbed, the speed increasing swiftly through Mach seven, ten, twelve...

"Uh, Gian?" Andra said.

"Not now, Andra... What?"

"Are all of these guys with us?"

"Who are you talking about?" Gian glanced at his screens to see a massive formation lifting off behind them. He looked out through the canopy. As far as he could see, all across the shipyard, a massive fleet of ships was building. Ships of every type and class were lifting off: fighters, destroyers, cruisers, even a battleship; it seemed as if there were hundreds of them, all streaking towards the sky.

"Domino to Ranger Squadron," Danis's voice said. "It seems we are part of something bigger. Stay sharp. Stay in formation. Looks like we are all together on this one."

"I guess they are all with us," Gian said, answering Andra's question.

His speed continued to increase through Mach 35

until the F32 reached escape velocity at thirteen-point-five kilometers per second, roughly forty-nine thousand kilometers per hour, into the black, at which point he eased back on the throttles and looked around. Seeing nothing other than the fleet rising around him, he checked his scanners, his screens, and his targeting systems.

As far as he could tell, the fleet numbered some one-hundred-thirty diverse ships spread out in a vast fan-shaped formation. Many of them in smaller, tight formations; most of them flying in singles or in pairs. It was a hodgepodge affair, like nothing Gian had ever seen. *Either this is going to be a massive victory,* he thought, *or a massive rout. Who's in command, I wonder? No one? Surely not! Oh well, there wasn't much time to plan anything. I guess we're going to have to play this one by the seat of our pants.*

Gian keyed his comms. "This is Joker. Do we have enemy numbers and location yet?"

"Nothing yet, Joker," Danis answered. "Stay alert and stay off the air."

Gian's scanners suddenly flashed red and his proximity warning buzzed in his ear. He glanced at his screens. They showed a large formation of several hundred enemy craft approaching from behind the smaller of Freyja's three moons.

"There they are," one of the Rangers said.

"I see them, Ranger Six," Danis said. "Ranger Squadron, go to flights of three. Watch each other's backs. Strawberry, Joker, you're with me. Good hunting, everyone." And she banked away to port. Gian and Strawberry stayed with her in close formation.

He reset his long-range scanner, synced his targeting systems, armed all eight of his Saber missiles—the F32s had been upgraded from six rapiers to the smaller but faster Sabers—and waited for a lock.

The swarm ships were approaching fast, coming straight at them. It seemed as if they were on them in seconds rather than minutes. His proximity alarm began to chirp. His targeting systems lit up, first red, then green, as they locked on to one of the leading enemy craft. He waited... and waited... holding the lock. He fired and two of his missiles streaked away, honing in on their target, but he had no time to see if they hit home. His proximity alarms were screeching. He glanced quickly at his screens. Two Swarm ships were coming at him from below and to starboard. *Where the hell did they come from? Damn! They're everywhere.*

He reversed his thrusters, hoping they would over-shoot. His speed dropped, and so did that of the two enemy craft. It was almost as if they knew what he was going to do before he did. He knew he couldn't outrun them. The only way to lose them was to...

"Joker to Domino, I have two under me. I'm going to have to break out."

"I've got two myself, Joker," Danis replied. "Deal with them and get back here as quick as you can."

"Copy that, Domino."

Gian's fingertips flew over the thruster controls, putting the F32 into an almost impossible spinning, twisting climb. *Damn!* he thought. *This is getting real busy real quick.*

And he remembered something he'd learned at the Academy: one of Telemanion's quips on space combat stated that "No strategic plan involving more than three people works once the chaos of battle begins." *Well, something like that,* he thought as he turned the climb into a loop that brought him below and behind the two Swarm fighters.

His targeting screens turned green. He switched from missiles to guns and thumbed the triggers. Twin streams of solid 50-caliber depleted uranium rounds impacted the closer of the two craft, shearing away its port gun platform and sending the craft spinning out of control. He adjusted his trajectory slightly and his targeting screen turned green again, but before he could fire, the Swarm ship, taking him by surprise, streaked upward and away at a speed he couldn't even begin to estimate.

He turned his ship around, looked for Danis on his hologram, found her and streaked after her. She was twisting and jinking, trying to dislodge a Swarm ship that seemed to be sticking like glue to her tail. Gian slid in behind it. His screens turned green. He had the lock. He fired his railguns. The rounds slammed into the enemy craft's fuselage, where he imagined the cockpit would be if it had one. The craft's blue halo flickered and then turned white, and the ship exploded in a brilliant flash of white.

"Thanks, Joker," Danis shouted. "I owe you one."

"You owe me nothing, Domino. I owe—"

"Look out behind you," Andra interrupted him.

Gian made a wide loop to try to get behind his enemy's six, but this time it didn't work. His proximity screen turned red and the alarm began to sound.

"Keep turning," Andra said calmly. "I've got this."

"You've got what?" Gian asked as he strained to hold the tight turn, watching his proximity screen. Suddenly, the Swarm ship veered sharply to starboard. Gian reversed his thrusters, rotated the fuselage, poured on the power and streaked after the now out-of-control enemy fighter. Now, less than fifty meters behind it, he obtained a lock and opened fire with his railguns and watched the rounds stitch from rear to front. The ship's halo died. It started to spin, slowly at first, then faster and faster until finally, all he could see of it was a caramel-colored blur.

It's done for, he thought. *No need to waste any more ammo.* He turned away and headed back to rejoin Danis.

"Hey," he said to Andra. "You did it!"

"I did," she said. "I told you I can help."

"Indeed, you can. Hang on, Andra," he said as he flipped the ship over into an inverted dive just in time to avoid a searing blast of brilliant blue energy from a Swarm fighter streaking toward him on his port side.

The enemy ship turned fast, matching his maneuver. He maintained his arc, flipped the fuselage, obtained a target lock on the enemy and fired one of his six remaining missiles. The Swarm ship had no chance. It ran head-on into the kinetic missile and exploded in a shower of brilliant white light.

Gian reversed his thrusters, rolled the F32 one hundred and eighty degrees to starboard and... He had no time to chat with Andra. He barely had time to think as a pair of Swarm ships appeared, seemingly out of nowhere, forward and slightly to port. He took out the nearest one with a long burst of railgun fire while Andra pushed the second off course just as it fired. Four bolts of blue plasma flashed by so close he could have sworn he smelled the paint on the F32's hull burning.

His fingertips flitted over his thruster controls, putting the F32 into a tight, hammerhead turn that put him less than a hundred meters off the enemy's tail. He switched from guns to missiles. His targeting screen turned from red to green and flashed, indicating target lock. He thumbed the trigger, then hauled the F32 into a hard turn to starboard, just in time to avoid the massive explosion as the Saber slammed into the enemy craft. *Four Sabers left,* he thought as he raced across the battle-field to rejoin Danis. *Let's make 'em count. Where the hell is she?* He looked out through his canopy. Things were getting tight. The battle was raging all around him, in all directions. The pirate ships were spread out over a vast area, many hundreds of kilometers in diameter in every direction. He could see fighters engaged all across the battlefield, all of the old classes, some of them he couldn't even identify, but he had no idea where Danis and the rest of the squadron were.

"More incoming, two o'clock high," Andra said.

Gian glanced up and to the right to see three Blues streaking toward him in an arrowhead formation, and his heart sank. He looked around. There was no one close, no one to help. He had been having trouble with two, let alone three, and they were going to be within firing range in a matter of seconds. It was Level E-9 all over again, only this time it was for real, and there would be no room for mistakes, Andra or not. If he went after the closest one, he would probably lose the advantage by the time the third one engaged him.

He almost hit full thrust and went after it anyway, but then he remembered: *What did Danis say? Get to a position where you can see your enemy and your enemy can't see you. Stack them up. Have patience. Yes, that was it... or something like it.*

So how can I use their positioning against them? If, instead of diving straight into the middle of them, I go low and then attack from below and to port... that would almost line them up.

"Hang on, Andra," he shouted. "This is going to be rough."

He poured on the power, put the F32 into a vertical dive, rotated his fuselage so he was, in effect, flying backward, but now he could see what his enemy was doing as they made the turn to chase him.

"Gian, what are you doing?" Andra asked. "You'll never outrun them."

"Hang on." Gian continued the dive, rotated the F32 twenty degrees to starboard, then rotated the fuselage and put the fighter in a tight climbing turn to starboard. He felt his inertia dampeners tighten around him as the G-forces increased. He couldn't see them. He hoped like hell he'd gotten it right. If he hadn't...

Suddenly, there they were, making the turn to follow him, but just a little too late. They were now almost perfectly lined up, wing to wing, one slightly above the other, and he couldn't help but smile to himself.

They must have seen their mistake because they began to break away in three different directions, but Gian was already firing his railguns. By the time the one nearest to him had exploded, he was already firing at the second ship. A hail of railgun rounds slammed into its left wing, tearing it off close to the fuselage, sending the craft spiraling away. The Swarmie was alive, but its machine, or whatever it was, was out of commission.

"Incoming," Andra shouted. "Gian!"

Gian's alarm sounded. His proximity screen flashed red. The third enemy craft had locked onto him and fired. Gian flipped the F32 to port, just as twin blasts of plasma streaked by. He reversed thrust. The F32 slowed dramatically. He waited two seconds, reversed thrust again and poured on the power just as the enemy craft streaked by. The Swarmie reacted almost immediately and went into an evasive pattern, but Gian stayed with him, waiting for a target lock. The two fighters spiraled, one behind the other, thousands of kilometers across the battlefield, Gian's targeting screens flashing red, then green, then red. Then it went green and stayed green, and Gian fired two of his four remaining missiles. Two seconds later, the missiles impacted the Swarm ship. It exploded, and Gian found himself streaking through a ballooning cloud of fire and debris.

Gian let out a breath and then yelled, "Yeehah!"

"Nice shooting, Joker," Danis's voice sounded in his helmet. "I was coming to help you out, but you seemed to be doing just fine."

"Domino?" he replied. "Where are you?"

"Coming up behind you. You all right?"

"Yes," he replied. "You?"

"We've lost Ranger Seven. But the rest of the squadron is still out there kicking ass."

"Hey," Gian said, "I finally passed level E-9."

Danis chuckled. "That you did, Joker. That you did. Come on. We still have work to do."

* * *

Gian battled at Danis's side for the next twenty minutes as they slowly fought their way back closer to the planet where a large number of Haven ships, including *Avenger*, a half-dozen or so Defender class battle cruisers, Class D destroyers and frigates, were holding their own against the enemy.

As the battle raged on, Andra continued to learn more of Gian's thought patterns and timing, growing more effective by the minute.

He and Danis were just swinging around *Avenger's* bow when they were surprised by a Swarm ship. It fired at Danis, but she was going so fast it missed. It turned sharply and came around behind her. Gian, some six hundred meters behind, increased his speed, caught up with it and his targeting systems locked on. His thumbs were on the triggers and he was just about to fire when he realized if he missed, if any of his rounds missed, they would probably hit Danis, so he had to wait.

He reduced speed, yawed the F32 to starboard, then adjusted all four of his thrusters slightly, putting the fighter into what would look to anyone watching as if he was drifting slightly to his right, and said into his comms, "I'm right behind you, Domino. Stay with it..."

The Swarmie fired just as Danis jinked to port. The bolt of blue plasma seared by, missing her by centimeters.

"Take your time, Joker," she said sarcastically. "It's not like I'm out on a date with this bastard."

"Keep moving. I got him."

But he hadn't got him. The blue ship was weaving and jinking with Danis, and he couldn't get a lock. He inched closer, willing the F32 to give him a lock. He tickled the thruster controls with his fingertips, fine-tuning his engines, but nothing seemed to work. "Damn, damn, damn!" he muttered.

He tried again, and again the enemy craft dodged and... fired... and missed.

"Joker, what the hell are you doing?" Danis yelled. "Get this son of a bitch off my back or he's going to take me out."

"I—" Gian began, but before he could say more, the Swarm fighter jerked violently to port. *What the hell?* His targeting systems locked on. Instinctively he thumbed the triggers and twin streams of 50-caliber depleted uranium rounds slammed into the enemy craft.

For a moment nothing happened. He was just about to fire again when the ship seemed to shatter, almost in slow motion. A nano-second later, the thing exploded in a tremendous blast of blue fire.

"About damn time, Joker," Danis yelled over the comms.

"You're welcome, ma'am."

"Andra," he said. "What happened back there? Did you do that?"

"Yes. I think I'm beginning to get the hang of this."

Gian grinned. Said nothing. He checked his screens, the hologram and his visuals.

Avenger, now some three-hundred kilometers to their rear, was firing broadside after broadside at the mass of Blues to starboard. But the massive ship was also taking fire, most of it absorbed by her second-generation shields, and what little was able to get through was handled by her upgraded armor. Not that she wasn't taking damage, she was, but her upgraded systems were clearly handling the plasma better than they had in the early days of the war.

"Joker to Domino," Gian said, staring at his hologram. "You see what's happening planet-side?"

The number of ships—on both sides—now engaged between them and the planet was staggering. The space around and across the battlefield looked as if it was on fire: flashes and explosions of orange, red, yellow, blue, white... There must have been at least a hundred Haven vessels engaged with double that number of Swarm ships, and they were spread out over a vast area of many thousands of cubic kilometers.

Gian was awed at the utter immensity of what he was seeing. Had he not seen it for himself, he would not have believed it possible.

"I see it, Joker," Danis replied. "Keep your mind on what you're doing. Don't let yourself—"

He didn't hear the rest. His proximity alarms sounded; his screens flashed red. Instinctively, he cut power to his engines, reversed thrust and opened all four throttles to the max. The ship slowed almost to a stop. His inertia dampeners clamped onto him, absorbing the crushing negative G-forces. The enemy craft that had had him locked screamed by so fast he barely saw it and was gone.

"You all right back there?" he yelled to Andra.

"I am, but there's a Blue approaching fast from behind and to port. He'll be on you in seconds."

He glanced at his proximity screens. She was right. He tapped the throttles and put the F32 into a long looping dive toward the battle below him.

The enemy fighter followed, slowly closing the gap between them. He tried to shake it. He couldn't. The problem was it was still too far away; far enough that it wasn't yet a huge risk, but Andra was right. It was closing fast.

His alarms began to sound. A second later his screens began to flash red, indicating the enemy had locked onto him.

"I can't shake it, Andra."

"It's too far away for me to reach," she said, trying hard not to panic.

"I'll try to..." He didn't finish the thought. Instead, he cut engine 3 to ten percent and increased the other three to full power and put the F32 into a crazy spinning dive. His screens turned from red to green, then from green to red again as the Swarmie stayed right with him.

Gian was just about out of ideas. His alarms seemed to be screaming at him. The hair on the back of his neck began to prickle. He closed his eyes. *I'm sorry, Andra...*

It was then, at what must have been the very last moment, that a missile slammed into the pursuing Swarmie and it exploded as another fighter came up behind him and did a victory roll.

Gian slowed. The fighter behind yawed to starboard and came up alongside him. The pilot, the big, bearded pirate with the mech boots, smiled at them and saluted.

Gian nodded back at him and touched his forehead with the fingers of his right hand and nodded his thanks.

The pirate fighter was a smaller craft with wings designed to allow it to fight in atmosphere. It looked to Gian like an old Veridian design or possibly even an older model.

The pirate waved a hand, then banked away to starboard and rejoined the battle still raging below, taking down first one enemy craft, then a second; its quad rail-guns taking a devastating toll.

As Gian watched, two Swarm ships moved in on the Veridian in a classic pincer maneuver. Thinking the pirate would need help, Gian immediately increased speed and put the F32 into a steep dive, but as he got closer, he could see he needed no help. The Veridian dodged the enemy's plasma blasts with ease. Then he double backed and fired on one Swarmie, ripping off its port wing, then the other, which exploded in a ball of white fire.

Gian was amazed at the pirate's skill. The Veridian fighter moved with such grace. He needed no help from Gian.

Gian shook his head, then looked around for Danis,

but the nearest USF fighter was more than a hundred kilometers away.

"Joker to Domino, I—"

"I'm right behind you, Joker," she said, interrupting him. "How's your ammo?"

That was something he hadn't thought about for a while. He did a quick check.

"I'm out of missiles and my rails are down to fourteen percent."

"That's about what I have," Danis said. "Time to go home and rearm."

"Copy that, Domino," Gian said.

"Domino to Ranger Squadron. All pilots check in."

As the rest of the squadron called in, she quickly learned that all had not gone well. She'd lost Rangers Seven and Eleven, and Six had lost an engine. She ordered the survivors back to *Avenger* to rearm.

Chapter Thirty-Two

Strange Bedfellows

Meanwhile, back on *Avenger's* bridge, Manda Haal stood at the command rail, grasping it with her right hand while staring down at the battle taking place on the giant hologram. There was no order to it. The pirate fleet—some ninety diverse warships of aging classes ranging from small, E-class frigates to a Class-B battleship and several hundred fighters—were spread out across a battlefield so vast it was breathtaking. There was no strategy, no teamwork, no organization. Each pilot fought alone. The number of casualties among them was, or would have been under a USF admiral, totally unacceptable.

The battleship had taken more than a dozen hits. For the most part, its antique armor had held, but two of its engines had been shot to pieces and its hull had been breached in three places she could see, but it was still intact, and it was still fighting.

At least two Defender Class cruisers had been destroyed and another disabled. Of the smaller craft... their losses, she estimated, were close to thirty percent. The enemy? The numbers were horrific. Was the pirate fleet winning? She couldn't tell. The battlefield was fluid, ever-changing. The hologram was a giant fishbowl full of animated green and blue dots.

She looked up and glanced around the view screens. Five flights of Swarm ships, fifteen in all, were off the starboard bow. They were still a thousand kilometers out but approaching fast.

"Divert all power to shields, sectors one, two and three; now," Omario Kingston's voice came over the open comms.

Manda inwardly nodded. Tactical had made the correct call. The forward shields and those to starboard went to full power.

The five flights of blue-haloed enemy ships came swooping in like a flock of eagles, three after three after three.

As soon as they came within range, *Avenger* launched a broadside of twenty, two-stage Rapier missiles fitted with ten-kilogram kinetic warheads designed to explode on proximity and split into twenty point-five-kilogram Dutrinium projectiles.

The barrage took out seven of the Swarm craft; the other eight continued their attack.

At fifteen hundred meters, *Avenger's* eighteen starboard point-defense turrets opened fire with 80mm rail-guns but, with the speed of the incoming enemy craft, they barely had enough time to fire, though they did manage to destroy three more of the blue-haloed ships.

The remaining five Swarm ships swooped in toward the starboard bow and then along the entire length of the ship, their plasma weapons blazing.

Avenger rocked as the plasma blasts ripped along the hull. The new, enhanced shields held as the first three enemy craft swept by, absorbing the heat and deflecting it out into space. But, as the fourth unleashed a devastating blast of super-heated energy, they began to fail. By the time the fifth and last made its attack run, the shields were down to thirty percent and the twin devastating blasts of blinding hot blue energy seared the hull almost from stem to stern. The result: two point defense turrets were swept from the hull and a third disabled and, with a final defiant blast of its two port-side weapons, it took out *Avenger's* outer starboard engine.

The failsafe system kicked in and immediately shut down fusion reactor six.

"Damage report, Mr. Volkov?" Morian shouted as he watched the screens.

"We've lost turrets twelve and fourteen," Volkov replied. "Sixteen is disabled. Engine One is disabled. Two, three and four are undamaged. Reactor One has shut down. Five through six are holding at ninety-four percent. No hull breach on any decks. Shields are back up to eighty-eight percent. Casualties as yet are unknown."

"Incoming," Kingston said over the open comms. "Six Blues at two-seven-nine point four-three. Distance seven hundred kilometers and closing. Speed Mach 22. Time to impact thirty-two seconds."

"Missiles, Ms. Fargo," Haal said. "Now, if you please."

"Missiles away, Commander," Fargo replied as ten twenty-five-kilogram, single-stage Lance torpedoes streaked away from the tubes in deck one, each locked onto one of the incoming enemy craft.

Morian watched as one by one, six blue lights on the hologram blinked out.

"Commander." One of the Engineering officers stood to get her attention. "We have non-USF ships... uh, pirate ships to be precise, requesting to dock in the *Avenger* for self-repairs."

"Check with Mechanical on that," Haal replied. "They can make that call. They'll have a better idea of what they can handle down there than we will."

"Aye, Commander."

"Mr. Kinston," Haal said, "keep an eye on that mass of ships in sector two-three-five."

"Aye, Commander."

Manda continued to watch the small portion of the battle she could see in the forward view screen. She wished she could see more. She glanced around the lower bridge deck, checking for signs of stress among the officers. There were none. With the exception of the disabled engine and gun turrets, all systems seemed to be running smoothly.

"Mr. Kingston?" she said. "Anything to report?"

"Sector four-three-one," the chief tactical officer replied. "They appear to be massing."

"How far out?"

"Eleven hundred kilometers."

Manda nodded. "Keep an eye on them, Mr. Kingston."

"Weapons?" she said as she left the rail and descended to the well deck and approached the weapons officer. "Be ready to unload on sector four-three-one."

"Aye, Commander," Corin Fargo replied.

"Are all missile tubes charged?"

"Not yet, ma'am," Fargo replied. "We're still charging the starboard tubes. Tubes one, three, five, seven and nine and thirteen port side are charged. Only eleven is empty, and they're working on that now."

Haal nodded. "Good. Railgun ammunition?"

"Port side is at fifty-five percent. Starboard is at twenty-three. Top side is at thirty-nine. Bow guns are at fifty-two, and our big gun is at ninety-one."

Again, Haal nodded. "Notify me immediately if anything drops below fifteen percent."

"Aye, Commander," Fargo replied without taking her eyes off her targeting screens.

"Commander." Morian beckoned for her to join him on the command deck.

"Yes, Captain?" she asked as she took her seat beside him.

"We need to be ready to take the momentum on this next one," Captain Morian said. "Where do we think our next attack is coming from?"

"Tactical has the next most likely sector at four-three-one where the enemy is massing. Distance... eleven hundred kilometers. They're not moving. I wonder..." She didn't finish the thought.

Morian nodded. "They will. You can bet on it." He paused, looked at the foreword screens, deep in thought, then said, "Ammunition? How are we doing?"

She shrugged. Morian didn't catch it. "We're good," she said, "for now, at least. Per your previous instructions, I'll let you know when levels drop to ten percent."

Morian nodded but didn't reply.

"Morian! *Avenger!* This is the IMFP cruiser Iron Cross. Do you read?" the pirate's voice squawked over the open comm.

Morian smiled at Haal, then said, "Put him through to me, Ms. Lowry."

Manda stood to let him take the call and stepped up to the command rail. She looked down at the hologram. The Swarm ships in sector four-three-two had still not moved. *What are they up to?* she wondered.

Suddenly, without warning, she felt dizzy, as if the deck had moved beneath her feet. She reached out, grasped the rail with both hands and took a small step sideways to keep from falling. The bridge seemed to spin before her eyes. She fought to remain upright, hoping no one could see her.

Instinctively, she knew what was happening to her. She gripped the rail with both hands. The bridge in front of her disappeared, replaced with a vision of the *Avenger* in space, in battle. She watched in awe as a mass of Swarm ships swooped in from the rear, all weapons firing. The bolts of plasma bit into her, slicing into her hull and taking out her engines, and God only knew what else.

The vision began to waver. She knew it wasn't happening, but after her visit with the seers, she knew that it would if she didn't do something to stop it.

The vision dissolved completely. She was back on the bridge, her hands still gripping the rail, a sinking feeling deep in her gut. She was overwhelmed at the thought of the *Avenger* taking a hit like that. It would take out the main thrusters if not the entire ship. And she knew it was going to happen soon. She glanced at the forward screens. The enemy ships in sector four-three-two still hadn't moved, but she could feel it in her bones that they would, and soon. Then, to her horror, the first of them began to move.

She almost panicked. She took a deep breath. *What to do first?* she thought. *There's no time to transfer power to the starboard shields. No, we have to move. Now!*

"Mr. Sen," she shouted. Every head on the bridge turned to look at her. "Come one-hundred-fifty-five degrees to starboard and roll the ship sixty degrees. Do it now!" Her voice had more urgency than any order she'd ever given.

"What?" Sen said, loud enough for all to hear. He was already carrying out the order but, instinctively, he still questioned it. As long as he was moving, though, she didn't care what he said.

"You heard me, Mr. Sen. One-hundred-fifty-five degrees, roll sixty."

"I did..." Sen said as the ship began to roll. The move was unheard of, but Manda knew in her gut it was the right thing to do. She needed to put *Avenger's* starboard side to the enemy so that her armored hull and shields would take the brunt of the attack.

"Tactical," she yelled, "you're going to have to cover topside on your own."

"Commander, what's going on?" Morian asked.

"There's about to be a massive attack from the rear, Captain. There's no time to transfer power—"

"What?" he said, interrupting her. "Mr. Kingston. What do we have on our six?"

"Nothing, sir. That sector is clear."

"Commander—"

"No, it's not, Captain." She cut him off. "You have to trust me. They are there; I know it. If we don't show them our starboard side, we'll lose our three remaining engines and suffer a massive hull breach."

Morian stared at her, his expression grave, then he nodded.

Manda turned again to the rail and watched the screens and hologram as the orientation of the battlefield changed, hoping she was in time and that the hull would be in place when the enemy attacked.

The ship stopped turning. Then nothing. For several seconds the bridge was deathly quiet as everyone waited.

Morian opened his mouth to speak, but before he could:

"Incoming," Kingston shouted. "Off the starboard bow, multiple enemy craft, range two-hundred meters. Stand by for impact."

The ship jolted. The bridge seemed to move beneath

them. There was an almighty rumble that could be felt throughout the ship.

"Massive hit to the hull," Kingston shouted. "Shields are holding."

"Missiles away," Corin Fargo shouted.

The ship shook again, seemed to stagger, then righted herself.

"Hull breach deck six, section three," Kingston shouted.

"Damage control?" Morian shouted.

"On their way, Captain," Maxim Volkov, the chief engineer, shouted. "I'm on my way, too."

"Mr. Sen," Manda shouted. "Hold your position."

"Aye, Commander."

She watched the hologram, counting as the blue lights off *Avenger's* starboard bow began to wink out, *six, nine, thirteen...*

The entire ship was shaking under the recoil of her railguns. *Fifteen... sixteen...*"

"They're turning away!" Kingston shouted. "They're retreating."

Manda, suddenly realizing she'd been holding her breath, let it out in a sigh of relief. They were safe.

"Long-range missiles locked on and away," Corin Fargo shouted. "Point defense, cease fire!"

"Hold your position, Mr. Sen," Manda repeated. "Damage report, please, Mr. Kingston."

"Minor hull breach on deck six. Other than that, we're good."

Manda and Morian looked at each other and smiled.

It wasn't the most professional report either of them had ever heard, but it was the most welcome.

"Commander," Morian said without looking at her. He seemed to be staring off into space.

"Yes, Captain"

"That attack came out of nowhere. It would have crippled the ship, if not destroyed it. You saved us. You have it, don't you? The Sight? Talk to me, Manda."

"Yes. I think so, and it's a little hard to handle, but at least I know."

Morian turned toward her and gave her a deep look. "I understand, Commander. It can't be easy for you. If there's anything... If you need to talk—"

"Captain, Iron Cross is asking for covering fire," Lowry said.

"Thank you, Ms. Lowry. Mr. Kingston. Give them what they need, and I need an up-to-date threat assessment, all sectors. I want to know where the next attack is coming from."

He looked at Manda, his eyebrows raised in question. She looked back at him, smiled and slowly shook her head.

"Sorry, Captain. It's not something I can turn on and off at will."

He smiled back at her, nodded and went back to his seat.

Manda took several deep breaths, trying to calm herself. The stress of what she'd just been through was something she'd not experienced before, not even when she'd steered the ship through the journey to Aries.

She closed her eyes for a moment, willed her heart rate to slow, then opened them again and, feeling a little less abnormal, she turned her attention to the momentum of the battle.

"We have company," Kingston said as a pirate battle cruiser with a Jolly Roger painted on its bow slid alongside and linked with them. Something Manda would never have thought possible, *but then again,* she thought, *don't they say adversity makes strange bedfellows?*

Slowly, the momentum of the battle began to change. As she watched the hologram and the datanet scrolling above it, she saw the number of enemy craft begin to dwindle. Unfortunately, also that of the IMFP fleet. The losses were heavily one-sided, though, but not in favor of the enemy and, all over the battlefield, the Swarm began to retreat. Slowly at first, then more and more until, finally, the last blue light on the hologram winked out, and Manda, her hands cramping, released her grip on the rail.

The battle was over, for now at least.

Chapter Thirty-Three

Jackknife

Danis's fighter, the last into the hangar, landed. She cut her grav engines, opened her canopy, removed her helmet and gloves and waited as Elio climbed down the ladder to the hangar deck, then followed him down.

It had been a long hard battle. She was glad it was over, but the adrenaline was still pumping and would be for at least several minutes more. Twice she and the squadron had returned to *Avenger* to rearm. Now they were home, all except for Rangers Seven and Eleven, and she was feeling somewhat... lost, as if she'd just read a great book without an ending.

She'd experienced the feeling before. Adrenaline was consumed in vast quantities in every battle, but nothing like this one, the longest and toughest she'd participated in to date. It would take a while for her to come down, for the adrenaline to stop coursing through her veins. She stood at the bottom of the ladder, either unable or unwilling to go to the Ready Room to take a hydro and change into a clean set of clothes. So she watched as one by one her pilots and copilots climbed out of their craft and headed out of the hangar, waving a hand at her as they went. She was a little surprised when she saw Gian approaching, and even more surprised when she saw who climbed out of his rear cockpit.

"Andra?" she asked, not knowing what else to say.

Andra shrugged. "I was just trying to—"

"It was me. I made her come with me," Gian said, the words coming out quickly. "Don't write her up. Write me up. I know I violated protocol. But I knew we were going to be challenged out there, and I'd seen how effective you and Elio were—are. Danis, her TK is amazing. She saved my life at least three times... and she saved yours too. You should have seen it when—"

"It's all right, Gian." Danis held up a hand to stop him. "Sometimes we do things because... well, we know they're the right things to do. I only wish you'd asked me first. I don't know what Captain Morian will say when he finds out you've taken a civilian into battle. Gian, she's not even in the Academy yet."

Danis knew she was going to have a fight on her hands, trying to persuade her brother not to ground Gian... and Andra. She also knew that her experiment with Elio and the use of his TK had worked better than she could have hoped, and now this. She'd already been thinking that it would be a good thing to equip more of her pilots with TK-enabled copilots. Now she was trying to persuade herself that it was happening quicker than she'd expected.

"Andra," she said, turning to her.

"Yes?"

"I want you to put in a request for flight approval. I'll sign it. Let's see if we can keep you in that fighter."

Gian and Andra looked at each other and smiled.

"Next time, you ask first, Joker," Danis said. "Well done out there, both of you."

"Thank you, ma'a... Commander. I had a lot of help."

"Consider yourself qualified on level E-9," she said. "I'll reprogram the computer to show that you passed. You're learning quickly, Gian. You'll be a great pilot one day. In the meantime, I've been watching you and would like you to brief the rest of the squadron on some of those moves."

Gian blinked and raised his eyebrows. "But? Me? Brief the rest of the squadron? Er... no, I don't think so."

"Why not? D'you have a problem with public speaking?"

"No, ma'am," he answered. "Well, yes, sort of. But I didn't do any of that stuff because I knew how to do it. I just did what I did instinctively, to get myself out of trouble. I didn't think about it... well, not much. And I'm still a rookie, still a second-year student at the Academy. They won't listen to me! And even if they do..." He tailed off, unable to think of any more excuses.

"Good," Danis replied. "They all need to learn from your adaptability. Your time in the simulator is paying off. You encountered a typical E-9 situation out there today. You thought it through, and you pulled it off."

"But—"

"No buts," Danis said, interrupting him. "I want you to take the rest of the squadron through E-9."

"They're not going to listen to me!" he replied emphatically.

"They will. Seniority doesn't come into it," Danis said. "I won't allow it to. You have a natural ability. Something few of us are blessed with. They can learn from you. We lost people out there today, and I don't want to lose any more. If the simulator helps, we'll use it. I want you to download the data from your ship and have IT program it into the template for a new level E-10. I want all of them to go through it and pass it."

"Yes, ma'am."

"And don't call me ma'am."

Gian was about to apologize when an alarm began to sound, and the green lights turned to red.

"Clear the hangar. Incoming ship." The voice was Krista's, *Avenger's* AI. It echoed around the hangar. "Clear the deck. Depressurizing in sixty seconds, fifty-nine, fifty-eight..."

They all turned and ran for the exit doors. The hangar sealed. The great door began to open, and they watched through the view windows as an unknown fighter entered too fast, slewed sideways, came to a halt, wobbled above the deck and then dropped heavily to the hangar floor.

The hangar door closed. The flight deck repressurized. The entry door lock clicked and Danis, followed by Gian and Andra, rushed back onto the deck.

The air inside the hangar was hot. The fighter's

engines were still running. The hot wind blew through Danis's hair as she held her hand in front of her face.

The fighter was a vintage Veridian C3 model. *What the hell?* she thought. *Who is this?*

The pilot lifted the machine off the deck, swung it around so it was facing the hangar door, its long wings barely missing the inner wall and Danis's F32A, then dropped back onto the deck, its landing gear squealing in protest before the portside landing strut collapsed with an earsplitting crack.

The Veridian's thrusters wound down. Its twin engines coughed, then spluttered, then died, and a pair of valves located under the fuselage unloaded two massive jets of steam and then, quite suddenly, all was quiet, except for some creaking and clicking. The Veridian was at rest.

It was at rest, but it was in poor shape. Two plasma blast holes were visible in the fuselage just forward of the wings. Danis could see right through them to the hangar wall beyond. Its engines were clicking and smoking.

The canopy swung open and a giant of a man flung one leg out of the cockpit, heaved himself up and over the bulkhead and dropped to the ground, landing with a loud clang on a pair of heavy mech boots. The man had just jumped out of a hot cockpit, some four meters above the deck, without a ladder.

"Hey, you," Danis raised her voice. "Who the hell are you?"

The big man turned to face her. He had a thick, black beard, a prominent nose, high forehead, brilliant blue eyes and a chest like a barrel... and he was wearing what appeared to be a USF-style flight suit with some sort of insignia on the shoulders that she couldn't identify.

"Me?" he asked, smiling broadly. "I'm Jackknife. Who the hell are you?"

"Jackknife?"

"Yeah, Jackknife," he replied, "and I need a damn fire extinguisher before this piece of shit fighter burns down your entire hangar bay."

Danis was irate. She couldn't believe the nerve of this... giant. Reflexively, she pointed to the bank of emergency extinguishers on a rack on the far wall behind the Veridian. She wasn't too worried because she knew the automatic fire system would kick in had there been any real danger.

Jackknife's mech boots clanged on the floor as he crossed the flight deck and grabbed one of the canisters.

"Danis?" Gian said.

"Not now, Gian."

Danis looked back at the fighter. It definitely had some damage. The two plasma holes were still smoking, but there was nothing flammable close to them, nothing that would start a fire. *This man knows less about fighter mechanics than he does about safe landing protocols,* she thought.

"Excuse me, Mister... Excuse me, Jackknife," Danis said angrily, her shoulders back. "You can't leave that... thing here. It's blocking the entire hangar. You have to move it. Now!"

He smiled again but ignored her as he walked quickly back to his smoking ship.

"Hey, jackass," she snapped. "Are you deaf? I'm talking to you."

Jackknife shook his head, set the fire extinguisher down on the deck with a thud and turned to face her. He glared at her, let out an annoyed sigh and said, "Look, lady, calm down."

"Commander—" Gian said.

"I said not now, Joker," she said. Then to Jackknife, "Don't you tell me to calm down. This is my hangar. And my name is—"

"In case you haven't noticed," he said, interrupting her, "I'm having a few problems with my rig here. I can't move it. It's not exactly fit to fly right now."

"I just watched you violate an entire catalog of flight safety regulations. What the hell were you thinking?"

"Listen, lady," he said, obviously aggravated. "I had two choices. I was hit and coming in hot. I could come in and do the hot landing, which may have broken one or two of your safety rules, or I could have waited for your approval and then crashed in here, destroying maybe half your squadron and killing as many members of your crew. Who knows?" He shrugged and looked around. "Yeah, or maybe I could have put the entire hangar out of commission. But no, I chose to bring her in nice and safe. No one got hurt. Nothing got damaged, except maybe for a couple of scratches on your newly waxed USF floor."

"Commander..." Gian tried again.

This time she gave him a look that would have frozen a lesser mortal. He shrugged and said no more.

"Who gave you permission to land?" Danis asked.

"I don't know. Somebody did. I requested an emergency landing and it was granted, as it should have been. You should know that. What are you bitching about anyway? We're in the middle of a war here. We would have done the same for you, damn it. Now get the hell off my case and let me try to fix my craft before it blows us all to hell and then some."

She hated this man and his arrogance, but she had to admit—to herself anyway—that much of what he was saying was true, *and if he had permission to land...*

"How long have you actually been a pilot, Mister... Jackknife?"

"More years than I can count, lady. Why d'you ask?"

"You're a pirate. You didn't get this far out here on your own? Why didn't you return to your own ship?"

He wrinkled his forehead, made a face and shook his head. He bared his teeth in a smile that sent chills down her spine, gave her an arrogant nod and said, "That wasn't going to happen."

"Why? Couldn't you find them?" she asked sarcastically. "You get yourself lost?"

"Screw you, lady, you tight-assed—"

"Hey, that's enough," she shouted. No one spoke to her like that. "Listen—"

"No, you listen," Jackknife snapped, interrupting her. "My ship, the battleship *Crow's Feet*, was blown up out there by those miserable Swarm bastards in their ugly as sin little ships. Oh yeah, and so was the rest of my team. My ship, all my buddies are gone... dead. Some of them I've been flying with for more than ten years. Now they're gone, thanks to those blue bastards. I was hit twice. I barely survived. I had nowhere else to go. I saw the *Avenger*. I heard comms traffic between your captain and the *Crow's Feet*, and the *Iron Cross*, the entire battle. So, I thought I'd head for here for help and maybe a little hospitality. Man, was I ever wrong. Let me get my ship at least operable and, lady, I'm outa here."

His rant caused her to put things in perspective. She didn't like him, but what he said reminded her of the friends she had just lost, She couldn't imagine losing her entire ship, losing the *Avenger*.

"Well, you're here now, and I'm... sorry for your loss." She looked at the still smoking Veridian and continued. "That ship isn't going to blow, not from just a couple of holes in her fuselage." Her tone was somewhat conciliatory.

"That shows just how much you know, lady. How long did you say you've been flying? Oh, you didn't, did you? I've a ruptured fuel cell, and I'm telling you—you watch—it's going to ignite any second, and if I don't put it out, it'll melt the entire rig."

Danis looked at the fighter, so did Gian and Andra. Nothing was on fire. Nothing was happening. The flight crew was watching her. Everyone was silent.

Jackknife turned, scooped up the oversized extinguisher in one massive hand and turned it on; foam blasted from its nozzle. *What the hell?* Danis thought, taking a step forward.

It was at that moment a high-pitched squeal erupted from the broken fighter and flames burst out of the port side fuel bay.

Danis felt a flash of heat on her face. Before anyone could move, Jackknife stepped forward and dowsed the entire thing with white foam, filling the Veridian's fuel bay and dowsing the fire.

How the hell did he know when that fire was going to start? Gian wondered.

"There we go," he said brightly. "That ought to do it." Jackknife turned off the extinguisher, took several steps back, snapped the cover back on the nozzle and set it down on the deck with a bang. He looked at the crew chief, pointed at it and said, "You should see that this is refilled. Thank you." He turned back to Danis.

"You want me to go? Fine, but how am I supposed to go anywhere when my ride is on fire? Looks like I'm not going anywhere right now. No fuel, no fly."

She looked at him and said, "No, I suppose not. Look, I understand you're used to doing things somewhat differently, but this is a big ship. There has to be an order to how we do things. The *Avenger* is a USF ship. We have rules and regulations we have to follow. If you're going to stay here, you're going to have to play by them too."

"Look, lady. I follow only one person's rules." He pointed to his chest. "Mine."

Danis crossed her arms. "Oh, yes?"

"Yes. We're in a war. It's every man for himself out there. We've been fighting and surviving against the Swarm for months on our own. We were doing just fine without the help of the USF and its rules and regulations and officers and uniforms, Lieutenant Commander Morian." He pointed mockingly to the name badge on her flight suit. "Sometimes you have to do what's right. Make a call and stand by it. You don't always have time to wait for permission."

"Don't lecture me about war," Danis said. "We've been fighting and dying... by the millions. You don't get to do it your way, not on this ship. You think you're better than us because you taught yourself how to fly this piece of crap?" She swung her arm and gestured at the wounded Veridian fighter. "Well, you're not. And you should also know that the last one of your kind we saved and took on board almost destroyed our mainframe spying for you people. So—"

"Domino," Gian said, angrily interrupting her. "You need to hold off. This is the pilot that saved my ass out there."

"Thank you, son, and you're welcome," Jackknife growled. "Now, if you'll excuse me, I need to speak to your captain." He turned to walk away, then turned back again and said, "But first, you got anything to eat? I'm starving. And how the hell do I get out of here?"

Danis gestured for one of the crewmen and asked him to take Jackknife to the mess hall, and then she watched him walk away, his heavy mech boots clicking on the floor. Never in her life had she witnessed such cockiness and disregard for authority.

Gian also watched the big man walk away, and he was smiling. It was obvious to Danis that he liked the man.

"Easy on the man crush, Joker," Danis said. "He's wild, bad news. You don't want to be like him."

"No, of course I don't," he said, overcompensating. "Of course not, what, are you crazy?"

"You're a horrible liar," Danis said and rolled her eyes. "Go after him. Show him to the mess hall before he starts to eat the grease tubes. I want you to babysit him, make sure he doesn't get into trouble. Got it?"

"Got it, ma'am," Gian said, then turned and ran after the big man.

"And make sure he's house trained," she called after him.

"Now, what to do with this mess?" she muttered, looking at the Veridian.

Chapter Thirty-Four

New Friends

The following morning, *Avenger* was parked in low, synchronous orbit over Haven. Morian was seated on the command deck of the bridge, thoughtfully, contemplatively watching Manda Haal confirm the final details for the ship's re-entry into Freyja's atmosphere.

She's a damn good officer, he thought. She's cool-headed, a competent leader, unflappable in battle, and she knows how and when to delegate. The crew... the officers... they all seem to like and respect her. That's a good thing too.

And then there's this new ability, this... Sight. How does she do that? And how can she be so precise? She knew we were about to be attacked from the rear, even before our proximity systems picked them up. Not only that, but she knew the exact angle and degree to turn the ship. Had she been a couple of degrees off, or a few seconds too late, those plasma blasts would have taken out our engines... and God only knows what else. It would have been a devastating hit.

He stood, went to the rail, and looked around the well deck below. Everyone was at work. Most of them, no, all of them seemed to have stepped up their game. The bridge crew had matured, a derivative of the many months fighting the Swarm. Of that, he had no doubt. *They've turned into a well-oiled fighting machine,* he thought as he watched them go about their various tasks.

He'd always known he had a good team, but after that day, that day fighting alongside the pirates—the IMFP—in what had turned out to be the biggest battle he'd fought to date, well, they'd really proved themselves... *The pirates?* he thought, *What of them? They fought well today. They lost a lot of good ships... men and women too. They gave their all. Maybe they can be more valuable, more useful to us than just a shipyard, factories, armored ships and weapons...*

"Captain," Prince Elio said as he joined him at the rail.

"Yes, my prince," Morian said and turned his head to look at him.

"Now that we seem to be in the clear, I think it is time we had a chat with our pirate friends."

"About the shipyards?" Morian asked.

"Yes. From what we've seen so far, they have more yards and docks than we thought. Better yet, they appear to have the manpower to staff them."

Morian knew this was an essential part of their original mission. They needed new resources, and it seemed they'd found them on Freyja. Unfortunately, they weren't abandoned as they'd expected. They were, by default, owned by the pirates and the IMFP. And Morian knew that the USF couldn't just walk in and take them over. They, the IMFP, had to be persuaded to allow the USF access to the vast facilities. And that would be up to Prince Elio; there was now a lot riding upon his success... or lack of it.

"I agree," Morian said, "but you do realize those resources don't belong to us, and we're going to have a hard time trying to convince these people to join us, to persuade them it would be in their best interest to do so?"

"I think we can make a good argument for that," Elio said. "One that will make them see the mutual benefit in an alliance with the USF."

"Agreed," Morian said thoughtfully. "The biggest challenge will be the Board of Directors. There are some tough characters among them, and very few of them will trust us, but I think I know someone who will. I think we should start with—"

"Tiger Wok?" Elio said, interrupting him.

"Exactly. And I think he has more influence than he's willing to admit."

"Very well," Elio said. "I'll go over my numbers again. Let's arrange a meeting with him as soon as possible."

"Why don't you do it, Elio? I think he likes you."

Morian turned from the rail and went back to his chair, leaving Elio staring after him.

The comm light on Morian's arm unit buzzed with an incoming message. He tapped the screen and brought up the image of Tiger Wok's face.

"Captain Morian," he said, smiling. "It's good to see you still in one piece, my friend. Unfortunately, I cannot say the same for many of my own people. You fought well today, so I understand, and I thank you for your help. Now... I trust you are making your way back to Freyja."

"Yes, we are on our way. And by the way, I've just been told we've taken in one of your fighters. The man you called Jackknife. His ship was lost in the battle, and he had to make an emergency landing. He saved one of my pilots, so I have been informed, so he is more than welcome here."

"Good," Wok replied. "Now I have to thank you personally. Jack is a close friend. I am grateful to you. But how about the *Avenger*? Did she take much damage?"

"We lost an engine, sustained some hull damage, and we lost several point defense turrets. We're also very low on ammunition. But today's damage, plus the damages we sustained during our journey to Beta Ariatis, has put us a little behind. Our fuel cells are stable, but our shields and targeting antennas are in need of an overhaul."

"Well, I have good news for you, my friend. I have heard nothing but praises for you since the battle. You alone are responsible for many of our ships being saved. We are more than grateful. And, the good news is that we have a repair berth available for you. Our people are offering the *Avenger* a full hull-repair. We have the materials and manpower available, and your ship can be as good as new in... well, not too long, my friend."

"That's wonderful news, Captain. I am happy to accept."

"Good. Follow the beacon as before to Dock Zero-two-five."

"Copy that. Zero-two-five."

"While you are awaiting your repairs, you and your crew are welcome to sample the meager hospitality of the station."

"Thank you again," Morian replied. "I'm sure the crew would enjoy some time ashore." *But if the hull is to be repaired, it could be more than just a couple of days. Giving them free rein in a misfit pirate colony might not be the best idea, Morian thought, especially as we still have our primary mission to complete.* But then, as he turned it over in his mind, it began to sound more and more like a good idea. *Hmm... It would enable me and my senior officers to learn more about their shipyards, dry docks and their manufacturing facilities.*

"That's incredibly good of you, Captain," Morian said. "I gladly accept your offer."

"Splendid, Captain, but please, enough of the Captain. You may call me Tiger. I'll be at the dock to meet you when you arrive. Goodbye for now, my friend." The screen went blank.

Less than one standard hour later, *Avenger* slid silently into one of the largest land-based dry docks Morian had ever seen. The great ship—almost fourteen hundred meters long and four hundred wide—settled onto the dock's antigrav supports and floated there like a giant bug.

No sooner had she settled, even before Morian was able to welcome his new friend aboard, than she was swarmed by a hundred small craft: antigrav lifts, inspection dories, service barks and repair boats. Within minutes, the hull was crawling with engineers inspecting the armor plating. *Avenger* was a hive of activity.

"You see, my friend?" Wok asked, waving expansively at the hologram of the ship he'd generated in Morian's Ready Room. "We will have you... what was it they used to say in the British Navy so many eons before The Purge? Ah yes," he continued without waiting for Morian to answer, "Shipshape and Bristol fashion, I think it was."

"It was indeed... Tiger." The name did not roll easily off the tongue, but Morian, not wanting to insult his new friend, used it anyway. "That was back in the seventeenth and eighteenth centuries, in the days of sailing the seas, long before The Purge... I have to wonder what Admiral Lord Nelson would say if he could see what we've become, if he could see the *Avenger*."

"Or even the famous Blackbeard," Wok said with a grin.

"An ancestor of yours, perhaps?" Morian replied, also with a grin.

"Ah, but who can say?" Wok replied. "But come, Captain. Please, my intentions are all good. I am not the rogue you think I am, I assure you."

Morian looked at him thoughtfully, then said, "No, my friend, I don't think you are." He picked up his glass, raised it and said, "To a long and fruitful friendship."

Wok raised his glass, clinked it against Morian's and said, "Aye, Captain. To friendship. Good friends, I think, are few and far between."

They drank their drinks in a single swallow. Wok

smacked his lips in appreciation, then said, "Let us eat, my friend. I know just the place."

"Isn't it getting a little late?" Morian asked looking at his chron.

"Late? No, of course not... Ah... I understand. You USF people live by the standard Homeworld twenty-four-hour day. Is that not so?"

Morian nodded and said, "Yes, Homeworld. Some of us still call it Earth."

"Well, we do not. You see, Freyja is a little larger than Homeworld, and her rotation is a little slower, thus our day is thirty-eight of your standard hours long. It is barely past noon, Haven time, and we are in the middle of summer so we have twenty-six hours of daylight." Wok stood and smiled and said, "So, my friend, we have all the time in the world. Shall we?" He held out an arm toward the door.

* * *

Later that same day, Manda Haal, Jiksar and Haltar Sen were off-ship on a one-day pass and were wandering the streets of Haven, taking in the sights and sounds of the bustling city. It was busy. The wide thoroughfares and plazas were crowded. The merchants at the small shops, stores and stands were hawking their goods to the passersby, just as they had for more than a thousand years, even longer than that on Homeworld.

Manda was surprised that Morian had allowed so many of the crew to leave the ship, leaving only a small security crew aboard. It wasn't something she would have done, but he was the captain, and she trusted him to know what he was doing.

She, herself, was a little nervous, being away from the ship, but with the repairs underway and the noise they would generate, it made sense and, so she supposed, it was always a good idea to give the crew a break whenever they could, especially after a major battle.

"D'you think these pirates will be able to complete the repairs in just seventy-six hours?" Jiksar asked as they wandered along the Western Boulevard.

"Two days? They're big talkers," Sen said. "Blowhards, if you ask me. Especially that big fellow, the one they call Jackknife... What kind of a name is that anyway?"

"We'll see how it turns out," Manda said. "And I think it's time we belay the word pirate. They may have their roots in piracy, but they've become much more than that. Most of them seem to be honest tradesmen: engineers, miners, fabricators, specialists, welders, armorers... Look around you. Look at the shops and merchants. We could be in downtown Paris, on Homeworld. Have you ever been to Homeworld, Jiksar? Or you, Lieutenant?"

Neither of them had. Both said they would like to, one day. Manda nodded, then stopped when a merchant at a food stand, having noticed their USF uniforms, called out to them.

"My friends, you must try my roast trihorn meat. It's delicious. Come on. Try it." He offered them each a small portion on a wooden skewer.

"No, thank you," Manda said and waved back smiling.

The jolly man bowed at the waist, kept smiling and turned to badger other possible customers.

"This place is amazing," Jiksar said. "I've never seen anything like it. How long did they say it's been like this?"

"They didn't," Manda said, "not to me anyway." She dodged sideways, out of the way of a rotund woman with a small child in each hand. "Let's find somewhere to get a drink and something to eat."

"How about here?" Sen pointed to a metal sign over a double doorway that proclaimed it to be the Hacker's Tavern.

Manda shrugged. "It looks as good as any other, I suppose," she said as she peered in through the glass panes in the door. "It looks pretty busy, so that's a good sign. Let's give it a try."

Jiksar held the door open for her, then followed her and Sen inside.

She was right. It was busy. In fact, it was packed. The place was abuzz. People were talking together, laughing, drinking. Some kind of strange music was playing, emanating from hidden speakers. And it smelled. Not a bad smell. A delicious smell of greasy food.

The three USF officers pushed their way through the crowd to the bar, and Manda ordered three mugs of the house brew. When they arrived, Manda placed a fifty-credit bill on the counter, which the barkeep instantly pushed back to her.

"Your money's no good here, Commander," he growled.

The people close by heard him, went quiet and turned to see what was happening.

"After what you did for us today, the drinks are on the house."

The crowd around them cheered and raised their glasses.

Manda was a little nonplussed, almost embarrassed. Never had she experienced anything quite like it.

She thanked the man self-consciously. He nodded, turned away, and so did the bystanders, who continued on talking together.

Manda had never been a big beer drinker but, every once in a while, she did enjoy taste testing the local flavors. The brew in her hand was a lager and obviously made the old-fashioned way, and it wasn't bad for such a backwater planet as Freyja.

That day, she was thirsty and quickly finished her drink, setting her mug down on the bar. She turned, put her back to the rail and her elbows on the bartop and looked around. Something caught her eye. Two men walked in wearing battle armor and helmets, face shields down, and she was suddenly aware that she'd seen several others similarly dressed in the streets outside, and even then, she'd thought it kind of odd.

"What are you staring at?" Jiksar asked, turning to try to see over her shoulder, which due to her height, was, even for him being almost as tall as Manda, difficult.

"Nothing really," she replied thoughtfully. "Just those two soldiers over there." She nodded in their direction. "They're in full battle armor."

Together, the three of them watched as one of the

face-covered soldiers joined a similarly dressed group and raised his face shield, revealing his face, then closed it again. The members of the group did the same thing.

"That's strange," Sen said, "that they flash their faces to one another like that. I wonder what that's all about?"

"It's a pirate tradition," the bartender said, overhearing them as he set down another round of drinks in front of them. "It's an old custom from back in the days of the Nerimium System war."

"What does it mean?" Jiksar asked. "Why are they wearing battle armor and full helmets?"

The bartender looked at them and smiled, taking in their USF uniform patches, then said, "You have to remember, most of these folk have been living on the edge for as long as they can remember, expecting a surprise attack at any moment. The pirates among us are all new to the alliance. Most of them are paranoid, so they wear their battle armor and remain ready for anything."

"That's a bit extreme, don't you think?" Jiksar asked.

The bartender shrugged, nodded, and said, "Perhaps, but it's happened so many times. Rivals killing rivals... it's happened here twice already. So, they remain on guard. The rest of my patrons don't seem to mind so, if it makes them feel safe, we allow it. But the fact remains, helmets and face shields are a great way to launch an attack... or assassination. Out here, it's not like you know who your enemies are. No one wears uniforms, and no one has to grant or approve an official declaration of war, as you do in the USF. These people have to be ready for anything. So, it's become a tradition that you show your face before entering a conversation."

Manda nodded. "I see, and I understand, but battle armor in a bar? That's more than extreme."

Again, the bartender shrugged. "I agree, but it is what it is. That's life out here on Freyja."

"Sounds like a tough way to live," Jiksar said after taking a sip of his beer.

"I agree," Sen said. "Not the way I'd want to live."

"They're used to it," the bartender said, "and it's not like they have much choice."

Manda nodded and pushed the strange way of life he was describing out of her mind. She looked around, taking it all in, impressed by the diversity among the customers. In this one small bar, smaller than the entire cafeteria on the *Avenger*, there were so many different nationalities, most of them identifiable by their dress and facial decorations: Bossians, Orsonians, Torians, Illithians and of course Arians. And those were just the ones she could positively identify. There were many others she couldn't place. And among those she could, there were subgroups, like the Arians, for instance; there were Arian pirates, easily identifiable by their colorful dress. There were politicians, merchants and so on and so on. An eclectic collection of true individuals that seemed to get along with each other and with everyone else. Freyja boasted a truly mixed-class society, something she hadn't experienced before.

The bartender, bar owner, or whatever he was, was clearly Bossian, yet he was making a killing serving Arian lager. The waitress with the serving tray was definitely Torian, and she was serving plates of brunzfish, native to Orso.

Manda sipped her beer, thinking of the number of worlds and systems represented by the clientele and staff in that bar. She and her two companions came from three different systems.

Truth be told, she was actually daydreaming, something she hadn't done in many a year. Images of the different systems floated around inside her mind like tiny holograms... and then, she had a thought, a random thought that came out of nowhere. It started as a thought, then changed into an image, an image of a large room, one she was familiar with, one she'd visited only recently. The image turned into a hologram. Soldiers wearing full battle armor burst into the room and began firing at the occupants at point-blank range. The room was soon awash with blood. Dead bodies littered the floor. The wounded squirmed, twitched, cried out. It was a massacre.

"Oh, my God," she said and slammed her glass down on the bar. "We have to go, now!"

"What? What is it?" Jiksar asked, jerking himself upright.

Manda put both hands to her face and massaged her temples. The vision dissolved, disappeared into nothingness.

"Something is dreadfully wrong," she said, still massaging her temples. "We have to go. Come, quickly. Follow me." She turned and walked quickly to the door, pushing through the crowd, with Jiksar and Sen close on her heels, both trying to get her attention, wanting to know what she'd seen.

Chapter Thirty-Five

The Art of the Deal

Tiger Wok escorted Morian and Elio into a large and obviously upscale restaurant on the north side of the city, not far from the municipal building where they'd met the board of directors earlier that morning.

"This is my most favorite spot to eat," Wok said as they stood just inside the ornate dining room, his arms spread as if he was welcoming the diners. It was built with two decks, if you could call them such. The center of the room was some two meters lower than the outer ring of tables. It reminded Morian of the *Avenger's* well deck, only it was a little deeper and filled with dining tables elegantly set with white cloths and nickel cutlery. The outer circle also had tables but was set out for more casual dining; about half the tables on both floors were occupied. The smell of fried food coming from the kitchen was intoxicating.

"Come, let us sit," Wok said and led them down to the lower level.

He greeted one of the waiters by name. Someone a few tables down called to Wok and waved. He lifted his chin to him and smiled in greeting. He stopped at one table and shook the hand of a man sitting with a heaping plate of food in front of him, clasping his hand in both of his and whispering something in the man's ear that neither Morian nor Elio could hear. Wok was obviously well known and popular with the staff and patrons alike.

Elio was curious to know how this pirate captain had become as influential as he obviously was. His boisterous personality was—or seemed to be—genuine enough, and his intellect and obviously better-than-average education were a rare combination of gifts. Elio was certain the man could have just as easily been a successful politician, businessman or even a royal, so why had he taken to piracy? How and why, it was immaterial. Tiger Wok was someone Elio wanted on his side.

"Here, my friends, sit." Wok stopped beside a vacant table and pulled out two chairs for them, then stepped around the table, pulled one out for himself, waited until they were seated and then sat down and cast a beaming look around the room.

A king in his court, Elio thought.

Wok looked around for a waiter, but before he could raise a finger one arrived at his side almost instantly.

"Ah, Rooter, my friend," he said. "Bring us three glasses of your finest brew. My friends are thirsty."

Elio looked around, then over his right shoulder, then his left. He felt exposed. He wasn't used to being seated in the center of such a busy establishment. But, after several minutes, he realized no one seemed to care, or even notice, that he was a royal. He liked that, and he liked the lack of formality here on Freyja. He liked how time wasn't wasted on formal introductions and frivolous customs. He liked the relaxed and informal style that Wok affected.

"So, Tiger," Morian began, seeming to have trouble with the informality of using Wok's first name. "You seem to have a great many Defender and Guardian class ships."

"Yes, yes," Wok replied. "And other classes too, though most of them are out of service, decommissioned. We out here on Freyja do not have access to the latest ships and technology, nor the manpower to service or fly them. But we learn what we can, when we can, and we grab what we can when we can. It is the way of things, my friend."

"As is evidenced by your First Mate, Mr. Clintok," Morian said dryly.

"True, true," Wok replied airily, either unaware of or caring little of Morian's obvious sarcasm. "But Clintok is a fine crewman." He shook his head and then continued, "No, I cannot lie to you, Richard. I thought he'd died out there on that rock, and I was both glad and a little sad to see him return. He is not the most reliable of men. But we must not dwell on such things, eh?" He reached over and slapped Morian on the arm.

"How many shipyards do you have access to, here on Freyja?" Elio asked.

"Ah," Wok said, tapping his chin and jutting out his

lip. "So for you it is all about business, my young prince." His dark eyes glittered with amusement. "Well, I will tell you this, we have access to many more than we have staff for. There are six independent shipyards here on Freyja, all capable of repairing *and manufacturing* the old Guardian and Defender class ships. Dutrinium and Core Ore are both plentiful here, which is why the shipyards were built here in the first place." He paused as the waiter set down another round of drinks.

Wok raised his glass, took a sip and continued, "Now, regarding size. We have ten dry docks that can each handle a Type-A Carrier."

Elio looked at Morian. Morian's face was expressionless. Elio's was not. He was dumbfounded at what he'd just heard.

"And we have docks in the north and south that can accommodate twenty Type-B battleships and as many more that can accommodate Type-C cruisers. Unfortunately, we are currently operating only eight at full capacity."

"That is very, very good news," Elio said.

"Perhaps," Wok said, "but you see, the problem is... we do not have the manpower to staff them all, nor even the need to do so, though we do try to keep them all in fully operational condition. But it is a trial, my young friend. It is certainly a trial.

"The yards are all run independently," Wok continued. "The ports are private businesses. But all work together and have a considerable business relationship with one another. They are extremely efficient at moving their workers around the different yards as needed. The free market is a wonderful thing, don't you think? We are not bogged down by system-wide regulations. Nor do we have to wait for off-planet bureaucrats to approve our decisions. So, we can operate a portion of the ports and yards we have, but we cannot staff all of them all of the time."

Elio looked at Morian. Morian nodded in a way that told him he agreed with moving the conversation to the next step.

"I think we can help you with that," Elio said.

"You do?" Wok asked, smiling, unconvinced.

"I do. We have an excess of manpower; tradesmen, designers, technicians, engineers, fabricators, mechanics, just about every trade you can imagine, and we're graduating more every month. We also have the capacity to get them here quickly."

"And where are all of these people now?" Wok asked before taking another drink of his beer.

"All of our USF ports and dockyards are over-staffed. Many of them are simply out of work."

"Tell me more?" Wok said, suddenly interested.

"Shortly after the initial Swarm attacks, it became apparent that our modern ships were... less than adequate; perhaps I should say effective but vulnerable. They need refits and upgrades, all of them. They need armor. None of our shipyards have that kind of capacity, so they too need to be upgraded. That alone will take at least a standard year and thus further limit their capacity to carry out the upgrade. This means vast numbers of shipyard workers have been laid off. Yes, we are building new yards, but again, the first of them will not come online for at least another year. And yes, Captain. We have manpower aplenty."

"More shipyards? New ones?" Wok asked. "You are right, my friend. That will indeed take a long time."

"It will, but if we can staff your shipyards, we can begin refitting our Angel Class ships almost immediately," Elio said earnestly as he leaned forward and looked Wok in the eye.

"That's why we, Captain Morian and I, volunteered for this mission," he continued. "We believe the misallocation of funds and resources throughout the Sovereign Systems—and the USF—is a huge mistake and our biggest weakness. Yes, it will take many months to bring our new shipyards online. In the meantime, who knows what the Swarm will do? No one," he said, answering his own question. "But what we do know is that the Swarm outnumbers us, and if we fall to them... so will you."

He paused again for effect, then continued, "We need that extra shipyard capacity now! We came here looking for abandoned shipyards we could recommission. But we don't need to, do we, Captain? You have them here on Freyja, already up and running. All you need is manpower, and we can supply it. In return, we would be willing to make our latest technology available to you."

"Yes, I see what you mean," Wok said. He squinted and steepled his fingers. "Please continue." It appeared their proposal was going well.

Elio nodded and said, "In addition, if we can come to a meeting of the minds, we would begin transporting personnel to Freyja. That would require two new Slipstream control stations for the Beta Ariatis System which, of course, would be constructed at USF expense. Furthermore, more people means more families. More families means a growing economy. All of which would be a bonus for Freyja."

"And you say all of this would be funded and logistically supported by the USF?" Wok asked somewhat skeptically.

"One hundred percent."

"Well, I see your point. I really do," Wok said, leaning back in his chair while still maintaining eye contact with Elio. "And I like what you have to say. I also understand your motives. It all makes sense, but..."

"What do you not like about it?" Elio asked.

"There is nothing I do not like about it," Wok replied. "But, well, it does seem... How shall I put it? What you're suggesting is a major transformation of our system, our way of life, which means I would have to convince the Board of Directors that such a transformation is necessary, beneficial and... that it would work. You must understand that I am but one voice among many. I do not make the decisions. I don't even get a vote. And then there are the people to consider. How will they receive it?"

"The people?" Elio asked.

"Yes." Wok spread his arms and looked over both shoulders, as if to encompass all of the people in the restaurant. "The people. All of them. Everyone. You see, the Board of Directors do not sit in that room and make decisions. Their job is to listen to the people, to their needs and wants. What you're asking for would require a referendum. And, for as much as I like and trust you, and for as much as I see the value of helping the USF in our fight against the Swarm, I cannot tell you the people of Freyja will see it as I do. It's most likely they will see it simply as a USF power grab."

"I can understand how it could look like that," Morian said, "which is why we want to go about it the right way."

"And what is the *right* way?" Wok asked.

Elio cleared his throat. "Well for one, there would have to be guarantees, on both sides, as one of your board members pointed out. Two, it is not our intention to replace Freyja personnel with USF workers. Three, we would open a vocational university here in Haven. In addition to staffing the shipyards, we would bring in instructors and professors to teach your workforce, and anyone else who wants to learn, the latest tech, weaponry, systems and techniques. This would provide the people of Freyja with endless new opportunities."

It was clear by Wok's expression that he liked what he was hearing, though he was doing his best to hide it. The man was a skilled negotiator. Nor did Elio believe he didn't have a vote. In fact, he thought Wok's word alone could seal the deal.

"In addition," Morian said, "the Beta Ariatis System itself would be protected by the fleet. Freyja would become a strategic ally to the USF; thus we would maintain a strong military presence."

"Again, I understand the value of that. But that in itself could be seen as a threat, part of the power grab, and I do not think, initially at least, the people of Freyja would like the idea of a permanent USF military presence."

It seemed to Elio that the discussion had reached an impasse. At a loss as to what to say next, he watched as the tables around them began to fill up.

Elio took a moment to sit back and take a break from negotiations, a tactic he had learned from his father, but, as the tables began to fill, he began to feel a little uneasy. Something about the placement of their table made him feel vulnerable. In any other circumstance he would have asked to be moved but, he was reluctant to disrupt the progress of the conversation. They were beginning to develop a rapport with Tiger Wok, or so he thought. He also thought that while Wok seemed to like what he was presenting, Wok didn't entirely trust them. And if that was indeed the case, and they couldn't turn him around, the conversation would lead nowhere.

"So you see, my friend," Wok said. "What you propose is a very grand idea and it does have potential. But I would need to persuade the board of directors, and that could take some time."

"Unfortunately, time is the one thing we don't have," Elio said.

"That is true," Wok said before taking another drink. "Fortunately, neither do the people of Freyja. And you are right, my young prince; humanity must come together if we are to prevail, and I will do my best to see that we do. And if the USF is willing to agree to certain... terms and guarantees, I think we have a chance."

"Thank you, Captain," Elio said. "It sounds as if we've come to a meeting of the minds. If so, and if you can pull it off, it will be a win for everyone."

"Ha, thank you, my friends," Wok said and raised his

glass. "Let us toast to it, yes? A win for everyone." And with that, he downed the rest of his drink in a single gulp.

Elio smiled and raised his glass. So did Morian.

"A win for—" But before Elio could finish the toast and put his glass to his lips, he was interrupted by the roar of blaster fire behind him.

The deafening roar of gunfire filled the restaurant, sending customers diving to the floor.

Elio leaped to his feet and started running, Morian and Wok right behind him. Never had twenty meters seemed so far. He dived over the ornately carved wooden bar, though little good it would do as protection other than to hide behind.

He hit the floor and rolled. Morian and Wok joined him a split second later.

He peered over the top of the bar. A helmeted soldier on the upper level was firing indiscriminately into the crowd. Tables and chairs were already burning furiously, filling the restaurant with acrid smoke.

Chapter Thirty-Six

Surprise Attack

Tiger Wok landed beside Elio to his left; Morian to his right. The pirate captain pulled a laser blaster from a holster on his thigh and rolled up to his knees. He moved from a kneeling position to a crouch, raised up above the bar top, took careful aim at the gunman and fired three quick shots and watched in awe as the shots were absorbed by the man's armor, doing no damage.

"What the hell kind of armor is that?" Elio shouted.

"Get down!" Wok yelled as the gunman turned in their direction and fired.

Wok dropped back down behind the bar as the blast seared harmlessly over his head.

"Looks like my blaster was a bad idea, my friend." Wok laughed as he re-holstered his pistol.

This guy's crazy, Elio thought, wondering what to do next.

There were several other armed customers in various locations around the restaurant, all returning fire, but nothing worked. The attacker's armor absorbed hit after hit, leaving him seemingly unharmed to casually shoot back at them. Within minutes, more than a dozen people, men and women, lay dead, and no one seemed to be able to do anything about it.

"Come on," Morian yelled. "We need to move." He was already moving towards the back of the restaurant, probably hoping to find a way out.

Elio got to his feet and surveyed the space between them and the front door. It was too far, almost twenty meters. They'd never make it.

Another customer screamed as a bolt of plasma impacted his chest.

What the... That's a plasma rifle. We don't use... Elio peered cautiously over the bar top. Sure enough, the assassin was holding what looked like a short, stubby weapon, similar to the ones he'd run into before in Pricus City. The armor looked off too. It was a fair copy of an older style USF suit, similar to those used by the pirates, except for the way it was absorbing laser fire.

It's a Blue! he thought. *Has to be.* Elio looked frantically around, looking for something that... *There, that's it.*

"Elio! Get down," Morian shouted and grabbed the prince by the arm and pulled him down as a blast of plasma fire flew over their heads.

"You two, run," Wok shouted. "Run for the door. I will distract him, yes? Go, now, my friends." And he leveled his laser pistol at the assassin.

But Elio wasn't about to lose his only contact with the

people of Freyja. He still needed Wok's help and support.

"Wait!" Elio shouted and made a wild grab for the gun and pulled it down. "I have an idea."

The screams of the dying echoed around the big room. He looked again for the assassin, the man he was now certain was a Blue in disguise. He... it was shooting at someone on the far side of the room but slowly backing toward them.

Elio turned his attention to the large kitchen knife he'd spotted on a shelf at the back of the bar.

"What are you waiting for?" Wok shouted. "Get moving. I will draw his fire."

"No, don't move!" Elio yelled back. "I've got this."

The assassin was closing fast. Elio, almost out of time, stared at the knife, remembering Ugo Tan's training, and with all his heart and soul, he willed the knife to lift, turn and fly.

He heard the plasma rip through the thick wooden bar front less than a meter away to his right. Another clipped his arm, but he was transfixed; he couldn't move, so deep was his concentration.

"Get down!" Tiger Wok yelled. "He will kill you." And he grabbed at Elio's arm, trying to pull him down.

Elio watched the knife raise a meter above the shelf. It flipped around one-hundred-eighty degrees. The point of the heavy knife was now directed at the gunman. Elio closed his eyes, and in his mind's eye he watched as the knife flew through the air as if it had been fired from a railgun. He opened his eyes to see the Blue stagger backward, its weapon pointing up at the ceiling, the knife deep in its throat. A final blast of plasma brought down a large section of the ceiling, then all was quiet, except for the moans of the wounded and the dying.

The armored being dropped its weapon, staggered sideways and fell to the floor clutching its throat.

"Hola! Nice move, my friend," Tiger Wok said as he slowly rose to his feet. "I am good, but you are better. You must teach me how to do that."

"It's not what you think it is," Elio said as he leaped over the bar and ran to the supine assassin, holding his wounded arm. He leapt up to the second level. Someone kicked the attacker's weapon away from the body. Elio knelt down beside it. It was covered from head to toe with what looked like an earlier model, dirty gray USF-style armor. He pulled the knife from its throat and dropped it to one side, then undid the clamps, pulled off the helmet and stared down into the cold, dead eyes of a Swarm soldier.

* * *

Manda Haal ran across the street, turned left, and ran along the sidewalk with Jiksar and Haltar Sen right behind her.

On and on they ran until they reached the municipal building where the Board of Directors had their offices. The doors were wide open. People were streaming onto the street.

She continued running, up the steps, into the building and into the lobby.

"Warning. Security breach. Please go to the nearest

exit. Warning. Security breach," the robotic voice repeated over and over.

People by the hundreds were running toward them, across the wide-open space of the lobby, down the stairs toward the exits, pushing, shoving, not quite panicking but close enough. Manda and her two companions fought their way through the oncoming crush toward the stairs at the rear of the building, red lights flashing and the emergency alarm blaring at every turn.

"Where are we going?" Haltar Sen asked breathlessly.

"To the lower level. Stay with me. We're almost out of time!" Manda yelled back.

They ran down the stairs, pushing their way through a crush of people rushing the other way. At the bottom, she turned right, ran along the long, wide corridor, rounded the next corner and ran on.

"Everyone else is running in the opposite direction," Jiksar shouted. "Shouldn't we be going that way?"

"No. Stay with me. We're almost there," she shouted. *Oh, dear God. I hope we're in time.*

And then they were running along the hallway with the blue doors. *Just a... few... steps... more.*

They rounded the next corner. *There it is!* The blue double doors where they had met the Seers were just steps away. The hallway was empty now, and deathly quiet, except for the sounds of their boots on the polished floor and their heavy breathing as they ran toward the doors. *Too late... Oh, God. I'm too late.*

"Hurry," she shouted as she ran to the doors, grabbed the metal handles and flung them open.

Inside the great room the scene was one of horror and heartbreak. Dead bodies littered the floor which was itself awash with blood. Not a single Seer was moving. Nor was there any sign of the Swarm assassins.

Some of the bodies were in pieces: arms, legs, heads severed by plasma fire. Most had died from horrendous wounds to the torso, shot at point-blank range, seemingly from where Manda and her friends were standing, just inside the double doors. There'd been nowhere for them to run. Nowhere for them to hide. Thus, they'd been ruthlessly slaughtered by the Swarm.

"They're all gone," she said, "all these people. I was too late... Too... damn... late."

The room stank of burnt clothing, of charred human flesh, ionized air and... of death. The walls, the screens and marker boards thereon, once covered with drawings, symbols and calculations, were now spattered with blood.

"What the hell happened here?" Jiksar asked.

"The Swarm," she said. "It was the Swarm." And she cursed herself under her breath.

"More to the point," Haltar Sen asked. "How did you know?"

"The same way I knew how to navigate the *Avenger*. I can't explain it. This time I was too late."

"Good job you were," Jiksar said thoughtfully. "If you hadn't been, we would have joined them. We're not armed."

Manda nodded absently, and then the reality of what had happened finally hit her. She not only felt the loss of those innocent people, but the people of Freyja had lost their greatest weapon in the fight against the Swarm. The

Seers had provided them with a strategic advantage, either to avoid battles or win them decisively.

Jiksar covered his nose and mouth with his hand.

"You say the Swarm did this?" Sen asked.

Manda simply nodded but said nothing as she stared at the bodies.

"But how did they get past security and all the way down here without getting caught?" Sen asked.

"I don't know," Manda said. "But we need to find out."

She stepped over one body, stooped down, squatting on her heels and felt for a pulse on the one that looked less severely wounded than the rest, but it was no use. They were dead, all of them.

The alarms outside in the hallway finally ceased and the emergency lights stopped flashing.

"However they did it, they must have left in a hurry," Manda said as she stood up, still staring down at the body. "They couldn't have gotten too far. Come on, we need to find the security people."

No sooner had she spoken than there was a flurry of feet and the sound of yelling voices coming from down the hall. The door was flung open and a small team of armored security personnel burst into the room with their rifles at the ready.

"Looks like they found us," Jiksar said.

Good, she thought. *Maybe we...* But before she could finish the thought, the sense of relief she'd felt at their arrival quickly turned into surprise and shock when the lead security soldier aimed his rifle at her and shouted,

"Get down! Get down on the ground! Do it now or I'll fire!"

Manda dropped to her knees and raised her hands above her head. Jiksar and Sen followed suit.

The guards surrounded them, their guns trained, yelling at them to get down on the ground. The three USF officers lay flat on the floor, their arms spread wide. One of the security officers knelt on Manda's back, forcing the breath from her body, and handcuffed her with a set of electronic restraints, then repeated the procedure with Jiksar and Sen.

"Don't move! Any of you!" an aggressive voice said.

"We got them, sir," someone said, obviously speaking to a superior via his headset. "Yeah. Three of them. Here in the Seer's room. We have them. Sir... they're all dead." There was a pause in the conversation while he listened. "The Seers." Another pause, then, "Yeah, all of them. They're all dead." Another pause, then, "Yessir, we'll bring 'em in."

"No, you can't do this," Jiksar protested.

"You've got it wrong," Manda said. "We didn't kill anyone."

"Tell that to the Board of Directors." The security officer said as he jerked the restraints, wrenching her shoulders as he hauled her to her feet.

Chapter Thirty-Seven

Deception

Gian and Andra— he in his cadet uniform and she in a lovely little flowered dress and neat, half-heeled shoes—were seated together at a table outside a small street café when the sirens began to sound and red lights on top of high poles began to flash.

Gian looked up at one of the poles, then at Andra. "What's going on?" he asked, his spoonful of kiscus fruit suspended halfway to his mouth.

"I don't know," Andra said looking around, "but it doesn't sound good."

People began hurrying to and fro, rushing by in both directions. The little café was just one of many, part of a long one-sided street of small shops that bounded a large open plaza, on the far side of which was a large church. Gian put his food down, stood and looked around, trying to see what was happening, but he saw nothing, which worried him. After what had happened to them on the outskirts of Pricus City, such situations always worried him.

Andra's right, he thought. *Something's wrong, bad wrong!* And the hair on the back of his neck began to prickle. He had no Psy or TK, and Andra's TK was of no use to them. Neither did he know what the emergency protocols on Freyja were or how to respond to the alarms, but he had a feeling that he was about to find out.

"Hey, Gian!" He turned his head to see Danis sprinting toward them. "Thank God I found you." She too was in uniform.

"What? What's going on?" Gian asked.

Danis stopped and looked frantically around. "Damn it. I'm trying to find Richard. Where is he, d'you know?"

"We haven't seen him since we were given leave," Andra said. "Have you tried reaching out to him?"

"Yes, but I can't reach him." She checked the screen on her forearm. "He's close." She looked up, looked around, shook her head, then dropped into one of the seats and looked up at them.

"What's going on, Danis?" Gian asked.

"I don't know. Something bad. I can't reach Richard, but I know he's in trouble. All I'm getting is feelings of panic... from everywhere." She looked up at the flashing red lights. "It must have something to do with these alarms. There must have been some kind of security breach."

Gian suddenly felt unprepared and vulnerable. They were unarmed. They were out in the open, in uniform, and more than ten kilometers away from *Avenger*.

"Where are the others?" Gian asked, backing up the two or three meters to the café wall.

"I don't know, but we have to find them," Danis said. "Richard's in pain and he needs help."

"What are you thinking?" Gian asked. "What d'you want to do?"

She looked around, then nodded in the direction of the tall buildings and pointed. "There," she said. "We need to go there."

She stood up and turned, but before she could move, a voice to their left said, "You three; stay where you are."

They all turned to look and saw three armed security officers walking towards them, their hands on their pistols.

"What is this about?" Danis asked.

"Do not move." The officer in the lead shouted and pulled his pistol and pointed it at them.

"What the hell is this?" Gian asked.

The three guards fanned out, as if they were anticipating they'd try to run.

"Just stay where you are and stand still," another of the officers yelled, his pistol in one hand, his other hand held high, palm out. "We need to ask you some questions."

Gian didn't like where this was going. Something, he knew, was very wrong, and he was becoming increasingly more nervous by the second, but he did as he was told. He stood still and raised his hands. *What the hell's going on?* he wondered. *Are we being double-crossed?*

Gian opened his mouth to say something, but before he could, a bolt of plasma from somewhere on the far side of the plaza slammed into the wall of the building behind him, showering him with debris and barely missing one of the three security officers.

Instinctively, he ducked, ran to Andra, grabbed her, pulled her to the ground and covered her body with his own.

All three security officers spun around and began shooting at something on the far side of the plaza. Danis ran to Gian and Andra and dropped to her knees beside them.

The blasts of plasma were coming thick and fast. The wall above their heads was taking heavy damage. They were covered with debris: brick dust and rubble. Gian lifted his head and looked across the square, trying to see who was shooting at them. In the distance, dodging from doorway to doorway, three soldiers in full battle armor were shooting at the three security officers who were doing their best to hold them off, but their puny laser pistols were no match for the attackers' plasma weapons.

One of the officers took a direct hit to his right shoulder, severing his arm and sending it spinning into the air, the pistol still in its hand, still shooting flash after flash in all directions as its trigger finger spasmed.

People were running in every direction. Laser and plasma fire flashed back and forth across the plaza.

"Stay down!" Gian yelled. "Wait for a break in the shooting and when I say run, we run together."

And they waited.

Chapter Thirty-Eight

A significant change

Manda, along with Jiksar and Haltar Sen, still restrained with their arms behind their backs, were escorted into a holding room where they were told to sit, stay still, and stay quiet.

They hadn't been there for more than a couple of minutes when the red lights began to flash again, and the emergency alarm began to shout its warning.

"Warning. Security breach. Make your way to the nearest exit. Warning. Security breach."

"Someone go kill that damn alarm," the leader of the security team yelled.

"There's still fighting in the food hall on Level Two," one of them reported after checking his data pad.

"Damn it," the leader growled to himself. "What the hell's going on?"

"You can't hold us here," Manda said. "We need to go back to our ship."

"No one's going anywhere until I get some more information from you." The security leader pulled off his helmet and set it on a counter, his laser rifle dangling on a sling at his back. "Where did you go when you left the *Avenger?*"

"What? What are you talking about?" Manda asked. "We were given a pass and told to enjoy ourselves in your city by Tiger Wok himself."

"That was his second mistake," the leader said. "His first was trusting you. He was told he couldn't trust anyone wearing a USF uniform—"

"Sir," one of the other officers interrupted him. "Section 7B on Level Two is locked down. The threat is contained but is not yet ended. Casualties are high and continuing to rise."

"Damn it, I want numbers. I need to know how many more of these USF sympathizers there are out there." He turned back to Manda and said, "You three are being held on suspicion of murder; you killed the Seers."

"What?" Haltar Sen said and burst out laughing.

"You can't be serious," Manda said. "How can you even think that?"

"You were found at the scene. No one else was even close. If you didn't kill the Seers, how do you explain how you got there before we did?" The leader rested his hands on his hips and looked around at his team, smiling as if he'd just won a debate.

Manda stared at the man, wondering how she could explain it to him so that he would believe her. She could tell the truth, of course, but she doubted that would work, considering the mood they were in.

She looked at Jiksar and Haltar Sen. Both of them looked back at her. Jiksar nodded.

She had to do something. The entire station was falling apart around them. They were in a mess and, somehow, she had to get them out of it.

"It was me," she said finally.

"See, I told you all so." The leader looked around at his team with a prideful smile on his lips.

"Not that, you fool," Manda said angrily. "Of course, we didn't kill the Seers. Why the hell would we? I mean that I was the reason we were able to get there so quickly."

"Oh yeah, and how was that?"

"I am a Seer myself," she replied.

The leader's eyes widened. Jiksar's and Haltar Sen's did the same. They'd suspected, of course; all of the bridge crew had, but to hear it from her own lips...

"You're a what?" the leader asked, his eyes narrowed, his head tilted slightly to one side.

"I'm a Seer," Manda said. "And, although the abilities of your Seers were somewhat... fragmentary, mine are not. Mine are quite precise. True, I didn't begin to experience them until a few weeks ago, but they are extensive, far-reaching. Though I never seem to have much time to act on them; today being a good example. But I do see things before they happen, and I saw the attack on the Seers and tried to stop it. Unfortunately, I arrived too late, as did you."

The security leader lowered his shoulders and slowly leaned his head back, trying to take it all in.

"You have to believe her," Jiksar said. "Why else

would we be here? What possible motive could we have to kill the Seers?"

"None of us know why the USF are here on Freyja," the leader replied. "All we know is, we were doing just fine until you arrived. You came and hours later so did the Swarm. That's just too much of a coincidence if you ask me."

"You're suggesting we're in league with the Swarm? Is that what you're saying? Preposterous!" Manda snapped.

"What I'm saying is, we were not attacked until you arrived."

Manda couldn't believe it. She looked around. "Think about it," she said. "The Seers were killed with plasma weapons, right?"

"Yes, but how do you know that?" the leader asked.

"Oh, come on. I was there in the room when you arrived... late," she said caustically. The leader looked away, obviously uncomfortable. "I saw the evidence, as did you... eventually. We saw the burns. We could smell the ionized air. We could see the wounds, damn it. Look at us." Manda tried to point but could only lift her shoulders. "How do you think we killed them? We're unarmed. Did you find any weapons? No, of course you didn't. Did you find any plasma rifles? No, you didn't. The USF doesn't have that kind of weapon, on any scale, and you know it. You didn't find a single weapon on us because we didn't have any."

The leader squinted, first at her, then at all three of them. Manda knew her logic was perfect and that it was working. These people obviously hadn't thought things through and had condemned them out of hatred for the USF.

"You want me to prove it?" Manda said. "Bring in one of your Psyops and have him read my mind. You'll see I'm telling you the truth."

The leader's eyes lit up. He clearly had not thought of that.

"Team Four Leader to Team Three Leader," he spoke into the comm unit on his wrist.

"Go ahead, Four."

"I need you to send us a Psyop to holding unit One, level One. Copy?"

Manda's head began to swim. She grew dizzy. The haze began to clear. The vision shimmered. More violence. More bloodshed. Portents of another attack. Images flitted through her mind. "Wait!" she shouted. "I have to talk to my captain. We need to talk to the Board of Directors. The assassins are still here, on Freyja. Another attack is underway."

Gian and Andra huddled together against the wall, Danis at their side, waiting for the gunfire to cease.

Danis wiped sweat from her forehead on the sleeve of her uniform jacket, instantly regretting it, then wondering why such little things always seemed to come to the fore in times of stress.

"We're stuck. We can't move," Andra said, her voice panicked.

Gian nodded and turned his head to look out across

the plaza just in time to see the last of the security officers take a hit to the chest. The officer jerked upright. His pistol fell from his hand, and he fell over backwards. This was their chance. They had to go now.

"Stay here," Gian shouted, then stood up and sprinted for the dropped pistol as plasma fire blazed over his head. He didn't know if they were shooting at him, someone else, or if he was just running into it.

He dove and rolled on the concrete, skinning his elbow, grabbed the pistol, turned and ran back to Andra and Danis.

He dropped down beside them, turned and looked across the plaza. The three armored soldiers were advancing slowly toward them across the square, guns blazing indiscriminately in every direction.

The brickwork above and around them was methodically being turned to dust. Only their small profile, low against the building, was saving them from being hit.

"Come on," Gian shouted. "We can't stay here." And he jumped to his feet, grabbed Andra by the arm, hauled her to her feet, and together the three of them ran through the shattered doorway into the café.

Once inside, he stopped dead and looked frantically around. They were inside a small restaurant with seating for maybe fifty or sixty people.

He heard something behind him and turned just in time to see one of the helmeted attackers stalk through the doorway.

Gian fired, three times. All three blasts of laser fire impacted the attacker mid-torso and he watched, stunned, as its armor flared bright blue and absorbed the energy.

Gian shoved Andra violently away from him, sending her staggering across the room, knocking over tables and chairs as she went. He barely saw Danis dive in the other direction. He was already firing blast after blast at the attacker's helmet.

More than a dozen blasts hit the helmet before Gian stopped pulling the trigger. The attacker still stood, motionless but unharmed, its armor pulsing brighter, then dimmer.

Gian turned and ran behind a steel support column and began firing again. Again and again his fire impacted the helmet.

The pistol clicked and then stopped working, its power cell depleted. He swore, threw it at the stationary attacker, then rushed it. He hit it hard with his shoulder. All one-hundred-twenty kilograms of him slammed into its chest and toppled it over backward, its weapon falling from its hands. He jumped on top of it, punched the helmet and yelped with pain as his fist impacted the steel-hard shell.

Gian looked around, searching for something he could use as a weapon. The only thing he could see that was close enough was the useless laser pistol. He grabbed it by the barrel and began to hammer the helmet with it. The grip shattered. He glared at it, tossed it away, frustrated. He grabbed the helmet and tried to wrench it off, but it was locked on tight.

Slowly, at first, the attacker began to recover. Gian tried banging its head on the concrete floor, but he could barely lift it. Then, suddenly, it grabbed both of his arms and threw him bodily halfway across the room. Then it reached for its weapon and aimed it at the now stunned Gian.

Danis and Andra jumped out from behind their cover, yelling and waving their arms, trying to draw its fire.

It saw them, swung its weapon toward them and began firing, just as the two women dove behind a large concrete planter. The planter shattered, leaving them exposed again. The attacker paused, swung its weapon back in Gian's direction, but Gian was already on the move, running for one of the steel supports.

Suddenly, a metal chair flew across the room toward the attacker. It saw it coming, raised an arm and fended it off. Another chair, then a table, then two more chairs. And each time it managed to fend them off.

Gian stuck his head out from behind the support. Andra was kneeling behind what was left of the shattered planter, her eyes closed, her fingers to her temples, Danis beside her with her hand on her shoulder.

A large metal table, somehow upside down, slammed into the attacker's knees. The armor held, but the attacker toppled forward and landed on top of the table between its legs, its weapon falling from its hands.

It struggled to its knees, reaching again for its weapon. A large chunk of the concrete planter slammed into its shoulder sending it spinning, but again its armor held.

Gian charged out from behind the steel pillar, ran to the attacker and grabbed its weapon. It was like none he'd ever seen before. As far as he could tell, there was no way to fire it, no trigger, no button, nothing. He flung it across the room, out of reach. He looked down at the helmeted soldier and could see that it was already recovering again.

Desperately, he looked around, spotted the piece of concrete Andra had hurled at it, grabbed it in both hands, raised it above his head and threw it down, as hard as he could, at its helmet. It must have weighed all of ten kilograms, but it bounced off the helmet high enough that he was able to catch it.

The attacker, now obviously dazed, fell back. Gian jumped on its chest, raised the rock above his head and slammed it down on the faceplate of the helmet. Then he did it again, and again, and again until finally the faceplate cracked, then shattered into a thousand tiny pieces.

Gian, breathing heavily, looked down into the large, almond-shaped eyes of a Blue. Those eyes were cold, expressionless... dead.

Chapter Thirty-Nine

Adaptation

It was almost an hour later when Danis, Gian and Andra entered the municipal building looking for Danis's brother, but he was nowhere to be found. After asking around, they were able to determine that Morian, Tiger Wok and Elio had spoken briefly to several members of the Board of Directors, and they'd then gone their separate ways: Morian back to the ship, Elio and Wok... well, they seemed to have disappeared somewhere into the depths of the building.

Again, she reached out to her brother. This time she was successful and was able to make the connection. "Danis, where are you?" he asked, sounding distracted.

"We're in the municipal building, looking for Elio."

"Don't worry about him. He's fine. I need you to come back to the ship, now. We have an emergency."

"But—"

"No buts, Danis," Morian said testily. "I don't have time to argue; just do it." And then he shut her down.

"What is it?" Gian asked.

"The Captain," she replied. "He's ordered us back to the ship. Come on. We have to go."

Meanwhile, Elio was sitting in an examination unit in the municipal building's medical bay, where a nurse was finishing up dressing the wound to his arm. The one good thing about the plasma wound—if there is such a thing— was that the heat had cauterized the deep trench as it plowed its way across the top of his right bicep, just above the elbow. It wasn't a deep wound but, as burns always do, it hurt like hell. However, it was nothing he couldn't handle.

He flinched as the nurse injected him with a pain killer.

"That should take the edge off," she said as she sprayed the injection site with a sterile compound that quickly gelled and formed a seal. "Just take it easy with the arm. Give it a couple of days and you should be fine."

"I will, and thank you," Elio replied.

The door slid open and Tiger Wok stepped inside, followed by Manda Haal, Jiksar and Haltar Sen.

"Ah, there you are, my young friend," Wok said effusively, his hand stretched out toward him. "I ran into your friends a few moments ago. We were worried about you. Are you all right?"

"Yes, I'm fine, just a small burn," Elio said as he rose to his feet and shook his hand.

"Elio," Manda said. "What a relief. It's so good to see you. We came as fast as we could. Have you heard anything from the Captain?"

"No," Elio said, "but I think we should get back to the ship."

"Agreed," Manda said. "Wok." She turned to the pirate. "D'you know if the roads are clear?"

"As far as I know, they are," Wok replied with a shrug and a grimace. "But who can know for sure after such a series of attacks?"

"How do we get there?" Elio asked. "Can you provide transport?"

"All in good time, my friends." He held up both hands, palms out. "First, on behalf of the Board of Directors and the people of Freyja, I take it upon myself to apologize for the mistreatment of your crew." He motioned to Manda, Jiksar and Sen.

"You see," he continued, "during the attack here inside the municipal building, tensions among the security personnel were... elevated, and several of them made some, shall we say, rash decisions. These three fine young officers were arrested and questioned but now, as you can see, they have been released."

Elio looked first at Manda, then Sen, then Jiksar. "Are you all right?" Elio asked.

"Yes," Sen replied, "we're fine, but the Swarm attack killed the Seers."

"No! How many?" Elio was stunned by the news.

"All of them," Manda said, almost in a whisper. The silence was palpable.

Manda then recounted her story, telling Elio how they'd rushed to the Seer's room only to find them massacred.

Elio shook his head. He was in a state of total shock. "How could this have happened?" he asked.

"That is a good question, my friend," Wok said. "This is what we know so far. Sometime around eight hundred hours, an unmarked freighter landed in docking bay ninety-seven. The ship was granted clearance to land, but once it did, the captain did not report its bill of lading to the transfer station. A pickup crew was dispatched, but when they arrived at the bay, the freighter was empty; its captain and crew of two were found dead on its bridge. It is believed the freighter had been captured by the Swarm and its crew forced to transport a company of Swarm troopers to Freyja. The troopers were disguised using an upgraded variation of the CR2C lightweight armor; thus they were able to hide their identity until the attacks."

"This is terrible. How many attacks were there?" Elio asked.

"Including the murder of the Seers," Wok replied, "there were five separate attacks in all. For some unexplained reason, the Seers were unable to foresee these attacks. In the past, they have always been very effective, but somehow the Swarm was able to find them and infiltrate our defenses. Now they're gone, and we have lost our first line of defense, our most powerful weapon. It is a very sad time... Of all the positive things an unregulated and free space port is," Wok said, "it isn't invulnerable.

Ships of all systems can come and go almost as they please, making it the perfect place for an undercover attack."

"I'm so sorry for your loss," Elio said, knowing those feeble words were inadequate to express his sadness or comfort Wok.

"Yes, yes... Thank you... Thank... you!" Wok said as he paced around the room. "Have we killed all of the invaders? I think so, but I don't know for sure. If we haven't, then where are they now? Will they attack again? Our Seers are gone. We can't know. We must be on guard."

"I agree, but I fear this may be just the beginning," Elio said.

"You do?" Wok asked. "Why d'you say that?"

"The armor they were wearing," Elio replied thoughtfully. "We've seen nothing like it before. You say it was an adaption of an early USF model. We know they're a silicon-based lifeform, but does that also mean they can change their appearance at will? If so, we're facing a challenge of almost infinite proportions. They could be walking among us and we wouldn't know it.

"From our many encounters with them," Elio continued, "we know they're learning, adapting: their ships, their technology, their tactics and, so it seems, they're doing so at an ever-increasing pace."

Elio stood, flexed the muscle of his right arm, then his fingers. Everything seemed to be working as it should and without a significant amount of pain.

"Our enemy is adapting quickly," he said. "They're

becoming more and more sophisticated. And I'm afraid we have little time left."

"Little time before what?" Tiger Wok asked.

"Until they grow more sophisticated than we can handle."

* * *

Manda stared at Elio, her mind in a whirl, filled with foreboding at what she knew she had to tell them. Yet she didn't want to tell them because she knew it would be yet another step toward... what, she wasn't sure. But she did know she didn't like the feeling of separation her rank of Commander gave her over the other members of the crew. They say high command is a lonely vocation and that, along with her physical stature, she'd found to be true. Now this... This new ability, she felt, would take that loneliness to a whole new level. She didn't want to be "othered," but she realized she had no choice.

Manda rarely, if ever, did anything without first thinking it through, but here she was; she was just going to have to say it and figure out the consequences afterwards. She knew life after her revelation wasn't going to be pleasant.

She stood. Elio, Tiger Wok and the others all turned to look at her.

"What you say is true, Elio. If we don't adapt, and quickly, the Swarm will overwhelm us." She paused for a moment, trying to find the correct words. "I... there have already been some changes or... advances on our side... to me... personally." She paused again, cleared her throat, then continued. "Some of you already know that over the past several months, and especially since we embarked upon this mission, I have been seeing things... I have been changing. I... I have the Sight."

Wok stared at her, his eyes wide with surprise. "But that is wonderful," he said. "Are you sure?"

She nodded. "Yes, I'm sure, but wonderful? Maybe," Manda said. "But the reason I'm telling you this now is because the visions are coming more often and... in more detail. And... because there's another massive Swarm attack coming."

"Are you sure?" Wok asked. "Where? When?"

"Now?" Elio asked.

"Yes, I'm sure, Captain Wok, and the attack will be here, on Freyja," she said somberly. "But when, exactly? That I don't know. All I know is... it will be soon."

* * *

Tiger Wok stared at Manda, stroked his beard and rested his chin in his hand. For a moment no one said a word. Everyone was pondering the gravity of what she'd just said.

Finally, Wok looked at the prince and said, "We have a vast number of civilians here on Freyja. Civilians that either cannot fight or have no ships. They must be protected. Our forces... those of us who have capable ships are their only protection."

"What are you saying?" Elio asked.

"I am saying that if we are attacked, our fleet can defend only one area at a time. If they attack on the surface, we must stay here and fight. If they attack outside the atmosphere, we would have to respond there, but we cannot fight in both places at once. The people of Freyja are counting on the fleet to help protect them."

"So what you're saying," Haltar Sen said, "is that you don't intend to fight with us."

Wok, when he had first met the helmsman, had not received a good impression of him, thinking him cold and standoffish. *Does the man have something against the free spirit of this community?* he wondered.

"It is simple logistics, I am afraid," Wok said. "Our fleet is small. We have but a few ships, and the ones we do have do not have the capabilities that your *Avenger* has."

"If we are going to survive this," Elio replied. "We must work together and fight together."

Wok, not wanting to create doubt among his new allies, replied, "Of course. And I understand what you say, my friend, and may I assure you, the Free People of Freyja will fight with you. But you must also understand that my duty... my obligation is to protect my people." He spread his arms, rolled his shoulders and continued, "I am just being honest."

"We all appreciate your honesty, Wok," Haltar Sen said. "And I, that is we, are being honest with you—"

"Sen!" Manda said, interrupting him.

"No! Let me finish. Like your fleet, our ship also can only be in one place at a time. And our weapon's systems and fighting capabilities are best beyond the atmosphere. If the *Avenger* is to have an impact on the outcome of the battle, we must fight the Swarm out there, in deep space." He pointed to the sky.

Wok nodded. He still considered *Avenger's* helmsman's tone harsh, but tensions were high. He had to be careful with his words so as not to give a false impression, but he needed these USF people to know he was loyal to his people before all else.

"I understand what you say," Wok said, "but I must reiterate, my first priority is to protect my people. They came to us for protection, and we cannot abandon them."

"We're not asking you to abandon them," Haltar Sen snapped. "We are just asking you to keep your word to us and fight with us."

Wok looked at Manda. She stared back at him, her face set. It was obvious to him that she agreed with her officer.

He looked at Sen, studied his face. Sen's expression was blank, and he couldn't decide if he was hiding something or not. He decided it was time for diplomacy.

"Rest assured," Wok said, "the fleet *will* fight with you, and we are expecting *Avenger* to fight with us. Where and how is yet to be decided, and much of that decision lies with your captain," he continued, artfully shifting the tide of the conversation. And it didn't go unnoticed. Sen smiled knowingly, shook his head and turned away.

"I am the leader of this mission," Elio said, "and I not only speak for myself, I speak for Captain Morian, and I tell you it only makes sense to meet the enemy in deep space. You could divide your fleet, and half could fight with us off-planet while the other half remains here to protect Freyja, but we both know that that would only weaken us. It's never a good idea to divide your forces. In fact, it's a recipe for disaster." He paused for just a second, then continued, "Now, let me ask you a question, Captain Wok. Who speaks for the Board of Directors? Who makes the decisions? Because if it's not you, sir, we are just wasting our time and I need to talk to whomever it is that *does* make the decisions."

Wok shrugged. "Rest assured, my friend, I have full authority over the fleet. They are loyal to *me!* Now, let me say this: What you say is true, but—"

"I don't understand the problem," Elio said, interrupting him. "We fought them together yesterday, and we defeated them. We worked well together."

"That is also true," Wok said. "but..." He trailed off, not wanting to deepen the growing rift between them.

"But what?" the prince asked.

Wok shook his head, looked at the floor and sighed, then looked up at him and said, "You must trust me when I say this, Prince Elio. Yes... We desire for us to fight together. And yes, I trust you. And many of my leaders and pilots trust you. Everyone was much impressed by your captain, ship and your crew. However, much has happened since then, and I am afraid that many of our people—especially since the assassination of the Seers —*do not* trust you as they did. Many of them have become suspicious."

"But we were cleared of that," Haltar Sen said turning again to face him. "Could it not be that it's you that's suspicious, as I believe you always have been?"

Wok shook his head emphatically. "No! You are

wrong, sir. I trust you all implicitly, and yes, of course you're innocent of the deaths of the Seers. I know that and so do our security teams. But word travels fast among the people and there is still much confusion. We are doing our best to alleviate the situation, but things are still chaotic out there."

"And that's understandable," Elio said. "But we must stand together. We must fight as one, and we must fight in deep space."

Wok knew Elio was right. No matter how much he hated the USF and what it stood for, when push came to shove, they needed the *Avenger's* firepower.

"Very well, prince," Wok said and held out his hand. "You are right. We will fight together. It is the only way."

Prince Elio stared into the pirate's dark brown eyes, wondering if the man could be trusted, but he, like Wok, had to take his word for it and shook his hand.

"Very well..." Elio hesitated.

"What?" Wok asked smiling broadly. "You don't trust me? I gave you my word and we shook hands. I expect you to keep your word, as I will keep mine."

Elio nodded then said, "Very well. We are as one. Now, let's get back to our ships and begin preparations." He looked at Manda and pointed to the door. She nodded and everyone began to file out of the room.

"My young friend." Wok tapped Elio's shoulder.

Elio turned to him and said, "What now, Captain?"

Wok smiled. "I was thinking: maybe the USF is not all bad, just like maybe it is not all good."

Elio smiled back. "I understand and, believe it or not,

I have been thinking the same about you and your pirates."

They both chuckled.

"You have my word, Tiger," the prince said, using his forename for the first time. "The USF and the *Avenger* will support you. We'll do everything we can to protect the innocent people of Freyja."

"Very well," Wok said. "Come. We must go to our ships, and quickly, while we still can."

Chapter Forty

The Calm Before the Storm

Back on *Avenger*, on the hangar deck, Gian pulled the thick nanowire gel cable across the floor towards Jackknife's ship. Fortunately, Maxim Volkov, the ship's chief engineer, had found an adaptor that would fit the Veridian, and they were able to charge the fighter's power cells. The holes in the fuselage had been patched, the portside strut had been temporarily repaired, her twin cyclon engines had been serviced and her weapons rearmed, though *Avenger* didn't carry any of the old Storm missiles she usually carried. Instead, they converted her launchers and loaded her with six Rapiers. All that was left was to charge the power cells.

Gian fitted the adaptor to the end of the cable and plugged it into the Veridian fighter's port, and the red charging light flickered and then glowed steadily. *Good,* he thought, *it's working.*

He backed away from the fighter and stood for a moment staring at it. There was something about its clean lines, its two swept-back wings and huge twin engines that excited him. The Veridian was old, more than sixty years old, but she was designed to fight in both atmosphere and space and... she was... beautiful, and he wondered what it would be like to fly her.

Jackknife dropped down from the wing, his metal mech boots clanging on the floor.

"I see you're admiring my lady," he said to Gian.

"She's beautiful. Are there any more like her?"

"One or two, in various states of disrepair."

Gian laughed and said, "And this one isn't?"

"Don't be fooled by her looks. She'll fly just fine," Jackknife said, dusting off his hands on his grubby flight suit.

"It looks like the cells are charging," Gian said. "You should be good to go in about thirty minutes, just as long as those patches hold."

"They'll hold. I patched them myself. Unfortunately, most of my onboard circuits are fried, but the backups are working. So long as I don't blow a nanobreaker, she'll fly just fine." He patted the side of the fighter like it was his pet. "We've been through a lot together. She has served me well, and she will no doubt continue to do so."

"Since we'll be going out there together," Gian said, "I have something I'd like to ask?"

"What is that?" Jackknife asked, grabbing a wiper from the wing.

"The last time we were out there, I noticed something. Your reaction times, your speed, the way you were able to maneuver, to anticipate the enemy's movements. I've never seen anything like it. It was as if... Something has to be giving you that edge. Have you ever considered that you might have the Sight?"

"No!" Jackknife snapped. His tone was sharp. Gian flinched back in surprise. "I do not have the Sight. I don't care what you saw out there. I'm able to do what I do because I'm a good pilot and a good fighter, and I make no apologies for it. My skill comes from good old hard work and experience. I grew up flying fighters. I was only fifteen when I flew solo for the first time. Life out here in the unregulated free areas is not like the peaceful upbringing you had back in your grand Sovereign Stars system. Out here we've been fighting and scrambling to survive our whole lives. One thing is for sure, I'll never end up like one of those sorry, drugged-up Seers, mumbling to myself all day. I belong in a cockpit, not a rubber room." Jackknife's eyes narrowed as he glared at Gian. He took several steps closer to him, his huge frame dwarfing him, and said, "And if you ever so much as mention something like that again, to me or to anyone else, I'll come down on you like a five megaton Storm torpedo, got me?"

"Umm... Yes," Gian stuttered. "My apologies, I didn't mean to offend."

"Good, then don't." Jackknife walked off.

Gian stepped back. *Oh yes,* he thought smiling to himself, *he has the Sight.*

He didn't take Jackknife's threat seriously, but he would, he decided, respect his wishes and keep it to himself. After all, people process and deal with their new abilities in different ways. Jackknife? He had a major chip on his shoulder. And whatever it was, Gian wasn't going to try and fix it for him.

* * *

Avenger's bridge was beginning to fill as one after another of her officers stepped through the door and went to their stations.

Manda, seated in her command chair next to the captain's, was already exhausted and they hadn't even lifted off yet. The ship was still in the dock. The repairs and upgrades to her hull had not yet been completed, though Manda had been assured she would be flight-ready in a little less than three hours. She could only sit and hope they would be done in time.

Haltar Sen finally arrived and took his seat at the helm while Simon DeLong began briefing his navigation team.

Manda rose from her chair, stepped up to the command rail, looked around the well deck, then decided to take a walk.

She descended the six steps and approached DeLong's station.

"Navigation is up and running, Commander," DeLong said. "We're just waiting for the objective."

"Good," Manda replied. "Thank you, Simon." And she moved on to Haltar Sen's station at the helm.

"Mr. Sen, walk with me, please," she said quietly.

Sen stood and followed her across the deck to the rear where she couldn't be heard.

"Haltar, I am going to need your help. You already know I have... I have the Sight."

She looked at him. He nodded but didn't reply.

"It seems," she said, "that my abilities are changing almost by the minute. I can't explain how I see what I see, but the visions are becoming clearer. I don't always get the entire vision right away, which means that sometimes I just know something, but I don't have time to explain it. So, if something like that happens and I need the ship to move, I will call you, understood?"

Sen nodded again.

"So, if I tell you to move the ship, you'll know why, and you must do it immediately and without question. I know that's asking a lot, but you must comply. You will not have time to think about it or question me, but I assure you, the survival of the *Avenger* will depend upon how quickly you act. Haltar, I need you to trust me."

Haltar Sen nodded. "Of course, Commander. I trust you completely."

"As do I," Morian said as he joined them.

"Captain, it's good to see you back," Manda said. Haltar Sen clicked his heels, nodded once to the captain and returned to his station.

"I heard only part of your conversation," Morian said. "Am I to understand your ability is evolving?"

"Yes, Captain, and quickly."

Morian nodded and said, "Tiger Wok has informed me of your prediction. I have infinite faith in you, Manda. Are we ready to go?"

"Thank you, Captain. I appreciate your confidence. I won't let you down. And yes, we'll be ready as soon as

Tactical arrives and we are released by the dock manager."

"Good, come with me. We need to talk, but not here."

They returned to the command deck and Morian dropped heavily into his chair. Manda sat down beside him.

"Tiger Wok will be our main point of contact for the Freyjian fleet. He says he's confident he can field almost twice as many fighters as he did yesterday."

"Good, we're going to need them... What is it, Sen?" she asked as the helmsman stepped up onto the command deck and approached them.

"If I might have a word with you both, ma'am?"

"Of course. What is it?"

"It's about the pirates, ma'am, sir."

"What about them?" Morian asked, looking up at him.

Haltar Sen looked down at them, hesitated, then said, "I didn't really want to go into the city. I only went because you, ma'am, and Jiksar asked me to. I'm not exactly comfortable rubbing shoulders with pirates. And to be honest, I..." He stopped, hesitated, opened his mouth and then shut it again.

"What is it, Sen?" Morian asked. "Come on, man. Out with it."

"Yes, sir... I know it worked out yesterday, but I have a bad feeling in my gut about working with these people. I mean, look how easily they turned on us and arrested us, accused us of murdering those poor Seers. We're not like them, sir. They're criminals, and we shouldn't be consorting with them. I just don't trust them, any of them."

"I understand your concerns," Morian said. "I wasn't too excited about trusting them myself. But remember, they don't trust us either. They think we're here to grab their shipyard. I had this very discussion with Tiger Wok less than an hour ago. But we can't do this on our own. All we can do is work with them but watch them and keep a sharp eye on them... There's a very old saying, pre-Purge, Russian, I think. It says, Trust but verify. Now, if that's all, please return to your station and make ready for departure."

Haltar Sen looked away. "Aye, sir. As you say, trust but verify." He hesitated for a moment, then said, "I understand, sir, and I apologize for my temerity. You have no reason to doubt my commitment to the mission. I am good to go, sir."

"Excellent, thank you, Haltar." Morian raised his arm, opened a screen on his data pad and began to read.

Sen turned on his heel and walked to the steps and then down to the helm.

Manda watched Sen go, then nodded and said, "Well said, sir."

Chapter Forty-One

Enemy Contact

Manda glanced up at the view screens. The sun was beginning to rise on a new Freyjian day, one she was sure would see a battle of momentous proportions.

"Commander," one of Volkov's engineers shouted, breaking into her thoughts.

"Yes?" Manda said as she stood and stepped up to the command rail.

"The shipyard engineers are requesting permission to pressure test the number three containment shields."

"Permission granted. Is the hull secure?" she asked.

The engineer went back to his com and relayed the question. "Yes, all sections have been pressure tested and passed one hundred percent. All four engines and the six fusion reactors have also tested one hundred percent. Shields are a little low at ninety-four percent but are fully operational."

"Very well," Manda replied, "but I am still waiting on the readouts for the new weight disbursement metrics. Krista needs those numbers before we can become operational."

"I checked. They said they've already sent them over."

"Krista, did you hear that?" she asked, well knowing that she had. She heard, recorded and entered almost everything into the ship's data logs.

"I did, Commander," Krista replied, her voice isolated and directed to Manda's immediate vicinity, "and, no, I have not yet received the metrics."

Manda nodded and said to the engineer, "Negative. I do not have those numbers yet. We need them now. Check with them again, Lieutenant."

"Aye, Commander. I'll let you know as soon as we receive them." The engineer leaned forward over his screens.

She stepped down onto the well deck and walked over to Maxim Volkov at the engineering station. "Maxim, what's the status of the maneuvering thrusters?"

"The thrusters are all primed, re-set with the new numbers, and tested. Everything is reading at one hundred percent, or close to it. It should be smooth sailing from here on out."

"'Should be' is the operative word." Manda smiled at the chief engineer and said, "Let's hope that all will indeed be smooth sailing."

Manda was one of those people who always hoped for the best but planned for the worst. Unfortunately, she knew they were about to enter a terrible battle. One that would bring massive amounts of damage and large numbers of casualties. If there was a way to spare her crew and the *Avenger*, she would take it. But there was no avoiding the inevitable bloodshed to come. She just wished she knew when.

Manda turned again to Engineering. "Lieutenant, I'm still waiting for those metrics."

"Nothing yet, Commander."

Logistics. Administration. Management. The military ran on bureaucracy. *Why oh why can't they ever just get it together?* she wondered.

"Wait," the engineering officer said. "They're sending them now, Commander." The engineer began tapping on his screen.

Manda's data pad buzzed. She looked at the screen. They were in.

"Upload them to Krista," Manda said, "and send me confirmation as soon as she's assimilated them."

She looked around, trying to remain calm, her back straight, her face expressionless, eyes flitting back and forth. She may have looked calm, but inside she was burning.

The Tactical officer arrived with his crew. Good. *We have to get off the ground! At least it looks like everyone is here.*

She raised her forearm, tapped the screen and said, "Haal to Commander Jadern."

"Go ahead, Commander," Jadern replied.

"I need confirmation that the crew are all present and accounted for."

"Confirmed, Commander. All decks have reported

in. We have two enlisted men in sick bay. Other than that, we're good to go."

"Thank you. Haal out."

Her final stop was at the Weapons station to check the status with Corin Fargo. That done, she turned once more to Engineering, but before she could speak, her data pad buzzed. She lifted her arm and tapped the comms icon.

"What do you have for me, Krista?"

"I have assimilated the new metrics, Commander."

"And?"

"And I have assimilated the new metrics. Lieutenant Marco in Engineering asked me to confirm with you when the process was complete. I am confirming. It's complete."

"No problems?"

"None, Commander. Is there anything else you need?"

"No. Thank you, Krista." She tapped the icon, broke the connection with the AI and returned to her chair next to the captain.

"All systems are at better than ninety-five percent, Captain. I think we're ready."

Morian nodded and began speaking into his comms, beginning the preflight sequence.

It was at that moment that Manda's vision blurred, and she grew dizzy. Her head cleared. She saw destruction, wreckage, burning buildings, blood, people running, screaming, dying... chaos.

Then the vision faded quickly. She jumped to her feet and ran to the rail.

"Lieutenant, Lowry!" she yelled for all to hear.

"Yes, Commander." She turned in her chair and looked up at her.

"Broadcast an emergency evacuation warning to the people of Haven. They must leave immediately or take cover. They are about to be attacked. Do it now! Before it's too late." And she listened as Lowry broadcast to the city on an emergency channel.

She staggered slightly as the electromagnetic clamps were released and *Avenger* lifted off on her antigrav engines. Had she gotten the warning out in time? She didn't know.

* * *

Elio clipped the lapel of his flight suit in place and grabbed his gloves and helmet, then ran out of the locker room onto the flight deck.

"Now hear this. Now hear this," Krista's voice echoed around the ship and in every department. "Secure all decks for takeoff. I say again, secure all decks for takeoff."

It was a command rarely heard on any USF ship. Once construction was complete, a ship would spend its life in space. But here, on Freyja, it was different. The ground-based dry docks were much more efficient than the space-bound docks used for the past century by the USF.

Elio ran to Danis who was at the ladder of her F32A.

"What are we supposed to do?" he shouted. Even in this situation, and no matter how many times he saw her, he couldn't get over how terrific she looked in her flight suit.

"Go on up, get into your seat and activate your restraints," she replied. "Make sure all of your systems are fully operational. I don't think we'll have time to do a full preflight check."

He nodded, pulled on his helmet and gloves, ran up the ladder, hopped over the bulkhead into the rear seat and began connecting his systems to the F32A. He checked his air supply, the sensors that would monitor his vitals, and confirmed his suit and forearm systems had paired with the fighter. Then he tapped the icon on his command screen, activated his restraints, then his inertia dampeners and felt the system close comfortingly around him.

He leaned sideways to look down over the port side to see what Danis was doing. She was talking to the big, bearded pirate, Jackknife, and in doing so he managed to catch the tail end of the conversation.

"I'm telling you, you're a great pilot," Jackknife said. "And you're almost as hot in person."

He saw Danis blush and look down at the ground.

Son of a... "Hey," he shouted.

They both turned to look up at him. Jackknife lifted his chin acknowledging Elio, then immediately turned his attention back to Danis.

"I'll be just a minute, Elio," Danis said.

Jackknife looked up at him and grinned, then leaned forward, closer to Danis, and said something to her he couldn't hear. They both smiled. Danis again looked down at the ground.

"Excuse me," Elio said. "The ship is about to launch."

"Oh, terribly sorry," Jackknife said as he took a step backward, turned slightly to face Elio and bowed from the waist. "I wouldn't want to hold you up, *my prince*." The sarcasm in his voice was not to be missed.

"I'll see you later, Danis," Jackknife said. "Good hunting. Stay safe." And with that, he gave her a smile and then turned and walked away.

The idea of Danis in a relationship with someone other than himself took him by surprise. He'd always liked her, but his affection for her was growing. His reaction at seeing her with someone she was obviously attracted to was, to him, a little disconcerting.

"What was that all about?" Elio asked as she climbed the ladder.

"Nothing. You ready to fly?"

He could see she wasn't in the mood for questions, so he let it go and watched as, without looking at him or saying a word, she climbed into the cockpit and secured herself in her seat.

The silence between them was awkward, and for once he was at a loss for words. The idea of the hotshot pirate hitting on her ate away at his gut. For one, he had no time for pirates; he didn't like them. And then he suddenly realized he didn't like *anyone* having eyes for Danis, and that for the first time in his life... he was jealous, and he didn't like that either. His head was filled with mixed emotions. This was not the time for such petty distractions. *Damn it!* he thought as he pushed them away and tapped the icons on his screens as the canopy closed over his head.

The entire ship shuddered, and as the magnetic clamps unlocked, *Avenger* rose quickly off the dock on its antigrav drives. At fifteen meters her thrusters took over and the ship rose in a matter of seconds to three thousand meters, at which point all four of her fusion engines roared into life, her bow lifted sixty degrees and her speed increased exponentially until it reached escape velocity, Mach 40, almost forty-nine-thousand kilometers per hour.

It was an almost infinitely unnerving feeling as the F32A's inertia dampeners closed around him. He closed his eyes, then opened them again, staring at his screens. *What the hell is that?* he wondered.

The proximity alarms began to sound. The orange warning lights in the hangar began to flash, flashing all over the hangar.

"We have incoming," Danis's voice resonated in his ears.

"So I see," he replied.

The bridge was quiet, except for the fluctuating, wailing sound of the proximity alarm. Morian was in his command chair with Manda Haal at his side. The preflight checks had been completed only seconds earlier, and they were only minutes away from launching out of the shipyard; too many minutes. Multiple Swarm ships were already approaching the upper atmosphere and coming in hot.

"The leading enemy craft are a little more than three-hundred-twenty kilometers out and closing fast, Captain," Omario Kingston said over the open comms.

"Get us out of here, Mr. Sen," Morian said to the chief helmsman.

"Aye, Captain. Stand by. Releasing clamps... Now!"

The ship shuddered, then rose rapidly, straight up. At three thousand meters, Sen said in a singsong voice, "Vector sixty zero degrees. Speed Mach nine... twelve.... Eighteen..."

Manda looked at the hologram and was happy to see that the majority of the pirate vessels were off the ground, though they were still vulnerable to attack from above. It would be several minutes more before they were in position to fight.

"Battle stations, Mr. Kingston," Morian said calmly. "Mr. Sen. Take us straight into that Swarm formation."

"Weapons hot, Ms. Fargo," Morian said.

"Aye, sir. Weapons hot," she replied.

"Shields up, Mr. Kingston," Manda said.

"Aye, Commander. Shields up."

Morian furrowed his brow, seemingly deep in thought. She looked sideways at him, laid her hand on his arm, and said, "Captain, there's no one close enough to protect our flanks. If we go straight in, we'll be on our own."

"I'm aware of that, Commander," Morian said without looking at her.

The ship streaked skyward, passing through Mach 30, her speed still increasing. Manda glanced at the hologram and was dismayed by what she saw.

She laid her hand on Morian's arm, leaned toward

him and said quietly, "Are you sure about this, Captain? There are hundreds of them out there. If we go in on our own..." Instead of finishing the sentence, she simply shook her head.

"We have to do what we can to give the people down there more time," Morian replied. "Every second we can buy for them could save hundreds of lives. We don't have a choice."

"Understood, sir." *A frontal assault*, she thought. *The Swarm won't be expecting it. But we're going to need all the help we can get. Where the hell is the IMFP fleet?*

"Morian to Domino."

"This is Domino. Go ahead, Captain."

"Deploy your squadron as soon as we break through into the black, Commander," he said. "We're making a frontal assault. You're to form a screen around *Avenger*. Copy?"

"Copy, Captain."

"Go to it, Danis, and good hunting. Morian out."

"Ms. Fargo," Morian said over the open comms. "Ready forward missile tubes and Big Charlie and fire on my command." Big Charlie was the ship's capital rail gun. It fired forward; its MOA adjustable only by five degrees in any direction.

"Aye, Captain."

"Mr. Sen. Steer three points to starboard and hold your course."

"Three points to starboard and holding, Captain."

The ship altered course slightly, aligning herself with the center mass of the Swarm fleet.

"Prepare to come about on my mark, Mr. Sen, and

steer ninety degrees to port," Morian said calmly into the comms, his seeming lack of excitement, or concern, designed to calm the bridge crew.

"Ms. Fargo," he continued, "load tubes one through thirty-nine with Rapiers and prepare to fire as we come about."

The Rapier missiles had been upgraded some months earlier and fitted with MIT—multiple independently targetable—warheads.

"Ms. Fargo," Morian said. "Confirm all missile tubes and railguns, including the capital weapon, are fully charged."

"Confirmed, Captain."

"Captain," Omario Kingston said. "Wok's fleet does not appear to be moving."

"He knows what he is doing, Mr. Kingston," Morian said. "He'll be here when we need him. Now, please focus on the task ahead."

Manda leaned toward him, raised a hand to her mouth so no one could see, and whispered, "Well said, Captain."

"Thank you, Commander." He clenched his jaw, as he always did when he was thinking, then leaned toward her and said, also in a whisper. "Let's just hope I'm right."

Avenger continued to claw her way upward for some several minutes more until finally she attained escape velocity at a little more than forty-nine thousand kilometers per hour and burst through the Exosphere into the blackness of space. At that point her main engines shut down and the crew's restraints slackened and then released.

The alarms began to sound in the hangar as it depressurized and the great door began to open.

"Ranger Squadron, deploy in numbers ascending," Danis said. "Ranger Leader first."

On the bridge, Morian leaped to his feet and stepped quickly to the command rail. Manda quickly joined him.

"Ms. Fargo," Morian said, "let go forward tubes."

"Missiles away, Captain," Fargo replied, and they all watched the giant hologram in silence as ten Rapier missiles streaked toward the oncoming Swarm fleet, quickly accelerating to Mach 40.

At five kilometers out from the leading Blue craft, the fifteen-kilogram warheads burst and the tiny thrusters of the twenty point-five-kilogram Dutrinium projectiles each Rapier carried fired and drove them onward; two-hundred of them in all.

But that wasn't all. The ship shuddered under the force of the recoil as Big Charlie also fired. The twenty-kilogram round—it looked like a fifteen-gallon drum—left the weapon at a muzzle velocity in excess of five thousand meters per second; at proximity, the projectile exploded, sending eighty point-two-five-kilogram Dutrinium orbs streaking out in all directions, turning Big Charlie effectively into a giant shotgun... with devastating effect.

Morian, Haal, and the rest of the bridge crew watched breathlessly as the tiny kinetic warheads approached their targets.

As the first blue light on the hologram winked out, the noise of cheering from the crew echoed around the bridge.

Morian smiled, held up a hand for silence, and watched as more blue lights winked out. As always, though, many of the warheads missed or, because of the angle of attack, were deflected. Nevertheless, he counted seventy-three enemy craft destroyed. That number was confirmed by the ever-changing datanet scrolling above the hologram. *Seventy-three down,* he thought. *Only two-thousand-nine-hundred-twenty-seven to go. I think we may be in a little trouble. Where the hell are you, Wok?*

The distance between *Avenger* and the Swarm fleet was closing fast.

Morian confirmed that his fighters were away, then turned again to the hologram and said over the open comms, "Bring her about ninety degrees to port, Mr. Sen. Ms. Fargo, let go the broadside as we come to bear, then reload and fire again; missiles and point defense fire as they close with us."

Sen reversed the ship's main thrusters and then adjusted them to bring the great ship about.

It seemed to Haal that the maneuver was taking forever, but in reality it took Sen only three minutes and twenty seconds to present the ship's starboard side to the enemy.

"Fire at will, Ms. Fargo," Morian said, a lot calmer than he felt. And twenty Rapiers burst from the portside missile tubes.

"Rapiers! Reload tubes one through thirty-nine and fire at will," Fargo shouted into the comms.

As the distance between *Avenger* and the leading ships of the Swarm fleet continued to close, she fired broadside after broadside of Rapiers with devastating effect. By the time they came within range of point defense weapons, Morian counted more than two-hundred-thirty of the blue-haloed craft had been destroyed, but he knew it wasn't enough; not nearly enough. The Swarm had the advantage of overwhelming numbers.

Avenger's point defense weapons came online. Railguns to starboard, topside and below began firing. Volley after volley of the small Saber missiles began to take their toll. It was, as they say, like shooting fish in a barrel. There were so many Swarm ships it was almost impossible to miss.

Ranger Squadron's remaining ten fighters were fanned out in five flights of two protecting her flanks. Jackknife, in his vintage Veridian fighter, was ranging back and forth picking off enemy craft, almost at will.

Morian nodded as he stared down at the hologram. The battle was going well, but *Avenger* was slowly but surely taking fire.

"Keep the barrage going, Ms. Fargo. We have to hold them until Wok and the fleet arrive."

"If they ever do arrive," Sen muttered over the open comms.

"What was that, Mr. Sen?" Morian asked. "I didn't quite catch it."

"Nothing, Captain. I was just talking to myself."

"Try to keep it to yourself, Mr. Sen. Damage report, Mr. Kingston."

"Nothing serious, Captain. Turret Seven took a hit and is inoperable, but there are no casualties... so far. There's a small amount of damage to the hull on deck three on the starboard side, but there's no breach. Power cell three is down to eighty-one percent. The shields are holding at... seventy-seven percent. Nothing to worry yourself about, Captain."

Morian nodded. *Nothing to worry about? There will be if we don't get help soon. We can't keep this up much longer. We'll be out of ammu—*

"Captain Morian, this is the Red Dragon. Do you copy?" Tiger Wok's voice echoed around the bridge.

"This is Morian. Go ahead, Captain."

"Ah, there you are at last, my friend. We have been unable to reach you. I have good news. Our people, most of them, have been evacuated from the city. Most of them are in the bunkers to the north. You have done well and, on behalf of the people of Freyja, I thank you. We still have a little cleaning up to do down here, but I should be with you shortly."

"We're relying on it, Captain," Morian said.

"Captain," Kingston said. "The Blues seem to be withdrawing... I think they are regrouping?"

Morian looked down at the hologram. It was true. The Swarm fighters were withdrawing, rejoining the main body of the fleet, and Morian had the awful feeling that the worst was yet to come.

Chapter Forty-Two

Cooperative Chaos

The Swarm's fleet was indeed regrouping. The everchanging numbers on the datanet scrolling above the hologram were fluctuating between a low of eighteen-hundred-fifty and a high of two-thousand-twenty. The hologram itself showed them spread out over a vast area just beyond Freyja's second moon some eight-hundred-twenty thousand kilometers out.

Morian was seated in his command chair gloomily watching the numbers slowly grow as, in small groups, the defeated spearhead rejoined the main body of the Swarm fleet. *They outnumber us almost ten to one,* he thought, *and most of the IMFP ships are antiques.*

"Commander Haal," he said, removing his hand from his chin.

She turned from the rail and looked back at him. "Yes, Captain?"

"Give the order to disengage and have the squadron return to the ship and rearm."

"Aye, Captain. How long d'you think we have?"

"I would have thought you would know that better than I," he said smiling.

"It doesn't work like that, I'm afraid," she replied. "It's not like I can turn it on and off at will."

"I know that," he said, "and the answer to your question is... I don't know either. Once they regroup, it will take them less than thirty minutes to get here, so we need to remain at battle stations. Tell Commander Morian she's to rearm as quickly as possible and be ready to deploy at a moment's notice."

"Aye, Captain." And she broadcast the squadron recall over the open comms and then contacted Danis on a closed channel and relayed Morian's orders to her.

* * *

Gian heard the transmission and glanced out through his canopy. Danis was fifty meters away to the left and slightly ahead.

"Time to go home to Momma, Ranger Squadron," Danis's voice came over the comms. "Well done, everyone." They hadn't lost a single pilot.

Gian maintained his position as Danis made the turn back to the ship and watched as Jackknife's Veridian joined them to her left. *Hah,* he thought, *that old bucket of rust is still in one piece.*

* * *

What the hell are they doing? Morian wondered as he sat and stared at the hologram. *Why aren't they moving?*

For almost an hour he'd sat there watching their numbers grow to more than twenty-one hundred. It was a daunting sight, a dense, blue blob just to the right of the moon.

"Weapons report, please, Ms. Fargo," he said finally, more for want of something to do rather than a need to know.

"With the exception of Turret Seven, all weapons are hot, Captain," Fargo replied.

"Ammunition?" he asked.

"Rapiers at seventy-three percent," she replied. "Sabers at eighty, twenty kaygee canisters at fifty-four percent—only one-hundred-sixty-three left—and 8omm railgun rounds are at seventy-seven percent."

Morian nodded and stared despondently at the stationary blue blob.

Inwardly, he shook his head and thought, *It's not enough. There are too many of them. We're outnumbered more than fifteen to one. Where the hell is Wok? If he—*

"Ms. Lowry," he said, interrupting his own thoughts. "See if you can raise Captain Wok." Then he sat back in his chair, steepled his fingers, touched them to his lips and waited.

"No contact, Captain," Lowry said.

"Keep trying, Ms. Lowry."

Damn! Morian thought savagely. *If he lets us down... There's no way we'll be able to hold them off.*

He stared at the hologram. *What the hell are they waiting for?* Then... he noticed something. He sat up in his chair, stared at the hologram, stood up, went to the rail and gripped it with both hands.

"They're on the move," he said urgently over the open comms. "I need their speed, Mr. Kingston."

"Almost thirty-thousand-kilometers per hour, Captain."

"Twenty-seven minutes, then," Morian said. "Give or take. Deploy the squadron, Commander. Anything from Wok yet, Ms. Lowry?"

"No, Captain. I'm still trying."

* * *

Gian glanced at his copilot's image on the small screen and said, "You ready, Andra?"

"I'm ready."

He tried to turn and look over his shoulder at his battle buddy, but his restraints were too tight.

"All right," he said. "Just stay calm. We're going to get through this."

"I have confidence in you," she replied.

The squadron had deployed in three flights of three and one of two, with Jackknife bringing the number of aircraft to eleven. Gian, Danis and Jackknife making up the lead flight.

The pirate flew up alongside, waggled his wings, grinned at him and gave him a thumbs-up.

"Get back in formation, Jackknife," Danis growled.

"Yes, ma'am." He gave Gian a wave, banked away and formed up on her left side and a little to her rear.

"Contact in ten seconds," Andra said.

"Bring it on," Gian muttered. Gian's scanners flashed red, and his proximity alarms buzzed in his ear. He glanced at his screens. *There they are...*

There were so many Swarm craft heading toward them at what he estimated at least Mach 15 that he couldn't count them.

Oh hell! Here we go! "Hold tight, Andra."

His fingertips flew over the thruster controls. He dropped the power to both starboard engines to ten percent and maxed out the two on the port side, sending the F32A into a crazy, spinning turn to starboard.

Out of the corner of his eye, he saw Danis go vertical and Jackknife peel away to port, just in time to see the swarm of blue haloed craft flash by.

He restored full power to his two starboard engines, reversed thrust, flipped the fuselage and went after them. He felt his inertia dampeners tighten around him as the F32 passed through Mach 20, putting him on the tail of the closest group of three Swarm fighters. He fired his railguns at the closest of the three and watched the projectiles hammer home, tearing the alien ship in half.

He eased back on the power, adjusted his trajectory slightly and fired again. "Gotcha, you bastard!" he yelled out loud as the second enemy craft went spinning away out of control. *Now for number three!* he thought as again he adjusted his trajectory. But number three didn't go down so easily. It began to twist and turn, going through a series of evasive maneuvers Gian thought vaguely familiar. He stayed with him, fired a short burst but missed. The two craft, one behind the other, rolled, banked, turned and climbed as Gian slowly closed the gap between them. He fired. A stream of 50-caliber slugs tore through the blue halo and ripped off the craft's starboard upper weapon platform, sending it spinning out of control. *Oh yeah*, he thought jubilantly. *I definitely have E-9 down.*

He looked around, looking for more targets, only to find he was on his own.

"Joker to Domino."

"Where the hell are you, Joker?" Danis yelled. "I have two on my tail and I can't shake them."

"I see you," Gian said. "Hang in there. I'm on my way."

He reversed his thrusters, flipped the fuselage, and poured on the power.

"Stand by, Domino," Gian said. "Go hard to port. I'll take lefty out first."

"Just don't shoot me instead," she said as she made a hard left turn.

Gian smiled to himself at the jab. *She's never going to let me forget that one,* he thought as he thumbed the triggers and watched as the Swarm ship exploded in a ball of blue fire.

He made a sharp turn to port and went after the second alien. Danis held the turn, so did the enemy fighter, and so did Gian; the enemy firing blast after blast of blue fire at Danis. But her turn was so tight they all missed. Unfortunately, the same held true for Gian.

"Damn, damn, damn!" he yelled.

"What is it? What's wrong?" Andra asked.

"I can't cut the angle. Its speed's too fast. The turn's too tight." He tried to decrease the MOA, but the F32 was at its limit and no matter what he did, he couldn't obtain a lock.

"Damn it!" he yelled.

"Gian. Get this son of a bitch off me before he kills me," Danis yelled.

"Let me try," Andra said. A couple seconds passed. They felt like hours to Gian as he held the turn. *It's not working!* he thought, but then, the Swarm craft jerked, its turn loosened and slowly it seemed to drift outward. Gian's targeting systems locked on. His screens turned green, confirming the lock, and he thumbed the triggers. The twin streams of slugs impacted the enemy fighter. Its halo flashed bright blue as it tried to deflect them, then turned white, then died altogether and the ship shattered into thousands of tiny pieces.

"Gotcha," Gian said. "You're all clear now, Domino."

"About damn time, Joker," she said. "But thanks."

"I thought for a minute you weren't going to manage it," he said to Andra as he followed Danis.

"It takes a little time," she replied, "and no little effort."

The three fighters, two F32As and the vintage Veridian, slipped into their designated position on *Avenger's* starboard bow, and for more than twenty minutes the great ship and her Ranger Squadron protective screen battled to hold off one attack after another with almost no losses or damage, but things were about to change; ammunition was running low.

The battle raged on. Twenty minutes in, Gian had personally destroyed seven more enemy craft for a grand total of twelve, but he was down to his last Saber missile and his railgun ammunition was down to less than ten percent. Danis had ordered him to dock and rearm.

It took Gian less than ten minutes to rearm before he was back out again and approximately a kilometer out from the doors when his proximity alarm sounded and his screens flashed red. He glanced at his screens, then turned frantically in his seat, trying to get a visual.

"There he is," Andra shouted. "He's on our five o'clock low."

Gian flipped the F32 and put it into a steep climb, trying for an Immelmann turn that would put him on his opponent's tail, but somehow the Blue anticipated the tactic and followed him, staying on his tail, closing the distance between them. Gian exited the Immelmann, flipped the F32, and tried to execute a rolling scissors maneuver and force the Blue to overshoot, again putting him on its tail. Again, it didn't work.

"Damn it, Andra," he shouted. "I can't shake the damn thing."

"I'm trying," she shouted back, "but I can't seem to grab this one."

"Warning. Target lock. Target lock," the dispassionate digital voice intoned. "Impact imminent."

"Come on, come on," Gian shouted as his fingers desperately flew over the controls, pushing the fighter to its limits.

He now had a visual. The enemy fighter was off his starboard side and a little to his rear. The enemy craft's portside weapons platforms were trained on him. He jerked the F32 hard to starboard and reversed thrust. The F32 veered toward the enemy craft and slowed. He thought he had him, but he didn't. The enemy fired. A bolt of blue lightning seared across his bow so close that for a second even his visor couldn't cut the glare, and it almost blinded him. His vision cleared. He shook his head and glanced to his right. The enemy craft was still there, its weapons locked on to him.

"Warning. Target Lock. Target Lock. Impact imminent."

"I know. I know, damn it," Gian shouted, glancing again to his right, expecting to see the enemy's weapons fire and tear the F32 apart. Instead, he turned his head just in time to see it explode in a flash of brilliant blue fire.

"You're all clear, Joker," Jackknife's voice came over the comms as the Veridian slipped up alongside him.

"Holy... where the hell did you come from?" Gian shouted. "He was about to shoot. I was done for. You saved us."

"You're welcome, but isn't that what we're here for?"

"Nice work, Jackknife," Danis said as she joined them on Gian's port side.

"Thanks, but listen, both of you," Jackknife said. "I need you to follow me. Go to my three o'clock; do it now!"

"What? Why?" Danis asked.

"There's no time to explain. Just do it."

Gian moved immediately but noticed that Danis was holding back. Clearly, as squadron leader, she wasn't used to taking orders from anyone, much less a rogue pirate.

Jackknife obviously wasn't used to fighting as part of

a team, but Gian trusted him and his instincts. He also knew something Danis didn't know: Jackknife had the Sight, though he'd never admit it. So Gian took a position on Jackknife's starboard side. Danis came late, but she eventually pulled into position to Gian's right.

"What the hell are we doing, Jackknife?" she shouted.

"Trust me. Stay with me," Jackknife said as he began a long sweeping turn to port, just as three Swarm ships came swooping in from above, right into their sights. Gian, taken totally by surprise, instinctively thumbed his triggers and fired, almost in unison with Danis and Jackknife. The three Swarm ships couldn't have known what hit them. All three vaporized in a single vast explosion.

"Oh wow, yay!" Gian shouted. "That was... damn scary, but a whole lot of fun. Yeehah!"

"Stay with me," Jackknife said. "There's more on the way, but we need to go to sector seven." And he did a barrel roll and took off with Gian right beside him and Danis trailing along behind them.

And Gian suddenly knew that fighting this still largely unknown enemy was going to be a whole lot easier with Jackknife on their side.

* * *

Meanwhile, back on *Avenger,* Morian was managing to somehow hold on, though for how much longer he didn't know, and the lack of support was beginning to worry him. The only thought that gave him a modicum of peace of mind was that Manda Haal had not yet issued any dire warnings. Still, he kept glancing sideways at her only to receive a slight shake of the head and a reassuring smile in return.

They were standing together at the rail, watching the progress of the battle through the screens and on the hologram.

The numbers were daunting. So far the enemy's losses were upward of eight hundred to his own losses of two F32As, three more gun turrets—one topside and two on the port side—a minor hull breach of Deck 7, with some minor damage to the hull on the port side of the keel. None of it more than was expected—less, in fact— but Morian had never been one to let his guard down, and he wasn't about to start.

"Comms. Anything from Wok yet?" he asked, already knowing the answer. Lowry would have informed him if there had been.

"Nothing yet, Captain," she replied.

He nodded and said, "Keep trying. Let me know as soon as you hear something."

"They've zeroed in on power cell three," Jiksar shouted. "Shields are at seventy percent, and we're taking multiple hits."

How could they know about that power cell? Morian wondered. *Do they have the same abilities we do? No, it must be just a coincidence.*

"Commander, keep an eye on that power cell and notify me if it drops below fifty-five percent."

Manda nodded.

"Weapons," Morian said. "Ammunition status?"

"Everything is running low, Captain."

"That tells me nothing, Ms. Fargo. How low is low?"

"Sabers at forty-one percent," she replied. "Rapiers at twenty-two. Big Charlie... seventeen percent, and railgun ammunition is down to nineteen percent. At the present rate of fire, we'll be all out in less than thirty minutes."

That was not what Morian wanted to hear, but there was nothing he could do about it other than to order Fargo to try to conserve her ammunition, something he didn't dare do in the face of such overwhelming forces.

And so the battle raged on and the damage reports kept coming in. Over the next several minutes they lost two more gun turrets, and Morian ordered the ammunition from the damaged turrets to be pulled and redistributed as needed. The one unexpected positive was that the new armor was holding up and performing better than expected.

"Captain." Commander Haal turned to face him. "Power cell three is down to sixty-four percent. Shields are still holding, but we'll begin to lose density on the forward shields if it drops below sixty. The Swarm ships are attacking our weak points. They're getting smarter. We need to change strategy."

"What about Ranger Squadron?" Morian asked.

"They've lost two fighters. They're still deployed and effective to port and starboard."

He shook his head thoughtfully, knowing that Manda was right, and that they couldn't maintain their static position for much longer. It was time to make a change. Everyone on the bridge had known that this moment would come. Morian just didn't think it would come so quickly.

"Pull Ranger Squadron in closer and prepare to stage for their docking," he said. "But don't have them dock yet. Just make sure Domino's ready."

"Captain, the numbers of enemy craft aft and topside are increasing," Kingston shouted.

"Stand by to come about and roll the ship fifteen degrees to port," Morian said, ordering a maneuver that would present his broadside to the enemy.

"Their numbers are increasing at twice the rate we anticipated, Captain," Kingston shouted again.

Damn it! We aren't ready yet.

"Fuel cell three is down to fifty-five percent," Jiksar shouted.

"Port side railguns are at eleven percent," Fargo shouted.

"Hold your course, Mr. Sen," Morian said. "Don't let up."

"Captain." Manda's voice was a little more tense than usual. "Ranger Squadron has lost another fighter, and they are too far out to dock. They are under pressure, Captain. They are being overwhelmed."

"Captain," Lowry said over the open comms. "I cannot make contact with Tiger Wok or his fleet. I think he must have abandoned us."

Chapter Forty-Three

Tiger Wok

An hour earlier

Tiger Wok was on the bridge of the light battle cruiser, the *Red Dragon*, at an altitude of six-hundred kilometers in low synchronous orbit. He was slumped in his command chair watching the air battle still raging above Haven's shipyards on his view screens; the *Red Dragon* had no hologram. Nor did she carry any fighters. She was just seven-hundred-fifty-meters long with a crew of sixty.

The buffer that Captain Morian and the *Avenger* had provided had given them just enough time to evacuate most of their people out of the city into the bunkers to the north. There were still a few stubborn holdouts, but even they had gone underground, into basements and dugouts.

One by one the fleet was destroying the last of the lingering Swarm ships. The opening battle for Haven was almost over. The battle for Freyja was about to begin.

Wok stirred himself, sat upright and shouted, "Why can I still not get hold of Captain Morian?"

"We lost power cell two on that last run," his pilot said. "All comms are down. Tech is working to bypass it. Comms should be back up soon."

"Good. What about Jackknife? We cannot communicate with him either?"

"No sir. Not yet. Soon."

"Damn it," Wok shouted. "Is anything at all working? What about *Avenger?* Where is she?"

"We don't know sir. Once they engaged the Swarm, the battle took them farther and farther away from Freyja. We won't be able to pick them up on long-range scans until we clear the magnetosphere."

"How much longer before we can get out of here and go to her aid?"

"The fleet is beginning to turn the tide over Haven," the pilot replied. "Not long, I think."

"You think? You think?" Wok muttered to himself. "I want to go now!" he shouted to no one in particular. No one dared to answer or even look at him.

Wok was desperate to get out there and go to the assistance of *Avenger*, but he couldn't leave the rest of the fleet; not until the battle for Haven was over. Nor could he split the fleet, and many of the pirates were off somewhere else, doing their own thing. Many more had hastily formed ad hoc fighting groups during the battle.

Yes, he had a verbal agreement and a plan to coordinate most of the senior captains, but now, with the comms down, he couldn't contact any of them. Some were even on different frequencies. Freyja's communications network was... chaotic. *Maybe,* he thought, *a properly integrated system and a clear chain of incident command as used by the USF might not be such a bad thing after all.*

"How long," he shouted, "until the bypass is completed and comms are back up?"

"Any minute now," the copilot replied. "The last ETA they gave us was six minutes, but that was seven minutes ago."

The ship shook as the shields absorbed a volley of plasma fire.

"Incoming. Two at two-six-three point one-nine," Tactical said. "Targets eliminated."

Wok loved the *Red Dragon* but wished she had the firepower of the *Avenger.*

"Captain," the copilot said, "we have one narrow line of sight channel open. We can send a message directly to any nearby ship."

"Finally. Thank the Gods. Send to... What's the closest ship?"

"We're locked on to an unidentified cruiser, Captain. over there." The copilot pointed to the forward view screens. "Stand by."

The copilot transmitted, "This is *Red Dragon.* Do you copy?" And then waited for a response.

"This is Kimura Fan of the *Black Witch.* What happened to you, Wok? No one has been able to contact you for almost an hour."

"Tell him we have comms problems," Wok said. "And then tell him I need him to relay this to the fleet: On my mark, all ships with TK abilities are to close on and form up around *Red Dragon*. Tell him to get back to me when he's sent the message."

The copilot relayed the message. Then turned again to Wok, nodded and said, "Message acknowledged, Captain."

This has to work, he thought as he stared at the *Black Witch*. *It must work. It's the only way we can get rid of the rest of these Blues fast enough for us get to the Avenger. She has to hold out for just a little longer.*

Wok really did love the *Red Dragon*. She'd been with him for more years than he could remember. She was old and cranky, but well-armored and her weapons systems were top-notch, considering her age. He closed his eyes and listened to the sounds of the battle raging around her. Again and again she shuddered under the impact of direct plasma hits, but the shields and her armor held. She shuddered under the recoils of her eighteen rail guns, and he was glad that he didn't accept the offer from the Stryker Corporation to upgrade her weapons systems a year ago.

"Captain," the copilot said. "Kimura Fan has relayed the message, and so far nineteen IMPF vessels with crew members with TK abilities aboard are heading for the rendezvous at our coordinates."

"Good, tell them..." He paused, then shouted for all to hear, "Where the hell are my comms?"

"They're up, Captain," the copilot said. "They just came back online."

"Thank the stars for that. Mr. Kadrie. Put me on an open channel to the fleet."

"Aye, Captain," Kadrie replied. "You are open to the fleet."

"This is Tiger Wok to all captains with crew aboard that have TK abilities. Let's put an end to this. Close in on *Red Dragon*. We'll combine our TK forces and wipe out the rest of the Blues. We can do this, but we need to do it together. Agreed?"

He didn't bother to count the responses. He could see on his screens that more than twenty ships had ceased firing and were beginning to gather around the *Red Dragon.*

It appeared, though, that the Swarm was going to try to take advantage of the close grouping of the IMPF ships, for they, too, were grouping together, lining up for attack runs.

"I think we're ready, Captain," the copilot said. "I mean, look at the screens. I've never seen so many ships grouped so tightly together. If we're going to do this, now would be a good time."

"Very well," Wok said. "Send this message: All captains converge on *Red Dragon* and assemble your TK operatives at your forward screens. Have them concentrate on the closest Swarm grouping. Let's see if we can do a little damage."

The copilot sent the transmission. Wok nodded and said, "Quiet on the bridge." Then he closed his eyes and began to concentrate.

Many of the enemy ships were too far away to feel the effects of Wok's enhanced abilities, but many more were close enough. Even so, the effort needed to move an entire ship, or group of ships, was immense. He was fighting not only their natural momentum, but also the thrust of their drives. The first few minutes were draining but, as the TK from the ships around him began to merge with his, he felt the strain of trying to push one ship into another begin to ease.

Wok opened his eyes and concentrated on the leading Blue craft. He stared at it, not blinking, not wanting to lose the line of sight. For a moment nothing happened, then it slowed and veered hard to starboard, impacting the one closest to it. Both craft exploded in a gigantic ball of blue fire.

Wok nodded and smiled, his dark eyes glittering. Then he turned his attention to the next in line. This time it was easier. The enemy drifted upward, slamming into the keel of the one above it; it, in turn, crashed into its neighbor, all with devastating effects.

Wok's bridge crew looked on in amazement as slowly the Swarm ships drew closer, their fleet turned into a vast debris field. Within minutes, the Swarm ships to the rear of the fleet, seeing what was happening ahead, began to turn and run.

* * *

"Aft shields are down to fourteen percent," Jiksar shouted from his station in Tactical. "We will not be able to withstand another major hit."

"Topside railguns are at eleven percent," Fargo called more calmly.

Morian stared first at the screens, then at the hologram, resisting the temptation to shake his head. The number of enemy craft was... overwhelming.

Where the hell are you, Wok? he thought. *If we don't get help, and soon, we're done for.*

He glanced to his left at Manda, his eyebrows raised in question. She pursed her lips and gave him a slight shake of her head.

"Anything from Domino and the squadron, Ms. Lowry?" he asked.

"They are still not responding, Captain."

"How about Wok?"

"Not much. Just some clutter..." Lowry replied. "Mostly odd words and partial sentences, all unintelligible. He appears to be having trouble with his Comms. I think he must still be engaging the enemy over Haven."

Morian took a deep breath, stared down at the hologram, then up at the datanet. *Still more than fifteen hundred,* he thought. *Here they come again...* He glanced up at the screens. The entire enemy fleet was on the move and heading toward them... fast. *This is it, then. The old girl can't hold together much longer... a few more minutes at most.* He took another deep breath, turned to Manda and said, "Not much longer, Commander. I'd just like to say—"

"Captain," Omario Kingston shouted, interrupting him. "We have incoming on our six."

Morian sighed deeply and said, "How many, Mr. Kingston?"

"Too many! A lot... sixty... eighty... it's... Oh my God.

Wait." Kingston sat back down, the fingertips of both hands flying over his screens.

Morian, waiting for and fearing the worst, stared at the screens through half-closed eyes, watching as the enemy ships approached.

"Captain Morian," Wok's voice on open comms echoed around the bridge. "It's good to see you are still in one piece, my friend."

The image of the *Red Dragon* filled the rear-view screens, along with more than two dozen IMFP ships of varying classes and sizes, the rest of the fleet in a vast fan formation following behind them.

Minutes later, they were alongside, all sides, topside, starboard, port, and below the keel, and they were engaging the approaching Swarm fighters.

"It's Tiger Wok," Haltar Sen yelled and jumped up from his seat waving his arms in the air. "It's Wok and the rest of his fleet. They came. They didn't abandon us after all."

The rest of the bridge crew also jumped to their feet, cheering, clapping, hooting and waving.

"Tiger," Morian shouted, waving for the crew to calm down. "Not one damn moment too soon. Where the hell have you been? We've been trying to reach you for more than an hour."

"I'm sorry it took us so long, Captain. Many more enemy ships attacked Freyja than we expected. But we took care of them."

"You couldn't have cut it any closer," Morian replied. "Another two minutes and all you would have found was a debris field. You arrived just in time."

"But we are here now, my friend, and you are still all in one piece, so all is good. Now you just sit back and witness the power of the free people of Freyja."

Morian and Manda looked at one another, wondering what Wok was talking about. Manda shrugged. Morian shook his head. They both turned to stare at the forward view screens. Wok's ship, easily identifiable by the Red Dragon emblem painted on her bow, was at the center of a formation of more than twenty ships, but they were all stationary. Not one of them was moving.

"What the hell is he doing?" Morian muttered as he gripped the rail.

It was a rhetorical question meant for nobody in particular, but Manda answered it anyway.

"Your guess is as good as mine, Captain," she said, not taking her eyes off the screens for even a second.

Not many seconds later, to their utter amazement, they watched as the four leading ships of the approaching Swarm fleet veered off course and collided with one another. The result was a spectacular chain explosion. One after another, the four ships exploded in gigantic bursts of brilliant blue. And, seemingly without Wok and his fleet firing a shot.

"They must be using TK," Manda said. "They've figured out how to combine their abilities."

For a moment, Morian said nothing. He continued to watch as dozens of Swarm ships destroyed themselves.

"I think you're right," Richard said. "That's exactly what they're doing... We've talked about it before. The theory that the abilities could be combined has been mentioned many times, but no one has ever tried to put it into practice. Now we're seeing it firsthand... and it works."

"It's amazing," Manda said, shaking her head.

"Red Dragon to Avenger. Do you copy?"

"Copy," Morian said. "Go ahead, Captain."

"It appears they've had enough," Wok said. "The Swarm is leaving."

Morian looked down at the hologram. It did indeed look like the bulk of the Swarm had withdrawn and was heading out into deep space, leaving behind a vast debris field that encompassed more than three-hundred-million cubic kilometers.

"That would appear to be so, Tiger," Morian said. "That was an amazing display with an unbelievable result. You must have destroyed more than a hundred of them."

"More than two hundred," Wok replied, "if you include those we destroyed over Freyja. Is it not sensational, my friend, this new extension of our abilities?"

"Indeed it is, Captain," Morian said and dropped down into his command chair and wiped his forehead. "That was a long one, Tiger... One I'll never forget."

Wok laughed and said, "You take these things much too seriously. What will be will be, and there's nothing we can do about it, so live life to the full and enjoy every minute of it, my friend."

Morian nodded, even though he knew Wok couldn't see him, and said, "You're right, and from now on I'll try to do just that. In the meantime, I'd like to invite you aboard, Tiger. We need to talk."

"And talk we shall. I will join you shortly." The

comms clicked off. Morian smiled, shook his head and saluted the image of the *Red Dragon* floating in space not more than a kilometer off *Avenger's* port bow.

"Nice work, my friend," Morian muttered. "I owe you one!"

"Domino is back on line, sir," Manda Haal said as she sat down beside him.

Morian opened a personal channel and spoke into his data pad, "Danis, are you all right? Where are you?"

"Yes, mostly. I lost another pilot. We're down to seven, eight if you include that crazy son of a... Jackknife. It's so good to hear your voice, Richard."

"You too, Danis. How did Gian do today? You didn't lose him, I hope."

"No. He was amazing. So was Elio. I'm going to miss them both. How about you? How's *Avenger*?"

"It was touch and go for a while. We've taken some damage, but nothing that can't be repaired. Thank God Wok finally showed up. It would have been a different story if he hadn't, but we can talk about that later... Come on home, Danis."

* * *

It was more than an hour later when Tiger Wok and two of his senior crewmen joined Morian and Manda Haal in *Avenger's* conference room, a huge smile on his lips, his dark eyes glittering, laughing, his black beard divided into five tufts each tied with a tiny red silk bow.

"Ah, my friends," he said, his arms raised expansively. "It is so good to see you."

He stepped quickly forward, grasped Morian's right hand in both of his and shook it vigorously. Then he stepped forward, wrapped his arms around him and hugged him. Morian was startled. This was something he'd never experienced before, and he didn't know how to respond. Fortunately, he didn't have to because Wok let go of him, turned to Manda, grasped her by the shoulders and kissed her on both cheeks, leaving her shocked and a little bemused.

"I think we deserve a drink, Captain," Morian said, removing the cap from a fifteen-year-old bottle of Orsian rum and pouring five large shots.

"To victory and good friends," Morian said, then tossed his down in a single swallow.

"To victory and good friends," the rest of the group repeated and tossed theirs down too.

Wok looked at his glass, smacked his lips, then looked at the bottle, picked it up, poured himself another and tossed that down too.

"That is some good stuff," he said appreciatively and set his glass down on the table. "Where did you get it? Ah, but never mind. I am here as your good friend," he said as they all sat down at the table. "And to thank you, Richard, for your sacrifice and for giving us the time we needed to evacuate the city. I also must thank you, Manda, for the warning. Without it, our people would all have been destroyed. I speak for the people of Freyja when I thank you both and, of course..." He looked around the room. "*Avenger.*"

"Your thanks are welcome," Krista, the ship's AI,

replied, "but they are not necessary. I was just doing my job."

The five people in the room looked at one another and burst out laughing.

"Seriously, Wok," Morian said, "you lost a lot of ships and good people today. We wish to express our sincere condolences for your losses. The *Avenger* and the USF will be forever grateful."

"Yes, it is indeed sad that we lost so many, but that is war, is it not?" Wok said as he looked down at his hands clasped together on the tabletop.

"You're a fine leader, Tiger Wok," Morian said. "You inspired so many people to follow you into... In some cases to their deaths."

"Ah, but you are wrong, Captain." Wok wagged his finger from side to side. "You see, the free people of Freyja are just that: they are free. They do not follow me because of my leadership. They do not follow me because they are told to. They follow me because they all are free to decide for themselves. Each person, each ship, knows what is best for them. And it is in desperate times like these that free individuals make the right choices. Yes, I asked them to follow me, but the choice was theirs to make."

"I understand and agree," Morian said. "But you shouldn't be so self-deprecating. It was because they trusted you and your leadership that they made the right choice."

"Perhaps you are right, Captain. Perhaps you are right... But you said you wanted to talk?"

"I do." Morian nodded. "It's time for us to leave

you. I must go back to Orso and report what we've found here on Freyja, and persuade the powers that be back home of the opportunities for a beneficial alliance."

Wok looked up with some concern, which Morian noticed.

"There's no need for you to worry," Morian said. "We have no interest in colonizing Freyja. It will always belong to the free people. We'll bring in people, resources and materials to help with the shipyards; that's it. And we'll build those two new Slipstream stations, but they too will belong to Freyja. In return, we'll contract your shipyards to update the USF fleet and build a whole new class of warships. And the USF will be here to protect you from future attacks. Your world will prosper, Tiger Wok."

Wok grinned, leaned back in his chair and opened his arms wide. "Yes. What you're offering and what you expect in return... It is acceptable. I, and the Board of Directors, will welcome you to Freyja. Go back to Orso, my friend, and we will see you again soon."

"They will?" Morian asked. "So you *are* the one who makes the decisions on Freyja!"

He smiled and said, "I am but a small voice among many. However..." He tilted his head, narrowed his eyes and showed his gleaming white teeth and, like Danis, Morian was reminded of a hungry krellfish.

Wok didn't bother to finish. His meaning was clear. He was indeed the man who made the important decisions on Freyja. Instead, he stood up, grabbed the bottle of rum, put it to his lips and took a huge swallow, then handed it to Morian and nodded for him to do the same. He did, then passed the bottle around the room.

"Goodbye, Tiger Wok," Morian said. "We'll return soon."

"Travel safely, my friends." Wok gave a slight bow of his head and turned to leave. The door slid open and then closed behind him.

Chapter Forty-Four

The Return Home

Several hours later, as *Avenger's* crew worked to complete the preparations for the long journey home, Manda Haal was seated at one of the navigation consoles, a hologramic map of the relevant star systems they would have to pass through floating in front of her.

Tiger Wok had arranged for the ship to be resupplied, and the deck crews were working hard to bring aboard and store millions of rounds of ammunition and hundreds of outdated, obsolete missiles which, in and of themselves, would require a copious amount of extra work to make them serviceable: they would fit *Avenger's* tubes, but the warheads had to be changed and electronic systems had to be reconfigured.

"How's it going?" Morian asked as he joined Manda at the console.

Manda looked up at him and rubbed her eyes.

Visions of the route, of the Slipstreams they needed to use, were flitting through her mind one right after the other.

"It's going well, Captain," she replied. "Just a few more calculations and we should be ready to go."

She stared at the hologram. It seemed to shimmer, something she'd not seen before. The star systems lay spread out in front of her. One by one she aligned them with those in the visions.

"The journey will require eight jumps," she said thoughtfully. "I'm still working on the entry and exit coordinates. My goal is to find a route that will allow for a smooth and rapid transfer from one Slipstream to the next while, if possible, avoiding contact with the enemy."

She began swiping her hands through the air, moving one holo image after another as if she was playing some kind of complicated game, tapping notes into her data pad, then swiping again. Morian sat down beside her and watched in awe as the content of the hologram grew ever more complicated, until finally, she leaned back in her chair, stared at her creation for a long moment, then said, "That should do it... I think. Eight slips, rapid transfers, forty-seven hours in all, if I'm correct." She finished typing the coordinates into her data pad and sent them to Simon DeLong, the ship's navigation officer. Then she turned to him and said, "Check your data pad, Mr. Delong, and enter the coordinates into the system."

Everyone stared at her, including DeLong.

Morian clapped his hands and said, "All right, Mr. DeLong. You heard the commander. Get it done."

* * *

It was almost three hours later, after a jump that lasted slightly more than an hour, that Morian, Manda Haal, and every member of the bridge crew waited with no little anxiety for the first exit.

The ship was at battle stations. The pilots of what was left of the fighter squadron were in their ships, their engines running, waiting silently, wondering... If need be, they would exit the hangar hot.

"Slipstream exit in three, two, one," Krista's pleasant voice echoed around the ship.

Avenger shuddered slightly and seemed to drop a little beneath them as if they were in an elevator, as it began its descent. The view screens turned from milky black to the stark black of the void studded with stars and a massive view of the Meridian Binary System. It was another of those systems where the gravitational forces generated by its two stars and eleven gas giants, including one supergiant, made it almost impossible to calculate the coordinates of the Slipstream entry points, making it the ideal spot for an ambush.

"Initiate flight path one," Manda said over the open comms. "Do it now, Mr. Sen. Flank speed."

"Aye, Commander. Flank speed it is. Time to reentry... seventeen minutes eight seconds."

"Swarm presence to our eight o'clock," Omario Kingston said. His words seemed to bounce off the walls. "Distance seven-thousand-two-hundred-kilometers and closing."

"Stay on course, Mr. Sen," Manda said. "They're

right where I thought they would be. If I've got it right, we should easily be able to outrun them to the next entry point."

Morian leaned on one elbow and flexed his fingers, making and unmaking a fist. He glanced sideways at her. Her face was tense. *She looks tired,* he thought. *And why wouldn't she? We all are, but I pray to God she's got this right.*

He trusted her. *When has she ever gotten it wrong?* he thought. *There's always a first time, I suppose,* he thought morosely, *but this would not be a good time for a first.*

Yes, he trusted her, but still, the idea of flying blind like they were was hard to get used to. And it was blind to him and the rest of the crew, all but Manda Haal. She was the only one that could see, and who knew where they were going.

"Distance to enemy contact is increasing," Kingston said. "Distance seven-thousand-nine-hundred-kilometers. We're losing them. Slipstream entry in ten... nine..."

The sighs of relief could be heard all around the bridge.

"Yes!" Manda said and fist pumped, then looked at Morian and smiled.

Richard simply nodded and smiled slightly, but deep inside he was elated.

"Seven more jumps to go and we'll be home," Manda said.

Chapter Forty-Five

Repatriation

Gian felt his stomach turn in that strangely familiar but unexpected way as the *Avenger* exited the first jump.

"All right, Ranger Squadron," Danis's voice came over the comms. "Stand by. Be ready to launch on my mark."

One by one the F32A canopies closed. Gian was just about to close his when he happened to look back out into the hangar and was surprised to see Jackknife sitting on the wing of his Veridian fighter. He was even more surprised to see that he wasn't even suited up. He was just sitting there, tapping on his forearm screen as if he was in the park on a lazy Sunday afternoon.

Gian's finger hovered over the icon that would close his canopy; he was intrigued. Was Jackknife not going to fly with them?

"Hey, Jackknife," Gian yelled down at him. "What

are you doing? We're about to launch. Aren't you coming with us?"

"No, we're not." Jackknife looked up at him.

"No, we're not what? What do you mean?"

"I mean, we're not launching," he replied. "There are no Blues within striking distance. The bridge is going to call and stand us down any minute now."

"Yeah but..." Gian looked around at the closed canopies of the rest of the squadron. No one could hear them. He looked again at Jackknife and said, "How do you—"

"Stand down, Ranger Squadron," Danis said over the comms, "and stand by for further orders."

Gian hopped over the bulkhead, landed neatly on the rungs of the ladder, and then slid down to the deck, where he ripped off his gloves and walked over to the big pirate who was still sitting nonchalantly on the wing of his fighter.

"You know, for someone who claims he doesn't have the Sight," Gian said, "you sure do have an uncanny ability to predict the future."

The big pirate looked down at him, stuck his lip out and shrugged. "What can I say? Just lucky, I guess."

"Lucky? That you are, Jack. So lucky, in fact, that all I know is that I want to be right next to you the next time we engage the Swarm. I honestly don't know how I would have survived that last attack without you."

"Don't put that stuff on me," Jackknife said. "I was just doing my job."

"Yeah, but..." Gian looked around. "Look, just between you and me, man to man. Thank you. I don't know how you do it. And I will never tell anyone. But whatever you're doing, keep doing it. You saved a lot of lives out there... and we're all grateful."

"I appreciate that, Joker. I really do." He pushed himself off the wing. His mech boots clanged as he landed neatly on the metal deck. "And who knows? Once I get used to life in the Orso System and all of this..." He waved his hand and looked around the hangar. "...USF-controlled crap... Well, who knows?" He looked around the hangar. "Maybe I'll learn more about myself and my... abilities." He winked.

Gian nodded. He knew what the big man was saying. If Jackknife wanted to help and felt safe doing so, he would make his abilities known, but only on his own terms and in his own time.

"I understand," Gian said. "I don't know why you decided to return to the Orso System with us—it was a surprise to us all—and I don't want to know. But if you ever need anything... If you ever need help, please don't hesitate to come to me."

"I may take you up on that, Gian," Jackknife said. "I'm not used to this USF life. I will likely have to register to become a citizen." He shrugged. "I'll also need a place to stay. I'll need to register with the USF if I'm to continue to fly my fighter. I haven't passed a pilot's test in over fifteen years. I'll have to do that. I have no Sovereign credits to my name. And the stars only know what other hoops I'll have to jump through." He shook his head. "This is going to be a bureaucratic nightmare."

"I'll help you through it all. Don't worry."

"Easy for you to say. I'll be breaking the law just by

entering the Orso System. I'll probably be arrested as soon as we dock."

"What?"

"Of course," Jackknife said. "I have no citizenship, and I'm entering the system without a Sovereign visa. Why do you think I had such a hard time making the decision?"

"That can't be right," Gian said. "Not after all you did to help the *Avenger*... And to save all of those people back there on Freyja. You saved my life, and Andra's. You risked your life to... They can't do anything to you."

Jackknife laughed and said, "I wish that was true, Gian, but I'm an outlaw." He grinned with a sly look of confidence. "They can do just about anything they want to me, and they would be well within their rights under the laws they created. So you see, it's not an easy path I've chosen to walk." And with that, he tilted his head slightly and then turned and walked away.

"Why the hell did you decide to come with us then?" Gian shouted after the pirate.

Jackknife stopped, turned to face him and said, "Maybe... maybe I was just tired of the kind of lifestyle I was living. Or maybe I was carrying a heavy weight on my shoulders and wanted to be rid of it. Maybe I just need a change." He paused, chuckled to himself, then turned and walked away.

And it was then that Gian knew with certainty that it was the Sight that was bothering Jackknife, that he didn't know how to handle it yet. *Maybe he doesn't know it yet, but I think he just wants to help, to put his Sight to good use... I need to talk to Danis. She needs to know, and maybe the captain too.*

And he did.

* * *

It was almost two standard days later and *Avenger* was about to exit the final Slipstream. Manda had planned the voyage to perfection. They'd seen Swarm activity at every exit point along the way, but not once had they had to engage.

Morian, seated in his command chair, shook his head and wondered at the importance of these new abilities, and how essential they'd become to the survival of the human race.

"Captain," Manda said taking her seat beside him. "Comms has just informed me that as soon as we enter the Orso System, we are scheduled to attend a virtual meeting with King Orson Lorne and his senior advisors."

Oh, that's just wonderful, Morian thought. He'd forgotten about the hell that was going to have to be paid for Elio's subterfuge. *The king and Ugo Tan are going to be furious when they hear all that's happened.*

Thirty minutes after they'd exited the final Slip and the ship had been secured, Morian walked confidently into the conference room, sat down at the head of the table and grabbed his halo. Prince Elio, Danis, Manda Haal, Jadern and half a dozen other officers were already waiting for him. He eyed Elio, sighed and shook his head. Elio, whom he could tell was also concerned, simply shrugged. They both knew how badly the meeting could go.

"I'm sorry, everyone," Richard said, "but Prince Elio and I will be the only ones present for this meeting. The rest of you may be called in later, but for now I need everyone else to leave, but please remain on call."

Looks were exchanged. Heads nodded. Everyone except Elio stood and quickly left the room. Once the door had closed and they were alone, Morian said, "Are you ready for this, Elio?"

Elio nodded, picked up the halo in front of him and said, "I am. But before we join my father, I was wondering, do you have a strategy?"

Morian shook his head. "No, and I must admit I haven't put too much thought into it. But what's done is done, and we can only explain why we did what we did. There's no reason to hide anything. And, as they say, the truth will set you free. That being so, we have to take ownership of what we've done, and I believe what we did was the right thing."

"Agreed," Elio said. "Let's get it over with." And he put on his halo, felt the familiar tingle as the nanoprobes pierced his skin and suddenly he, along with Morian, were in his father's office where Marshal Ugo Tan, Duke Rutta, and his father, King Orson Lorne, were waiting with impatient looks on their faces.

"Captain Morian, Prince Elio," Duke Rutta said. "Let me be the first to welcome you home. That said, I must inform you that *Avenger's* data files were downloaded and sent to our analysts the minute you entered the Orso System—"

"Just a damn minute, Rutta," the king said. "Do you mind if I have a moment with my son before you hang him?"

"I—" the duke stuttered.

"Shut the hell up," the king said and then looked at his son. "It's good to have you home safe, Elio." Then he turned to Morian and said, "And I thank you for that, Commodore Morian. Then he looked again at his son and said, "What the hell have you been up to, son? You have some serious explaining to do."

Morian pretended to clear his throat and sat up straight, resting his forearms on the table in front of him in what he hoped was a confident posture.

"Now that you have the mission data," he said, "you'll observe there are two primary factors to consider. One is that the mission became vastly more complex than we anticipated. And two, the mission was a total success. You will note that our investigation into the Beta Ariatis System discovered a massive complex of functioning shipyards, ports and manufacturing facilities on the planet Freyja—"

"Yes, yes," Rutta said interrupting him. "But before we get to that, I would like to bring up the fact that not only did you encounter stiff resistance..." He checked the data on his forearm screen. "...on at least three separate occasions that would have qualified for an immediate abort of the mission, at the very least, you chose not to do so. Your actions, Commodore Morian, resulted in major damage to the *Avenger* and... the loss of five F32A Fighters and their five pilots. Regardless of what you found on Freyja, that alone is an offense subject to court-martial. What do you have to say for yourself?"

Duke Rutta and his political weaseling was going to be a challenge. He didn't care about the five lost lives. He cared only about making himself look good in front of the king.

"Duke Rutta," Morian began. "Nothing burdens my heart more than when I lose a crew member. Those fighter pilots that valiantly gave their lives in the battle against the Swarm are heroes, and they will be recorded as such. How very deeply that affects myself and my officers cannot be expressed. But this is not about them and their sacrifice. Their sacrifice is the reason the mission was successful, and the reason that I am alive and sitting before you today. I would also point out that yes, we encountered strong resistance, much stronger than we anticipated and—"

"We ran into pirates," Elio interrupted. All eyes turned to him.

"What?" King Orson asked.

"It was my fault," Elio continued. "In my initial research I found there was significant pirate activity in the Beta Ariatis System, but I removed that data from the Intel reports that I presented to you and provided to Captain Morian. Captain Morian didn't know anything of the pirate threat until we were well beyond the point of no return."

The king's mouth dropped open. "Captain, is this true?"

"Yes, your majesty," Morian said.

"Well, that's even worse," Duke Rutta said. "We

cannot have that. Intelligence data of this magnitude cannot be manipulated to suit the needs of anyone; not even by you, Prince Elio. Had we been aware of it, we would never have approved the mission. This is a blatant disregard for military protocol and—"

"And I will handle military protocol here, Duke Rutta," Marshal Ugo Tan said, interrupting him.

"I know that you wouldn't have approved the mission," Elio said, "which is why I hid the data. Captain Morian himself would not have accepted the mission, had he known."

"That's true," Morian said and nodded. "However, I want the record to show that it was my decision to move forward once we did know of the pirate presence. And I can say with confidence that we did the right thing."

"So, you admit it." Duke Rutta pointed his finger at them. "You admit that the mission was wrong and should never have been allowed to proceed."

"Not at all," Morian said easily.

The duke threw up his hands and said," You see? What did I tell you?"

"What the duke is trying to point out," Marshal Tan said calmly, "is that for a mission to proceed under such... difficult circumstances, there has to be a great deal of benefit. Is there such a benefit? If so, perhaps you would like to elaborate."

"Yes, Marshal, there are indeed a large number of benefits. There are six huge shipyards on Freyja, all bigger than anything we have and all of them are fully operational, though largely undermanned. While they are indeed undermanned, there are large numbers of skilled operators and technicians who are presently running the outdated machinery. They have the capacity to absorb multiple teams of qualified technicians supplied by us. These shipyards are large enough to handle as many as ten Class A carriers at one time and double that number of battleships, along with B, C, D, or E Class ships. Better yet, they have the capacity to manufacture new Guardian and Defender class ships. They also have access to unlimited quantities of Dutrinium and Core Ore. And, one thing more: these ground-based shipyards are vastly more efficient than our orbital yards."

The king's eyes lit up, and he leaned forward and rested his elbows on the table. "Is all this true?" he asked.

"Yes, Your Majesty," Morian continued. "But the colony population of Freyja does not have the required numbers of qualified people to staff each and every facility. They do, however, have the managerial capacity and the will to do so. Indeed, they have been doing so. All six shipyards and five ports are fully operational and expertly maintained. All they need is an influx of trained personnel to become fully operational; personnel we can supply. It is a perfect match. If we supplement their staff and resources, we can have every facility on that planet running at full speed within the month." Morian paused for a second and looked around the room.

"And let me guess," Duke Rutta said. "Every one of those workers is unregistered. Is that correct?"

"Yes, that's correct," Morian said. "They are free peoples outside of Sovereign control. But that doesn't make them incompetent or any less dedicated to the eradication of the Swarm."

"And how do you suppose an entire pirate colony is going to accept it when the USF takes over?" Duke Rutta asked.

"That's not going to happen," Elio said.

"What did you say?" the duke asked.

"It's my recommendation," Elio continued, "that the best course of action is to do as I said, bring in supplemental personnel and oversee the manufacturer of a new Slip gate control tower at the Slip point. Other than that, the USF should refrain from trying to take over control of the entire system, and treat the free people of Freyja as allies."

"You're suggesting we send USF personnel into a system to live freely under the supervision of whatever criminal pirate happens to be in charge?" Rutta asked, obviously outraged.

"Essentially, yes," Elio said. "But you have it wrong. Tiger Wok is not a criminal. He's an honorable man with whom I had the privilege of serving shoulder-to-shoulder against the Swarm."

"And this man is loyal to the USF?" the king asked.

Elio was silent for a good five seconds and then said, "No, Father, he is loyal to the people of Freyja, but they are not our enemy. We are fighting the Swarm, not the IMFP. We are all fighting for all Humanity, and the people of Freyja know that."

"The prince is correct," Morian said. "The entire population of the Freyja colony is fully supportive of the USF goals and have agreed to let us use their shipyards, their facilities, and their factory workers and engineers.

"I should also mention this," Morian continued.

"They have a fleet of more than a hundred Guardian and Defender ships and, thank God, at least that many more are lying in dry dock waiting for us to refit them." He paused again and then continued.

"They are older ships with railguns, projectile technology and Dutrinium armor. They have been maintaining them for more than fifty years. So, not only can we retrofit our existing fleet faster than we ever thought possible, but they are willing to fight their fleet alongside ours."

The king chewed on his lip and looked at Duke Rutta and Marshal Ugo Tan. The two men exchanged glances.

Elio knew the tide of the conversation had turned.

The king leaned in and stared at Elio. "Son, are you sure about all this? Are you sure it's the right thing to do, for everyone?"

"Absolutely." Elio didn't hesitate.

"Commodore Morian?" the king asked.

"Yes, Your Majesty. As prince Elio said. Absolutely."

"Very well, then," the king said, sitting back in his chair. "Commodore Morian. You will submit your mission after-action report to Marshal Tan as soon as possible... I would also like you to work with my son, to draft a proposal to transport the first contingent of qualified shipyard personnel to Freyja."

"My king, you cannot possibly make such a decision so quickly, so easily," Duke Rutta protested. "We should debate it first."

"I can and I will." He banged his fist on the table and said, "It... is... done!"

And so the king had decided. Morian kept a straight

face, but deep inside he was more relieved than he ever would admit. It had been worth it.

* * *

Gian watched Danis marching with long fast strides, her arms swinging, across the hangar deck, obviously with a purpose and with two of *Avenger's* security officers close on her heels, blasters in hand. They were headed towards the locker room, where Jackknife was sitting at the table doing something on his data pad.

Wondering what was happening, Gian ran after them.

"Jackknife." Danis stopped in front of him and stood, feet apart, her hands on her hips. Her uniform was crisp and clean.

What the hell is she doing? Gian wondered.

"What?" Jackknife looked up at her and the two officers. "Oh, come on. We've only been in Sovereign territory for a couple of hours and you're already here to arrest me? Hell, the USF works faster than I thought." He lifted his chin at the two guards.

"Jackknife," Danis began and handed him several sheets of paper. "I am here to inform you of your official status under sovereign law, USF Regulation five zero nine, article seven, paragraph three A."

"Which is?" Jackknife gave a sarcastic shake of his head.

"Well, if you would take the time to read paragraph Five A, you would find there's a provision that explains that in time of war, and undue hardship, any person can be granted Sovereign citizenship upon volunteering for USF duty, provided the said individual has demonstrated unusual and heroic acts on behalf of the USF and the people under its protection."

"What?" Gian asked.

"Does all of that USF gobbledygook mean what I think it means?" Jackknife asked.

"Such citizenship status can only be granted by a battlefield commander who has personally witnessed such heroic acts. The request must be submitted through the USF chain of command and approved by the wartime theater's senior officer. The new citizen then has an obligation to fulfill a four-year commitment of duty in the USF."

Jackknife stood up. "You lost me at 'citizenship.'"

Danis didn't miss a beat. "I, as the battlefield commander who witnessed your acts of heroism on the battlefield in the Beta Ariatis System, submitted the request to Commodore Morian, who was the senior ranking officer in the said theater of war. My request was just approved." She stepped forward and reached out to shake his hand. "Congratulations, Jackknife. You are now a citizen of the Sovereign System of Orso."

Jackknife looked at her, then at the two security officers. "So, you're not here to arrest me?"

"No. These boys came with me as a favor." She pointed her thumb at the guards. "I just wanted to give you a hard time."

The pirate reached out and took her hand and shook it.

"But there is one thing more," Danis said as she

tossed a USF jumpsuit at his chest. He caught it with one hand. Looked down and let it unroll. The navy blue jumpsuit had the USF patches on its shoulders. "The paperwork's not yet gone through so you're only legal if you arrive in port wearing the USF uniform and carrying your USF ID. So, put that on so they don't arrest you when we go planet side." She handed him his small, white and blue ID card. "Don't lose it."

"I... I don't know what to say."

"And, since you're going to have to pick an occupation," Danis said, "I suggest you pick fighter pilot. You'd make a lousy cook."

"I can do that."

"And it so happens I have an opening in Ranger Squadron. So, on behalf of the entire crew, may I say we would be honored to have you serve with us."

Jackknife nodded and grinned. "Thank you... uh, sir or whatever your rank is... I accept."

"The title is Lt. Commander, call sign Domino, but off duty you can call me Danis, just like everyone else does. Do *not* call me ma'am! Welcome aboard, Jackknife."

She turned to walk away, then had a thought, turned back again and said, "And lose those damned mech boots. They're not regulation, and they're too damn loud."

Jackknife looked at Gian, pulled a face and winked.

* * *

Danis stopped by the hangar door and told the two officers they could go, then she turned, and with her hand on the door frame, she watched as Jackknife turned the

USF ID card over in his hands. She couldn't tell if he was disappointed or excited. What she did know was that he was a handsome and mysterious man, and she remembered how he'd flirted with her.

She saw Gian and Andra smiling and laughing together. They'd made a good team, and she was happy for their USF success, and for their relationship. They seemed happy together, and she was sorry she was going to lose them both.

Her thoughts turned to Prince Elio. She'd enjoyed having him fly with her. But, as they say, all good things must come to an end, and her time with Elio as her copilot was almost over, and that saddened her too.

Epilogue

After the meeting with King Orson Lorne, Duke Rutta, Morian and Prince Elio, Marshal Ugo Tan made his way down the Level Two staircase of the royal palace to the basement, where he turned to the left and continued on along the long, bare corridor. Motion sensor lights flicked on and off as he passed by them.

Eventually, he came to the end of the corridor and a large metal door. He placed his right hand on the biometric scanner and then offered his forearm screen with his code to a second scanner.

The door swung open, and the two security guards just inside came to attention.

"Welcome back, sir," one of them said as he opened the next door.

Marshal Ugo Tan walked inside and approached the white-coated doctor who was standing at the long, narrow horizontal window.

Tan joined him at the window. The doctor, his hands

clasped together behind his back, glanced sideways at him but said nothing.

Tan looked through the one-way glass at the more than a dozen people who were wandering around inside. Whiteboards covered all four walls. They appeared to be muttering to themselves, slowly swaying back and forth. Occasionally, one of them would stop walking, step over to the wall and write something on one of the boards. Tan knew these people were kept in a drug-induced state under close guard.

These people were the Seers of Orso. Their presence was unknown to all but the king, the doctor and Ugo Tan.

The drugs were custom designed to enhance their abilities... and their obedience.

"How is everything tonight, doctor?" Ugo Tan asked.

"Fine, sir. But I'm glad you came," the doctor replied. "I have something to show you. Come."

Ugo Tan followed the doctor to the far end of the window.

"There." The doctor pointed. "You see?"

Ugo Tan stared at the whiteboard on the far wall at the end of the room and nodded. He remembered this spot. It was crucial. That particular board was blank except for a date and a time written in large black letters. The numbers had been written down many months ago by the Seers.

But something had changed, and Marshal Ugo Tan felt his stomach turn over in fear. "No!" he said. "It can't be. We're not yet ready."

The date and time of the Swarm's next attack had

changed. It had been moved up. *But why?* he wondered. *Was it Elio and his reckless though fruitful mission?*

He didn't know. Nor was there anything he could do to change it. The battle to end all battles was coming, and they were almost out of time.

The End

Thank you reading *Gods of War*. I hope you enjoyed reading it as much as I did writing it. It was a new venture for me, and for you. If you did enjoy it, I hope you'll go ahead and take a chance on Book 3, *Armored Fleet*. I think it's even better than *Gods of War*, but that's just me, and I don't count. It's you who will decide. Anyway, to grab a copy you can CLICK HERE. The link will work anywhere in the world.

Thank you again.

Blair Howard.